The Miranda Complex

Volume 2:

Poppies

Barry Smolin

For the Zoo, too

CONTENTS

Interlude

1

"Georgie Porgie," the voice nudged me out of my Miranda meanderings, "pudding and pie."

I attempted to focus on a face in the haze.

The holy countenance I beheld just beyond the veil of pot smoke belonged to this dreadlocked dude with John Lennon glasses named Waldo who'd been in my AP English class in 12th Grade, and he was thrusting a joint toward me.

Apparently it was my turn.

I took a hit and handed it back.

"Good shit," Waldo grinned as my eyes reacted to the immediate buzz, "Right? There's angel dust mixed in there, man."

"The hell you say."

"Have fun."

"Yeah but, dang, dude, I could've sworn you were a chick just now," I said, refusing to panic.

"Nah, that's just your repressed latent homosexuality trying to avoid admitting lust for a handsome black man," Waldo said as if he'd rehearsed it.

"You sounded like a chick calling me Georgie Porgie, I swear, dude."

"I didn't call you Georgie Porgie, man, *she* did," Waldo pointed to the girl who crouched to my left, her face right up in mine when I turned.

"Chick?" she cocked her eyebrows at me and went right on, "Hey, Georgie Porgie, who said he was gonna call and never did."

I was still feeling the quaalude heavily.

My dick was numb.

And now I was allegedly on angel dust also.

It was a tremendously fucked up moment.

"Lily Adams," she said, "Dr. Acorn's class? Oviatt Library? Book of Thel?"

Holy crap, I was looking into the aqua-mauve eyes of the girl from Zody's.

"Hey," I said, coming out of my slouch, "Yeah, your number rubbed off my hand before I could write it down and I just–"

"–said fuck it."

I offered a mea culpa shrug.

"Guys," she shook her head.

I was still at Madeline's party and I remembered I'd said goodbye to Miranda Savitch a while ago, though I could still hear her voice like maybe in another room somewhere.

I had been (not sure how long) sprawled in a wide green velveteen chair.

The air was richly aromatic, woodsy sweet, cannabis plus nag champa.

"I thought I might see you at this shindig," Lily said.

"What are you doing here?"

8

"Madeline Baker is one of my oldest friends from Jew camp. She used to talk about you. I was gonna make the connection but you never called me. S'anyway."

"I, um," I stumbled.

I was barely sort of friends with Madeline Baker.

She only went to Fairfax in 11th & 12th Grade.

I never had any classes with her but she was tangential friends with girls I knew in the *Chick Clique* and also she and my pal Sandy Clay were boyfriend-and-girlfriend for a while, and so our paths crossed now and then. And I was invited to the party, so.

"Why would Madeline Baker be talking about me?"

"Like I told you in Oviatt, you're one of those people people talk about. And I believe Maddy was a confidante to someone who was majorly into you, but I'm sworn to secrecy."

"OK."

"I dunno, dude. You make an impression. What can I say?"

"Writing poetry these days?" I shifted.

"Hell yeah, and songs too. Girly-Q's at the Bla-Bla next Saturday. On Ventura. You should check us out. You missed the last one," she bore into me.

"That's your band, right?"

"Yup. It'll pop your rocks off if you come, I promise."

"Definitely possible," I said now in full-on aubergine eye lock with the girl from Zody's whose irises kept changing colors the longer I gazed, "Still stalking Tony Crumb?" I had to ask, which did a nice job of breaking the spell.

"Yeah, I can't help it," she said, getting up, "S'anyway. I'll come back when I'm drunk. Don't go anywhere, Georgie Porgie. I'm not done with you yet.

I have plans for your future," she got up and ventured forth to find alcohol, "Stay."

As Lily was worming her way through the crowd–I watched her sway for as long as I could–three younger girls came downstairs together.

I immediately recognized Mildred Rust, Whit's younger sister, and waved.

"It's Lance Atlas," she said, approaching me, "How's it going?"

"Pretty good," I said, "and how about for you all?" I asked all three of them.

"Pretty good," they straggled out together.

"This is Madeline's sister Ginger," Mildred said of the girl to the left, but I can't remember now if it was her left or my left.

I think it was my left.

"I get to have a sleepover because my sister got to have this party tonight," Ginger said, "My parents are out of town."

"Cool," I said because that's all I could think of.

Then Mildred said, "And this is Annie, but wait oh yeah, you two–"

I made eye contact with the girl on somebody's right and we both realized who we were.

"Yeah we know each other," I said, "Hey," half-waving, "Crazy to see you."

She smiled.

Annie was sort of a pen pal.

"You look different," I said, "It took me a sec."

"Braces," she smiled.

"I liked your goofball teeth."

"Eh, too Bugs Bunnyish," she said.

"What are you doing in L.A.?" I asked.

"We're here visiting my grandmother."

"Not in Cambria?"

"No no just here in town. We're staying in Park La Brea."

"Don't get lost in there."

"I think I've got it figured out. I know how to get to the Tar Pits and back so far. I like roller skating there."

"Are you still reading Charles and Mary Lamb?"

"Yes, I love those stories. I'm not all the way done though. Thank you for recommending them."

"What's your favorite so far?"

"Oh *The Tempest* for sure. Magical," Annie said.

"You'll read or see the play one day."

"For sure, for sure," she said. "I also understand *Romeo & Juliet* better now."

"Ahem," Mildred Rust interrupted, "Have you seen my loser brother here anywhere? I left my toothbrush in his car."

"You can use mine," Ginger said.

"Ew I'm not doing that," Mildred shooed.

"Uh, no, I haven't seen Whit, but that doesn't mean he isn't here," I said. I hadn't talked to Whitman Rust since clapping his back in a guy-hug at graduation a year ago. He went to Berkeley and we didn't keep in touch.

"Dang. Oh, and Taryn told me to say hi to you if I saw you," Mildred said, "So hi from Taryn."

"Say hi back," I said, "I haven't seen her at Aron's in a long time."

"She doesn't work at Aron's anymore. She's going to Valley College and wants to be like a music librarian or something."

"An archivist," I said.

"Yeah, that's it."

"That's perfect for her."

"I guess," she shrugged.

"But please say hi back from me."

"I will," she said which meant she might.

"No you won't," I said, "You'll forget."

"Dude, the first thing she's gonna ask me is if I saw you, so, you know, yeah, I will tell her, believe me."

"Haha," I gave it my usual.

"We came down to get punch," Ginger said.

"I don't think you guys should be drinking that punch," I said, "It's for grown-ups."

"We're not guys," Annie said, "And you're not grown-ups either."

"Sorry. You girls."

"Young women."

"Yes, of course. You young women."

"That's better," she said.

"You young women shouldn't be drinking that punch."

"My sister said we could," Ginger said.

I weighed the morality of waiving my authority over their behavior. Would I be contributing to the delinquency of minors?

I decided to foist all responsibility onto Madeline. So if anything happened it would be her fault.

But what if Ginger was lying and Madeline hadn't actually OK'd their consumption of the rum punch?

And then of course there was also the fact that, as Annie pointed out, none of us in the room were of legal drinking age so what did it matter? We were all breaking the law.

"Go for it then," I said, "As long as Madeline said it was OK. Enjoy."

"We're gonna," Annie said as all three began making their way to the punch bowl and then she added, "Good to see you in person. You owe me a card."

"I know. I suck," I said.

"Nimnork," she waved me off and vanished into the dining room.

2

I had met Annie three years before, summer of 1976, when she was a very kooky smart-ass bucktoothed 9-year-old kid.

Whitman Rust's family had a house in Cambria up the coast past San Luis Obispo, and Whit invited me to spend a week up there with them. Whit's older brother Bigelow drove me up. Everyone else was already there.

Annie's family rented the house next door.

The first couple of days I only encountered Annie in passing when she was hanging out with Mildred around the house.

But then on July 4th I ran into her outside when I was going to take a late afternoon stroll down to the ocean and maybe sit and watch the sunset which is something I feel like doing pretty much every afternoon of my life.

"How's it going," I said as I walked past, "Lance. Lance Atlas."

She came over and began walking alongside me.

"Annie." she said like a guy on TV, "Annie De Milo."

She was kind of giggling at the same time and making this imp face like Giulietta Massina in *La Strada* but with freckles.

Neither of us said anything for a while but she kept trying to stifle her giggling.

"You're the boy from Angel's Flight," Annie broke the silence.

"Say what?"

"What," she giggled looking away.

"The boy from Angel's Flight?"

"We were on the last Angel's Flight together," Annie said.

I had gotten high with Big and Whit right before my walk, and so her observation brought to mind some celestial scene of ancient knowing, when she was actually referring to the cable car in Downtown Los Angeles.

"I have a picture on my dresser," she said, "the last group of people to ride on Angel's Flight. You're in it. So am I. I was 2. In the picture I'm sitting on my dad's lap. It was in the *Herald-Examiner*."

I had in fact been on the last Angel's Flight ride before they shut it down in 1969.

I remembered we had that picture too from the *Herald-Examiner* only my dad left it intact, just put the newspaper itself beneath the linen closet in a drawer where we kept photo albums and other mementos.

"I was 8 years old on the last Angel's Flight," I said, "How can you possibly recognize me from a picture taken 7 years ago?"

"'Cause I look at it everyday so it always feels like it just happened. And plus our names are listed."

"Wow," I said, "I know the picture. We have the actual newspaper at home in a drawer. I'll have to pull it out and take a look when I'm back home."

The sound of the ocean forced us to raise our voices.

"Where do you live when you aren't here?" I asked her.

"Wales," she said.

"Wales, like in England?"

"The United Kingdom," she said, "but yeah."

"You don't have an accent," I said.

"I was born in Los Angeles," she said, "We moved when I was seven."

"And you're, what, nine or so now."

"Yeah."

"So two years."

"Duh," she giggled again, "You're good at math."

With hands clasped behind her in this really awkward extended position, she arched her back and leaned forward.

"Where in Wales?"

"Hay-on-Wye," she said, "but we just call it Hay. It's along the Wye river."

"Why'd you guys move to Wales?"

"We're not guys. Just my dad is."

"Sorry, you guys and dolls."

"I'm not a doll."

"Sorry."

"My mom kind of is though," she giggled and looked away. "God, I can't stop laughing," she said and laughed, "God."

"What's so funny?"

"I don't know I'm nervous or something," she kept laughing.

"Nervous?"

"I'm talking to the boy from Angel's Flight. It's freaky."

She kept doing her mermaid-yoga thing and giggling.

"So, why did you and your mother and father move to Wales?"

"My dad inherited a bookstore there, and my parents decided that they would try to run it instead of just sell it. There's like a hundred bookstores in Hay. It's cray-zee. Everybody's really into books. And cheese."

"Are you into books?"

"Reading is my favorite thing to do," she said, "It's what I do the most. Besides breathing and swallowing and blinking my eyes."

"What's your favorite book?"

"Um, probably . . . *From The Mixed Up Files of Mrs. Basil E. Frankweiler.*"

"Oh, far out, I remember that book. The brother and sister living in the museum."

"I love Peter Pan stuff too."

"Totally. I sometimes feel like Peter Pan is real–"

"–Oh, and I just read *The Phantom Tollbooth.* That's actually my favorite right now for sure for sure. *Mrs. Basil E. Frankweiler* is second."

"*Phantom Tollbooth* was my favorite book when I was nine," I said.

"Really? Neat. It's the best. Plus, my dad's name is Milo, so."

"Your dad's name is Milo De Milo?"

"Hey, my mom's name is Venus, so."

"No way."

"No really, I swear. My mom's name is Venus De Milo," she laughed right after she said it which made me laugh too.

"Your dad is Milo De Milo and your mom is Venus De Milo," I said.

"Isn't that cuckoo bazookoo?"

"Cray-zee. How did you come out normal?"

She made this slack-jawed face with her tongue hanging out and her eyes crossed.

"I take that back," I said.

"I sometimes think the only reason my mother married my father was so she could be Venus De Milo," she giggled some more.

"Instead of?"

"Venus Dipchunk," she laughed again and her eyes opened really wide.

"Eek," I said.

"That was her maiden name," she laughed, "Venus Dipchunk."

She couldn't stop giggling for a minute.

"My mom is funny. She already has a Welsh accent."

"Venus De Milo fits her," I said.

"I guess."

"She looks like a Venus De Milo."

"But with arms," she giggled some more and then eventually it all subsided.

"You are a goofball," I said.

"Nyeah, and you're a nimnork, so," she said and raspberried. "Ooh, you farted," she giggled again.

"What did you just call me?"

"A nimnork."

"What's a nimnork?"

"You don't know what a nimnork is? It's what *you* are," she was trying not to laugh.

"And what am I?" I said making a dorky duck face at her.

"A nimnork," she giggled, "I already told you."

I laughed too because at the time I thought it was funny.

But I was also pretty high so it's also possible it wasn't really that funny.

"It's not quite as bad as being a noogie-noo," she said.

"A noogie-noo."

"Yes, being a noogie-noo is much worse than being a nimnork."

"Like what I am."

"Yip. Yap. Yop," she said, "And the very worst thing you can be is a nimnork noogie-noo. Avoid that at all costs, Mr. Lance Atlas of Atlantis," Annie said.

"I will most definitely avoid that fate, Annie De Milo of Cambria."

"Wales."

"Lady De Milo of Wales."

I crossed my arms and let the warm breeze make me feel less mutant.

"You know Mildred from previous summers?" I asked her.

"Yeah. And other times too. We were in this drama class thing where we did a play version of *Alice In Wonderland* and *Through The Looking Glass* together. I got to be the Red Queen. Yay! I love the Red Queen!"

"The card or the chess piece?"

"Both! Queen of Hearts and the Red Queen. Who would you want to be in that story?"

"The Caterpillar, for sure."

"Ooh yeah he's neat. And the Chesire Cat!"

"Totally," I said.

"Nyeah but I'm not really friends with Mildred. Our parents are friends, and we're the same age, so we're supposed to be friends too or at least play together while the grown-ups talk."

"I know how that goes."

"I don't really like her very much. She's kind of mean and she also always takes credit for everything and I just let her because if I don't, you know, like I said, she's mean. Our moms went to school together or something, I'm not sure. Gum?" Annie asked and held out a Band-Aid box, the metal kind, which she'd pulled out of this dorky black plastic purse she was wearing.

"You keep your gum in a Band-Aid box?"

"Yeah, I thought it was funny," she said, "One time I cut myself, back when we were still living in Los Angeles, and when my mom opened up the tin I thought each band-aid looked like a stick of chewing gum. So I asked her if I could have the tin to keep gum in and she also thought it was a funny idea so she gave it to me to use for my gum. Want some? It's Juicy Fruit. I love Juicy Fruit."

"No thanks," I said, "Gum gives me a headache."

"What a nimnork," she put a stick of gum in her mouth.

"You don't call your mom mum."

"I told you, I'm American. I just live in Wales. God. You are cuckoo bazookoo," she made a spiral around her ear, "*loco en la cabeza*," and then she giggled again.

The stick of gum was still slightly hard in her mouth when she said that.

I laughed a little because it made her sound kind of like a deaf person, but when she asked me why I was laughing I didn't want to tell her 'cause it was too fucked up to say out loud even though it was true.

She stuck the gum out of her mouth at me.

"What else do you have in your purse?"

"Well, let's see," she dug around, "a yo-yo," she held up a yo-yo made of purple transparent plastic, "because you should never leave the house without a yo-yo."

"It reminds you of what you are."

"A yo-yo?"

"Yuh huh."

"Nuh-uh, get this straight. I am a goofball. You are a nimnork. And this," she released it downward and then let it roll back up, "is a yo-yo."

Then she pulled out a deck of cards.

"We should play hearts or war sometime," she said and rummaged some more.

"Aren't those pretty much the same thing?" I said to myself.

"A superball. Catch," she suddenly tossed a ball my way and I missed it and had to go chase it.

"Only a nimnork would miss that, right?" I asked her as I brought the ball back.

She crossed her arms and looked at me but said nothing.

"Noogie-noo?"

She went akimbo and gazed at the horizon.

"You . . . are . . ."

I fell to my knees in a mock plea for mercy.

" . . . a nimnork," she half–laughed, "but I forgive you."

The two houses were on this gradual slope that started out as forest and ended up as beach.

We had wandered down to the shoreline.

There were a lot of rocks in the sand near the water.

One sherbet orange stone caught my eye and I picked it up as the tide receded.

I examined it more closely in the waning daylight and saw these darker tangerine colored bands swirling around its circumference and here and there shades of white.

I decided I'd keep it and give it to Miranda when I got back to L.A.

It'd give me an excuse to call her.

I would tell her it came from Asteroid B-612 like in *The Little Prince*.

"What do you think of this?" I showed Annie the rock, though the dusklight dimmed our vision.

"Neato," she said, "Looks like Jupiter, huh? Kind of?"

I shrugged.

"Can I have it?" Annie asked.

"Nah I've got something else in mind for it."

"What?"

"I have someone I want to give it to."

"A girl I bet."

"May be."

"Lance has a girlfriend," she intoned in the familiar melody, "Lance has a girlfriend."

I shuddered at the memory of my penultimate fuck-up with Miranda at the Observatory when we went to see Laserium.

"Cheshire Cat moon tonight," I steered the conversation elsewARD, to that supine crescent glowing white against a darkening blue.

"Yeah," she said, "look, neat. I get it. The smile."

"You get it, but do you dig it?"

"I dig it. I dig it."

"You dig it, but do you dig it the most?"

"I dig it the mostest," she said and crossed her eyes at me, "Doyoyoyoy."

"Annie!" we heard the echoing call of Venus De Milo, "Annie, come help carry!"

She and Annie's dad were toting picnic stuff.

Further up the beach we could see the Rusts, or at least Mildred and her mom and dad already laying out picnic paraphernalia.

"4th of July fireworks on the beach tonight. We're having dinner out here," Annie said.

She started to trot toward her folks.

"See you later maybe!" she turned and then moved on.

When I got back from walking with Annie, I lay down on my designated guest bed in Whit and Big's room. It was actually Whit's bed—Whit volunteered to sleep on the floor 'cause Whit was the kind of guy who didn't give a shit about stuff like that. He'd sleep on the floor and be like whatever, same difference.

I turned on the radio.

Whatever local station it was tuned to was playing England Dan & John Ford Coley's "Nights Are Forever Without You" at that weirdly coincidental moment.

Lying in bed with the radio on,

Moonlight falls like rain.

Soft summer nights spent thinking of you,

When will I see you again

And, as I lay there in bed with the radio on, I conjured images of Miranda Savitch and pictured myself giving her the rock from Asteroid B-612 I'd found and imagining how and where I'd give it to her—like maybe sitting on her bed or standing on the beach at night—and how it might play out and stuff like that.

I wasn't planning to go to the fireworks picnic thingy that night.

Fireworks are too much like war and they make me think of the world ending 'cause that's what I think it might look like for a few seconds. I've dreamed it that way several times.

Normally, July 4th week would've been my Older Sister Fuck-O-Rama week wherein I'd a take on a different friend's older sister each night The Pleiades—but I decided that I'd instead, due to her proximity, devote all of my lustful attention to one older sister this time, Taryn Rust, whom I had finger-fucked on her parents' living room couch several months before.

Plus Buzzy said he heard Taryn say that she wanted to have sex with me so the hope thing, the thought that it could actually happen in real life, made it seem in advance like it could potentially bring about the greatest bone explosion ever.

Taryn Rust was 19 and ooh did thoughts of her fuel my horny.

I didn't know it would be so strong,

Waiting and wondering about you.

I didn't know it would last so long,

Nights are forever without you

But even as I lay waiting for an opportunity to empty my testicles into a mental approximation of Taryn Rust's vagina (based on the essential topography I'd mapped out with my hand during the aforementioned finger-fucking episode on her parents' living room couch in December), I kept tying the song lyrics back to Miranda Savitch and the fact that I missed her like I missed being excited about Chanukah and birthday cake and the new season of *Love American Style.*

My thoughts became too sad for radio and so I switched it off and listened instead to the music blaring from Taryn's tape player across the hall.

It was The Runaways.

Manny had just turned me on to them so I was somewhat keyed in.

I journeyed to the room Taryn was staying in and found her standing up bopping to the music.

"Cherry Bomb," I said, leaining in her doorway and breathing deep her aroma.

I'd had many conversations about music with Taryn Rust while standing in the doorway of her bedroom back in Los Angeles, so the scenario felt familiar.

"The Runaways, yeah," she said.

"Cool," I said.

Down the street I'm the girl next door

I'm the fox you've been waiting for

"I taped it off KROQ. You know KROQ? Weird station."

"Yeah yeah, Manny Shepherd loves KROQ. That's what we listen to when we hang out at his house."

I was memorizing her for later. Her curves. Her crotch. Her mouth. Her breasts in recline.

She was wearing a t-shirt and a bikini bottom. Her breasts seemed to be unharnessed.

I could not wait for the house to empty so I could go into the other bedroom and enjoy my catalogue of newly minted images.

Taryn and I waited together for the chorus and sang along when it arrived.

Hello Daddy, hello Mom

I'm your ch ch ch ch ch ch ch ch cherry bomb

Hello world I'm your wild girl

I'm your ch ch ch ch ch ch ch ch cherry bomb

"What's that?" she pointed at the bulge in my pocket.

"Oh, a cool rock I found on the beach," I pulled it out and showed it to her.

"It's like from Jupiter or some shit," Taryn said as she took it in her hand.

"Nyeah, I don't think there are rocks on Jupiter. Jupiter is mostly gas."

"I thought that was Uranus, haha . . . psych," she teased.

"Ba-dum-tchhh."

"Can I have it?" she asked.

"N'I've got something else in mind for it."

"All right, *be* cryptic then," she said and put the rock on the nightstand and looked at me, "Whatever. I don't give a shit what you do with that rock."

I'll give ya something to live for

Have ya, grab ya til you're sore

We listened to the end of "Cherry Bomb" both nodding our heads and smiling at the shared groove.

About a week before I came up to Cambria I'd gone with Manny Shepherd to try and see The Runaways at an all ages show at The Starwood up on Santa Monica & Crescent Heights.

They were already kind of too famous to be playing there, so we knew it was going to be way crowded but we thought why not go up to The Starwood and at the very least ogle some girls who maybe like sex even if we don't get in.

Manny and I walked up to The Starwood from his house and shared a joint along the way.

We were already pretty high by the time we passed this place called The

Institute of Oral Love and busted up and couldn't stop laughing.

"Blowjob lessons," I said.

"Please, fellatio, it's an institution of hired learning," he laughed at his own turn of phrase.

"Fellatio lessons," I said and then, I don't know why, "Fellatio ice cream cone."

"Like pistachio."

"Nuts included."

"Haha, yeah, and they also teach pussy-eating I'm sure," Manny said.

"Please, cunnilingus," I intoned like William F. Buckley, "Hired learning."

"Dang, dude, I love how it's all on purpose up here," Manny said.

"What is?"

"The names of the places."

"The gay humor is like an acknowledgement you mean?"

"Yeah. Don't you think?"

"So, are the names then ironic? Or un-ironic?" I asked.

"Maybe both?"

"I think the fact that we laugh makes them ironic," I said.

"But they're also proclaiming their gayness which isn't ironic all but just, like, mundane fact, dude."

"May be," I said.

The myriad business establishments along Santa Monica Blvd rolled past us like a Hannah-Barbera background, a grungy empty bar called *Jack Hammer's*, a residential motel *The Bedrock Inn*, ("You'll have a gay old time should be their advertising slogan," said Manny), across the street a furniture and interior design store *Back To Front* adjacent to the beerhouse called *99* (when we passed it Manny said, "Dude, Barbara Feldon from *Get Smart* was a fox"), some mysterious door that just said "Privates Club" and right below it "Members Only," next door to *Well-Hung Frames & Mountings*, and then what we guessed was some kind of sex club called *Kingdom Come* whose sign had an arrow pointing down toward the front door and the phrase in flashing neon "Get Blown Here," and finally the infamous lesbian bar *Miss Jane* which stood inexplicably next to the *Pussycat Theatre*, a bastion of fiercely heterosexual X-rated movies.

"What were we just laughing about?" Manny asked several minutes later when we came back from our separate head spaces.

During that time I'd experienced several moments of thinking we were on a side street in Las Vegas.

"The Institute of Oral Love," I said with exaggerated flair like in a TV commercial, somehow suddenly remembering.

"Oh shit yeah, that's right," Manny wheezed, "dang, dude."

"What kind of grass is this, man? 'Cause it is way strong."

"Yeah'mmm, it had one of Bigelow's flagrant names like Krakatoa or some shit."

"Krakatoa, East of Java," I thought to myself because I found it impossible to think the word Krakatoa without East of Java following.

I knew *Krakatoa, East of Java* was the title of a movie and that Sal Mineo was in it, but I'd never seen the movie, so to me it was just this weird phrase that I kept in my head for some reason and whose images I couldn't separate from each other. I even knew that Krakatoa was actually west of Java. But still. *Krakatoa, East Of Java* laid claim to my brainwaves.

"That makes a lot of sense," I said, "calling this shit Krakatoa."

East of Java, I thought.

"The earth does some crazy shit sometimes," said Manny, "I mean, like, OK, the fucking volcano Krakatoa," East of Java I thought, "dang, dude.

Krakatoa," (East of Java), "was some majorly fucked up shit," he paused, "right?"

"I dunno, all I know is this Krakatoa East of Java shit is doing some crazy shit to my head right now," I said.

"Totally. This is more stay at home and watch *Saturday Night Live* type shit."

"Right, not walk through West Hollywood and stand in a crowded club type shit."

But we crossed the street and headed over anyhow.

We made our way through the crowd where there were various clusters and cliques on one side of the Starwood parking lot, kids who'd bonded over hairstyles or fashion or sexual preference, and then on the other side of the parking was a spot where all the loners hung out together in bashful silence.

When we got up to the club entrance, we learned via a hand-scrawled sign the show was sold out and if you weren't inside already you weren't going to get inside. Someone was also saying words to that effect through a megaphone.

Some of the excluded were hanging out near the door so at least they might be able to hear some of the set.

This girl came up behind us and said, "Is it really sold out?"

The comely lass turned out to be Evelyn Childs, the reason I got a C in Geometry, she with the crotch I longed for, a massive distraction.

"Oh, hey," I said and blushed a little.

She recognized me enough to say, "Hey. Geometry."

"Yeah," I said, thinking it excellent that she knew who I was or at least where she knew me from.

"Bummer, I wanted to see this," Evelyn said and looked around at the milling crowd.

"Major drag, yeah," I said and looked down at the ground.

The only other time we'd spoken was in Geometry class once when she asked if she could borrow my eraser.

I didn't know she was into music.

She wandered away after a couple of minutes of us not saying anything. I think she sort of said see ya or maybe she just waved bye.

The song "Cherry Bomb" reminded Manny and me both of the cherry bomb incident a week before also involving Buzzy Lagniappe and Claude Moss.

"Man, I thought for sure we were going to jail," Manny said as we walked home from The Starwood having had no interest in listening to the muffled shell of sound that leaked outside through the door of the club.

"Oh, dang, dude, I ran away from there so fast. I even went really far in the wrong direction from my house just to get as far away as possible from the explosion," I said.

"I ran down Detroit toward Beverly, but this old man tried to stop me and he told me to wait for the police but I just kept running till I got home," Manny said.

Claude Moss had gotten a cherry bomb from his uncle who'd brought some back from Tijuana for July 4th which was coming up in a couple of weeks, and we were gonna do something goofy with it like blow up a detergent box on Detroit Street where Claude lived, but Buzzy Lagniappe said no we should do something crazier like blow up somebody's drainpipe and then he accused us of being pussies in advance if we said we didn't want to do that so we ended up all doing it rather than become pussified.

We scouted out a worthy drainpipe, in back of one of the houses that abut the alley just west of La Brea.

Claude used masking tape to affix the cherry bomb to said drainpipe.

It was about 9pm.

The plan was to run in different directions and back to our own homes and then debrief on the phone later.

Buzzy lit the fuse with his Bic and backed away quickly.

The blast was louder than I expected—my ears were hurting—and the damage far worse.

The lower half of the drainpipe was mangled, a window above the garage had shattered and the garage door was blackened, a shadowy stain apparent even in the darkness.

We four scattered like the paper shreds of the cherry bomb in the air, dashing our separate ways into the overcast June night.

Neighbors were coming out of their houses and yelling what the hell.

I headed west on 1st Street, the opposite direction from my house, and got all the way to Martel before cutting up to Beverly Blvd and backtracking my way home.

I was worried about setting off heart fibrillations and even sensed a mini-flutter and fluctuation in my chest like butterflies or shooting stars but nothing sustained.

"Yeah, man, I thought for sure we were going to jail," Manny said again, "That old man who tried to stop me, he kept yelling, 'I can describe you! I can describe you!' Dang, dude, I'm pretty sure I dreamed about it that night. 'I can describe you!'"

"It's a good thing you look like every other dude in the Fairfax area."

"Be on the lookout," Manny said like an all-points-bulletin, "for an adolescent male, olive complexion, kinky hair, prominent nose . . ."

Buzzy had actually gone to jail before, or at least got arrested and had to be bailed out, for staging a fake gunfight on Rodeo Drive in Beverly Hills on a Saturday afternoon. Whitman Rust was with him in that escapade.

Buzzy chased Whit down the street firing at him while Whit fired back.

They used air guns that looked and sounded real.

The scenario ended with Buzzy shooting Whit and Whit sprawling out on the sidewalk as if dead and apparently people were freaking out all around them even though there was no blood.

After further freaking out the bystanders by getting up and running, Whit, with Buzzy alongside, attempted an unsuccessful getaway down one of the side streets, but they were nabbed easily by the cops and taken to the Beverly Hills Police station and booked, on suspicion of what I have no idea.

Whit had told us that when they were leaving the police station Buzzy asked the desk clerk if he could get a copy of his mug shot to take home with him as a souvenir and she called him a little twerp which Buzzy said was a sure sign that she wanted to climb on his dick.

Buzzy's dad was a lawyer and eventually got the charges dropped in both cases.

"They are getting way too dangerous for me," Manny said.

"Yeah, I don't enjoy that kind of stuff," I agreed.

"Plus when Buzzy starts talking in voices and shit," Manny said.

"Yeah," I agreed, "Flippy Killbones. Out there, dude."

Manny and I were simpatico in temperament.

He was really the only guy I hung out with regularly anymore.

When we got to Santa Monica and Vista we couldn't decide whether to eat at Astro Burger or Oki Dog—Pioneer Chicken never being part of the equation—but eventually the onion rings at Astro called in a more alluring voice.

We both got double-cheeseburgers, onion rings and shakes. I was in the mood for strawberry but it reminded me too much of Miranda so I got vanilla instead.

We ordered our food to go so we could get back to Manny's house in time to watch *Saturday Night Live*, but the rerun was of a boring one so we ended up listening to KROQ in his bedroom and falling asleep.

The next day Manny had to run errands with his mother so I took the bus down to Sorrento Beach, where I again bumped into Evelyn Childs who was with this other girl I didn't know.

She didn't introduce me to her friend because there was no reason to.

And anyway I'm pretty sure Evelyn didn't actually know my name.

"You again," she said, "Two days in a row. It must be destiny."

I blushed and cleared my throat in this annoying old man way.

"Small world," I said.

"I hate that song," Evelyn said.

"Which? The one from the Disney ride?"

"Of course. What other one is there?"

"The one from *Gypsy*," I said.

Both girls shrugged.

"*We've got so much in common, it's a phenomenon*," I sang, "Stephen Sondheim? The greatest internal rhyme of all time?"

They had no idea what the fuck I was talking about.

"Sounds pretty gay," Evelyn said.

"But yeah, the Disney ride," I moved on, "me too, I hate it," I said, "It reminds me of 'Nights In White Satin.'"

"Yeah! Exactly," she said and looked at her friend, "So what are you up to?" she asked me.

"I was just going to catch a few waves," I said.

"You surf?"

"Well, bodysurfing I meant. Huge waves today," I said though the waves weren't particularly huge.

"Oh, far out, go for it," she said.

"Totally," her friend added and looked at me like someone I might fantasize about later.

I wanted to make both of their libidos twitch with my mastery of the elements.

I strode into the water feeling all muscly and male, in good shape from a year of basketball and track, and after a couple of false swells caught a wave whose crest I rode for several seconds until it broke and tumbled me head over heels downward and then face-first onto the sandy ocean floor, which I thought might up my heroism in the fair damsel Evelyn's estimation.

In the tumult I lost track of which direction to swim in order to reach the surface.

I experienced a few seconds of drowning-panic before finding air and breath via natural accidental flotation.

The kind of thing that happens when you finally give up.

I just let nature take me to safety.

Alas, when I emerged from my near-death experience in the waves, Evelyn and her friend were nowhere to be seen, or rather nowhere to be seeing me.

I thought maybe that was them heading toward the pier, but I couldn't tell for sure because I wasn't wearing my glasses.

Whit and Big came out of the living room, where they'd been watching TV, as I stood next to Taryn's bed.

"You're not trying to fuck my sister again are you, Atlas?" Whit jibed as he and Bigelow passed us in the hall and started heading out the front door.

"You guys coming to the fireworks?" Big asked us, "Mom and dad are already there with Mildew. They've got food and shit. Partying with the De Milos. We're heading over now. We can probably find beer around."

"Fuck that," said Taryn.

34

"I'm not into it either, man," I said, "Fireworks freak me out."

"Pussy," Whit said, exiting with a shrug.

Bigelow looked at Taryn and me.

"Yup," he said as he exited.

Taryn was lying on her right side.

"Here, boy," she patted the spot next to her on the bed.

I sat down cross-legged on the bed facing her.

She rose to her knees and nudged me onto my back thereupon proceeding to lock lips and tongue with me and so we were at it.

"What's that?" Taryn asked, touching my cock through my cutoffs, "Another rock in your pocket?" she said reaching in via the bottom of said cutoffs and touching the tip of my dick with her fingers then unbuttoning the fly and maneuvering it out into the open while I ran my lips along her neck and earlobes, occasionally tugging with my teeth and groping her loosed boobs a little bit through the shirt. It was practically like touching her breasts directly.

I had gotten a hand job from her that same night in December I finger-fucked her on her parents' couch, and I was remembering that encounter while feeling my way through the one at hand.

I felt her stroking my cock as I went in under her shirt and, for the first time, held bare tit in both hands.

I wasn't quite sure what to do with them though so I hurried on to what I knew.

I sent my right hand into her bikini bottom and found her expecting me.

I remembered her instructions from last time, *make whirlpools*, and got that motion going gently.

She alternated breathy whisper and quiet moan.

I could smell the musk of her groin emanating.

After a time she prodded my hand and guided me deeper.

"Up and in," she whispered, helping me rub up and tug down in steady rhythm while continuing the whirlpools on her clit with my thumb like I was playing a Chopin étude or tiddlywinks or something.

I still had boob in my left hand but wasn't really doing anything with it as my tiring right hand kept its rhythmic vigil at her swelling pudendum.

Her vocalizations were gaining volume and her hips were moving to meet my polyrhythmic digits, maximizing the leverage and the friction and the centripetal force involved in gaining the desired synaptic release.

I tried kissing her on the mouth while she was moaning but she'd pull away each time and press my face into the crook of her neck.

She built to a series of ever more emphatic emanations ending in one long squeaky moan during which her cunt clamped down on my fingers for a few moments as she held my hand still and then in a few seconds relaxed.

The air was rank with our sweaty wrestlings.

"Do you have a rubber?" she whispered after we'd made out with each other's mouths a little and her breathing settled.

"No, I–" I said, my wettened right hand now up under her shirt and playing gently with her nipples, "I don't have any reason to carry a rubber."

"Dang, that's unfortunate," she said and began making her way down my body until like a memory of heaven her tongue was on the underside of my cock, the 'flapjack,' I used to call that hot button wedge of skin for some reason, though Buzzy always called it the man-clit, and then her lips went all the way around the circumference of the head and I was in her mouth and everything was how it was supposed to be.

I arched my hips toward her and tried to thrust my cock at her mouth, but she held me still and took over the tempo and the motion.

"Let *me*," she said.

My full enjoyment of the sensation was occasionally disrupted by my recurring meta-awareness of the fact that I was getting a blowjob. I wasn't masturbating. Taryn Rust's mouth was sucking my cock for real.

I was living one of those confessional sex letters at the front of *Beaver Slam* magazine.

Instead of a small midwestern college I was in a posh west coast summer rental.

I looked down and saw Taryn Rust's mouth on me like the girl from Zody's.

Surprisingly, at times the blowjob got a little boring.

If I'd been jacking off I probably would've jizzed all over my belly already.

I think maybe part of it was I didn't know the protocol about coming during fellatio and so I was semi-consciously postponing.

I mean, were you supposed to give some kind of warning signal? I bet they teach that stuff at the Institute Of Oral Love.

Taryn must've been able to tell from my intensifying gutturals that I was getting close because she removed my cock briefly from her mouth, said, "Go for it," and went right back to bobbing.

"Totally," I said or maybe just thought.

The sound of the fireworks show outside along with Taryn cradling my balls with her left hand while she gave me head and also, admittedly, closing my eyes and pretending she was Miranda for a few moments sped the momentum toward a great unleashing into Taryn's cashmere mouth.

I clutched her hair with one hand and held her cheek and chin with the other as I felt myself about to climax.

Just at the moment when I groaned openly and crossed the threshold of the event horizon I could also hear the TV still on in the living room, some 4th of July ceremony in Washington DC being interrupted by a special bulletin about an Israeli raid on Entebbe airport in Uganda to defuse the hostage situation there.

I'll have to find out more about Entebbe later, I thought to myself as my jettisoned spunk splashed the back of Taryn Rust's throat and trickled along her uvula.

When I came I made the kind of groaning noise guys in movies make when they get knifed in the back.

Happy fellated birthday, America, I thought, my balls bursting in air, my cock spouting sparks like a Roman candle.

Wowie Kazowie, as Bozo the Clown might say.

Dang, dude.

The road to Hell is depraved with older sisters.

Taryn crept up my body and kissed me.

Her mouth still held some of my seed.

I lay supine to her genius.

It was one of those indelible devotional hyperaware moments, almost too real to believe.

Just then, as Taryn cuddled into my embrace, I started to feel a fibrillation episode coming on. My heart was quavering.

Of course.

Dang, dude.

It tickled at first and then I started to hyperventilate.

"Are you OK?" Taryn said, a bit panicked.

"I don't know," I rasped short of breath, "Let me . . . lie here . . . a sec."

The darkness broke up into globules and glowworms and gamma rays.

Cold perspiration gathered at my temples and hairline.

I'm not sure if I passed out or not. I think I might've. It was dark in Taryn's room and she couldn't tell either. Plus she was also really stoned.

"Lance?" Taryn asked, and I heard her but I don't know if it was the first time she'd asked, "You OK?"

She seemed worried.

"You're all clammy," she said when I opened my eyes.

"Hey, no," I said, "I think I'm all right. It was just—"

"We should get you to the other room. They'll all be home soon now that the fireworks are over," Taryn said, "You probably shouldn't be in bed with me when they get here."

"Agreed," I said.

I rose as slowly as I could to avoid a head rush and what it might set off.

"You sure you're OK?"

"Nyeah I'm cool. I just need to lie down," I said, "and sleep."

Taryn walked slowly with me back to Whit and Big's bedroom.

I put my arm around her and reached all the way over her shoulder and grabbed her left breast gently.

"I'd say you're just fine," she said and moved my hand away but I let it fall back upon her left breast again and she snickered "Yep" and let it stay there this time.

Then we had an extremely slow wet kiss after she helped me lie down in Whit's bed even though I didn't really need her help.

"What happened exactly?" she asked, sort of sitting next to me on the edge of the bed, "What was that just now?"

"I dunno, my heart gets weird sometimes."

"A little too much excitement maybe?"

"May be," I said trying to be casual and ironic but then let slip, "That was amazing. Thank you."

I reached up and touched the side of her face.

"Your turn next time," she said as she rose to leave, "Cool? You down?"

"Mmm-cool, yes," I said, presuming she meant eating her out one day.

"Down to go down," she said, "Grooviness," thumbs in air.

She stayed a few moments in the doorway.

I slipped into or was rather seized by sleep.

I was so conked out I didn't hear Whit and Big come into the bedroom when they got back from the fireworks on the beach.

My dream was of a frozen landscape, a place where I didn't have to speak. Everything was understood. It was just like that dude said in the *Upanishads*.

As soon as I woke up I dreaded the inevitable awkwardness with Taryn.

I was subtly freaking even though I thought I wouldn't.

That morning, when Bigelow said he was going to be driving back to L.A., I asked if he'd give me a ride home and he said yeah no problem.

Oh, I would masturbate the shit out of that scenario for weeks. I received that Bicentennial Blowjob scores of times in my mind's cock.

But right then I knew that every time I'd look at her I'd be thinking, "You swallowed my cum." I mean every time I'd look at her for the rest of my life. I mean if I ran into Taryn Rust decades hence at some old age home or something, like when we're both in our nineties and shit, I'd probably look at her drooling in her wheelchair and gazing into space like a demented vegetable and be thinking to myself, "You swallowed my cum." If I myself were senile in that same old age home, unable to recognize my own family even, I know I'd still look at Taryn Rust and think to myself, "You swallowed my cum." So, at the very least, I needed to get out of that house.

But what was I going to tell Meryl Rust about why I was leaving so suddenly?

"I finger-fucked your daughter to, I'm presuming, orgasm and then she gave me a blowjob and swallowed my cum and now everything's all weird," I knew I couldn't say.

"Should I call your mom and tell her to come get you?" Meryl asked after I told her I wasn't feeling well and should go home.

"No no, Big said he's driving to L.A. today and offered to take me."

"I got bidness to attend to anyway," said Big.

"I don't want to know anything about it," Meryl said, "that business of yours."

"No problem," Big said, and then to me, "We'll leave in like an hour or so, dude. Cool?"

"Cool, thanks. I'll be ready."

I hadn't brought much with me, so I packed it all up quickly in my backpack and went outside to read.

I was deeply into *Of Human Bondage*, trying to squeeze in a British novel before an entire year of American Lit that lay ahead in 11th Grade.

There was a perfect spot on the back porch for looking at the ocean through the trees.

Annie De Milo came over to say bye.

"Milly told me you're leaving already," she said.

"Yeah, I'm not feeling that well really," I shrugged.

She had brought a pad of paper and a pen with her.

"Give me your address so I can send you a postcard from Wales," she said. "So you can see sort of what Hay looks like."

"Oh cool," I said, taking the pad and pen from her, "Send me a postcard with the Wye River in it."

"OK! And then you'll have my address and you can write back if you want."

"May be," I said, thinking I was unlikely to do such a thing.

"It was very nice to meet you," she said and held out her hand and we shook, "You're funny. For a nimnork."

"You are funnier," I said.

A long silence was smoothed over by the sound of the waves in the distance.

I never know what to say in goodbye situations so finally I resorted to my dad's old favorite, "I'll see you when I look at you," which made Annie laugh and say duh.

"Let's do it, dude," Bigelow beckoned as he walked to his car.

As I was putting my bag in Big's trunk, Taryn made an appearance on the porch.

"Here," she came toward me, "You almost forgot this," handing me the orange rock from Asteroid B-612.

I didn't want to say something stupid or committal, so I chose silence as a survival tactic.

"Ciao," she said and waved nonchalantly as she backed away.

I know I blushed. I'm not sure if anybody other than Taryn saw but she definitely saw.

She was crazy on my mind for weeks afterward.

She'd swallowed my cum.

Flagrant.

3

The angel dust in that joint Waldo had given me was working in synergy with the quaalude, and, dang, dude, I was trying to find my way back to the present tense.

When I looked down for a second I thought Lily was sucking my cock like a frozen banana from Zody's, but I realized that memories of the Taryn Rust Bicentennial Blowjob were overlapping with my actual position in the time-stream wherein I remained at a party at Madeline Baker's house and Lily Adams was standing next to the chair I was slumped in, holding either her third or fourth glass of punch.

"I'm back, Georgie Porgie," Lily said and crawled onto my lap.

She tried to get me to drink some of her punch but I declined.

I didn't really want her to be on my lap, partly because I kept thinking she was some kind of sea-monster as her face was doing like this Scylla-baring-her-teeth type shit from *The Odyssey* and then her mouth was suddenly like Charybdis, the whirlpool, the giant sucking vortex (even though I maintained enough meta-cognition to know it was the angel dust causing that), but also because I couldn't stop thinking about the possibility of getting a blowjob from the girl from Zody's which gave me a vague sort of half-hard quaalude erection probably feelable through my jeans, and also Miranda Savitch had entered the living room and was now in my line of sight and I figured she was bound to look over just as Lily was pouncing on my mouth which seemed like it was about to happen.

Dang, dude.

"Oh yeah, I forgot, you've met," Madeline Baker said, seeing Lily draped across me and rolling her eyes.

"Cal State Northridge," Lily slurred.

"Oviatt Library," I added, raising my index finger as punctuation.

"Whatever," Madeline tutted and walked away seeming perturbed.

Waldo was over by the stereo putting a new cassette in the tape deck.

"You turned me on with 'The Book of Thel'," Lily said, still holding her punch while lying against me.

"I turned you on *to* 'The Book of Thel'," I said.

"That's what I said, meant. Said meant. Sediment," she said with her eyes half closed.

She was majorly drunk, and I started to harbor, through the PCP warp, a creeping fear that she was going to throw up on me, which is right when we started kissing.

I disengaged after a minute or so even though it was quite enjoyable and said, "You know I'm not Tony Crumb."

"I know who you are. Don't make me cry, Georgie Porgie."

We started kissing again but I don't know I just wasn't into it.

My thoughts were swimming upstream.

To the music that Waldo'd just put on.

My ears were grabbed by the groove of "Disco Inferno" which came rattling through the speakers and set lots of bodies in motion.

In fact Lily left my lap and got up to shake her booty to it which was a welcome respite.

She was wearing a denim skirt that hugged her ass tight even though it was nearly knee–length and not at all sexy, more like something you'd wear to your bubby's 80th birthday party at a restaurant on a Sunday afternoon.

"White people dancing," said Waldo, "heh," as he returned to his spot on the couch.

"There oughta be a law against it," I said.

"Most definitely," he sort of slurred, "You ever heard this?"

"Uh, yeah," I said, "about a billion or so times on the radio."

"Nah, man, I'm not talking about that crappy radio edit," he said, "This is the long version. Listen to some of the trippy-ass shit they play when it breaks down and opens up. Dude. Listen. Check it out. I made this tape that's playing right now."

He spoke with his eyes closed and nodded to the beat.

The first 3 minutes were just the song I'd heard in saturation quantities on the radio.

"*Burn baby burn*, dude," said Waldo, "They're invoking the Watts Uprising, 1960s, the Magnificent Montague, KGFJ, man," he paused, "*Burn that mother down*," he sang, and then he slurred something about this song being way more subversive than people give it credit for before lying down sideways on the couch.

People getting loose y'all, getting down on the roof

I was mostly watching Lily's ass dancing.

I could see Miranda's ass too, in those white jeans, across the room.

Miranda was talking to Madeline Baker and that had me all paranoid.

They both looked over at me a couple of times while they were talking so yeah I was feeling it.

I had the rock from Asteroid B-612 in my pocket.

I'd brought it thinking I might see Miranda.

One last opportunity to give it to her.

But right then I was thinking nyeah never mind she stopped being into me a long time ago it's stupid.

I turned my attention back to the dancing ass of Lily Adams, the girl from Zody's.

I couldn't get enough, so I had to self-destruct

For some indefinable flurry of time I felt like I was getting head from Lily again.

My eyes were closed and I had the sensation of her pillowy lips on my dick.

Then I had a sudden panic that maybe I was masturbating in public.

I opened my eyes to find neither was true.

Dang, dude. Angel dust.

But see the thing is I had always heard angel dust made you want to walk into traffic and fly out of windows and stuff but I just wanted to listen to music with Waldo and look at girls' asses so maybe there wasn't really any angel dust in that joint 'cause people often claimed joints were laced with angel dust but it was only true some of the time.

Lily was still dancing, and next to her were Eddie Gurges and his girlfriend who must've just come in.

I remembered I needed to talk to Eddie about something.

He was going to UCLA and we hung out on occasion and shared our current creative projects with each other. I looked at his drawings, he listened to my music.

We were going to be seeing Monty Python at the Hollywood Bowl together and his girlfriend Judith had this other friend who wanted to go and Eddie had asked me the day before if she could use my other ticket and I just wanted to tell him that I'd thought about it and yeah of course that's cool I don't have anyone to bring anyway so sure especially if she's cute but even if she's not.

I looked to my right and Waldo had sat back up.

"*I just can't stop*," he sang along, "*when my spark gets hot.*"

The familiar radio version of "Disco Inferno" gave way to something new. The groove remained the same, but the air and the sea within it changed.

"Right here comes the breakdown," Waldo pointed toward the speakers, "Dig. Hear that guitar plunking funky as hell, chakka-chakka chakka-chakka."

I just can't stop when my spark gets hot

It would be cool to make out with Lily under the full moon, like at the Tar Pits, I thought. I had a blanket in the trunk of my car.

That would have been on the agenda were I not blitzed beyond the galactic barrier and had I not committed myself to a vow of celibacy.

I couldn't tell whether my eyes were open or closed at times.

The music kept bringing me back.

"And horns, hello," Waldo said, "like classic R & B."

Burn it burn it burn it burn it burn it burn it burn it

We were sailing on the same wavelength, Waldo and I, in the middle of the jam.

Our eyes acknowledged it a couple of times.

We were both gone to one place.

"Now the keys enter," Waldo pointed again at the speakers, "Dig . . . Right . . . Here."

"Laying it down," I said like a lame-ass whiteboy.

"Fender Rhodes, baby," Waldo said, letting me have my lameness and leaving it at that, "And here come the horns again, yes, hello hello hello hello . . ."

He started crossing his hands in front of each other.

"And now it's just all intertwining," he said and leaned back, "Dig that shit."

I caught eyes with Eddie and motioned him over and he flashed one minute at me.

"And I love the synth here, bringing it all back home . . . to . . . the . . . *Burn baby burn,*" Waldo sang.

He was playing with his dreads.

As "Disco Inferno" faded, Waldo said, "Now wait, check it out," raising a finger in holy notice, "My favorite disco band," he smiled and closed his eyes and pointed.

I recognized the opening vamp.

"I don't know about this transition, man. Eh. Could've been smoother. Oh well," he shrugged, "But still . . ."

"*You tell me this town ain't got no heart,*" Waldo sang and looked at me, pointing again.

"The Grateful Dead are your favorite disco band?"

"Well, what is this we're listening to? This is disco. Dig," he said, miming the drums.

Well well well, you can never tell

I had just recently started getting into the Grateful Dead after not liking them at all for a number of years after my uncle took me to a Dead show at the Universal Amphitheatre in 1973 and I fell asleep it was so boring.

But last year at the Shrine Auditorium I went to see the Dead mostly because Manny and I had heard it was easy to get LSD there which is something we had been most anxious to try.

We did indeed score two blotter hits and my first acid experience was in that midst and I found a deep connection with the band and the people who liked them.

"I remember I saw you at the Shrine last year," Waldo said, "Your eyes were twirling."

"Must've been the acid," I said.

"Which? The shit *I* was on or the shit *you* were on?"

"I would imagine a combination thereof," I said and listened to the music for a minute, "I remember you were the only black guy there."

"Yup. Most definitely. I have that same experience when I go to reggae shows. But, dude, that 'Estimated' into 'He's Gone'?" Waldo gestured as if I should get it.

That concert'd taken place like 18 months before and it seemed as if he could still hear every note.

I wasn't *that* into the Grateful Dead.

I nodded as if I got it even though I hate when I do that bullshit just so cool dudes like Waldo will think I'm cool too.

49

"Where's Shepherd these days?"

"He's at Northridge also, like me, but he's spending the summer in New York right now. We have a band together called Tin Man Alley, kinda on hiatus while he's back east."

"Oh, yeah, I heard you guys were playing the Troubadour, right?"

"Yeah, we did, that was back in April."

"Emmett Beall's in the band, right? I went to Pasteur with that dude. Why'd he stop going to Fairfax?"

"I'm not really sure, to be honest."

"Where'd he go?"

"Hami," I said.

"Emmett's the coolest of cats, man. Keep me posted on gigs, and I'll come check you out when I can."

Miranda was now talking to Claire Farnaway, Sharon Rose, and Justine Balthazar, and they too kept looking over at me.

Luckily, I knew I wouldn't have to deal with seeing Lorelei Lux because she had dropped out of UCLA after 1 quarter and moved up to San Francisco to write and escape the "mind–forg'd manacles" as she put it.

She'd come over unannounced one night back in January right before she left for the Bay Area to say goodbye and also to apologize for something but she wouldn't say what, she said I'd know.

Typical Lorelei.

We were in my bedroom and I was lying on my bed and she sat in the chair at my desk and it was gnawingly awkward because we didn't really communicate at all anymore and she just blurted out, "I really want to apologize to you."

I had no idea what she had to apologize for, but I didn't want to get into one of her Lorelei Lux mind games where if I couldn't guess what was going on in her head via telepathy I didn't deserve to know.

So I just said "OK" and shrugged.

That was the last time I spoke to her.

Anyway, I knew she wouldn't be at the party.

"Were you at the Dead show at Pauley Pavillion last December?" Waldo asked me.

"I was there, yeah. And you go to UCLA, right?" I asked.

"I do."

"English major?"

"Duh. What else? The Megiddo Effect. You too?"

"Duh huh," I said and crossed my eyes but that hurt so I stopped and wondered if everybody's eyes hurt when they fake being cross-eyed. My dad used to tell me if I did that too often my eyes would get stuck like that and even though I knew it was bullshit I thought about it with some level of trepidation every time I purposely crossed my eyes at someone just to be goofy.

"Is this the 'Shakedown Street' from the Pauley show?" I asked.

"No, man, this is from Giza, when they played at the Pyramids last September, huge sweet jam, Jerry just being completely tender but also free and intense."

"How did you get this?"

"The cosmos sends these things to me, dude. It's all about synchronicity," he said, "and having a roommate who's a hardcore Deadhead."

"Right on," I said, "this is great."

Meanwhile Lily had landed back in my lap and started snuggling into me again.

She had sour punch breath.

Maybe that's 'cause it's midnight, in the dark of the moon besides

"I want to get out of here," she said as I listened to Bob Weir's rhythm guitar part and really locked into it.

Maybe the dark is from your eyes

"You should go," I said, "You've got nothing to lose but champagne."

"But I want you to come wif me," she pouted in borderline baby talk which is always an effective way to shut down my system.

"Where do you want to go?" I hated myself for asking.

"I was thinking we could go somewhere," she said in my ear, "and do sumfing."

I pushed her away a little.

Nothin' here that could interest you (well well well, you can never tell)

"I, um," I squirmed, "I dunno, I, I'm really high and you're really drunk and I don't think you really know who I really am. Really."

"I know who you are, Georgie Porgie," she said, "you're the fat kid from *Willy Wonka & The Chocolate Factory*, what's his name, Buzzy something."

"Augustus Gloop."

"Buzzy Lagniappe," she said, "that's who I meant, that's who you are."

"Augustus Gloop is the fat kid from *Willy Wonka & The Chocolate Factory*."

"Nuh-uh, that is so not true. Hey," she said to Waldo who seemed to be conversing with invisible spirits using only his eyes and eyebrows, "Isn't Buzzy Lagniappe the fat kid from *Willy Wonka & The Chocolate Factory*?"

"Where did you go to elementary school, lady?" Waldo asked, "Augustus Gloop is the fat kid from *Willy Wonka & The Chocolate Factory*. Buzzy Lagniappe is a Danny Partridge-looking motherfucker we went to school with. He went crazy or something last I heard."

"I live next door to Buzzy Lagniappe and yeah he's pretty out there now," I said.

"Dude, I'm so wasted," Lily said, "You live next door to the fat kid from *Willy Wonka & The Chocolate Factory*?"

"No, but I live across the street from H.R. Pufnstuf," I said. "Maybe you should lie down for a while," I said.

"I am lying down," she said into my chest.

"I mean like on the couch or something else that's not me."

"Are you twying to get wid of me?" she slid toward baby talk again.

"Nyeah, I just, um, you know, can't," I stumbled.

"Can't what?"

"Um."

"I'd probably fall asleep in the middle at this point anyway so whatever," she said and lay back down on me.

"That's why they call me the Sandman," I whispered.

After a couple of minutes just listening to the music I looked down and she had in fact fallen asleep.

"Hey, how's it going?" Eddie Gurges said as he leaned over and embraced me as best he could with Lily in the way, "My *landsman*," which is what Eddie always said after he hugged you if you were of the tribe, the requisite acknowledgement that, yes, we are both Jewish.

"Pretty good," I drawled, "how's by you?"

"*Es geht mir gut*," he said, "*Du?*"

"Nyeah, pretty good, I guess," I said, "But, dude, I wanted to tell you by all means let Judith's friend use my extra Monty Python ticket. I have no one to invite anyway."

"Great," Eddie said,

"Is she cute?" I asked him.

"I heard that," croaked Lily.

I covered her ears.

"Is she cute?" I asked Eddie again.

"I can still hear you," Lily said and pinched my shoulder.

I spanked her butt.

"Ow," she said and laughed.

"*Potch in tuchis*," I said and slapped her ass again a little harder and then our mouths met and we started kissing rather passionately by my best reckoning, at least enough so that my cock started to get reasonably hard.

"See you later, man," Eddie said and patted me on the head while I was thus enlocked with Lily, "I'll tell Judith about the ticket."

I'd have to get more information on my Monty Python date later I thought to myself during the exchange of tongues and lips and teeth with Lily.

I began to feel like Lily was going to swallow me, as if her mouth were about to widen like a serpent's and take me all the way inside her.

But then her lips went limp and I realized she'd fallen asleep again, this time mid-kiss.

Georgie "Sandman" Porgie.

Dang, dude.

"Lily?" I tapped her.

"This music sucks," she grunted, I think, in her sleep.

I slowly maneuvered myself out from under her and joined Waldo on the couch.

Lily unconsciously curled up in the chair by herself.

"What're you reading these days?" I asked Waldo who was still pretty enrapt with the music.

"*The Fan Man,*" he said.

"Great book. Manny turned me onto that one a ways back."

"It's like an intricately patterned mosaic. Everything's accounted for. It's way cool. And fucking funny as heck."

"I gave it as a present once to this girl who'd already read it." I said.

Don't tell me this town ain't got no heart

You just gotta poke around

"This song is about Los Angeles," Waldo said.

"I dunno, man, I don't think so," I said. "Aren't the Dead from San Francisco?"

"Yeah, dude, I'm just feeling it. You know. I'm not thinking it, I'm feeling it. Dig?"

"It's a mythic every-city, man."

"Like Terrapin," he raised his fist, "Part of the misfit mythos."

The tape ended but Waldo didn't move. I saw Madeline Baker go over to the stereo to put an LP on the turntable.

"So, Waldo," I said, "what's the first thing that comes to your mind when I say Krakatoa?"

"East of Java," he said.

"Really?"

"What the fuck else is going to come into my head when I hear Krakatoa?"

"I thought it was just me."

"Nah, dude, it's the universal human condition. Every motherfucking motherfucker on the motherfucking earth knows this phenomenon. You could go into like the most secluded tribe in the Amazon rain forest in fucking Brazil or some shit and walk up to one of those long-balled tribesmen and say 'Krakatoa' and that dude will immediately say 'East Of Java.' It's like Jungian and shit. You should try it. It is heavily studied by the anthropological community."

"Even though Krakatoa is actually west of Java?"

"Yeah, man, geography don't mean shit in Jungian terms. We're talking archetypes, dude. Archetypes."

"And what do they say is the cure for this collective tendency?"

"Seeing the movie," said Waldo, "Of course."

"Of course," I said because I was supposed to, "Sal Mineo's in it."

"What other reason do you need then?" Waldo added and we slapped hands.

By way of experiment, I yelled out "KRAKATOA!"

"EAST OF JAVA!" shouted back the multitude who'd heard me so like 30 people.

Madeline had put on *The Best of Bread* and everybody started hooting.

"The soundtrack for every kissing game in 8th Grade!" Madeline said, to more laughter and, I'm sure, assorted sordid memories.

If a picture paints a thousand words then why can't I paint you?

The words will never show, the you I've come to know

Waldo rose.

"You splitting?" I asked.

"Yeah, man. You've heard of 'white flight'? Well, this is my flight *from* the white," he held a hand-as-gun to his temple.

I gave him thumbs-up, that whitest of all hand gestures.

"Take her slow," he bowed with hands together and headed toward the front door, saying bye to a few people on his way out, mostly people I'd grown up with and gone all the way through school with and played kissing games with but who now were pretty much strangers to me and it made me wonder if they always had been because it felt the same either way.

And there was Lily asleep on the green velveteen chair, possibly the girl from Zody's but also possibly just some neurotic Jewess I had already let way too far in.

And there was Miranda across a crowded room, some enchanted mythos, holder of my assorted memories, some sordid, some sweet, some painful and perfect at the same time, some indelible, some delusional, some primary, some secondary, some tertiary, some guilty, some lustful, some infused with the shame of wanting, some that're more like wishful thinking, some unlikely to've ever actually happened but are fostered anyway like orphans from someone else's head or else from the dreamer's own muddy subconscious.

Memories, like the images in a rear-view mirror, are always closer than they appear.

Miranda looked over her shoulder at me just for a second and then looked away when she saw I was looking in her direction.

I extended my legs and lay back and closed my eyes and listened to the music.

Floating on the vestiges of the 'lude.

I had the couch to myself and I for damn sure was gonna monopolize the shit out of that thing.

If the world should stop revolving spinning slowly down to die,

I'd spend the end with you, and when the world was through,

Then one by one the stars would all go out,

And you and I would simply fly away

Pandora's Box

1

Despair took hold a mere 3 weeks into 11th Grade upon my having seen Miranda Savitch making out with Freddy Snow during the screening of *Pandora's Box* we'd all attended one Saturday morning in late September.

Afterward I sat at the bus stop on the corner of Wilshire and La Peer, across from the Motion Picture Academy theatre, wanting to grok the fullness but grokking only that Miranda was a shadow now, off to something new.

Dolly Ferris crossed Wilshire and joined me at the bus stop.

"Hey," she said.

"Heya hey," I answered without looking her way.

"Why so glum, chum?"

I shrugged.

"Death of Chairman Mao got you down?"

"Haha," I let her get a chuckle out of me.

"Mandy and Freddy?"

I shrugged again.

"They're pretty much together, yeah."

"Sure looks like it," I nodded.

"I feel like we've been here before, eh?"

"Hyup," I remembered the sock hop.

The bus arrived and we both dug out our passes.

After we got on board Dolly said walking backwards in front of me, "What are you doing now? You wanna come over?"

"I was thinking of hanging at the Tar Pits," I said.

"Come hang out at my house," she said, "sit by the pool, eat grapes, tell me your troubles. I've got Wheat Thins."

"I dunno," I said with a little less glumness as we made our way down the aisle, "But, dang, dude . . . Wheat Thins."

We sat in those seats on the RTD where you face each other.

"Hey," she said, kicking at my foot.

She was trying to get me to look at her instead of out the window.

"Hey," she said again, still nudging.

I met her beckoning.

She looked at me like we were already kissing.

"I take it you've broken up with Aaron."

"Uh huh," she said.

"What happened?"

"I dunno," she shrugged, "it was winding down for a while. We both wanted out, I guess."

"That makes it easy."

"Nyeah, not so easy," she said, "I still freak out when I think of him with other girls and stuff. He's everywhere in my head basically. But, yeah, I'm glad it ended on a mellow note. We'll probably even hang out or something when he's in town for Thanksgiving. Or maybe not. It doesn't matter. Does it?"

"Where's he go again?"

"Stanford."

"Right."

Her eyes had this sparkle about them like crushed gemstones brownish and powdery in the sunlight.

The bus opened its doors at Fairfax.

We got off and stood on the corner of Wilshire and Fairfax in front of the Thrifty, and the better part of me said offer to buy her an ice cream cone and go hang out with her at her house and you know you will totally end up making out with her on her bed, but my dominant demon self said out loud, "I think I'm gonna go hang at the Tar Pits."

"Come over," she countered with low-key allure.

Dolly oozed it like an ancient tree.

Dolly Ferris always enflamed me, especially if we were alone. I had let her slip from the fantasy pantheon over the past year because she had a boyfriend, and that killed the whole hope thing that's so integral to successful mental revels. But now and then I'd look at her in class and get all het up again and crave that mercury mouth of hers.

"Come over and play," she said.

The whirl was all before me.

Mine for the taking. Once again.

And I said, "Nyeah I think I'm gonna go hang at the Tar Pits."

Dolly smirked at me.

"You are crazy and you suck," she said, "but I love you anyway."

"Haha," I said.

"I'm serious, Lance."

She looked at me while I looked across the street at the Ohrbach's sign and remembered when it used to be Seibu.

"I've meant that a lot of different ways over the past few years," she continued, "but no matter how else I mean it I always also mean it as a statement of sincere friendship," she said, "Really and truly. Lance . . ."

We stood a moment longer in the ochre afternoon sunlight.

" . . . Come over," she said one more time.

"Rain check," I said.

"It never rains here," Dolly frowned, blew me a pouty good-natured kiss and waved as she turned to head home.

I watched her ass for a while as she walked away and wondered if she was aware that I was doing that.

I crossed Wilshire to the Johnnie's corner and then across Fairfax past May Company heading down Wilshire to the Tar Pits.

En route I stopped to hail and salaam the mighty KMET even though it no longer sizzled like it once had.

I walked slowly through the park, inhaling the intermittent whiffs of tar that have always made the place feel like home.

I had come to the Tar Pits so I could lie submerged in self-pity for however long was left of daylight.

Miranda wasn't into me anymore.

Does it matter? I wondered.

I wouldn't even describe it as a sadness.

It was a bewilderment, a lostness, an orphanage.

It stung worse than shampoo lather dribbling down your chafed ass-crack in the shower.

11th Grade had gotten off to a mostly good start right up until I saw Miranda and Freddy making out at the *Pandora's Box* screening.

The highlight of the school year thus far was having Period 1 American Lit with Mr. Megiddo, the English teacher who would make forever irrevocable my connection to literature.

Harvey Megiddo entered the classroom on the first day of school looking mythological. He was about six feet tall and had thick brown hair, parted on the side, that hung to just below his ears, a droopy mustache, rectangular wire–frame glasses on a heroic Roman nose, plaid shirt, tan cords, Wallabies.

Also on that first day of class Miranda walked right past me without saying hello to sit in the back with Dolly Ferris and Arabella Mayflower.

Miranda had sat next to me in English class every year since 7th Grade.

My stomach tumbled.

Claire Farnaway ended up to my left again just like in 10th Grade.

Gina Dichlich chose the desk to my right, usually Miranda's, and Whitman Rust claimed the desk behind Gina upon whom he was crushing at that time and kept swearing to us that he was just about to ask her out which he never did. Manny Shepherd sat in back of me and Claude Moss sat in back of Claire.

I was totally bummed about Miranda not sitting next to me, though it all made sense 3 weeks later when I saw her making out with Freddy at the *Pandora's Box* screening.

"Together again!" Claire said to me smiling broadly and dragging me out of my downer.

"Yeah!" I said, quite happy in fact to be sitting next to Claire once more–we always had laughs—yet hyper aware that Miranda was back there instead of up front next to me.

Above Megiddo's desk there was a poster that said *Pope Springs Eternal* with a gnomish man emerging from the ground like a plant.

"Like on *Rocky and Bullwinkle*," Claude observed.

"That doesn't look like the Pope," I said to Mr. Megiddo.

"That's because it's not *the* Pope, though it is *a* Pope, *A* as in Alexander Pope, the great British writer. And you know what, why don't we start with Pope because he had a lot of great things to say about art in general and literature in particular, what makes it good and not so good, and that's mostly what we're going to be doing in here, talking about art in general and literature in particular and what makes it good."

"What about the not so good?" I asked.

"We don't have time to waste our energies on the not so good," he said and walked to the blackboard, "That's true of life in general and love in particular."

"*True wit is nature to advantage dress'd,*" he wrote as he spoke slowly, "*What oft was thought but ne'er so well express'd.*"

We looked at the couplet for a moment.

"What does he mean by that?"

We sat in fearful silence.

Nobody wanted to go first.

"What's 'true wit'?"

I raised my hand.

"What's your name?" Megiddo pointed to me.

"Lance Atlas," I said.

"Lance, what's true wit?"

"I am," said Whitman Rust to assorted laughters.

"What's your name?" Megiddo asked him.

"Whit, W–h–i–t."

"OK, well done, sir," Megiddo acknowledged, "But what's true wit, w–*I*–t? Lance?"

"I know *True Grit*," said Claude Moss, "Good movie."

"Not really," said Mr. Megiddo, wincing. "Lance, save me. What's true wit?"

"Uh something that's legitimately maybe funny or clever?" I asked.

"I like the legitimately part," Megiddo said, "Yes, and you're on the right track. Wit has a broader meaning here than just humor, though that can be part of it definitely and many times is, but think also of all kinds of inventive or creative expressions that are intended to enlighten or inform or stoke revelations. From the German *wissen*, to know, and also the Sanskrit *veda*, knowledge. Wit."

"So true wit is something that's legitimately . . ." I couldn't find the word.

"Art maybe?" Mr. Megiddo said, "Art, discourse, observation, human creativity, when it's the real deal, is 'nature to advantage dress'd.' What does that mean? Don't be thrown off by the syntax. And what's syntax by the way? Mr. Beauregard taught you this I know."

Gina Dichlich raised her hand.

"What's your name?" Megiddo asked her.

"Gina Dichlich," she said.

"Pardon?"

"DICK–LICK," Gina said again followed by her timeworn smile.

"I meant your first name," Megiddo replied unfazed, "What's syntax, Miss Dichlich?"

"Word order," Gina smirked.

"Correct. Word order. Good. Don't be thrown off by the syntax of this line. Put it in a more familiar sequence. Nature dress'd to advantage."

Claire raised her hand but without waiting to be called upon blurted out, "Things are made to look better than they really do?"

In Megiddo's, you could say stuff without raising your hand and he didn't care unless you interrupted people.

"I'm Claire, by the way."

"Hmm . . . not quite that, Claire, close, but not quite better than they *really* do, but rather . . . what?"

Miranda raised her hand.

"Your name?" Megiddo asked her.

"Miranda Savitch," she said.

"Things are made to look . . . what?"

"Better than they *usually* do."

"Bingo," he pointed, "And what's the effect of that?" he asked.

"Well, it's like they . . . shine."

"Yes, and what's the effect of *that?*"

"It . . . makes . . . you . . . notice it better?" she tried.

"Yes!" he said and paused, "Art is the universe calling attention to itself. The artist is the conduit, the one who takes us there, to that moment of noticing," said Mr. Megiddo, "and Pope underlines the notion with 'what oft was thought,' what has been thought about a lot, *oft*, the ideas that are always out there, 'but ne'er so well express'd,' but have never, *ne'er*, been put into such illuminating or dazzling or profound or exquisitely beautiful words or whatever medium."

"Saying it in a way that's never been said before in other words," I spoke without raising my hand.

"In a way that's never been said before, yes," Mr. Megiddo echoed, "*Tell the truth but tell it slant*, as Emily Dickinson put it. Give it that shine, that shimmer, that glow. It's the same with people by the way. You know how we describe pregnant women and brides as 'glowing?' Why do they seem to have a glow about them?"

"'Cause they're having a baby or getting married, like big milestones," Whitman Rust said.

"Oh I don't think it's because of the milestone aspect. I don't think a bride is glowing because she is going to get married per se or that the pregnant woman is glowing because she's going to be a mother, no."

"Then why?" asked Claude Moss.

"They're glowing because they are doing what they want to do. Believe me, a pregnant woman who doesn't want her baby or a bride who doesn't want to get married will not be glowing," Mr. Megiddo said.

"But marriage and having babies are something that women are supposed to do so maybe they are glowing because of the milestone aspect to it," Manny said.

"Hey," Miranda hooted from the back, "Uncool. Who says women are *supposed* to do anything? It's 1976, dude."

"Perhaps," Mr. Megiddo said, "they are glowing because they've found that blissful nexus," he interlocked his hands, "where what you want to do and what you are supposed to do becomes the same thing. We can continue this discussion another time. I'm supposed to collect your emergency cards today. Please pass them forward."

"Can I bring mine tomorrow?" a couple dozen students asked, at which Megiddo rolled his eyes and said, "Of course."

Art is the universe calling attention to itself

Mr. Megiddo's phrase fastened itself to my thought stream.

The artist is the conduit

"The one who takes us there," I said to myself, *"to that moment of noticing."*

It felt like something I should have known already.

Knowledge had been hitting me that way a lot lately, like, "Yeah, what took you so long, dude?"

That semester was also the first time I didn't have any classes at all with Lorelei Lux. She was in Megiddo's other American Lit section, the Period 2 class, and nothing else in our schedules matched up either.

I was aware of her on campus, but we didn't interact.

An excellent unexpected surprise that term was a Cinema class some of us got to take as an elective.

Mr. Simmons—a new English teacher who was really into movies—got to teach this one cool non-English class, a history of film starting from the very earliest.

When we first walked into his classroom and saw him, Buzzy pointed and said, "Hey that's the dude from the *Exorcist* line!"

Claude was also in the class and he said yeah it was him for sure.

"It is!" I agreed.

That story was part of our shared mythology. He came up all the time. Walter Simmons. The dude from the *Exorcist* line. And there he was, our teacher now. Mr. Simmons. It was trippy.

We told him who we were and he sort of pretended to remember but there was no glint of true recollection.

It's weird how someone can be a mythic figure in your conversations and consciousness yet you play no role at all in his.

It's always kind of like that with teachers.

We remember *them* way better than they remember *us*.

In his first lecture Mr. Simmons said of movies, "What you see is an illusion. That motion is really a series of stillnesses," he paused, "and what your eyes see is nothing but a blurring together of those stillnesses in sequence."

We saw great shit in that class. "A Trip To The Moon" blew our surreal cool-nerd pothead minds.

And Charlie Chaplin became one of our deities, especially *The Gold Rush* but *City Lights* also.

It was Mr. Simmons who arranged it so we could attend the *Pandora's Box* screening at the Academy where I saw Miranda making out with Freddy Snow for the first time.

I was immediately mesmerized by Louise Brooks whose face was like Dorothy from *The Wizard of Oz* only slutty.

About halfway through the movie I looked at the row in back of me, like right when Lulu shoots her new husband, and saw Miranda and Freddy frenching and they were very clearly boyfriend and girlfriend and I hadn't noticed until that moment and nobody'd told me.

I was able to watch the rest of the movie and even love it but Miranda and Freddy frenching right in back of me cut into my pleasure in a major way.

Hence my solitary sulking among the fossils that afternoon.

I watched the bruise-blue sky turn black and the leaves on the trees become more shadow than substance before I thought about heading back to a mopey night of emotional blurgh in my bedroom.

When I got home from the Tar Pits I went up onto the garage roof and smoked a bowl of Bigelow Rust's School Night pot, kept hoping Penelope Lagniappe would climb up and join me, then, when she didn't, I slunk into my room and put on *Blonde On Blonde* and the exquisite heartache which permeates that album turned my sadness into inspiration.

We sit here stranded, though we're all doing our best to deny it

I realized I was totally capable of simultaneously being heartbroken over Miranda while imagining Penelope Lagniappe sucking my cock on the garage roof.

Dang, dude.

That is some flagrant sleazebag slimeball sluthood right there.

Now, little boy lost, he takes himself so seriously

He brags of his misery, he likes to live dangerously

I kept the rock from Asteroid B-612 in my underwear drawer with all the other memorabilia and relics of the various enthusiasms that inhabited my past.

I had wanted to give the rock to Miranda once upon a time many weeks ago.

Name me someone that's not a parasite and I'll go out and say a prayer for him

I wanted to jack off but an overwhelming agony about Miranda brought me to a stall.

The shame of wanting applied only to Miranda, I realized, and I also acknowledged how fucked up that was and how impossible it had therefore been from the start.

It didn't happen because it never could have.

The ghost of electricity howls in the bones of her face

Dang, dude. Holy scripture, that line.

I wanted to create such imagery and set it to music. Or create such music and set it to imagery.

I was ready to do the work.

I was ready to make it everything.

The Miranda complex became a catapult.

While my conscience explodes

Two daughters of Mnemosyne yclept Calliope and Euterpe descended unto me in my Dylan-drenched despair that night (and they were both stout *carlas-for-the-nones* those lasses), and Calliope was dressed like a ginger-haired dominatrix in a leopard-skin mermaid skirt and Euterpe looked like Mary Ann from *Gilligan's Island* and they commanded me to serve only them from now on.

"We'll fill your heart with enough phantom love to float you alone forever,"

Calliope implied with her stern glance while Euterpe rode a bicycle in circles around my bed. Neither of them spoke out loud.

That Mexican shake I'd inhaled on the garage roof earlier had more of a kick to it than I was expecting.

I mean, I could smell Calliope and Euterpe in my room, like the dankness of an ancient cave. Like they were *there*, dude, I swear to fucking God. They were *there*.

When Calliope leaned over I could totally see down her aquamarine bustier too.

And Calliope got some tig ol' bitties, dude. Flagrant.

The spigot opened.

I was 15 years old.

Halfway to almost dead.

I lay on my back in the dark after Side A ended.

A cacophony of melodies warred in my head.

Outside my head only silence.

The moment had a mournful beauty I would learn to nurture.

I was an artist.

I had seen Calliope's breasts and lived.

My loins were yearning.

Shedding the Miranda sadness, in my bedtime fantasy that night I got off the bus and went home with Dolly Ferris and pretty much fucked the shit out of her on her bed, or at least my porno-forged version of what fucking the shit out of someone would look, feel, and sound like.

On Sunday I sulked around with my guitar and wrote this hallucinatory dirge in G7.

And then it's all over . . .

And then it's all over . . .

And then it's all over . . .

And then it's all over . . .

This opening could be repeated as many times as felt relevant.
It was music to be sung while looking away with your eyes closed.
I moved to C7 for the verse.

It starts like an accident

It leaks like an artery

It grabs you like gravity

It spreads like the angelstream

It grabs you like gravity

And then it's all over . . .

And then it's all over . . .

And then it's all over . . .

And then it's all over . . .

It was the trippiest thing I'd yet written. Stone age. Calliope and Euterpe
were in my body like spiders.

It feels like a miracle

It washes your thoughts away

Like everywhere nature

And then you go under

Like everywhere nature

And then it's all over . . .

And then it's all over . . .

And then it's all over . . .

And then it's all over . . .

I pictured Miranda in a lake, treading water, looking back at me doing the same, something I'd dreamt before. We were hominids in Eden.

A very cool place

All this presence

The edge of normal

The God collective

The edge of normal

And then it's all over . . .

And then it's all over . . .

And then it's all over . . .

And then it's all over . . .

The song had nothing to do with Miranda and yet she was all I thought about throughout the composing process.

More and more my songwriting was operating parallel to my engagement with consensual reality, kind of always going on in the background even when I wasn't actually in the conscious act of writing.

In such a condition eventually there arises an invisible barrier between you and the world you're supposed to be living in.

You start to feel like a Martian.

In Cinema class that Monday after the screening, Mr. Simmons started off talking about *Pandora's Box*.

"So what'd you guys think?" he asked, which is what he always asked after every movie we'd see in class.

"It was pretty depressing," said Rich Harte, this dorky-smart senior I knew from Librocubicularist Society meetings, "It was more of a downer than I was expecting from a silent movie."

"It's dark, yes, but I don't think it's depressing," Mr. Simmons said, "This is a film about clinging to hope despite every degradation. Lulu always thinks everything is going to be OK. Did you notice that?"

"That's 'cause she's a slut," Claire Farnaway said, "always ready to move on to the next guy."

Like me, thought I, slut of the imagination and inveterate crush whore.

"She loves everybody," I said, based on personal experience.

"That's another way to look at it," said Mr. Simmons.

"She never commits to anybody. She's not generous. She's selfish," Claire said.

"I know one of the judge guys talked about the Pandora's Box story from mythology, but I don't see what it has to do with the movie," said Heaven Sender, Buzzy Lagniappe's most agonizing crush for all eternity.

(Buzzy made no dent in Heaven's heart and he knew it but still he loved her deeply and pretty damn monogamously, at least outwardly, for a long time. "One day I'm going to marry her," he said to me more than once and I could tell he meant it even though, as far as I know, he never once spoke to her.)

"Well, who was Pandora?" Mr. Simmons asked.

"The first woman," I said.

"In Greek mythology, yes," he said, "and what about her box?" he asked.

"She opened up a box that held all the Evils, and they flew out," Miranda said, the first time she'd spoken in that class.

"She allowed evil into the world in fact," Mr. Simmons said, "according to the story."

"Like Eve," Manny Shepherd said, "Pandora's Box, Eve's Vagina, same portal to evil."

"Wrong," Miranda said to Manny, "The men who wrote the Bible used that story to scapegoat women."

Mr. Simmons nodded his head at Miranda and turned to Manny for rebuttal.

"That's what the judge guy was talking about," Heaven interrupted and thus extinguished an impending heated exchange, "her bringing evil into the world."

"But Hope remained in her box," Miranda backed off, "Safe."

"Elpis," I said, flaunting my mythology chops.

"Yeahzackly," Miranda said. To me. Directly. Which felt weird.

"Just as in the movie hope remains safe in Lulu, you see?" Mr. Simmons tried to make the connection.

There's always hope. Remember that, monsieur

After school I found a note crammed into the slats in my locker.

There was an inscription on one of the outer folds.:

I still have your signature in my dictionary, but like Dolly says—that was a long time ago. Was it really?

It was from Miranda.

Dang, dude. The dictionary. *Postscript.* 8th Grade. Ping pong. Fish sticks. 3 years ago.

Lance,

I know Dolly said something to you about Freddy and me and I would like to explain something for my benefit, I hope. I like Freddy because he's fun and I have a good time with him, except I could never like him or anyone else like I like you. You are more special to me than anything else. I don't know what we have left anymore—I only know what you mean to me. Whatever it is we have I don't want to lose it. I would like it to grow so that maybe someday, once again, we can have what we once had. Until then, or forever, I'll always be here waiting for you—and no one can change that.

Love,

Miranda

Later that night, while I was mulling over how to respond to the note, Miranda called.

"Hi, Lance," she said.

"Hey," I said, "How's it going?"

"Pretty good," she said, "You got my note?"

I maintained utter silence because I truly did not know what to say other than yeah and that seemed superfluous.

"So when did you start up with Freddy?" I asked finally, breaking the silence, which used to be her job.

"A while ago," she said.

"You two have always had kind of a thing."

"Yeah, I guess," she said, "but."

"Hey, it's cool," I attempted an illusion of detachment.

"I love you, Lance," Miranda said abruptly and then paused a few moments, "There is a place in my heart that is yours alone. You didn't seem to want to occupy it. That's all."

I nodded into the telephone.

"Git it?" she asked, "Lancelot Link, Secret Chimp?" and giggled nervously, trying to connect one last time.

The shame of wanting haunted me.

"When did you guys know you were a couple?" I did my usual diversion.

"Lance, please," she said, "Let's leave Freddy out of it for now."

"When did it become official?" I persisted.

"Jeez, OK, we went to the Tar Pits near the end of summer vacation," she volunteered, "Do you really want to hear this?"

"Yeah yeah," I said. "What'd you do at the Tar Pits?"

"We sat under a tree. We did what people do . . . I don't–"

"–Yeah yeah. I know. I know," I felt bad for being an asshole, "I'm sorry,

I–"

"–I've spent a lot of energy on you," Miranda said and she was slightly crying I think, "At times, like when we'd be out together with no one else around or talking on the phone, I'd think wow this is the greatest connection of all time and I felt like you were mine and we were us and this was it and then suddenly, always, like the next day you'd be really distant or awkward or obviously into some other girl or whatever. And I finally wondered, why am I doing this? Freddy's into me. Freddy starts conversations with me. He actually calls me on the telephone. He calls me by my name. Freddy's fun. He takes me places. We laugh. He acts like a boyfriend. You know?"

"I know," was all I could muster, "You–"

"You don't need anything. You could sit in a room all alone or whatever and be cool with it. I'm not like that. I need to be needed."

"I know," I shrugged to myself.

"I need the whole thing," Miranda said.

"I know," I said, again.

"But still . . ."

I let our future together shrivel in silence, an agonizing instant.

"Ugh. Forget it. Bye, Lance." She hung up before I could say goodbye back.

Dang, dude.

I totally knew which tree they sat under at the Tar Pits, too, and I kept picturing it.

2

A few days later it was Yom Kippur, and I was afraid that services might push me into a really dark confrontation with the absence of Miranda, but I felt like I wanted to put myself through that, like maybe it could be useful.

My parents still made me go to services on High Holidays anyway, so I figured I should put it to a meaningful purpose.

Services were one of the few occasions you could see girls wearing dresses anymore except for the cheerleaders when they were in uniform and also Gina Dichlich who continued to delight the male population with her daily minuscule ensembles.

Otherwise it was just all pants everywhere.

Pants can be good for ass-gazing, but for the overall ogle dresses get it better.

Pants take away the promise.

The youth services were upstairs in this expandable multi-purpose room that could accommodate b'nai mitzvot receptions, makeshift Hebrew school assemblies, youth services, and also fucking horrible-ass cotillion.

Fucking cotillion, dude.

When I was in 6th Grade, my mother made me go to fucking cotillion, an introduction to socializing with the opposite sex, like dancing and chatting and stuff.

Temple made the barest imprint on my consciousness. I never thought about it when I wasn't there.

HaShem spoke not to me in those environs.

The kids around me could sense my indifference and stayed away.

I remember mostly my own silence while on the premises.

And always having to sit next to that gnarly bitch Yocheved in Hebrew school.

The previous year during Confirmation class I alternated between hating Yocheved and fantasizing about fucking her, and sometimes it would be both of those at once.

I never did my Hebrew homework. Ever. I'd show up on Sundays and Wednesdays and fill in the worksheets as we'd go over them in class.

The teachers didn't really give a shit as long as you were able to read from the Torah in time for your bar mitzvah.

I would sometimes skip Hebrew class and go across the street to St. Mary Magdalen's to get some fascination out of the mass.

Or maybe to Copper Penny for hot chocolate when I was in 10th Grade if I had any allowance money left at the end of the week.

I dug the music at temple, though.

The music director was a hepcat named Jack Sylvan with a beatnik daddy-o goatee, just a shade or two away from Vegas.

He had set the liturgical songs to hooky pop melodies and he was very into what he was doing and I love when people are very into what they're doing because that's the source of true happiness and everyone could have it if they could only find something to be very into doing.

Jewish fucking cotillion meant Jewish boys and Jewish girls learning dance steps only white people would ever do in public and being forced to talk to each other while dancing, with scripted questions you had to memorize ahead of time. "What school do you go to?" was always the 2nd question after "What's your name?"

One time I was paired up with this girl I carpooled with to cotillion named Anita who was also in my 6th Grade class at Melrose Avenue Elementary School, and when I asked her that question about what school do you go to, she said, "The same one as you, dodo bird," and it was difficult to proceed from there until Anita started laughing and called me a silly-billy and she was almost beautiful for a second.

The man who ran cotillion and taught the hokey dance routines was a little balding guy who was kind of like Billy Barty, maybe a little taller.

I don't know what his real name was but we were instructed to call him Mr. Fred.

The kids all referred to him as Mr. Fred Mertz.

I would often take refuge at the table along the back wall with the sugar cookies and fruit punch and dollops of eternal sadness.

I carpooled with Anita—she lived 2 blocks away on Orange Drive—and on the way home that night, the night we danced and she called me dodo bird, I looked at her as her dad drove us home.

I couldn't tell if she was as miserable as I was about having to go to fucking cotillion.

Maybe she wanted to go, maybe she even liked it.

I knew such creatures existed.

Anita, who was normally quite talkative and filled with gossip, had her head pressed up against the window and wasn't saying anything.

She looked all the way beautiful in the fluctuating streetlight for a long stretch of Wilshire.

Those vague early stirrings warmed my starry cockles.

Fucking cotillion was nearly worth it that night.

My sister Mimi and I were sitting together waiting for the Yom Kippur service to start in the multi-purpose room where the temple youth were gathering, some gleefully, some reluctantly, some begrudgingly, some just high enough to be resigned to it.

The most gung-ho kids all sang in the choir, the same kids who also went to Jew camp together every summer.

And I was there to transcend Miranda.

Before I could get into that groove, however, I was distracted by the incongruous appearance of Evelyn Childs, ongoing crush and fantasy but also a classmate in Algebra 2 with Mr. Fudd, this like ultra-strict hard-ass who graded you down for everything including wrinkles in your paper and smudges and shit. He'd circle them and write –5 next to each one. Just a few weeks into the semester and I knew I'd be busting my ass to get a C in that class and hating every minute of it.

"Hey," Evelyn said coming to sit down next to me.

"Uh, hey," I stumbled.

"Runaways, beach," she thought she had to remind me.

"And Geometry last year," I added, "and Algebra 2 this year. Period 2. Mr. Fudd. You sit next to me."

"Oh, yeah, huh."

"You go to this temple?" I had to ask though 'cause there's no way she wasn't full on *shiksa*.

"No, my mom's boyfriend does, and he's really into being Jewish, and she's really into him, and so here we are. Ugh. This is my sister Julia," Evelyn pointed at the girl sitting next to her, "She's in 10th Grade."

"Hey, I'm Lance," I said with the usual froggy mucus voice I automatically get around beautiful girls, "I've seen you around, yeah."

Evelyn and Julia had the same sultry essence, partly due to their identical pillowy lips that promised the softness of a proxy vagina.

I think Julia was actually more beautiful than Evelyn but it was Evelyn's throbbing whatnot that called me.

I had a great fantasy in mind for bedtime involving the three of us.

The crazy thing is I almost got the opportunity to live that fantasy in advance of the planned jack-off session.

Not long into the service Evelyn leaned over and said, "Wanna leave?"

"You mean like ditch Yom Kippur services?"

"Yeah," she whispered.

"And go where? To like the Copper Penny or something?"

"No no. I've got the keys to my mom's car. We can go hang at our apartment for a couple of hours and get back before services end."

"I don't know," I said.

"Dude, do it," said Julia over Evelyn's shoulder.

The prospect of their lips convinced me.

Justine Balthazar was singing in the choir so she wouldn't notice my absence, and Mimi would get what was up and'd be cool, though I knew I'd be teased about it later or maybe even threatened with blackmail when she needed a favor. But still, she'd be cool about it in the moment and would cover for me if I was late getting back.

"I'll be back before services are over," I whispered to my sister who saw Evelyn and Julia slipping out the side door.

"You are a fucking slut," Mimi said to me as I scurried down the row.

I too slipped out the side door of the multi-purpose room into the eerily empty hallway and down the stairs to anticipated blasphemous escapades.

Their mom's car smelled like spilled horseradish and dirty gym clothes.

It only took 10 minutes to get to their apartment in the Miracle Mile area so I just breathed through my mouth until we arrived 'cause, dang, dude, that shit was nasty.

They lived in a really drab and kind of sad apartment, more like a hotel suite, with generic landscape art and hard uncomfortable furniture that probably stayed the same no matter who lived there.

"How long have you been in this place?" I asked them.

"Uhm, what," Evelyn said and looked over at Julia and shrugged, "a year and a half maybe? We moved in the summer before 10th Grade started, so yeah."

"Where did you live before that?"

"Different places," Evelyn said and looked at Julia again.

"Around," Julia added.

"Depending on mom," Evelyn said.

"And who she was fucking at the time," said Julia.

"What does your mom do?" I blushed.

"Convinces men to take care of her," Evelyn said.

"She's good at being taken care of," Julia added.

"Even if it means fucking really gross guys sometimes," Evelyn said and looked at Julia, "lots of times."

"Most of the times," Julia laughed.

"And who never have foxy sons I might add," Evelyn said.

"Ever," said Julia.

They had the mom thing down like shtick.

I wanted to kiss them both really hard on the mouth.

I'm pretty sure I would've been able to also, I mean kiss Julia and Evelyn both really hard on the mouth, and who knows what else, but I started to get this really distressing stomach trouble, as in the gurgly-churning internal squirt of imminent diarrhea.

It came upon me suddenly and with great liquid vehemence burning in my bung.

I tightened my sphincter to its maximum resistance against the flood.

All the naughty possibilities evaporated in my crippling horror at possibly having to shit loudly and wetly in the bathroom of their very small apartment.

Perhaps, if I asked to be taken back to temple right away I'd make it there in time to release my aching bowels in the bathroom in the Religious School building which I could sneak into and which would be good and deserted.

"Hey, I know this is a total drag, but could you drive me back to temple?" I winced at Evelyn.

"What?" Evelyn said, "We just got here. We're not even having fun yet."

"That sucks," Julia added.

"Why?" Evelyn asked.

"I just feel weird about this," I said, not mentioning that I needed to shit loudly and wetly somewhere and I'd rather it not be their very small apartment, "It's Yom Kippur."

"Dang, dude, guilt-tripping yourself," Evelyn shook her head but could see my desperation, "But I get it. I'll take you back, yeah," she turned to Julia, "You coming?"

"Not yet," Julia said.

"Haha,"

"I think I'll just hang out here," Julia said, flipping through a magazine for effect, "Ciao, losers."

"I'll come back and get you," Evelyn said.

"You don't have to."

"Yes I do. I will be back soon to get you."

Julia gave her the finger without looking up.

Both young ladies were rightfully disappointed by my wimpotence.

"Bummer," Evelyn said on the way back to temple.

I tried not to clutch my belly and wondered if she could hear the churning.

"Shit, don't feel guilty, dude," Evelyn said, "God doesn't give a shit about shit like this. Just be a good person. That's what matters. Don't be an asswipe to people. You didn't hurt anybody today, right? That's God's path," she said as she pulled up to the curb, "See you in Fudd's!"

"Speaking of God," I joked and made a desperate dash to the bathroom.

Because my gastric distress had put a stop to the would-be debauchery and cut short my time with the exquisitely kissable Childs sisters I had gotten back to temple well in advance of the conclusion of morning services.

The contents of my bowels belched from my butt in one fine gush of grainy river.

I let myself sit on the toilet for a while, long finished with business, simply relaxing in the silence and solitude.

I had sopped up the wet remnants. I had flushed. The water beneath me was clean.

I was just sitting there, my cheeks hanging low, my ass wide open.

The only graffito on the wall of the stall read:

YHVH watches you masturbate

Rather than go upstairs only to make it look like I was coming downstairs with the crowd who'd actually been at the youth service, I just hovered in the halls downstairs and pretended to look at the pictures of past congregation presidents and Confirmation classes—my own included—and then met my parents and Mimi as planned out in front of the sanctuary.

Mimi smiled at me for making it back in time.

"So dad's going to stay," my mom said, "and I'm going home. It's up to you."

"Home, please," Mimi said.

I pondered for a moment—because I really wanted to stay and flagellate myself—whether or not it was worth it to gamble on another stomach eruption in public.

"I'll stay here with dad," I said.

"Pick you up at 4pm?" my mom asked.

"No, I want to stay for Yizkor and the final shofar blast, so 6," my dad said, which was really weird because he was not in the least bit religious.

"You still want to stay?" my mom asked me.

"Um, yeah," I said.

My dad put his arm around me, pleased.

I figured given our ultra-reform congregation nobody would much stick around for the afternoon service, but I was surprised at how many stayed.

The sanctuary wasn't completely full, but damn near.

Neither Rabbi Saks nor Rabbi Hamlisch gave the sermon that afternoon. They had a guest speaker, not a rabbi at all but a member of the congregation.

Rabbi Hamlisch said his name, *Ben Schlicht* it sounded like, but I know that's not what it actually was.

"Good yontif," he said upon taking the bima, "I don't know whether I should thank Rabbi Saks and Rabbi Hamlisch for giving me this great mitzvah or if I should be cursing them for burdening me with its delivery. But here we are. I have lived to tell the tale, and a whale of a tale it is."

Mild supportive laughter echoed through the sanctuary.

He resumed, "We began the Kol Nidre service last night by staring into the empty ark, which, as Rabbi Saks explained to all of us, without the Torah inside it, is a coffin. Not some abstract coffin. But our coffin. My coffin and your coffin. We too are asked to confront and accept the reality of existence, to realize that death is always here right now. We are told to remember death. On Yom Kippur this understanding is necessarily intensified for the purpose of repentance, but, actually it's available to us every Shabbat, when the Ark is opened on Saturday morning and we see the Torah, Life, ensconced in a coffin. Even when the Ark is closed they are thus intertwined; life and death are at one with each other."

He paused a moment to let it sink in.

"Our task today is atonement, or, as many before me have pointed out, at-one-ment. We need to be at one. We need to be at one with life and death. We need to be at one with ourselves. We need to be at one with each other. We need to be at one with God. Adonai Echad. Your task today has been to find your "inner Echad." Your at-one-ment. The reunion of everything. My task leading up to this day has been to find a way to be at one with the Book of Jonah. I will admit the first few times I read the Book of Jonah I didn't understand it. I mean, you have this extremely unlikeable protagonist, the reluctant prophet, Jonah, who never fully realizes the truth of his calling. We are left with a failed hero being scolded. 'What am I to learn from this scripture?' I wondered with each re–reading. I conjured up memories of my first encounters with Jonah, when I was a child sitting on a Sunday morning at religious school. As the teacher told us the story of Jonah all I could picture in my mind was Pinocchio in the whale's belly from the Disney movie. In my child-mind Jonah was the puppet who wanted to be human; the story of Jonah was a mere cartoon to me for most of my life. When I started doing my first serious readings of the text in order to attempt this *d'var* today, I just simply kept hitting an impasse. I couldn't figure out what made Jonah so great. He's kind of a jerk. And yet, it's the chosen haftarah to read and think about on this the holiest day of the Jewish liturgical year. So the mythic and spiritual power of the Book of Jonah isn't in dispute in my mind, but I just simply couldn't pin it down. It began as a frustration and then turned to panic. And then, just as I found myself about to be swallowed up . . . Jonah's confrontation with mortality, though not, ultimately, what I found most fascinating about the story, was the hook that allowed me to reel in this *dag gadol*, this big fish called the Book of Jonah. Shedding my panic, I went off in search of guidance, a path to understanding. I knocked on Rabbi Hamlisch's door."

The speaker paused a minute and nodded at Rabbi Hamlisch.

Rabbi Saks looked displeased.

"Rabbi Hamlisch gave me a book of Hillel's wisdom and bookmarked the great sage's discussion of Jonah. To be honest, I didn't find Hillel's exegesis to be that helpful. However, having the book in front of me reminded me of Hillel's three famous questions: *If I am not for myself, who will be for me? If I am only for myself, what am I? If not now, when?* These questions became my way into grasping something in Jonah to hold onto. These 3 immortal questions, I realized, outline and illuminate the process that Jonah must go through. From self-awareness–If I am not for myself who will be for me?–to awareness of community and others–If I am only for myself what am I?– along with the always underlying lesson against the postponement or avoidance of one's calling–If not now, when? Jonah avoids God's initial call to go to Nineveh and prophecy against the Ninevites by boarding a ship that is sailing the opposite direction of Nineveh, toward Tarshish. There is no question of Jonah's defiance. Just when God wants him to face the world, Jonah flees to the interior. It is from the very beginning of the story that Jonah begins his journey inward. When the storm overtakes the ship, Jonah is not on deck but rather down in the innards of the ship, the interior. Not only that, but he is asleep. He is asleep to his own calling and he is asleep to the struggle of his fellow human beings above. Jonah is all the way inside, only for himself. After he's thrown overboard, he ends up in the belly of the big fish, which proves a kind of rescue and salvation; Jonah remains in the interior. And his prayer is a signal of this interiority, the frightening power of confronting one's self, one's soul, all alone, with nobody to lean on. 'You cast me into the deep,' Jonah cries, 'in the heart of the seas; and the floods surrounded me; all your billows and your waves passed over me . . . the waters surrounded me, even to the soul; the depths closed around me, the weeds were wrapped around my head. I went down to the bottoms of the mountains; the earth with her bars closed on me forever.' Jonah is all alone. He continues, 'When my soul fainted inside me I remembered the Eternal.' He becomes at-one with God's presence. Jonah gains some level of self–awareness. It is Hillel's 1st question. If I am not for myself who will be for me?"

There were nods of acknowledgement and recognition.

"Jonah is in the belly of the great fish for 3 days and 3 nights. It is during this 3-day sojourn that Jonah, in fact, makes the transition from being at one with himself to reaching out and being at one with others, even those who are his enemies: the Ninevites. Jonah is vomited back into the world with a willingness to reach out. He journeys to Nineveh and prophecies to the Ninevites. They repent, which in turn causes God to repent of his decision to destroy them. The reluctant prophet done good. However, God's sparing of the Ninevites upsets Jonah. Jonah thought his prophecy was simply advance notice of their inevitable death and that God would destroy these enemies of Israel. Jonah's repentence, therefore is incomplete. He fails to be completely at one with others. In fact, he goes and sulks outside the city of Nineveh. Apart, not at one with his fellow human beings. 'Do you do well to be so angry?' God asks. Jonah is being scolded and doesn't realize it. God repeats the lesson when he destroys the gourd he gives Jonah in Chapter 4. Jonah is angry that God has destroyed the plant, to which God responds: 'You have concern for the well-being of a plant yet you have no concern for the lives of 120,000 human beings in Nineveh?' Hillel's question rings clear. If I am only for myself, what am I?"

The congregation was all the way with him now. He was carrying us along.

"Like Jonah, as a people, we Jews don't like to be told what to do. Jonah's resistance to God's call echoes a behavior pattern we see throughout the TaNaKH. We spend much of our time in the Holy Scriptures turning our backs on God's call. From the Israelites dancing around the Golden Calf through the succession of the alternately wise and corrupt Kings of Israel and Judah to eventual exile in Babylon and elsewhere.. So what is it that the Book of Jonah is calling us to accept and fulfill? The Book of Jonah contains a vision of a united world and challenges the separateness we have always sought to maintain as Jews. Certainly, we have good reason to be suspicious of the world. I needn't go into a historical recounting of attempts made by the Gentile world to destroy us. We attach ourselves justifiably to Hillel's 1st question: If I am not for myself who will be for me? Our survival as a people depends upon our vigilance and industry. But we mustn't ignore Hillel's 2nd question: If I am only for myself, what am I?

God wants Jonah to help the Gentile sailors and the Gentile inhabitants of Nineveh, enemies of Israel. This is the task Jonah is resisting. He's not avoiding personal or physical difficulty. He's avoiding a God that requires him to help the enemies of his people. Jonah's name in Hebrew–Yonah– means "dove." Like a dove, Jonah is fiercely loyal to his people. But clearly, very clearly, God is displeased with the recalcitrance of Jonah, his unwillingness to connect beyond the insulated community and be a representative of God's chosen people in the Great Big World. When Jonah grieves over the death of the gourd when earlier he had been hoping for the deaths of 120,000 Ninevites, God's sore displeasure is profoundly expressed. The Book of Jonah ends with this scolding, with Jonah's failure to transcend self and immediate community and face the world. On this day of at–one–ment, when we try to reunite all that has been torn asunder, within ourselves and within our immediate community, we should also make an effort open our hearts to the possibility of reuniting all that is asunder in the Big World. It really is a desperate necessity. It is our responsibility. Looking inward must eventually steer us toward looking outward and connecting, perhaps unpleasantly at times, but willing to compromise, in an effort to rescue human civilization from the brink of catastrophe. It just simply must happen. We can no longer resist that call. We are out of time. We must emerge from the belly of this big fish ready to answer Hillel's 3rd and final question: If not now, when?"

I saw Schlicht after the service and I said, "*Yasher Koach*" to him because that's what I heard everybody else saying to him.

I wanted to get home and give sound to this song that had been festering in my head since the middle of Schlicht's Jonah *d'var*.

I actually wrote it in one sitting that night after the family breaking of the fast gathering.

I ended up calling it "Death Shuffle."

We all go there together

We all go there alone

Death is not forever

Death is not a stone

It just is, it just is

Death's not a secret

Let it be what it just is

Death is not a killer

Death is not a town

Death is not a call away

Death's not always around

It just is, it just is

Death's not a secret

Let it be what it just is

Death is not a terror

Death is not afraid

Death is not an error

That our fucking parents made

It just is, it just is

Death's not a secret

Let it be what it just is

Death is not a trouble

Death is not a crime

Death is not a bubble

From the bottom of the slime

It just is, it just is

Death's not a secret

Let it be what it just is

Death is not a tangle

Death is not a friend

Death is not a dangle

From a darkness with no end

It just is, it just is

Death's not a secret

Let it be what it just is

Although I had gone to temple to wallow in Miranda, I realized I had not thought about her at all pretty much the whole day.

My dream that night had something to do with military graveyards.

3

After the Yom Kippur connection Evelyn became someone I said hi to in the hall.

That's actually a pretty big deal in the tableau vivant that is my social life.

I'm not one of those people who says hi to everybody.

For me there's a kind of unspoken thing that has to happen between two people before they start acknowledging each other in the hall.

If we haven't had that unspoken thing happen, I don't say hi or even nod.

I'm not talking about strangers. I never say hi to strangers.

I'm talking about people I know but whose relationship with me is just distant enough to not require the hey-how's-it-going head-bob.

I like it like that.

It's always a relief not to have to acknowledge someone in passing.

How many unnecessary aisles have I walked down in the supermarket in avoidance of having to say hey-how's-it-going to someone I hardly know but who might be insulted if I ignore him?

How many times have I pretended to be shopping for tampons rather than stand in line behind my neighbor at the checkstand and have to make small talk?

I was once in line at Rexall behind my across the street neighbor Mr. Wilson, and he recognized me and then out of nowhere he said, "How about that Billy Carter huh? Wacky stuff."

I pretty much had no choice but to say, "Yup."

And then the joint realization that we had nothing else to say to each other amplified the already audible silence but luckily it was his turn in line and so he rescued both of us by talking to the cashier.

"How about that Billy Carter huh? Wacky stuff," he said to her.

"I guess," said the cashier after biting the bubble she'd blown and licking it off her upper lip, "whatever."

He turned to me, raised his eyebrows and pointed at her as if she'd actually said something meaningful.

I smirked and gave him the most noncommittal thumbs-up since the moment before the Big Bang.

"But you know behind closed doors President Carter goes off on him though, like 'What the fuck is wrong with you, cracker? I'm the President of the United Fucking States now. You can't be talking all crazy to the newspapers and radio and TV and shit. That shit don't fly now. The rules have changed,'" the cashier said and then blew a new bubble that covered her nose when it burst.

"That comes to $19.84," she said after her tongue couldn't reach and she had to use her fingers.

"Oh, my. Ominous," said Mr. Wilson as he handed her a $20 bill.

"I guess," she said, "A penny makes it 85 and a nickel 90, and a dime is 20 dollars."

Then Mr. Wilson raised his eyebrows and pointed at her again and I had no idea what the fuck he meant so I just nodded knowingly and gave him another limp thumbs-up.

I try to avoid such situations whenever possible.

Evelyn and I now had enough of an interactive thing to wave to each other on the quad and stuff.

We kindled a vague friendship, occasional exchanges of music—she made me Best of Iggy Pop and Best of Velvet Underground tapes and I turned her on to Leonard Cohen and Tom Waits—but also just goofing around.

Occasionally we'd listen to Rodney Bingenheimer's new show on KROQ while talking on the phone.

Rodney was playing lots of newer stuff, some of it from Los Angeles bands but also some of the punk rock that was starting to come from England and New York.

Sometimes she'd throw a wadded up piece of notebook paper at me when Mr. Fudd was obviously looking down Heaven Sender's blouse in Algebra 2.

"Heaven's working it," I heard Evelyn say once to Stephanie Pedersen, the wannabe chola with Charon mascara who sat in front of her, and Stephanie just said, "Ay, puta," like a white girl.

I remember this time Evelyn and I were talking at lunch and we saw Deirdre Lux walking with Mr. Hill across the quad, and Evelyn said, "They have to be fucking. Don't you think?"

"I can't help you there," I shrugged.

"Trust me."

"Why on earth would I do that?"

"Because I make you kick-ass tapes. Trust me. They're fucking. They're fucking like we should be."

"Why on earth would I do that?" I said again and we both started laughing.

A little later Evelyn came back to it.

"You don't want to fuck me? Not even a little?"

"Uh, no," I said, "Fraid not."

"For real?"

"Yeah."

"You're not just trying to be some saint or something?"

"No, for real," I said even though I had sometimes constant thoughts of fucking her.

"And you are heterosexual," she said.

"So far."

"And you really have no interest in fucking me."

"I have thought about it once or twice. But you're too cool."

"What does that mean?"

"You're too cool to fuck."

"You are a very weird boy," she said.

"I am aware of this fact, yes."

"And a liar."

Dang, dude.

For weeks I had been listening exclusively to Bob Dylan because I was determined to learn the craft from him.

On one particularly perfect afternoon after listening to "It's Alright Ma, I'm Only Bleeding" like 10 times in a row, I sat up on the garage roof and started picking a Dm chord on my guitar, finding a groove, a piano-player groove but a groove nevertheless, and I just picked it over and over again and began to summon what I wanted to be an avalanche of language, à la "It's Alright Ma."

My girls Calliope and Euterpe showed up and whetted my amplitude into writing this song I called "Frailty And The Naked Wrist."

Give me your tired, your pure

The muddled mess you must endure

Abate this suicide allure

Though the guide-like light remains obscure

Frailty and the naked wrist

One time around, the last chance missed

Six feet under and never been kissed

You'll be one soul fogged by misery missed

Then I changed the cadence and added an A7 at the end of each phrase.

The future's laughing backwards

We're the joke on which it thrives

While we cast ballots in the sewers

And vote on human lives

I wrote rough drafts of those first three stanzas that night and then labored at the song for days after, sometimes during class, and constantly after my homework was done at night, carrying several pieces of folded notebook paper in my back pocket with me wherever I went. That was my gear. Eddie Gurges had his sketchpad. Lorelei Lux had her notebook. I had my Bic 4-color pen and several pieces of folded up notebook paper in my right back pocket, a habit I've never kicked since. I like to write my rough drafts in green.

The rest of the song unfolded slowly but I was pleased.

From a rational tantrum in a flag-clad room

Once reborn, twice resumed

Feet-first back into the womb

Descending toward a blue-sky tomb

Clasping hands in a kneeling stance

Motionless in a ritual dance

Wear uniforms, a vague form of trance

Form prayers, vain airs of chance

The worship house is up for sale

Though the property's condemned

Here, don the shredding shroud

Knit and purl your own amends

The menace never vanishes

We're threatened as we try

Equality is a parody of what it's like to die

The only ends have been rebuilt

The means of which are strewn with guilt

Our nation chokes on silt

Stock customs other nations spilt

Death's your decision friend, your boast

You'll have second-guessed our gracious host

And those who loved you most

Will raise their glasses in a eulogy toast

Like the horizon that ends but never starts

Look forward now in anguish to the past as you depart

We were reading "Bartleby the Scrivener" in Megiddo's class, a warm up for our journey through *Moby-Dick*.

I loved "Bartleby" from the introduction of the characters on.

"I would prefer not to," we all said to Megiddo every time he'd assign us work for a couple of weeks afterward until it wasn't funny anymore.

"A man utterly alone in the universe," Megiddo said, Melville's very words, "*But he seemed alone, absolutely alone in the universe. A bit of wreck in the mid Atlantic.*"

"That gives me shivers, that image," said Gina Dichlich, "I'm terrified of the ocean."

"But does it make your nipples hard?" Buddy Feigenbaum asked almost inaudibly but loud enough for Gina to hear.

"Fuck you, Buddy," Gina said.

"OK, I'm cool with that," shrugged Buddy, "Shiver me timbers," he said miming a cock stroke.

"That's enough," Mr. Megiddo tutted, "Many more people have that fear than admit it, the fear of the ocean, the scrotumtightening sea, James Joyce called it," Mr. Megiddo said, looking around at some of us, me especially, while the class collectively giggled at Mr. Megiddo's use of the word scrotum, both because the word scrotum is funny unto itself and also because a teacher had said it outside of Health class.

"Flagrant," said Claude Moss.

I was, in fact, like Gina Dichlich, afraid of the ocean and still am.

I thought about "Bartleby the Scrivener" nonstop for days after we read it.

Of course "I would prefer not to" ran through my head constantly, but even more than that it was the "absolutely alone in the universe" image that haunted my conscience.

A bit of wreck in the mid Atlantic.

Another thing was that Bartleby reminded me of Buzzy.

Buzzy was moving beyond any ability to interact with the external world.

He still had stretches of lucidity but we could all tell they were getting harder and harder to sustain.

Buzzy would often not quite finish a point.

When pressed on this issue, that of not finishing his point, he'd rationalize it by saying, "That way you can participate in the making of the point instead of me just making it for you."

"Okey-Doke, Shmoke," would be my typical answer, or some other indirect way of saying I didn't know what the fuck he was talking about.

But then he'd diverge into private language meant only for his internal associates all of whom bore linguistic similarity to Bugs Bunny.

He understood that these episodes happened, these incidents of "disappearing into the wilderness."

"What do you do there?" I asked him once when I saw him sitting on his front porch and writing in a spiral notebook, ". . . in the wilderness?"

"A lot of times I go to visit the family in the house next door. I have dreams about them."

"But I live in the house next door," I said.

"No, it's a different house. Like a shack in the middle of nowhere, but it's also next door. I can't really explain it. At first I thought it was a dream thing. But it's always there, dude. It's like a cabin in the woods."

"And there's a family in there?"

"Totally."

"And you talk to them?"

"Well mostly I'm just eavesdropping from outside the windows. They don't know I'm there. I never get to go inside the house. I want to go inside but I'm also really afraid that I'll get trapped in there and never get back out. Ooh, and dang, dude, this one time I really freaked out because I could actually see in the window and it was *my* house, *this* house. That was some trippy-ass shit, dude. Occasionally I follow them to this underground city. It's really molten metal looking, like all the buildings glowing orange and shit, and the Eiffel Tower is there and the Statue of Liberty."

If I was over at his house and he would disappear into the wilderness, there to vegetate in catatonia or speak in maniacal geysers of language, I would use the opportunity to play records of his I didn't have at home, and, if I didn't just go home (to the house next door), I'd maybe try to flirt with Penelope, faithfully waiting for me, just across the hall, in the alien galaxy of an older sister's bedroom.

This one time, dang, dude, I went into Penelope Lagniappe's room and she was listening to the radio and we got royally stoned because her parents weren't home and she did this flagrant wiggle dance to the song "Play That Funky Music, White Boy" which launched the most flagrant erection that I know she saw and I was a little embarrassed but I was also kind of turned on when I saw her see it. We didn't do anything but the possibilities kept me flush with fantasy for many nights thereafter and that's just as good anyway.

When Jimmy Carter was elected president we were all really excited to be leaving behind Gerald Ford's purposely dull America and the last vestiges of Nixon and were looking forward to where the plain-spoken governor from Georgia would lead us.

Claude had a poster up in his room that was a picture of Jimmy Carter, bearded and looking like white Jesus, and beneath the picture it said "J.C. Will Save America."

Right before the election, like the weekend before, Miranda had shown up at our front door with her mother.

They were canvassing for Jimmy Carter.

It was the Saturday before the election, and when I first heard the doorbell my impulse was to turn off the TV and hide behind the couch because I thought it was the Jehovah's Witnesses.

But then I heard Miranda's voice saying, "This is Lance's house," and so I answered the door.

"Hi, Lance!" Miranda's mother said to me, "Are your parents home?"

"Hey," I said, "No, they are out and about somewhere."

"Hey," Miranda said to me.

"Hey, how's it going," I said back.

"Pretty good," she nodded and rocked nervously.

Tamar started her spiel about how we can't endure 4 more years of the status quo under Ford but I told her both of my parents were voting for Jimmy Carter so she didn't have to convince anyone.

"Excellent! Campaign button?" she asked.

"Yeah, sure," I said and Miranda handed me one.

"Thanks," I said, "and can I maybe have two more for my sisters?"

"Absolutely," Tamar motioned to Miranda, "and also for your parents."

"Thank you thank you," I said again.

"You're welcome," Miranda answered and looked at me only for a second.

"Well, onward," Tamar said, "Nice to see you, Lance."

"Take it easy," I said and sang it to myself.

"Remind your parents to vote on Election Day!" Tamar waved.

Miranda was already walking away.

In the week or so following the election, with politics buzzingly immanent and me still under Dylan's sway, I decided to write a political song called "When Shall We Be Free?"

The concept was actually ripped off from "Won't Get Fooled Again," but I figured that song was just invoking a universal truth so it's not really copying, just adding my angle on the tendency of revolutions to eventually spawn a new authoritarian regime.

Dormant inside for many years

The build was slow but sure

It happened just as I had feared

But how much longer can it be endured?

There's no escaping the power you possess

Will it transcend your all too certain death?

When shall we be free? When shall we be free?

The prophets speak of a savior

A messiah to save our souls

I don't see how our behavior

Affects in any way the final toll

The family business thrives on what you preach

Love God and country, that's what you teach

When shall we be free? When shall we be free?

I'm the guy, you've seen me before

My brother died in the middle of your last war

Take it all then take some more

After all that's what we're here for

I can't stand the heat in the kitchen where it's warm

Rising swelling waves and tides are turning true to form

The books are burning to be unknown to the unborn

No silver lining surrounds the cloud of your radioactive storm

No more lies! When shall we be free?

Lose your disguise! When shall we be free?

Newspaper stories they don't tell us

Who's talking behind those doors

And this world you've tried to sell us

Can't be bought in any store

And all the broken windows and burning building deaths

To you were only inconsequential threats

When shall we be free? When shall we be free?

Of your politics I'm growing weary

You move in a paradox

Your plan for independence works in theory

But in practice it lies lamely on the rocks

Here's your final warning

Listen very hard

The deck is stacked against you

As soon as you pick your first card

When shall we be free? When shall we be free?

After the second verse I wanted there to be a long guitar solo, symbolizing the revolution itself, followed by a half-verse, the aftermath.

And now the flag is ours

We own the people too

Now we wear shirts and ties

Just like they used to do

This is our vision

And we dictate what is true

One by one we'll win

And own the world before we're through

Our revolution has only just begun

Why are they shouting then

"My God what have we done?"

And the final insult

Our prize for having won

Is the people that we fought for

They're all crying in the sun

They're crying:

When shall we be free?

When shall we be free?

When shall we be free?

When shall we be free?

Later that night I was watching Part 1 of this new TV movie called *Sybil* about a woman with multiple personality disorder.

It had been much anticipated because Sally Field was going to play Sybil, and we were all curious how she'd do in such an intense role because to us Sally Field was, well, Gidget, but also, maybe even more significant to us, she was Sister Bertrille from *The Flying Nun.*

Dolly called right in the middle of *Sybil*, during one of the long commercial breaks.

"Hey, what's up," she said.

"Nothing much," I said.

"Watching *Sybil?*"

"Isn't everybody?"

"I guess, yeah," she said, "haha."

"Sally Field is great," I said.

"Oh definitely," she said and paused, "She's pulling it off for sure. Hey, Mandy's here and has a question to ask you."

It had been like 5 or 6 weeks or so since Miranda and I had our ugly phone conversation and we'd only exchanged a few words since then, all of them unpleasantly awkward, like when she came to the door canvassing for Carter.

"She talks like Buzzy Lagniappe, don't you think?" Miranda took the phone from Dolly and talked to me like nothing had happened.

"Sally Field's people have more variety in their voices," I said, bewildered by her friendly tone but trying to tap into it.

"*The people, the people,*" Miranda said and then laughed.

"*The purple,*" I said in the same voice which was kind of like my munchkin voice.

I could hear Dolly's TV in the background and it sounded like Dolly was having some kind of argument with her mother.

"How are you?" Miranda asked.

"Pretty good," I said.

"I miss you."

"Likewise."

"Here's Dolly," Miranda said and handed the phone over.

"This is really weird," Dolly sort of whispered. It sounded like she was walking with the phone into another room.

"What is?"

"Well, Mandy's here and, you know, I don't know, it's weird."

"Why is it weird? I mean it's weird that Miranda talked to me just now like everything was normal."

"Nyeah—and, I don't know. It's weird. I feel weird."

"You *are* weird," I said.

"Shut up," she flirted back, "See? It's weird. I want to play with you right now and I can't."

"Is she telling you all the details of her relationship with Freddy?" I asked.

"Well yeah but."

"Maybe we should talk another time," I said.

"Nyeah nyeah you're no fun," Dolly said, "That's not true, yes you are. Sibyl's coming back on anyway so yeah."

"Later," I said.

"Maybe we'll actually hang out one day," she said.

"We will for sure," I said because that one always worked for a while.

"OK bye," she said and added "I love you" quickly as she was hanging up.

The next day after school when I went to Aron's to get *Radio Ethiopia*, Patti Smith's new album, Taryn Rust was working.

I'd seen her there a few other times since she'd given me that blow-job up in Cambria and we'd make eye contact and smile and stuff, but this time she came over to talk to me while I was flipping through the $1 bins.

"New Patti," she saw me holding the album.

"Oh yeah," I said, "Just checking to see if there are any other treasures in here today."

"Aren't there always?"

"Pretty much," I smirked.

"You wanna come listen to it at my house?"

I shrugged.

"We're overdue for a rendezvous," she bumped my butt.

"Uhhm, your family," I said.

"I got my own place in September, I moved out," she said.

"Ah," I said, "But I promised Manny I'd listen to it first with him," which was the truth actually although I probably would have said it anyway even if it weren't.

I wasn't quite sure why I was rejecting Taryn's offer. I just felt weird about it.

"Bummerooni," she said.

"What are you doing these days besides working?" I asked her.

"I'm taking a music history class at LACC."

"You're just taking one class?"

"Yeah," she shrugged, "I tell everybody I'm going to a 4-year college, which is true 'cause LACC is a college and it's going to take me 4 years to get my AA."

I smiled but remained silent.

"Well maybe some other time," she said, "I have to get back to work. Your turn, remember," she reminded me with her tongue, "See ya."

4

On Saturday night I went over to Manny's house to give a listen to *Radio Ethiopia*.

We warmed up for the event with a ritual pre-listening toke session out in

Manny's old playhouse of course.

"Is your sister home?" I asked him, partaking of the smoothest Thai stick.

Manny lay back and closed his eyes.

"Dude, you always ask me that question. She's away at college."

"Oh yeah. Brown, right?"

"Yeah yeah, Miss Perfect Grades. Cal State Northridge for me."

"Me too, dude. C in every math and science class."

"C as in CSUN," he drawled.

"Dang, dude," we said to ourselves separately.

I kept forgetting Leah was away at college. I'd have to derive my imagery from elsewhere later alas.

We talked about our music a little bit.

Manny had been writing a bunch of really great melodic rock songs which he played for me whenever I went over.

I'd already played him my newest tunes and he suggested we form a band to do my stuff and his stuff.

"You'll sing your tunes and play rhythm guitar. I'll play piano and sing my tunes. We just need bass, drums and lead guitar."

"Let's do it," I said.

"For sure," Manny said, "We have to. We need a name."

"42 Kims," I said.

"Girl On Girl would be really funny."

"Crush Whore."

"Sorry No Beaver," Manny grabbed one from the way past.

"Terminal Highway."

"Echo Echo Echo."

"The Loch Ness Munsters."

"Dang, dude, Herman Munster in a kilt."

"Totally."

"Yeti Vs. Sasquatch."

"Highly Salami."

"Jewish reggae band."

"YHVH Rastafari, mon."

We both tried to come up with others but it all got too cloudy.

"Dude, it's Patti time," Manny said and started to hoist himself against the preeminence of gravity.

And thus we slogged from the backyard into the house.

"Immanuel!," his mom called from the back bedroom, "I think I left my pills on the what's-it-called! Can you bring them?"

"Yeah!" he shouted and went to the kitchen.

I poked my head into Leah's bedroom which had lost her scent in the weeks since she'd left for college.

I felt like I was floating down the Shepherd hallway for a second.

I had to navigate my way through the dining room to Manny's bedroom because the dining room table was too big to allow unhindered passage around the chairs.

Manny had a really small bedroom compared to his sister and parents.

There was just pretty much room for his bed and a dresser. Just enough floor space to lie down on during music listening sessions.

His stereo sat on top of the dresser.

LPs and open books were strewn across his bed..

Manny had trouble keeping track of his personal environment.

I knew he was currently engrossed in *The Electric Kool Aid Acid Test,* but there was also a collection of Schopenhauer essays by his pillow as well as *Autobiography of a Yogi, A Season In Hell, The Knee of Listening* by Bubba Free John, and, of course, *Moby-Dick* which he was reading for Megiddo's class.

Following the sublime crackle of needle lowering onto vinyl, Radio Ethiopia came out ripping.

Ask the angels who they're calling

Go ask the angels if they're calling to thee

Ask the angels, while they're falling

Who that person could possibly be

Both our heads were bobbing and we were smiling and pointing at each other throughout.

And rock and roll is what I'm born to be

We gave each other five in agreement and then sang together:

and it's wild, wild, wild, wild

"Guitar solo," said Manny moving his fingers to the riff.

For a while we were too absorbed in the music to speak.

Her poetry was more spaced out than the music.

Hey Sheba, hey Salome, hey Venus eclipsin' my way. Her vessel, every woman is a vessel, is evasive, is aquatic.

"Beautiful," I said.

"Women," said Manny.

"That line," I said, "*Every woman is a vessel, is evasive, is aquatic.*"

When, when will you be landing?

When, when will you return?

Feel, feel my heart expanding

I was reminded of "Goodbye Yellow Brick Road."

When are you gonna come down?

When are you going to land?

And that of course reminded me of Miranda and our only real dance together.

Coming in the airport, coming in the sea

Coming in the garden, got a conscious stream

Coming in a washroom, coming in a plane

Coming in a force field, coming in my brain

"Dang, dude," I said.

"I love when chicks talk about coming," Manny answered.

"Totally."

"In a major way."

"Coming in my brain . . . dude. Flagrant."

"She's like Rimbaud," Manny said. He had gotten really into French symbolist poetry and so the analogy didn't surprise me. "And Leonard Cohen is like Verlaine, and Dylan is like Baudelaire."

"I guess maybe," I said 'cause I didn't feel qualified to say anything else.

I didn't know much of that stuff.

I think I'd read maybe one Verlaine poem by then.

Rimbaud I knew a bit better because Manny always had *A Season in Hell* on his bed and I would flip through it all the time, and, yeah, I could see the connection to Patti Smith's imagery and attitude. So that part worked.

I'd skimmed a cool collection of Baudelaire poems one afternoon when I was killing time at Papa Bach waiting for *Children of Paradise* to start at the NuArt but I don't recall any Dylanesque imagery at all.

Deep in the heart of your brain is a lever

Oh deep in the heart of your brain is a switch

Oh deep in the heart of your flesh you are clever

Oh honey you met your match in a bitch

"Right on," Manny said.

"Dang," I said, "Bitches, dude."

"So who's the current crush?" Manny asked me.

"Oh, everybody, you know," I said, "I think about them all."

"Every single one of them has a pussy," he said, "You ever think about that?"

"Dude, it's the underlying basis for every conversation. Of course."

"I mean, that's the first thing I think when I look at a girl. 'She has a pussy,' I say to myself," Manny said.

"I'm more inclined to say, uh, 'nice eyes.'"

"But you're really thinking, 'She has a pussy' I mean come on dude admit it."

"It's all about the eyes for me. That's where it happens, dude."

"I thought Miranda would always be into you," Manny said unprompted.

"Me? Haha."

"I was surprised when she started up with Freddy."

"I wasn't."

"Really?"

"Nyeah, I knew it was gonna happen."

"How?"

"They've always had a thing."

"Well I was surprised," Manny shrugged.

"Who's your current masturbation muse?"

"Whoever I'm into that day," he said, "You know exactly how it is. Hey have you read that Samuel Beckett book *How It Is?*"

"I've seen it in bookstores but I've never read it."

"It's trippy. There's no punctuation. I've got it here somewhere but good luck finding it."

Neither of us tried to.

We both lay on our backs in the dark, Manny on his bed, I on the floor, listening to the final track, the title track from Radio Ethiopia, a magnificent piece of apocalyptic space-performance.

Feel so fucked up

I walked home from Manny's house still majorly stoned but held alert by the chilly night air.

I ran into Gina Dichlich on Oakwood and Fuller. She was with this boxy girl in an L.A. Kings jersey who, I think, went to Fairfax the year before but I hadn't seen her around campus lately.

"Lance, Wendy," Gina introduced us and we said hey. "Lance sits next to me in English," she explained.

"And we have been in school together since Kindergarten," I said, "don't forget."

"I remember you from last year," Wendy said. She had a nose ring.

"You wanna get high?" Gina offered.

"Already there, man," I said, laughing and they laughed too.

"Right on," Gina said, "So what're you up to?"

"Oh, I was just hanging with Manny Shepherd listening to the new Patti Smith album."

"Cool," Gina said.

"She's a dyke, isn't she?" Wendy asked.

"Not as far as I know, no," I said.

"I heard she was," Wendy said, "but it was from this asshole chick who doesn't know shit about shit so never mind," she then cackled like a toucan.

"Sure you don't wanna smoke out with us?" Gina held up a joint.

"Nah, I'm well fueled already. I wanna get home and work on this song idea."

"Do it," Gina said.

"Inspired by Patti, you know."

"Righteous," Gina said, "Rock on."

"Nice to meet you," I said to Wendy and she said yeah back.

I thought about veering up to Melrose to get an apple fritter, but then I decided to head straight home and work on this new song that had been bubbling around in my brain for a few days and which I had just realized what to do with once I'd heard *Radio Ethiopia*.

My dad was tuned into Johnny Carson when I got home.

"Howdy doo, Mr. Lance," he said, "Johnny's got Raquel Welch on tonight if you still carry that flame."

"Ah, cool, no."

"Do you know about the time Raquel was on and she had her cat with her and she said to Johnny, 'Do you want to pet my pussy?' and Johnny said,

'Yeah but you'll have to move the cat first?'"

"Yes you've told me that one before."

"Dirtiest thing I've ever seen on television."

"I'm gonna work on a song before I go to bed," I turned down the hall.

"Even better," he said and went back to the tube.

I sat on my bed with my 3-way lamp on dim and sandalwood incense burning.

I strummed A-minor to E-minor until I got a rocking hippie groove going.

Watching God watching us watching us

Watching God watching us watching us

Watching God watching us watching us

Watching us watching God

That would be the chorus, open enough for great rich harmonies and also some cool round-singing at the end for sure.

The verses would freeze in time between choruses.

The song seeped out slow and easy.

We can't fly

There's not a Jesus in the sky

We can't stand

We've been banned from Buddhaland

We're designed

So inclined

Watching God watching us watching us

Watching God watching us watching us

Watching God watching us watching us

Watching us watching God

We are lame

Armageddon never came

We are trapped

The Apocalypse collapsed

We're confined

To the mind

Watching God watching us watching us

Watching God watching us watching us

Watching God watching us watching us

Watching us watching God

We can't pray

Allah's heart has given way

We can't see

Hidden myth or mystery

We're consigned

To be blind

Watching God watching us watching us

Watching God watching us watching us

Watching God watching us watching us

Watching us watching God

Manny was really into that one when I played it for him.

"Dude, we could totally jam out on this. Gotta find that ace lead guitar player. Hey I talked to Yigal Frumkin about playing in our band."

"Drumkin," I drawled Yigal's nickname. He played drums in both orchestra and jazz band. "That'd be fantastic."

"Hell, yeah, in a major way," Manny said, "I told him maybe we could talk at the Librocubicularist Society meeting tomorrow."

"Totally," I said.

I wasn't one for joining clubs at school, but that year a club called the Librocubicularist Society had formed. It met in Mr. Megiddo's class during lunch once a week, and I felt like I had to be part of it.

Its ostensible purpose was to be a once-a-week gathering place for the appreciation of strange words.

The club was started by this 12th Grader named Herman Q. Levine, a brilliant, fast-rapping Jewboy, part Groucho Marx, part Monty Python, who really used the club to free associate out loud.

Normally, school clubs, in order to be approved by Student Council, had to agree to a democratic process of electing officers. But somehow the Librocubicularist Society bypassed that requirement or else lied on the approval request form and then ignored it because the Librocubicularist Society was an absolute monarchy, with Herman being the King, naturally.

His Loyal Shyness King Herman, self-described son of Moses and Zipporah, created his royal court from those among us, dubbed with such titles as the The Prince of Prolix Poetry, the Princess of Penis Envy, the Duke of Dime-Store Novels, the Earl of Existential Angst, The Suzerain of Saucy Sidekicks, the Kaiser of Keystone Kop Kapers, the Comtesse of Closet Dramas, the Grand Poobah of Pedantry, the Marquess of Movie Novelizations, the Queen of Saturnalian Roman Orgy Scenes, a title bestowed upon none other than Herman's girlfriend Sheba Neville who looked just like Herman, and indeed they were kind of like the same person, the only differences between them being Sheba thinking Valentine's Day was important and Herman thinking the Three Stooges were funny.

"You can either call us Sheba and Herman or Sheba and Her Man," she loved to say to any new listener.

King Herman dubbed me the Baron of Pornography & Ribald Humor.

"Because therewith thou hast no peerage," said his majesty as he tapped my shoulder with his scepter wrapped in purple and gold tinsel that he got at a Lakers game.

One of the rituals of the club was that whenever the name of poet Gerard Manley Hopkins was uttered, everyone in the room was supposed to shout "Boo! Hiss!"

I liked Gerard Manley Hopkins. We'd read "Spring and Fall" in Beauregard's class in 10th Grade and I dug the way he played with language and sound.

It is the blight man was born for

It is Margaret you mourn for

That poem got right to the gist of it.

Apparently the 12th Graders in Megiddo's AP English class didn't share the fondness.

Another one of Herman's tropes was every time he'd shout, "Bad Mother!" we all had to shout back "Shut Your Mouth!"

Occasionally he'd respond, "Well I'm talking' 'bout Shaft," but mostly he'd point at us and then try to dance like James Brown which is something white guys should just simply never try to do, because, sorry, but dang, dude.

Every meeting would begin with the official Librocubicularist Society chant:

Genuflect we'd all say and kneel and make the sign of the cross.

PRO–lix, PRO–lix, PRO–lix, PRO–lix was chanted while snapping fingers.

Snapping fingers continued:

Librocubicularist, Brobdingnag, Brobdingnag

Librocubicularist, Brobdingnag, Brobdingnag

Triskadecaphobia, Brobdingnag, Brobdingnag

Triskadecaphobia, Brobdingnag, Brobdingnag

And then making the motion of pushing someone out the window we'd grunt:

De–fe–ne–stra–tion! De–fe–ne–stra–tion!

And back to snapping fingers:

Pro–LIX, Pro–LIX, Pro–LIX

Herman entered the room with his scepter but also wearing a paper crown from Burger King.

"Our featured word this week, latelies and gentlebens," King Herman pronounced, "is *smegma*. I command my royal page to bring hither the holy *Funk & Wagnall's* so that we, that is the *Royal We*, might look it up therein."

Several people in the room were already going ew because they knew what smegma was.

I know I did. The unfortunate result of reading the dictionary for fun.

Jim Lord gave me a thumb's up from across the room and mouthed the words 'head cheese.'

Jim Lord always knew stuff like that too and knew I knew also. That was the basis of our early relationship. Word recognitions across the room.

The "royal page" was this intense scrawny dude named Clarence Hellsworth. I think he was a 10th Grader. The dictionary was actually a little too heavy for him, but he made it to Mr. Megiddo's podium where King Herman located smegma and then said, "I deem it fitting that this week's definition be recited to us by the very Baron of Pornography & Ribald Humor himself."

He beckoned me with his scepter.

"Lance Atlas, Baron of Pornography & Ribald Humor, arise and come forward."

"But I am circumcised, my liege," I said bowing low, "I suffer not the genteel indignities of smegma."

"We'll forgive you your shortcomings in this instance and beseech you to grace us with your lofty wickedness, O worthy Hebrew. Title or no you are my subject and must obey my command, or off with the rest of your head, *verstehst du noch?*"

"I will oblige, m'lord," I came forward.

The King pointed to *smegma* with his scepter.

"I feel like I'm at my bar mitzvah," I said to much laughter due to the preponderance of Jews in the room, and then I read out loud in mock-heroic tones, *"The secretion of a sebaceous gland; specifically the cheesy sebaceous matter that collects between the glans penis and the foreskin or around the clitoris and labia minora."*

"Gross!" shouted one of several girls I didn't know.

I looked over at Claire to gauge the look on her face.

She didn't make eye contact in that moment. She seemed to be humored though.

Claire and I would go to Librocubicularist Society meetings together and then we'd walk down the hall to Cinema class Period 5 after lunch.

I found myself opting to hang with Claire in a variety of interim situations lately, like between classes, Madame Couchée's room at lunch, occasionally in the hall outside Megiddo's room before school on the mornings she'd arrive early enough to sit and gab.

We had a beautiful little groove going.

I first knew something was up and funny with my feelings for Claire when Claude Moss asked her out and I felt all twinged about it.

Pre-jealousy.

I remember Whit and Manny giving him a hard time the day Claude and Claire were supposed to be going on their date.

We were at Claude's house doing bong hits and listening to *The Royal Scam*.

"So where are you taking her?" Whit asked Claude.

"We're gonna go see *Logan's Run* at the Pan Pacific."

"Dang, that's *still* playing there."

"Doesn't Claire work at the Pan Pacific?" Manny asked.

"Yeah, that's why we're going. She can get us in for free. I'm going there when her shift ends."

"Dang, dude, chicks like it when you spend money on them. And you're taking her to a free movie at the place where she works? That's dog, dude. You've gotta make it special," Whit said, "or you're not gonna get anything off her."

"How far you think you're gonna get?" Manny asked, "First base?"

"Buy me some penis and jack her crack," Whit sang, "I won't care till she's down on her back. and it's root root root . . . ."

Claude laughed at that.

"I don't know," he said, "far as I can I guess. Definitely 1st base. Maybe 2nd?"

"Sacrifice bunt probably," I said.

"Base on balls for sure," Whit snickered.

"Intentional walk," Manny added, "Just don't strike out looking, dude."

Dorky guy giggles mingled and rumbled among us, the easily amused.

I was trying to stay upbeat despite my bumming over Claire going out with Claude.

I was surprised at how much it niggled at me.

Luckily (and also really weirdly) neither of them ever spoke about that one and only date they had. Not a single word about what happened.

A few days later Claire was blowing on my face during Mr. Megiddo's class causing me to look over.

I was falling into her essence.

"So what do we take away from *Moby-Dick* other than it's long and hard?" Mr. Megiddo asked us in class.

The class was silent after a brief laugh.

Mr. Megiddo sat in a student desk but facing us. He extended his long legs and crossed them at the ankles.

"Come on, tomorrow you're going to be taking a test on it."

"What's the format of the test?" Gina Dichlich asked.

"There will be 4 I.D. questions-passages that you have to comment on in short-answer form and one full-length essay on some aspect of the book."

"Like what aspects should we be preparing for?" Arabella Mayflower asked from the back.

"The things we talked about in class would be a good place to focus."

"Could you please be a little bit more vague, Mr. Megiddo?" Jim Lord asked to random laughter.

"You know very well what to study," Mr. Megiddo said, "If you were paying attention in class you'll be fine. But go over some things tonight. Talk to a classmate about it. Share ideas. But what do we take away from *Moby-Dick*? Come on."

I raised my hand.

"Lance," Mr. Megiddo pointed.

"It's kind of like 'Bartelby' only just about everybody in *Moby-Dick* is all alone in the universe."

"Especially Ishmael," Mr. Megiddo said.

"When he's floating on Queequeg's coffin it's like that image 'a bit of wreck in the mid Atlantic' in 'Bartleby.,'" I said.

"That's great," Megiddo said, "Nice catch."

"I like Lance's idea that everybody's alone," Miranda said, "Ahab is the loneliest of all, I think."

I looked at her and she was right there waiting for it. She tilted her head and glanced at me briefly.

"In a way there never is any real camaraderie among the crew," Mr. Megiddo said.

"I was gonna say," Miranda agreed, "Everything's a secret on the Pequod."

"Is this gonna be on the test?" Gina Dichlich asked.

"You bet. A new essay question is being born as we speak," Mr. Megiddo said.

The class mumbled amongst themselves debating whether or not Megiddo was joking about the new essay question being born.

You never knew with Megiddo.

Sometimes he'd come into class and say, "OK, sheet of paper out, everything else off your desk, quiz on last night's reading," and when we'd complain that he said we weren't going to have a reading quiz today, he'd answer, "Oh, did I say were weren't going to have a reading quiz today? Well, I lied. Question #1 . . ."

With Megiddo, you were always wise to presume.

"What are we doing today?" Claude Moss asked because everyday somebody had to ask that stupid fucking question and that day it happened to be Claude.

"Walt Whitman," said Megiddo.

"Whitman!" Whitman Rust said.

Mr. Megiddo smiled and handed out a sizable packet.

"These are excerpts from his poem 'Song of Myself.'"

"This is all one poem?" Whitman Rust asked.

"Excerpts from one poem, yes."

"Dang, dude," Whit answered.

The day we did Whitman in Megiddo's class was the last day Buzzy Lagniappe was in school for the rest of the semester. I stopped seeing him next door too for a while.

Megiddo read from the massive swath of excerpts, bringing it alive and making it immediate, as if Whitman were in the room with us, as only Megiddo could do, words on the page became ideas in the air.

I was enraptured by the dance of language as well as the transcendent imagery.

Walt Whitman was equally free wandering lonely hillsides and striding through the streets of Manhattan.

His ability to love everything seemed to me a revelation to be emulated.

My heart wanted to find that openness so that all the stars inside it might finally shine.

"*Urge and urge and urge, always the procreant urge of the world,*" I said out loud as I exited school that afternoon, out the side gate via the cafeteria onto Genesee.

I felt the whole horny planet tilting in the same direction.

No matter the pretext, it's always about fucking.

I was really inspired by the Walt Whitman poetry, and my journey home that day was electrified by Whitman's ecstatic vision as well as by increasingly prevalent thoughts of Claire Farnaway.

Walking home from school could sometimes be a drag but other times it was a space for reverie and revelation and freedom and all kinds of hope.

"*Trippers and askers surround me,*" I said and embraced my fellow freaky citizens in all their warbling mania.

The Fairfax area was blessed with a stable of unusual characters who all added to the experience of walking home from school.

There was Martel Morrie, who shook his legs as he walked down Beverly Boulevard taking notes on a little pocket pad.

Morrie usually seemed to be in a state of great amusement.

Like the voices in his head were Borscht Belt comedians or something.

There was also Lava Lady who lived in an obsidian stone house with no windows on the corner of Detroit and Clinton.

She wore her hair straight up in a cone and walked around in enormous platform shoes which made her seem about 7-feet tall.

Her long coat complemented a pair of purple corduroy bellbottoms which flared out drastically from under the coat.

She moved along the sidewalk with infernal confidence.

The hellsparks in her wake shielded her from unwelcome interaction with the straights.

Bad-ass biker dudes were always hanging out in her front yard. She'd stand outside and laugh with them.

It was weird to see Lava Lady smoke a cigarette and laugh.

Like she was making an unnatural connection with humanity or something.

There was also Grampus, the fat old man who'd say to us as we'd journey past his fetid bivouac in the doorway of the long abandoned Spanish Kitchen, "Heh heh heh, I like little girls like you; I put 'em on my dick and twirl 'em aroun'. Heh heh heh heh."

Then he'd go back to masturbating and shouting at us as we'd walk away, "I wouldn't fuck you with a dog's dick! Heh heh heh heh . . . that's beautiful, baby."

There was Ripley The Stripper who'd stand all day on the corner of 3rd and Fairfax by the Town & Country shopping center, across the street from Farmers Market.

He was a man of great flabby girth who'd pose shirtless for the tour buses as they queued up to turn into the Farmers Market parking lot.

His jiggling midlands were on display while he'd stand at curbside and wave and roll his belly.

Every so often a cop would come by and laugh with him for a while and make him put his shirt on.

Then Ripley'd take it off as soon as the cop would leave and get back to shaking his funky groove thing.

There was Valentino the Vietnam vet, a hyper-intense weirdo who'd get all amped up on caffeine at Fiddler's coffee shop on Beverly.

He kind of moved like he had cerebral palsy, but I'm pretty sure he didn't have it. It was more like a nervous twitch type thing.

Valentino would sit at the counter at Fiddler's and sometimes just go off.

"Valentino, tell us about your latest girlfriend," one of the other counter regulars would prompt, and Valentino would rant away.

"So I told her straight up, I said, 'Look, the only reason I came here is to fuck your pussy, baby, so let's dispense with the ceremonials and get right to it' and then she gets angry at me like I'm the bad guy in all this and so I just flat out tell the bitch, 'Listen, hon, I'm not the bad guy in all this, you are, because you know why? You know why you're the bad guy in all this? You're the bad guy in all this because you're the one, not me, you, you're the one who's being dishonest, right? You claim you want to go out to dinner and see a movie and all that crapola when we both know all you are thinking about right now is having my hard dick inside you,' and then she gets even more furious and shrieks like a viper 'cause they're all vipers, every single fucking one of them, she shrieks, 'I can't believe my mother duped me into going on this blind date, I'm gonna fucking kill her,' and then I was happy to leave asap 'cause I realized that if that bitch was crazy enough to kill her own mother then you fuckin' know she could easily be giving me the praying mantis treatment by the end of the evening. I mean I want my cock to be worshipped, but not like that. No way."

The brothers who owned Fiddler's would laugh and give him his daily coffee and bear claw.

After exiting school I'd usually walk down Genesee Avenue past the tennis courts where the girls team would always be practicing.

"Both in and out of the game and watching and wondering at it," I thought more Whitman to myself as I watched the girls volley for a while.

I recognized in that Whitman line my own eternal role, that of the removed participant, the involved observer.

In and out of the game.

My thoughts were interrupted by Claire Farnaway calling out "Hey!" to me as I walked past, "Lance!"

Claire was on Varsity.

I went up to the fence to see what she wanted.

"Hey," she said, gripping the chain links that separated us.

"What's up?" I asked.

"Nothing," she said, "I just wanted to say hi."

"Well, hi," I said.

"Hi," she said back, and we both abided the silence a while, "Uhm–"

"I'm heading home," I said.

"Cool. You ready for the *Moby-Dick* test?" she asked.

"Mostly, yeah, I really dug the book."

"Ew, even those boring technical chapters that keep interrupting the story?"

"OK, I admit I skimmed those," I said.

"Everybody skims them!" she said.

"I bet Megiddo even skims them," I said.

"No doubt," Claire laughed, "What do you think Megiddo might have us write about on the essay part?"

"Oh you know it'll have to do with all the allegorical religious stuff," I said, "He hit that really hard in class. Unless he goes for the stuff we talked about today."

"That was so cool, the connection you made to 'Bartleby' and everyone being alone," Claire said.

"Thanks."

"Miranda sure liked it."

Chicks. Dang, dude.

"I guess," I said.

"Hey, maybe we could talk about the test and stuff later like on the phone or something if you're around tonight."

"I'll be around, yeah," I said.

"I'll call you. I'll get your number from Miranda."

"No, don't do that."

"Oh, yeah, huh," she said but I couldn't read the tone.

I nodded at her.

"Dolly then," she said.

"Nyeah, uhm, don't do that either."

"Dang, dude," Claire said.

"Here," I pulled a piece of notebook paper out of my backpack and wrote down my number. I'm usually too lazy to do that, but I wanted to prevent a further listing of girls in my orbit..

You are a fucking slut

"Ah, you're a WEbster, too," she saw the prefix.

"Yeah."

"Miss Farnaway," Coach Hathaway called, "tear yourself away from your boyfriend and get back to working on your far from adequate serve!"

Claire smiled at me.

"Bye, boyfriend," she said.

"See ya."

Claire did call that night and we talked about *Moby-Dick* and stuff.

"Man, Megiddo was getting pretty sexual today," Claire said.

"Oh, you mean when he described *Moby-Dick* as 'long and hard'? That was just a joke."

"Haha, yeah that, but also earlier about *Moby-Dick* being a sperm whale and Ahab's missing leg being an emasculation image and all that."

"Totally, and, ooh, dude, remember early on the shit about Ishmael and Queequeg in bed."

"Yeah yeah," she giggled.

"Ishamel afraid of getting stabbed by Queequeg's big harpoon! Isn't that what he said?"

"Yes!"

"That was flagrant."

I told her what I was anticipating doing on the essay portion of the *Moby-Dick* test and we went over all the allegorical stuff Megiddo brought up in class.

After that first encounter, I began visiting with Claire at the fence every day on the way home after school.

One afternoon I was peeling apart a flower I'd picked up from the ground while I talked to her.

"What are these bushes that grow along the fence anyway, do you know? I see them everywhere, like even on the freeway."

"Oleander," I said, "We have some of this growing along our backyard wall. Oleander is poisonous actually."

Claire nodded her head and then sort of laughed to herself.

"That makes sense," she said.

"What does?"

"Oh . . . when my sister and I were being bad or loud or whatever, my dad used to tell us to behave or he'd give us oleander salad for dinner. We had no idea what he meant."

"Whoa."

"Yeah. What an asshole," she looked into the distance, "Luckily I don't have to see him much anymore."

"How often?"

"Oh, like every other weekend though sometimes not if things come up. I always get the feeling he's relieved when I can't go over to stay at his place for the weekend. He has another family now."

I hadn't known of her sadness until then. I knew she had sadnesses because everyone does. But I didn't know that particular one.

One day I walked past the tennis courts and there was no practice going on. The courts were deserted.

I was majorly bummed. It was, in fact, an extraordinary amount of major bummage.

Claire was my daily treat.

I kept walking forlornly down Genesee when Claire emerged from an apartment building just as I passed.

"Hey," she said.

I looked up from my sulk and smiled.

"Oh, wow, hey, I was just thinking how majorly bummed I was that I wasn't gonna get to see you," I said.

"Aww," she said, "You were?" and sat down on the grass, "No practice today. We kicked Pali's ass so Coach Hathaway gave us the day off."

"Is this your building?"

"Yeah," she said, "I was just coming outside to water the roses."

"Good timing!" I said.

"Random chance," she shrugged, "yeah."

And dang, dude, right at that moment, right when she was saying "random chance," we locked eyes like cats do.

Hers were sky-blue and burning, and mine–all shit-brown and gooping–got really lost in them.

The world was doing flip-flops in the periphery.

I wanted to kiss her but I thought it better not to because maybe the moment was just a delusion on my part.

"*Round and round we go, all of us, and ever come back thither,*" I thought more Whitman to myself as I remained locked up in looking at her.

"Uhhm, I've got to go," I said and kept sitting there.

"OK, bye," she said and sat there too for a while.

Eventually I stood up and walked the rest of the way home, dizzy with the rhythm of Claire's eyes.

That night I wrote a song inspired by the shift in my vibe with Claire though it took on its own life and ended up not being about us at all really except maybe in the smallest way.

Something here is different

Something here's off normal

Verging on significant

We're awkward now and formal

Yesterday you looked at me

With something like a history to unfold

Would it were told

Don't be afraid

Please don't disappear

I'll propose a question

Straightforward and sincere

You provide an answer:

Is there something here?

Something here has begun to change

Something here's getting stronger

Only slightly rearranged

Each glance keeps lasting longer

I find it hard to break the gaze

And carry on with my own hazy day

I can't turn away

Don't be afraid

Please don't disappear

I'll propose a question

Straightforward and sincere

You provide an answer:

Is there something here?

Something here's not what it was

Something here's all aquiver

A deeper shade or a subtle buzz

Like a tickle or a shiver

When I behold your sweet mystique

I lose the useless need to speak at all

I'm caught in your squall

Don't be afraid

Please don't disappear

I'll propose a question

Straightforward and sincere

You provide an answer:

Is there something here?

At school the next day, in History class, Claire leaned across the aisle and showed this new girl Darla something she had written in her notebook.

Darla sat in front of me.

Looking discreetly over Darla's shoulder, I saw that Claire had written on a piece of notebook paper, "*I have the hots for Lance's bod.*"

Green light. Go.

And I went.

After school that day I made my appearance at the tennis court fence and Claire came running over.

"Miss Farnaway!" Coach Hathaway barked.

"Hi!" she said to me.

"I think your coach wants you."

"The old dyke can wait a sec," Claire said.

"Real fast then, I–uh, do you want to go to the Songwriter's Showcase with me tomorrow night? Over at the Improv? I'm thinking of auditioning for it when I have enough good songs, and I want to check it out, take an inventory of the talent, you know, and-uh I'd love it if you'd come with me."

"Yes," she said.

"Yes you want to go?"

"Yes!" she said as she ran back to tennis practice and mimed a telephone.

Dang, dude. Now what?

I did call her as per her gestured request.

"So tomorrow night?" she said.

"Yeah. The Improv's just over on Melrose near Fred Segal. We could walk there maybe?"

"Totally, easy, yeah. What time?"

"Uhm, I'll come over to your house around 6:30?"

"Cool," she said, "I'll be ready."

"Yeah it'll be fun," I said.

We were silent for half a minute or so.

I actually wanted to hang up already but I figured I was supposed to keep talking to her because I'd asked her out and that was kind of like being her boyfriend or something and when you're someone's boyfriend you've gotta stay on the phone with her until she's satisfied which takes longer and longer each time.

Dang, dude.

We didn't interact much at school the next day except in English a little and when she said "See you tonight" at the tennis court fence after school.

When my dad dropped me off at Claire's he handed me two $20 bills while saying, "Show the young lady a good time. Buy her a Coke. Girls like it when you buy them things. Will this be enough?"

"For a coke?"

"For the whole night."

"Yeah . . . More than. Thank you."

"Girls are expensive."

"I know."

"Except the ones who are cheap."

I chuckled enough to satisfy him.

"Buy her a coke," my dad reminded me as I exited the car.

Claire saw me from the upstairs window and motioned that she'd come down.

Maybe she didn't want me meeting her mother.

Our greeting was awkward, half-almost kiss, stiff embrace, a blushy "hey how's it going" in unison followed by a joint "pretty good" and tentative laughter.

On the walk to the Improv we held hands.

My palms were predictably sweaty.

"Nervous?" Claire asked.

"I guess," I looked down.

"Me too," she said, unclasping my hand and holding me by the arm instead, wiping her palm on my sleeve and laughing.

I felt like I had a real girlfriend for the first time.

I was hoping my stomach would behave and I wouldn't have to shit loudly and wetly in the Improv bathroom.

The admission was $5 and I paid for both of us, so I still had $30 left to spend on Claire.

A waitress came and asked us if we wanted anything.

"You want something to drink?" I asked Claire.

"A Coke?"

"Same for me," I smiled in acknowledgement of my dad's wisdom though he didn't tell me Cokes would be $6 each. And we both had 2. Dang, dude.

The Songwriter's Showcase was a weekly event at the Improv run by Reginald Paraffin and Ian Mulcahy, two extremely cool cats who were utterly dedicated to the craft of songwriting and providing a venue for aspiring songwriters to get the work heard.

I hoped to perform there eventually.

It probably wasn't Claire's ideal destination for a date, but she acted like it was and I couldn't stop staring at her.

The music ended up being irrelevant to the evening.

Somebody sang a song about carbon monoxide. And this one songwriter did a tune whose only lyric was the word *rush*.

Claire and I mostly just looked at each other in the flickering candlelight, clasped hands across the table, and said things like, "I'm really glad we're doing this" and "me too" and "we're on a date" over and over.

I also noticed there was this really cute girl sitting by herself in the corner.

After the Showcase ended I called my dad from the pay phone at the Improv and asked him to pick me up in an hour on Genesee. We walked back to Claire's apartment building, for a while holding hands, then I put my arm around her, and after that we went back to holding hands.

When we got to the foot of her stairs we stopped and faced each other, leaning against the stucco newel post.

"I'll wait here with you 'til your dad comes," Claire said.

"Cool," I said and leaned forward to kiss her and she held my face.

Our mouths melted together in a first exploration of tongues, teeth, cheeks, lips.

It was a beautifully mutual smooch, long and passionate.

"You are so cute," she said upon separating.

"What um?" I tried to kiss her again and she held me back a little.

"The way you asked me out," she said, "It was adorable. You were blushing. I've been wanting you to do that."

"Well I did it."

We kissed.

"Yes you did."

We kissed again.

"I had to."

"Yes you did," she said and laid her lips back on mine.

"Luckily you reciprocated," I garbled.

"Yes I did," she mumbled through her nibblings at my mouth.

We had our arms completely around each other in a oneness.

"When did you know?" I asked, leaning my forehead against hers, "I mean, what this was and stuff."

"Nyeah, it's been growing for a while I guess, but I always figured you weren't all the way into me so I didn't let myself."

"Ah," I said.

"But like even last year hanging out with you in Madame Couchée's room at lunch, and sitting next to you in Megiddo's this year for sure."

"Yeah I love that," I said.

We kissed some more.

"But most recently, um, at the fence during tennis practice a few days ago."

"Which day?"

"Oleander."

"Oh yes."

"You were standing at the fence talking about something or other–"

"–Oleander–"

"–No, it was just before the oleander salad thing, but it doesn't matter because I wasn't listening. I was just looking at you and my stomach was jumping. I don't know. It was a really simple moment. I just said, 'Yeah. Him.' So. Yeah. You."

She hooked her fingers through two of my front belt loops.

"When did *you* realize?" she asked.

"I dunno," I said, "I guess sitting on the front lawn of your building."

"That was amazing," she said, "Yeah."

"And I remember a particular moment in Couchée's room at lunch last year where I thought someday maybe."

"Jacques Brel was playing," Claire remembered.

"Oui. 'Quand On A Que L'Amour.'"

"*Mon amour, toi et moi,*" she sang, "Yes, I remember that. Yes," she patted my pectorals with her palms.

"But your front lawn was like crazy," I stared her down.

"Yeah. that was pretty much the only thing I thought about for the rest of the night," she said, looking into me, "And all day yesterday. And all day today. And like right now because we're doing it again and it's real."

"Yeah."

"Eyes."

"Eyes."

"Yeah."

"Dang, if I hadn't been walking by your house right when you were coming out . . ."

". . . You stepped right into my trap, my pretty," she said.

"Haha," I said.

"You think I'm joking," she said.

I didn't answer.

"You were waiting for me to walk by," I finally said, "and emerged on purpose."

"Boys are so simple."

"Oh yeeeeeah?" I scrunched up my fist like in a Three Stooges movie, "Sez who?" and I threatened to show her a little chin music.

We went back to frenching.

Our fingers got all tangled up in each other.

My dad pulled up in front and gave the shave-and-a-haircut honk.

"Bye," I started to move and she held me back.

"Are you walking to school tomorrow?" she asked. Our hands were interlocked and she wasn't letting go.

My dad honked again.

"Yeah, I think so," I said.

"Stop by here on your way and I'll walk with you," she said.

"OK, cool," I said.

We kissed again and I ran to the car.

"Have fun?" my dad asked.

"Yeah," I said, "I think I have a girlfriend."

"Mazel Tov," my dad said, "Enjoy it while you can."

I didn't know what he meant by that, though I do now.

"Did you buy her a Coke like I told you?"

"I did."

"Works every time," he said and patted me on the shoulder.

That night in bed I kept saying, "I have a girlfriend" over and over. I even got up briefly and looked at myself in the mirror and said it. "I have a girlfriend!"

I thought I'd take myself to dreamland by fantasizing about fucking Claire, but, much to my flabbergast, I didn't feel like jacking off and instead just went to sleep.

5

The next morning I stopped by Claire's apartment on the way to school in the morning and she joined me the rest of the way.

We made out in the hall before school to the teasing of various friends.

Then we made out again up against a window at the end of the hall during nutrition.

Then we made out again sitting at her locker during lunch.

Then we kissed goodbye through the chain link fence by the tennis courts after school.

"Miss Farnaway, PLEASE!" Coach Hathaway shouted, "The only balls you need are here on this tennis court!"

"Ugh," Claire pouted and returned to practice.

That weekday ritual took hold quickly.

On the weekends sometimes I'd hang out at her house or sometimes she'd hang out at my house or sometimes we'd go to the Tar Pits or to whatever movie was showing at the Pan Pacific where we could get in for free after her shift or maybe to Canter's for a nosh but always with the goal of making out eventually, which for us was kissing.

I found that I wasn't compelled to touch her body at all.

I just loved kissing her.

And I loved being around her.

Her heart opened wide.

Claire Farnaway made birthday brownies for every person whose birthday she knew.

Claire Farnaway would let you look at the answers on her science test if you needed to.

Claire Farnaway was always the first one to ask what's wrong.

Claire Farnaway brought every teacher presents every year on the last day of school before Christmas vacation and again on the last day of school in June, not because her mother made her but because she wanted to.

Claire Farnaway called you if you were sick to ask if there was anything she could bring you.

One never questioned Claire Farnaway's ulterior motives.

I was enthralled by her loving warmth, her humor, and her azure irises.

Recently I'd seen a rerun of *The Waltons*, the episode where John Boy is temporarily blinded and has to endure a sightless existence for a time, and the heightening of his other senses, the hyperawareness of the multilayered complex of neurons that navigates us through the physical realm, the intensified perceptions that John Boy experiences, struck me as an experiment worth trying.

I decided I was going to spend an entire day like that, blind, like John Boy, from waking to sleep, and I asked Claire to spend the day with me as my companion and guide.

And the thing about Claire was not only did she do it, but she didn't act like a dutiful girlfriend or anything; she was totally into it. She contributed. She didn't think it was stupid.

"Dorky maybe, but not stupid," she said.

We took several walks around the neighborhood in different directions.

Claire led me up to flowers, trees, had me kneel next to storm drains, walked me down an alley allowing the smell of empty beer cans and exhaust fumes and sounds like the sound of electric poles buzzing and the crunching of gravel underfoot to get accentuated with the lack of visual input.

She even had me crouch down and smell some dog shit in the vacant lot on Mansfield and Beverly.

"Gee thanks," I said rising from the pile of poop.

"Shit's all part of it, dude," Claire said, "Breathe deep the gathering gloom."

"Please don't," I begged.

"Watch lights fade from every room."

"Claire," I leaned over and kissed her between each word to shut her up, "Do not. Do. The rest. Of. That. Poem. Please."

"Whoa shit, look," Claire said.

"Um."

"Oh yeah, oops. No, there's a freaking turtle in the grass."

"A turtle?"

"Yeah, or a tortoise. It's pretty big," she said, "Here," and she dragged my hand to feel its shell."

"Whoa," I said, "and it's alive?"

"Hell yeah. It's looking right at us."

"You should keep it," I said.

"No, it probably belongs to someone," she said, "We should try to find the owner."

I didn't really want to do that.

I hate dealing with shit like that. Like knocking on strangers' doors and stuff.

That's why I always came in last place in the magazine subscription drive in school every year, 'cause I hated knocking on strangers' doors and so I never sold any magazine subscriptions.

My parents always subscribed to a couple so I wouldn't have to submit zero sales, but I still knew I sucked.

Don't parents know that shit doesn't work?

"Just keep it," I encouraged, "You'll love it."

"No, I'll be thinking of the little kid who's crying 'cause she lost her turtle," Claire said. "I bet it came through the backyard fence of that building right next to the field. Let's go ask."

She handed me the turtle and led me to Orange Drive.

"It has one of these thingies," she pressed my hands against the doorpost of the downstairs unit.

"A mezuzah," I said, "Jew thing."

"Ah," she said as she knocked.

A lady said "Yes?" from behind the door.

"Excuse me, ma'am," Claire said, "we were wondering if you lost a turtle? Or a tortoise?"

The door opened and I caught the unmistakeable smell of chicken stock in a crock pot, an aroma that pervaded the neighborhood on Friday nights and Saturdays.

The woman gasped, "Shlummy!"

"It's yours?" Claire asked.

"Shlummy's here!" the woman shouted and footsteps came running from the back of the house.

Another voice said, "Lance?"

"Yeah?"

"What happened to you?"

"Just an experiment in blindness," I could almost place the voice.

"Is this your turtle?" Claire asked.

"It's my little sister's. She's not home from shul yet."

Naomi Richter. Had to be.

"Thank you for finding him!" Naomi's presumed mom said, "Ruthie will be so happy! Shlummy disappeared yesterday morning."

I could hear Naomi's mom take the turtle from Claire and go back inside the house.

"So, wait," I said, "We live two blocks away from each other? I'm on Citrus."

"Yeah," Naomi said, "That's weird. All this time. I've never seen you around here."

"Bizarre," I said.

"I'm the girlfriend," Claire said.

"Ah," said Naomi, "Well thank you for finding Shlummy. That was very kind of you to bring him back. Bye, Lance. Good Shabbos."

She closed the door abruptly.

"What a bitch!" Claire marveled on the way back to my house.

"Nah," I said, "What'd she do?"

"So . . ." said Claire who had ascended to her full power as my official monogamous girlfriend, "Who is she?"

"I'm pretty sure I told you about her," I said even though I had not in fact ever mentioned Naomi Richter.

"Um, no."

"Naomi Richter?"

"All this time,' she said. What does that mean, 'all this time'? How do you know her?"

"She was my math tutor for a while in 10th Grade," I said, leaving out the part where I tried to finger-fuck her while she was on her period behind the pool at Gardner Park.

"OK, you are lying to me right now, but I'm going to be patient because I know that eventually you will confess," she said.

I pictured how Naomi was probably getting similarly grilled by her own mother at that same moment. She could so easily have pretended not to recognize me.

"That was very you, to go looking for the turtle's owner instead of keeping it for yourself. You are a nice person," I tried to steer.

"I remember Lori kept telling us last year about this Orthodox girl you were hanging out with at the library," Claire said.

I swallowed self-consciously..

"Yes," I said with a forced calmness, "Our tutoring sessions were in the library. What's the big deal? You did a mitzvah returning that turtle. You are amazing."

"I saw the way she looked at you when she thought you were hurt."

"She. Was. My. Math. Tutor," I said very slowly and with heroic snarling reserve on behalf of all men.

"That's not what Lori said."

Dang, dude. Chicks are always on the lookout for each other. Like even in advance.

Chicks are psychic.

When we got back, *Dusty's Treehouse* was on TV, a little kiddy show featuring a nebbishy Jewish guy who lived in a pastel treehouse and talked to animal puppets and showed them all sorts of arts and crafts projects and also read stories to them.

It was a very sweet-hearted show and I always found it to be a great comfort in the midst of those indefinable sadnesses that inevitably crop up on a Saturday afternoon.

We sat in my living room and I listened to *Dusty's Treehouse* while Claire described what everything looked like.

She seemed to have dropped the Naomi trope.

But of course those things don't actually ever go away. They just get warped and woofed into the fabric of things.

"I never realized how gay he sounds," I said of Dusty.

"Duh," Claire laughed.

After *Dusty's Treehouse* we walked over to Fiddler's to have lunch, and Claire said that the cloth around my head made everyone look at me like I'd been injured or something.

"You know, like your Orthodox girlfriend thought you were," she said, resurfacing.

I heard a voice saying, "So I said to her, I said, 'Look sweetheart I don't have time for your timid rigmarole.'"

And I said, "Dang, dude, Valentino's here."

"Huh?" Claire asked.

We were holding hands across the table.

"There's a crazy guy at the counter. Valentino. I know his voice."

"How can you hear that?" she asked, "We're on the other end of the restaurant."

"I don't know, I think it's working."

"What is?"

"The heightened sense of hearing," I said.

"Yeah?"

"I feel like John Boy," I said, "My hearing is totally fucking intense right now."

"Like you could hear dog whistles and stuff?"

"Totally," I said, "Do you have one?"

"No. But maybe Naomi Richter does."

"Claire," I said abruptly, "She. Was. My. Math. Tutor."

"Cool, whatever," she said and put my hands on the milkshake glass, "What am I whispering right now?"

I wanted to be able to say something totally foul like "fuck me hard," but I was already in too much dog doo because of the Naomi Richter encounter, so I decided to hold off on joky stuff until she retracted her antennae.

"I love you?" I said, "Or at least that's what it sounded like."

"Dang, that's amazing," Claire said, "yes, I love you," though in actuality when trying to listen for her whisper all I could hear was Valentino at the counter.

"And when she took off her clothes she was all scaly like a reptile and I'm not into bestiality, you know, like some dumbfuck hillbilly, so I said, 'Get thee behind me, Satan,' and she called me a goddamn Jesus freak, and I should've walloped her right then and there in the name of Christ our Lord but I restrained myself because the only guy who'd care about bailing me out of jail is my dad and he's fucking in jail himself right now, so I'm screwed if I get arrested."

But I got the "I love you" right on a lucky guess and that submerged the Naomi problem for a time.

Claire was biting on my fingers.

"Let's go back to your house and make out," she said.

"Lead the way, m'lady," I said like Herman Q. Levine.

When we got back to my house we went into my bedroom to make out, i.e., kiss.

I was not particularly into exploring Claire's body.

It wasn't inexperience. My two liaisons with Taryn Rust certainly taught me how to establish and bring to completion intimate contact with the female anatomy. I mostly knew what to do, up to a point.

But, I guess, part of it was I couldn't really tell if Claire wanted me to touch her for real.

I knew she wrote that note to Darla about having the hots for my bod, but did she even know what that really meant, with my hands all over her breasts and maybe my fingers getting inside her vagina for a decisive and ecstatic thrumming?

I was afraid of ruining something by going too far and both of us getting embarrassed.

Taryn was really demonstrative regarding her penchant for sex.

A certain amount of aggression from a girl is what flints my ignition, I admit it.

At the very least I need the green light to be crassly obvious, like utterly obscene, so as to render all sexual congress inevitable.

Sometimes even the green light wasn't enough. Evelyn Childs, for example, who straight up asked me if I wanted to fuck her and I said no without having any idea why I was saying no considering the amount of time I'd spent fantasizing about her.

"OK," I said, pulling out of the current kiss, "Full confession . . . I saw that note you passed to Darla that said you had the hots for my bod."

"Haha, yeah, you saw it because I wanted you to see it," she taunted.

"Dang, dude."

I had K–LOVE on, the soft-rock station, because I thought that'd be the most conducive to smooching.

They loved John Dawson Read on that station.

We must've heard 4 John Dawson Read songs while we were making out all afternoon.

I definitely remember "One Road For Angels" and "Some People Are

Crazy."

"A Friend Of Mine Is Going Blind" came on and we both caught the irony and started laughing but kept on kissing too.

"Make the laughter part of the kiss," Claire said and that became really the motto of our relationship.

Every kiss began and ended with laughter.

I don't remember what the 4th John Dawson Read song was, but I know they played it.

"You have turkey lips," I said to her, running my finger across her narrow mouth.

"What?"

"You have turkey lips."

"Great," she said, "Just what a girl wants to hear from her beau."

"Turkey lips," I said again with flirtatious cruelty.

The Elton John song "Someone Saved My Life Tonight" came on, and Claire said yay because she loved Elton John and *Captain Fantastic* was her favorite album.

We lay on our backs side by side and listened.

I was already turning south on Elton John at that time—*Goodbye Yellow Brick Road* was like a farewell—but Claire's enthusiasm for *Captain Fantastic* reminded me of what I used to love about him, how much of my piano playing was learned listening to *Tumbelweed Connection* and *Honky Chateau* and *Madman Across The Water*, and so she won me over to an appreciation for *Captain Fantastic* just by her sheer beautiful wide-hearted embrace of it.

I started calling her Sugar Bear in jest.

When she wasn't Turkey Lips, she was Sugar Bear.

"Miranda's not talking to me now," Claire said one day when were hanging out in the hall during Nutrition.

"Why?"

"'Cause I'm with you."

"What does she care?"

"You're still her property."

"But she's with Freddy."

"That doesn't matter, silly. She still owns you too."

"That's cray-zee," I said even though I had already been taught that lesson, back in 8th Grade, by Miranda herself, who told me I would always be the property of Candy Stoner.

It was prophesied I would die with many owners.

Owned by many, possessed by none.

My mission, my destiny.

Accumulate intimate distances.

Romance at arm's-length.

"I think Miranda was only friends with me because of the French connection," Claire said.

"That doesn't seem like a movie she'd like. You either!"

"No, I mean that my mom is French and I know French and all that stuff and Miranda wants to be French."

"Really?" I said.

"The way she's always hanging out with Madame Couchée after class and now she has *Le Petit Prince* in French. Have you noticed?"

"No," I said.

It gave me stomach cramps when I thought about the changing details and new additions to Miranda's life since our essential severing, the shit I wasn't privy to anymore.

"Freddy got it for her," Claire said.

"Maybe he reminds her of the Little Prince," I said and then felt ridiculously sorry for myself.

"Huh?"

"Nothing," I said.

"Inside joke with Miranda?" Claire sighed.

"Kind of," I said even though I knew I should've dismissed it with an 'of course not, silly.' But too late.

Claire turned away.

Ugh. Dang, dude. I always fuck up like that.

In late November, right before Thanksgiving, Mr. Simmons gave us the option of a term paper or a film project. The film could be about anything but had to make reference to films we'd studied in class.

I immediately formed a group with Claire, of course, and Claude Moss, Mitchell Goodman, a film buff with a tartly skewed sense of humor, and also, amazingly, Heaven Sender, known mostly for her generous vagina but who turned out to be deadpan funny and a great asset to our film project.

Mitchell wanted to direct and we were all cool with that. He knew his shit.

We agreed we wanted to make reference to Charlie Chaplin and The Marx Brothers and the Keystone Kops, but we had to figure out a story.

"Everybody try to come up with a concept by tomorrow and let's see if something clicks," Claire said.

That night Claire invited me to hang out at her apartment because her mom was going to be out all evening and we could work on film ideas together.

"Plus we can make out on the couch in the living room!" Claire said as if picturing it.

"What about your sister?" I asked. Claire had an older sister, Natalie, who passively and unwittingly aroused my secret fetish by the purely accidental virtue of being born before Claire.

"Oh she practically lives at her boyfriend's house these days," Claire said, "I guarantee she won't be around."

When I first got there, for a while we just talked about ideas for the movie.

"I think Claude would be a great sad-sack hero," I said.

"Oh, totally," she said, "He'd nail it. And he could have encounters with the Little Tramp and the Marx Brothers."

"Yeah yeah," I got excited, "and, like, a beautiful ingenue."

"Heaven, in other words," Claire said.

"Zackly," I said, knowing I'd pay for that one. I should have hesitated. Dang, dude. Again.

"And I get to be?"

"Harpo?"

She stared at me.

"You have the hair," I said, "and the adorable face. And the turkey lips."

"You're saying I look like Harpo Marx."

"No I'm saying you would do a very good job playing Harpo Marx in the movie we're going to make, sugar bear."

I was trying to get her to think I was adorable which usually worked in such situations.

"I hate you so much," she said as she started kissing me.

We kissed until neither of us wanted to anymore.

"So the sad-sack wakes up in the morning in his sad little room and then goes out into the big sad world," I said.

"Where would he encounter characters from slapstick comedy though?"

"It could be just walking down the street."

"Nyeah, that's boring. I think a park would be better 'cause then we could use like the swings and the slide and the basketball courts and stuff. Stuff to do stuff with. You know?"

"Totally, yeah yeah, better," I kissed her, "right on. You're a genius."

"La Cienega Park would be perfect," she tried to say mid–kiss.

We let our tongues roll around together.

I had the idea he slips in and out of intense daydreams, so when he sees Chaplin and the Marx Brothers and stuff you don't know if he's daydreaming it or if it's really happening.

"Yeah," Claire said, "so he's like sitting on a park bench and Chaplin comes up with a broom and dust pan and starts sweeping around the bench and he's all freaked out that the guy cleaning up at the park is Charlie Chaplin and he moves away."

"For sure. We should be writing this down."

Claire ran to her room to get her notebook and she was wearing these short shorts that let me see her ass bounce as she moved.

Claire returned, notebook in hand, wearing very loose gray sweatpants.

Why do chicks have to change every time they go into their bedroom?

"So he wakes up in the morning looking all–"

"–sad-sacky," I said.

"Sad-sacky," she wrote down.

"Oh, he should look at his Farrah Fawcett poster and get an erection."

"No. That's gross."

"We can use like a baseball bat or something. It'll be high–larious."

"Ugh. That's nasty. And why Farrah Fawcett?"

"Claude has a Farrah Fawcett poster in his room, *the* Farrah Fawcett poster."

"So we're filming it at Claude's house. You just decided this."

"Yeah. Write that down too. Location: Claude's bedroom."

She did, eyes still rolling at the erection idea.

"And then he's maybe shooting baskets," I said, and the Marx Brothers come and steal his ball."

"With me as Harpo."

"Correct."

"Just making sure."

"Deal with it, Claire de Lune."

"I am, obviously," she said, "And Mitchell will want a Keystone Kop involved."

"Played by him," I said.

"Of course. Mr. Mack Sennett himself."

"So, easy, the Keystone Kop comes and chases the Marx Brothers away. Funny chase scene around the park, like on the jungle gym equipment and down the slide and stuff," I said.

"Perfect, yeah. Then what?"

"Sad-sack walks over to the playground and sees a beautiful ingénue on the swings," I said, "Or, no, wait, La Cienega Park has those little horses that rock back and forth, even better, she'll be rocking back and forth on one of those little horses."

"Heaven'll like that," snarked Claire and then we started kissing again though I knew she was irked that I kept referring to Heaven as beautiful.

"And the girl turns out to be real," I said, ignoring Claire's snarkings.

"For sure. And . . . they end up back in his bedroom maybe?" she's the one who suggested.

"Yeah yeah." I said, "And they, like, sit on the bed together and then pan up to Claude's hand tearing down the Farrah Fawcett poster and it's implied that they're kissing or something."

I really wanted to say we should see them under the covers looking like they're fucking, but I knew that'd get me sent home immediately.

"This could be really great," Claire said.

"I can do Chaplin and Groucho," I said.

"Definitely. Duh."

"And Heaven can play the—"

"—beautiful ingénue."

"I guess, Yeah," I said.

She looked me at me like come on, dude.

"And I get to be Harpo," she said.

"You will be the foxiest Harpo of all time," I said.

"A foxy Harpo."

"The foxiest."

"Haha."

"Of all time, sugar bear."

"Are all guys the same?" she asked and I shrugged. I had no idea what she meant. "You totally had sex with Naomi Richter. Don't even waste energy

163

denying it."

Dang, dude. That turned the corner fast.

I dunno, I think–in fact I know–the sexual imagination of the human female is just as promiscuous as that of the human male and there is some kind of enormously successful con-job going on here that leads us to believe otherwise.

Fake outrage is but one timeworn technique girls use to disguise their own indiscriminate lusts. They've all got multiple boyfriends happening in their minds and fingers.

Jealousy is projection.

And speaking of timeworn techniques, I tried to change the subject by telling her about the movie Manny Shepherd and I made when we were twelve.

"The summer between 7th & 8th Grade," I said, "we made this movie called *Judo Jew*. A Jewish kung fu movie. It was like 20 minutes long or so. Oliver Gelding was in it. He played the bad guy."

"Of course you made the black guy be the villain."

"Hey, Manny played a bad guy and Buzzy also played a bad guy in the film and he's whiter than Casper's mom, so shut up. And, dude, Buzzy did this totally hilarious like 5-minute death scene where he was like twitching and convulsing. We were all busting up. He was Gus back then. It's weird calling him Gus now."

"Dang, Gus Lagniappe, that's right. He's been Buzzy for, what, like a year now?"

"Yeah, around that, I dunno."

"Seems like he's been Buzzy forever," she said. "He hasn't been in school for a couple of weeks. Have you noticed?"

"Nyeah, I don't know what's up. I haven't seen him on the front porch next door even. Maybe my mom knows. But anyway *Judo Jew* grew out of us being into the TV show *Kung Fu*. We created this Jewish hero, yarmulke and all. I played him."

"Good casting," she yucked and slapped her knee.

"I remember in Hebrew school Rabbi Hamlisch was once talking to us about the word Israel, which means 'he who strives with God.' Jacob is given that name after he wrestles with the angel. Rabbi Hamlisch said that story really describes the core of the Jewish people. Who we are. 'The Jewish people are those who wrestle with God,' Rabbi Hamlisch said, "Israel." That's why I've always loved watching professional wrestling. It like gets me in touch with my own people."

"Wrestling and kung fu movies. Two things I don't understand," Claire said.

"Oh," I said, recognizing an irreconcilable difference certain to doom us.

When I was a but a lad, I was deeply into professional wrestling, that orchestrated struggle between man and uncertainty, a preternatural choreography, albeit one whose outcome was always predetermined.

"Wrestling is fake," my dad said one Saturday when I was watching KCOP Channel 13 like when I was in 6th Grade or somewhere around there, "a put-on. The winner is decided way in advance. They might as well be doing it on *The Flip Wilson Show*. Or *Sonny & Cher*."

I didn't believe my father when he told me that again the next night over dinner, obviously annoyed at my obsession with the sport.

Wrestling was my latency period pornography.

I subscribed to wrestling magazines.

I collected autographed pictures of wrestlers.

Occasionally, Whit's father would call the immortal phone number RI–9–5171, RIchmond–9–5171, and make reservations for us to go to the Olympic Auditorium, where the gods on high dwelt, there at the corner of 18th & Grand, and see wrestling matches in the exalted palace of the sport, heavenly peak among the clouds, in reality a totally run-down shithole filled on Friday nights with a strange mixture of dorks, drunks, lunatics, families, jocks, and freaky little boys like me, a mix of ethnicities unseen anywhere else in Los Angeles, a potpourri of people united by their willingness to believe in nonsense.

Roller derby, another entertainment product disguised as legitimate competition, also took place at the Olympic Auditorium. We occasionally went to see The Los Angeles Thunderbirds skate live, but mostly we watched roller derby on television.

A regular in the audience was this old black lady named Nellie, who always sat in the front row, yelling at the wrestlers, hitting them with her purse when they'd fall out of the ring, casting spells on them with her collection of voodoo dolls that hung from a long bamboo stick. Nellie was a show unto herself, queen of the whole Pinocchio hoax.

Most of my live wrestling experiences, however, happened in the TV studios of KCOP Channel 13, at the corner of La Brea and Willoughby, across the street from Bargain Circus.

Every Saturday night was live wrestling on Channel 13, with Dick Lane and his sidekick Bill "Hoppy" Haupt who did all the live post-match interviews with the wrestlers.

The ring announcer was Jimmy Lennon.

The KCOP wrestling show was taped at 6pm for broadcast at 8pm, but you had to start lining up at like 2pm to get a seat for the taping, and there was always a mess of humanity sitting in lawn chairs who'd been there since noon. So, we were never first in line.

To kill time we'd take turns going across the street to Bargain Circus, a hodgepodge of unrelated items at cheapshit prices. Several significant notches below the merchandise at Zody's.

You didn't want to admit you shopped at Bargain Circus.

All the customers were there incognito.

You'd joke about seeing a gym bag for $1.99 or something and be all laughing like "Yeeeah that's some ratty-ass crap" out loud to your friends, but also be thinking *Hmm I'd kinda like to have that* in your mind and maybe even be thinking about sneaking back during the week and buying it, which in fact I did a couple of times.

After the Bargain Circus visits, two of us at a time would walk down to Pink's to get chili dogs and Mitz soda. You never saw Mitz soda anywhere but at Pink's.

At 4pm the wrestlers would start arriving at the KCOP parking lot.

They were dressed in street clothes, though if they were masked wrestlers they would, of course, be wearing their masks already.

Our hero Mil Mascaras, never showed up at KCOP. We had to catch him on *Lucha Libre* on Channel 34 or see him live at the Olympic Auditorium when he came through.

One time Bigelow Rust said to me, "You do know there are like a thousand Mil Mascarases all over the country and in Mexico too.

We didn't believe him.

Each wrestler carried a gym bag with his wrestling gear inside.

The "good guys," the ones who were in favor with the audience and had that knowing heroic persona, were always friendly to the crowd lined up at the fence.

The "bad guys," the lying cheating sons-of-bitches, always with a flamboyant, arrogant impresario manager escorting them, would grimace and scowl, on cue, at the fans on their way into the studio.

Rarely did any of those dudes, heroes or villains, possess a body-type that could be described as "athletic."

For the most part they were thick, big-bellied behemoths stuffed into unflattering ring garb, but to us they were as grand and noble as Achilles and Ajax and Hector and Aeneas.

A tribe of warrior galoots.

Entering the small studio at KCOP, we'd all take our spots in the rows of bleachers, which held about 100 people, and Nellie would go to her special folding chair on the floor next to the ring and start setting up her voodoo shit.

I remember the night she swatted Kenji Shibuya with her folding chair when he got knocked out of the ring by Freddie Blassie.

Dick Lane would take his place ringside and launch into his gattling-gun narration of this weekly opera of human grit and struggle.

"Whoa, Nellie!" he'd scream as the wrestlers would begin bouncing off the ropes and onto each other in the confines of the blue canvas ring.

The show let out in time for us to rush home and watch it on TV and look for ourselves, which was fun except for the long, boring Zachary All commercials and also the ads for another stodgy men's haberdashery called Barr Clothing on the corner of 6th and La Brea. It was at Barr Clothing that we'd pick up our free tickets to Saturday Night Wrestling at KCOP Channel 13.

Herein lies the crux of my ultimate disillusion with wrestling:

I thought John Tolos and Freddie Blassie actually hated each other.

Their feud was vicious and steeped in legend.

In my understanding of the cosmos, The Golden Greek John Tolos and Classy Freddie Blassie were the bitterest of enemies.

I was to find out differently.

My Aunt Faye worked for a time as a bookkeeper at the Peniel Motel on Ocean Avenue in Santa Monica, a spot where, as she learned, many professional wrestlers would stay when they were in L.A.

Knowing of my obsession with the sport, an obsession her own sons, my cousins, shared, she very sweetly invited me to spend a day at the motel playing with my cousins in the pool and meeting some of the wrestlers.

One summer morning my mother dropped me off at the Peniel Motel where my aunt escorted me out to the pool.

I saw a whole bunch of wrestlers there. Masa Saito, Victor Rivera, Killer Kowalski, Bruno Sammartino, Black Gordman, and, to my world-shattering disbelief, John Tolos and Freddie Blassie, on chaises longues together at poolside, laughing like palsy-walsy soul-brothers instead of the archetypal enemies I expected.

Whatever awe I felt at these larger-than-life gladiators collapsed under the weight of its own fantastic gravity.

A vortex opened in my innocent mythos, draining me of all romantic dazzlement.

This blasphemy was exacerbated by the niceness with which Tolos and Blassie greeted me when my aunt came out to introduce me to them.

The Golden Greek a sweetheart?

Classy Freddie Blassie a teddy bear?

I had my one and only chance to be called a "pencil neck geek" by Freddie Blassie and instead he called me "honey," as in "Very nice to meet you, honey."

There was also a plain potato-faced bronze girl with enormous breasts lounging next to them.

"Naphtali," she said, extending her hand.

Her name, as it turned out, was actually Natalie and I'd misheard her when she introduced herself.

After I shook their hands, John Tolos said to me, "Hey, maybe you can settle this argument, you're about the right age."

"OK," I said.

"Blassie here keeps saying that the fat kid from *Willy Wonka & The Chocolate Factory* is named Buzzy something."

"Lagniappe," said Blassie, "Buzzy Lagniappe."

169

They both looked at me.

"Augustus Gloop," I said, "Augustus Gloop is the fat kid from *Willy Wonka & The Chocolate Factory*."

"Unh?" Tolos pointed to his forehead and tapped it triumphantly, "See what the kid says?" Tolos then pointed at me with his middle finger, "I win."

"Son, you let me down," Blassie said and reclined in the lounge chair.

Then they both started laughing.

"I still say it's Buzzy Lagniappe," Blassie added.

"I have a friend named Gus Lagniappe and his real name is Augustus and we sometimes call him Augustus Gloop."

"Is he fat?" Tolos asked.

"Nyeah, kinda," I said. "Chubby at least. He's also my neighbor. He lives in the house next door."

I had brought my brand new gym bag, the one I kept my fake wrestling clothes in, the ones I'd wear when we'd have pretend wrestling matches in my backyard.

I wanted to have every professional wrestler possible sign it.

But I didn't think I'd ever encounter big names like John Tolos and Freddie Blassie.

Blassie took the bag first. I gave him the black Flair pen I'd brought.

"Hey, I have a bag just like this," said Blassie, "I got it for a $1.99 at Bargain Circus."

Tolos inserted, "Only Blassie would admit he shops at Bargain Circus."

"This pencil neck geek here likes giving me a hard time. But if he's not careful I'm gonna make that handsome face of his look just like my old granny's did after I kicked her down the stairs," Blassie blustered.

"Was that the time she brewed your coffee too weak?" Tolos asked.

"That's the time, yeah. That useless prune just couldn't seem to get it right. I yelled at her as she lay at the bottom of the cellar stairs, 'Any pencil neck geek can learn how to make coffee the way Blassie likes it. What's your excuse?' You better believe she made my coffee the way I like it every day since."

"Aw, that's cold-blooded," scolded Tolos.

"I'm just kiddin' around," said Blassie. "You don't believe I'd really do something like that, do you, kid?"

I didn't know what to answer. Because of course I could imagine the Freddie Blassie I knew from wrestling kicking his grandmother down the stairs for making weak coffee. But this Blassie at poolside, clinking lemonade glasses with John Tolos was a completely different character. Which one was real?

Blassie handed the gym bag to Tolos, who also signed it. I shivered with the loss of all that was sacred, a breaking matrix, an illusion revealed as just that and nothing more.

"Very nice to meet you, honey," said Blassie.

"Take care, kid. Be careful in the pool," added Tolos.

I laid my bag down next to my towel and dove into the deep end to splash around with my cousins.

My father was right.

It was like the death of every mermaid.

At Peniel I saw the faces of the lords of wrestling and was crushed by their gentility.

It made me feel like an asterisk.

I didn't bother telling Claire about my wrestling moment now that I knew she didn't like wrestling.

We were making out on her couch, horizontally, when her mom came home earlier than expected.

"Non! Non! C'est impossible!" she shrieked at us as we lay *in flagrante de–lip–to* on the living room couch, "Ce. N'est. Pas. Possible. Non."

"I think you better call your dad to come get you," Claire said after returning from a private conference with her mother in the other room.

That was a tense night overall, not just the thing with her mom walking in, but, I don't know, something got broken for good.

A broad smear across the glow.

6

The next day Claire and I laid out our scenario for the film, which met with consensus approval because no one else thought of anything and so we set filming for Saturday of Thanksgiving weekend at Claude's house and La Cienega Park.

We decided to call it *Down In The Dumps*, which was Claire's idea and we knew it was right as soon as she said it.

We filmed the first scene and the last scene together, as they both took place in Claude's bedroom.

For the last scene we decided to have Claude and Heaven be under the covers together at the end and maybe have the final shot be Claude getting an erection like in the first scene.

"I think I'm going to excuse myself from this shot. I'll be in the living room," Claire said and exited.

"You know what would be better?" Heaven asked after Claire stepped out.

"What?" Mitchell asked back.

"We should make it look like we're fucking at the end," she said, "like under the covers and stuff but you'd still see the humping."

I felt validated.

"I'm in," Claude approved immediately.

"I'm sure you are, and I dig the idea too, even have had that very same idea in the privacy of my own mind, but I don't think Simmons would be cool with that," I said.

"Probably right," said Mitchell, "but let's film both endings and decide later."

We all just wanted the soft core porn even though we knew we couldn't use it.

The erection shot was easy. As in the first scene, Claude raised a baseball bat he brought under the covers with him to a vertical position and then he and Heaven smile at each other. It was really funny.

For the alternate take, Claude climbed on top of Heaven and started pumping and man they got into it.

Heaven started fake moaning.

It was, collectively, the single greatest thing we'd ever heard in person in our lives.

"This is a silent film, Heaven," Mitchell said, pretending to be unfazed.

"Oh yeah, huh," she said while Claude continued to dry hump her under the covers.

"But, uh, could I get a close up of your face with the moaning and everything?"

So we all got to hear it again, dude. It was flagrant.

Afterward, Claire came back into the room.

"That sounded like fun," she said.

"How would you know?" Heaven sassed back.

Claude admitted privately to me and Mitchell that he almost came, just from the dry humping.

"Because, dang, dude," he explained, "Heaven's pudendum, I could feel it. It was right there, like angel clouds."

We ended up using the erection ending of course, though Claude asked if he could have the footage of him looking like he's fucking Heaven.

In addition to the film for Simmons, we were also all busy working on our Emily Dickinson papers for Megiddo. Each of us had to pick one Emily Dickinson poem and do an *explication de texte* and also lead the class in a close oral reading and discussion of our chosen poem.

Miranda did "Hope is the thing with feathers" of course.

"Hope" is the thing with feathers —

That perches in the soul —

And sings the tune without the words —

And never stops — at all —

"Any questions before we start taking it apart?" Miranda asked after she read it through once.

"I read somewhere she was in love with her brother," said Misty Winters whose voice I hadn't heard in maybe 2 years even though I always had classes with her.

"I tend to steer away from the gossip school of criticism," Mr. Megiddo said, "It's pointless and reductive. How does your knowledge of Emily Dickinson's personal life add in any way to your understanding of her

174

work? You have to jettison the presumption of autobiography. It's just you and the text."

Miranda did a really nice job with the bird metaphor and then brought in two other poems for comparison, Paul Laurence Dunbar's "Sympathy" and Thomas Hardy's "The Darkling Thrush" and really did a mindblowlingly great job tying them together, showing how that bird metaphor is also used in those two other poems, always as a symbol of the capacity for hope.

I wanted to watch *Kung Fu* reruns with her.

"Why a bird though?" Megiddo asked her. "You've done a spectacular job showing us other bird-as-hope metaphors. But get to the why."

"Um," Miranda considered, "That a bird always sings no matter how dreary the circumstance."

"And why is that, do you think?"

"It's the only way they know how to communicate," Miranda said, "and I was also thinking the fact of having wings gives them the knowledge of an escape that's always available to them, it's just a matter of timing it right."

She shrugged uncomfortably as Megiddo let the moment sit.

"Well said. And these poets are maybe getting at . . . what?"

Miranda looked down.

"You've already said it yourself."

"About having wings?" she asked.

"Yes, what about having wings?"

"Escape," she said.

"I believe you described it as an escape that is always—"

"—always available to them, yes. Yes."

"Yes. Tell me."

"As with the birds, our means of escape—"

"—or our road to happiness or whatever—"

"—Yeah that too, it's always available to us. It's inside of us."

"Like a song, like wings, it's part of who we are. Hope springs eternal where?"

"In the human breast," I said, invoking one of the many Pope quotes Megiddo had laid on us since September.

"The heart. Right here," he said. "Miranda that was fantastic. Above and beyond. Brava."

I grabbed Miranda's arm as she walked by.

"Amazing," I said. She pulled away and nodded.

Claire gave me a stare-down and then looked across the room.

Gina Dichlich did a typically Gina explication of "Come slowly, Eden."

COME slowly, Eden!

Lips unused to thee,

Bashful, sip thy jasmines,

As the fainting bee,

Reaching late his flower,

Round her chamber hums,

Counts his nectars—enters,

And is lost in balms!

"This is all about the irresistible allure of the vagina," Gina said, in an instant imprinting herself in everybody's head forever.

It's one of those images you know you'll remember on your deathbed.

the irresistible allure of the vagina

"Gina, where are you going with this?" Mr. Megiddo interrupted.

"Well, just look at it."

"No, *you* show us how to look at it."

"You've got 'lips' in the second line," she said.

"You've got lips on your mouth too," Megiddo answered.

"OK, umm . . . the 'fainting bee' metaphor."

"Explain," he said.

"The bee is perched on the *lip* of a flower."

"And . . ."

"I don't know."

"What's the flower?"

"I don't know."

"What's this poem about in your view?"

"The vagina."

"So what's the flower?"

She smiled.

"You already knew that," he said.

"Well, yeah, but."

"Go on."

"I mean, 'round her chamber hums,' and it's very specifically *her*."

"Dickinson uses the female possessive pronoun."

"Zackly," Gina said, "And then it goes, 'he enters.'"

"He enters her."

She blushed.

"That's all right, finish," Megiddo said, "You can do it."

"'And is lost in balms,'" she said and covered her face a little.

"Meaning?"

"Really?" Gina said.

"What are the balms?" Megiddo pressed.

"Pussy juice," Buddy Feigenbaum said loud enough to become everybody's hero, though luckily Megiddo didn't hear him.

"What's this poem really about then?"

"Getting lost in love?" Claire said.

"Or lost in God? or Death?" I said.

"Or someone's coochie?" said Buddy.

Mr. Megiddo interrupted, "I look forward to reading your paper where I'm sure you finish the thought. Excellent job."

I could see Gina mouth 'thank you' to Megiddo before she sat down.

When Jim Lord, in his explication, tried to use the line "might I but moor/

To–night in thee!" to claim that the poem was about "the irresistible allure of the vagina," Mr. Megiddo laughed but also curbed the laughter.

Manny did "Much madness is divinest sense" and dedicated his presentation to Buzzy.

"Where is Buzzy?" Sharon Rose asked and everybody turned and looked at me because I lived next door to him.

I shrugged.

"Do you know, Whit? You're his best pal," Claude Moss said.

"He's been having trouble keeping it together," Whit said, "that's all I know."

This girl named Celeste Nova from Brazil—she'd just moved to the States from Brazil in September but spoke English with no accent which was completely weird—did "This is my letter to the world," and her presentation was sadder than the poem.

She started crying after reading the first two lines.

This is my letter to the world,

That never wrote to me

"I chose this poem because it's me," she said and started crying again.

Mr. Megiddo let her sit down and moved right along.

Claire went over and stroked Celeste's hair and was whispering to her.

I watched in wonder both at Claire's goodness and at how she no longer had me enraptured.

I did "There is no frigate like a book" because I knew it from the sign over the door of The Frigate, my favorite store in Los Angeles, but class ended before I got to do my oral presentation, which was kind of good because Miranda's was so much better than mine would have been.

That night I wrote a song for the film.

We didn't want the song to be narrative, so I decided to make the lyrics about dreams being places you actually go. It really had nothing to do with the film but it worked in context when we presented it to the class.

I set the words to a wonky set of minor chords with dissonant harmonies, borderline atonal, though it most definitely had a melody.

A dream is more than mere continuation

Mere flashy aftermath mere thoughts that glow

A dream is real travel

A distance to unravel

A dream is a place where you go

A dream is a place

Off you go

Dreamward Ho

Sometimes a dream's a place of no dimension

Sometimes a dream's a place where you can fly

Everybody sings

Everyone's got wings

A dream is a place like the sky

A dream is the place where you go when you die

Sometimes a dream is a place like the sky

Sometimes a dream's a place above the river

Sometimes a dream's a place to watch it surge

Slipping off the wall

Down a waterfall

A dream is a place like a verge

A dream is a place where you go to submerge

Sometimes a dream is a place like a verge

Sometimes a dream's a place where you are running

Sometimes a dream's a place without a sound

A thousand hazy ways

A single crazy maze

A dream is a place all around

A dream is a place where you go underground

Sometimes a dream is a place all around

Sometimes a dream's a place of suffocation

A place you can't escape the chasing threat

Where memories ensnare you

And strangle as they scare you

A dream is a place like a net

A dream is a place where you go to forget

Sometimes a dream is a place like a net

Sometimes a dream's a place without a history

Sometimes a dream's a place without a guide

The darkness under boulders

Protects you from the soldiers

A dream is a place where you hide

A dream is a place where you go back inside

Sometimes a dream is a place where you hide

Sometimes a dream's a place that is familiar

A city that you visit on your own

An echo in the air

No one else is there

A dream is a place you have known

A dream is a place where you go all alone

Sometimes a dream is a place you have known

Sometimes a dream's a place without a limit

Lambent as the starlight on a rose

Where conscience won't contain

The orchard in your brain

A dream is a place where it grows

A dream is a place

It's the place where everything goes

We presented the film to the class on the last day of school before Christmas vacation.

My song was played on a shitty LAUSD cassette player which kept changing speeds.

Mr. Simmons said, "Oh my" when the film opened with Claude's erection while looking at the Farrah Fawcett poster but otherwise he was quiet.

As I watched I was bothered by the flaws in my Chaplin and Groucho imitations.

Claire was indeed the foxiest Harpo of all time. I should have smeared my Groucho/Chaplin mustache makeup all over her sugar bear face and turkey lips that day, though I did not do that because I was all stressed out about the film coming out ok.

Afterward, Mr. Simmons said, "Very clever references to Charlie Chaplin, The Marx Brothers, and the Keystone Kops, but I thought the story was pretty weak overall. Why were his fantasies all of slapstick comedians? You could've established that in some interesting way in the first, um, bedroom scene," he raised his eyebrows at us, "Instead of the Farrah Fawcett poster . . . correct?"

"He should have had Chaplin, Marx, Sennet posters on his wall," Mitchell said.

"Uh huh, something like that," Mr. Simmons said. "I had no problem with the erection, though I was surprised by it. My problem is with the choice of

Farrah Fawcett as she has really nothing to do with the character. The camera angles and the choice of shots were uniformly excellent," Mr. Simmons credited Mitchell who held two thumbs up and said, "Cool."

"Oh, and you should have made it look like they were fucking at the end" is what we were all hoping he'd say but alas we didn't get our wish.

Miranda, Dolly, and Arabella made a film about a dashing rogue who seduces women and then kills them, played by our classmate Godfrey Dirth, the handsome strapping *shaygetz* with goyboy strands of blonde hair hanging across one of his seductive green eyes.

In the opening scene Arabella, carrying a balloon, gets taken into the bushes at the Tar Pits by Godfrey, who is her date, and, just as in the movie *M*, we see her balloon rise up out of the bushes and know she's been killed.

Next, Godfrey drowns Dolly in her swimming pool and then we see her floating in the pool like William Holden in *Sunset Boulevard*.

And then Miranda gets stabbed mid-embrace in a scene that echoes the death of Lulu in *Pandora's Box* with the hand going limp and everything.

The twist comes at the end when Godfrey encounters a beautiful ingénue (played by Heaven Sender, moonlighting in another group's film) who ends up killing the rogue with poison lipstick.

"Why doesn't the lipstick kill her too?" Claire asked after the film was over, "It's stupid," which was, I'm pretty sure, directed at Miranda Savitch and Heaven Sender simultaneously.

Claude Moss said, "Like in the *Gilligan's Island* episode," which everyone ignored because he's Claude.

"Magnificent work," Mr. Simmons said, "Great, dark images. Spot on film references. I can tell you've been paying attention. Though, again, the story wasn't very strong and the characters were undeveloped. But this isn't a filmmaking class so. All of you could benefit with some storytelling practice, however. Pay attention to the stuff you're reading in English class. Learn from the masters."

Miranda's work was better than mine and always would be and yes I still cared about that fact.

I wanted to tell her how great I thought her film was but I didn't.

When Christmas Vacation started I was uneasy about the Claire situation.

Claire and I went to the movies now and then when she got off work and most definitely still had some good times hanging out together, but our outings had taken on a presumed quality, with more and more moments feeling obligatory, like we were just automatically spending all our free time together because we were supposed to.

Our relationship had become the default state of being.

I found myself feeling guilty but also resentful about feeling guilty about wanting to just stay in my room and work on songs and listen to music and read and maybe, if my homework was done, go up on the roof and get high and possibly get to joke around with Penelope Lagniappe and ogle her freckled breasts.

I'm at my best when things are going nowhere.

For example, Claire was extremely put out one night when, instead of getting together with her, I went to see the Kings play the Montreal Canadiens with Rudy Tuesday.

Rudy was the only other hockey fan I knew, but also one of the greatest dudes to talk to because he knew how to riff on a joke but then get really serious also and go deep and he could move fluidly back and forth between the two which is what I always like to do.

Rudy and I went to Kings games together whenever we could, but this was the first time I'd gone to a game with Rudy since getting together with Claire.

Rudy was already driving and had a car, so whenever we'd go to games he'd pick me up in his yellow Honda Civic and we'd both be clad in our gold Kings jerseys and Rudy wore this yellow helmet with a spinning red light on top which he'd switch on whenever the Kings scored a goal and we'd usually discuss that night's game on the way to the Fabulous Forum in Inglewood and segue seamlessly into school gossip.

Rather than pay for parking, Rudy put his car in the lot behind a medical building on Prairie, a secret free parking area for fans in the know. Just meant a brisk walk to the Forum from several blocks away and back afterward with a large group of nervous white people moving briskly to sanctuary.

That night, someone else was in the car when Rudy came to pick me up.

"Hey, you remember Wendy from Fairfax?" Rudy asked.

The girl turned around to the back seat and I recognized her from when she was smoking out with Gina Dichlich over on Oakwood and Fuller that night.

"Oh, yeah, hey, how's it going. Good to see you again," I said.

"Yeah," she said.

As usual we got the $9 Colonnade seats and sat up near the ceiling of the Forum.

The Kings looked pretty decent early in the season. They were fun to watch.

Marcel Dionne was on his way to a 53 goal season, Rogie Vachon was a monster stopping the puck, Butch Goring was kicking ass nightly.

To be an L.A. Kings fan was to live on hope because usually they absolutely sucked.

"Every new season is another possible shot at the Stanley Cup," Rudy said during a lull in the action. The refs were conferring on a disputed call.

"Yeah, let's hope," I said as play resumed, "looking decent so far."

"Oops, Bert Wilson just tripped over the blue line," Rudy joked, "So maybe not."

But we just kept going back, game after game, still do, hoping for purple and gold glory.

"I hope I get to hear Bob Miller say 'The Kings are the Stanley Cup Champions!' really loudly on national television one day," I said.

"It'll happen, dude," Wendy promised.

"Believe," Rudy said and the three of us clinked Coke cups knowing we'd keep the faith. We were Kings fans forever.

I debated whether or not to call Claire when I got home from the game, but it was after 10 and I was afraid of getting her in trouble with her mom.

The next day I was in the middle of reading *Without Feathers*, the Woody Allen book, which my aunt had given me for Chanukah, when Claire called.

"Hey, stud, what are we doing New Year's Eve?" she asked.

"Stud?"

"Yeah. Just trying to be funny."

"Haha," I said.

"So?"

"Uh, my parents are going to a party 'til late if you want to come over and hang out," I said in my ever evolving role as the worst boyfriend of all time.

"I guess," she said, "OK."

"We can have some bourbon maybe."

"Sounds fine."

"I can show you *Judo Jew*."

"The film you made when you were 12? Cool," she said most unenthused.

I couldn't muster much myself.

New Year's Eve Claire came over after my parents left for their party and we pecked hello at the front door.

It was a cold night in Los Angeles.

"Whiskey?" I offered trying to be all nonchalant about it.

"Sure," Claire said.

I brought a bottle of Jack Daniel's from the liquor cabinet and two glasses.

We sat on the couch together, knees touching.

Mimi was out at a party and Joy was watching TV in her bedroom and was unlikely to come to the front of the house save for maybe a snack in the kitchen.

We could have done anything, Claire and I, but neither of us seemed to want it.

It was my first encounter with the tepid emptiness of dragging out a situation that had run its course.

I poured the whiskey and we clinked glasses.

We should have toasted "To us" together but instead I said *L'chaim* and Claire said *Salut* and we both took sips.

I sort of shivered from the harshness of the liquid going down.

Neither of us wanted to admit it tasted nasty.

"Mmm," we smiled at each other.

My stomach was uneasy knowing how disappointed she was that this was her New Year's Eve.

I had set up the projector and screen so I could show her *Judo Jew* and I thought we'd also watch *Down In The Dumps* again.

That was the exciting evening I'd planned.

"Look at you," Claire said as 12-year-old me appeared on screen with painted on beard and crocheted blue and white yarmulke.

The opening sequence had me dancing the *hora* alone side-to-side in front of my garage door.

Manny had written a song for the opening credits but I didn't have the tape anymore so I sang it a cappella for Claire.

When he walks he looks like other people do

When he talks he sounds like me and you

But when he fights the criminals are through

Judo Jew

God loves you

Claire laughed politely.

Neither of us wanted to be doing what we were doing in that moment.

I was rapidly downing the glass of bourbon and a certain sense of stable selfhood was getting away from me.

Claire was sipping more slowly.

We were both quite drunk by the time we got to the scene in *Judo Jew* where Manny plays three different characters.

"Oh shit check this out," I slurred, "Manny's an ensemble with himself."

"Groovy," Claire said, becoming less forgiving of my pathetic nature.

We had set up Manny's back patio to look like a saloon in the scene.

I poured myself another glass of Jack.

"*L'chaim*," I said and raised my glass to Claire who sat at the other end of the couch. She raised her empty glass and turned down my offer of another pour.

In the scene Judo Jew enters the saloon and sits at the bar to drink a glass of Manischewitz.

The bartender is played by Manny looking like he normally looks only with a red gingham cowboy shirt on.

Two bad guys are playing cards at a table adjacent to the bar, both played by Manny (thanks to the miracle of splicing), one a gray-haired mustachioed man in a stetson and the other a shirtless dirty scumbag in tight blue jeans.

"Manny's coming over to the bar to pick a fight," I pointed out to Claire.

"Ah," she said while yawning.

"Now watch me kick his ass," I said.

Claire lay back on the couch. Her vagina had probably never been drier.

"I'm not into kung fu movies," she said and reached out to me.

I turned off the movie.

I realized how bad it sucked so I couldn't blame her.

"C'mere," she slurred.

I lay on top of her and we started kissing.

I nibbled on her neck and earlobe and she began to stir a little, but when I unbuttoned her blouse and reached around to unclasp her bra I couldn't find the hook.

"It's in the front," she said.

After that I blacked out.

I have no memory beyond her saying, "It's in the front."

Mimi coming home woke me up.

"Dang, dude," Mimi said as she looked at the bottle of bourbon and the two glasses and me passed out on the couch, "Have fun? Where's your girlfriend?"

Claire had gone.

"I dunno," I mumbled, sitting up, "I don't remember."

"Oh," Mimi said and started cleaning up a little, "We should probably hurry."

It was 1:00am and luckily my parents weren't home yet.

Mimi put the bourbon bottle back in the liquor cabinet and washed the two glasses.

I packed up the projector and folded up the screen.

"Thank you, sis," I said.

"Just trying to help you out, brohan," she said and started heading down the hall.

"How was your party?" I asked.

"Oh, it was pretty cool. Miranda Savitch was there and told me to say hi to you."

"What?"

"Hi from Miranda," she said.

"What?"

"That's all," Mimi said and ambled down the hall.

I checked the living room for any incriminating evidence and then went to bed but didn't sleep very well because I knew I had to call Claire in the morning.

The next day I procrastinated until about 11:59am at which point I could no longer say it's still morning and called Claire, initially to apologize.

"You fell asleep as you were reaching for my boob," she said. "I tried to wake you up for a while, but when you got too heavy and weren't coming out of it I peeled out from under you, made sure you were breathing, and called my mom and asked her to come pick me up 'cause she said I could call whenever I wanted to come home. She was just staying in and was gonna watch the ball drop and then maybe some *Twilight Zone* reruns on Channel 5. It's cool, dude. You drank too much booze. No biggie."

She was being too nice. I also got the feeling she was about to invite me over or something and I didn't feel like it.

"Uh, hey," I said, deciding this was the moment to break up with her, "I don't, um, I don't think I want to do this anymore."

"Do what?" Claire said.

"I mean this, us, we've been together for quite a while now."

"2 months is quite a while?"

"I dunno, it just doesn't feel right."

"In what way?"

"I mean, you don't like professional wrestling and kung fu movies."

"What?"

"That sort of thing. You know," I shrugged, which she couldn't see over the phone but I'm sure she could hear in my voice, "We're sort of incompatible in some ways."

"Because I don't like professional wrestling and kung fu movies? Are you joking? You don't really care about that stuff anymore do you? When's the last time you watched wrestling *or* a kung fu movie? Really, Lance. This is bullshit."

"I'm sorry. No no. I'm just . . . not into it."

"Why are you doing this?"

I could hear the burgeoning cry in her voice.

"I don't know," I said.

"What is wrong with you? I don't care about last night. So what. New Year's always sucks anyway. I hate it as much as you do."

She paused and I didn't fill the silence.

"I don't know," I said again.

"Lance, this is ridiculous," she said. "You don't like me anymore suddenly? Say what it really is? Are you bored? Do you like someone else? What is up?"

"It's not someone else, it's everybody else," I wanted to say.

"It's not someone else. I don't know. I'm just. I just wanna hang out by myself and do shit alone. I still want to be friends with you though," I said, "That's the thing."

I figured it was already bad enough that anything else I said would only make it worse so I shut up and let the silence hang.

"Ugh, this sucks," she said and she was definitely already crying, "Well, happy New Year, I guess. See you at school," she seemed to be waiting for me to say something, which I didn't. Then all she said was "Bye" and hung up.

I am the bringer of pain.

I lay on my back hating myself for a while and then pulled out my newly acquired copy of *Captain Fantastic & The Brown Dirt Cowboy* and put it on the stereo, lowering the needle onto "Someone Saved My Life Tonight."

You almost had your hooks in me didn't you dear

You nearly had me roped and tied

Altar-bound, hypnotized

Dolly called me in the afternoon.

"Hey, I was practice-driving with my mom, and we saw Claire walking down Beverly Boulevard crying. Did you guys have a fight?"

"Uh we kind of broke up yeah."

"In other words you dumped her."

"Nyeah, I guess. I dunno."

"Come over," Dolly said without hesitation.

"I dunno," I said.

"Come over and tell me about it. Talk it out."

"Ice cream cone at Thrifty?" I offered.

"I'll meet you there," she said.

"Hour?"

"Yes!"

Sweet freedom whispered in my ear

You're a butterfly

And butterflies are free to fly

Fly away, high away, bye bye

I didn't want to take the Beverly bus to Fairfax for fear of seeing Claire, so I took La Brea to Wilshire and transferred.

Dolly was waiting in front of Thrifty on Wilshire & Fairfax in a leather jacket and jeans.

"Happy New Year," she tried to look appropriately sad for me.

We hugged and held it a while, staying embraced even as we talked.

"Likewise," I said, "Can I buy you an ice cream cone, mademoiselle?"

"Oui, oui," she nodded, "Let's share one. I'm not that hungry."

"I want chocolate," I said.

"Uh–uh, vanilla."

"Strawberry then. Compromise."

"Right on," she said..

We walked down Fairfax to Dolly's house, sharing the cone back and forth, watching each other lick it.

"So tell me," she said, "You and Claire."

I shrugged.

"I wasn't into it anymore, I dunno."

"I know that feeling. Bored?"

"No no not at all. Claire's amazing. It was really feeling obligated to always be together and me just wanting to hang alone and do music or just read all day and not be interrupted and also not feel guilty about it."

"Yeah, especially Saturdays, right?"

I smiled at her knowledge.

"Having to be with someone all the time."

"Even someone you like to be with usually."

"Right on, I get it," she said.

Back at her house I played piano while Dolly did the dishes which she was supposed to have done earlier but forgot and which her mother insisted she take care of immediately.

I had just finished writing a song called "This World" which was inspired by this really weird dream I had where I was performing on stage and my singing voice sounded like Leonard Cohen.

When I woke up I remembered two lines from the song I'd been singing in the dream. One was "Death won't take us out of this world" and the other was "That is why I have not understood this world."

I fleshed out the rest with an apocalyptic scenario.

Cohenesque chords and melody, consciously so because I was him in the dream.

I sang "This World" in the Ferris living room, playing their comfortably warm Steinway baby grand.

This world is over

An empty nest

An orphaned boulder

Come to rest

This world is leaden

And all bereft

Forgetting Armageddon

Nobody's left

That is why I have not understood this world

That is why I have not understood this world

I'm the by-product of nuclear fission

Conduit spawn of the bombs that were hurled

Ignorant heir to a lifeless condition

Death won't take us out of this world

This world is broken

From apocalypse

Every wisdom ever spoken

Has been eclipsed

This world's dismantled

A stagnant sphere

Ransacked and abandoned

Nobody's here

That is why I have not understood this world

That is why I have not understood this world

I'm the result of primordial friction

Vegetable essence whence life first uncurled

Perched on the verge of the earth's crucifixion

Death won't take us out of this world

This world is sterile

A vacant waste

Carelessly imperiled

By the human race

This world is barren

A pillaged stone

Withered womb of Sarah

Nobody's home

That is why I have not understood this world

That is why I have not understood this world

"Bravo," said Leonard Ferris, Dolly's dad, from the hallway, "Yours?"

I waved and nodded.

"Yeah. New one."

"We haven't seen you in ages, Lance. Glad you're back."

"Dad! Please!" shouted Dolly from the kitchen.

"What are you reading right now?" he asked. He usually asked that question.

"I just started reading *Pale Horse, Pale Rider*," I said, "Katherine Ann Porter."

"Know of it but haven't read it," he said.

"I'm liking it a lot," I said.

"I'll have to get my hands on it."

"And set your eyes on it."

"*Pale Horse, Pale Rider*," he said to remind himself.

"Yeah," I said.

"Play on," he gestured at me as he made his way upstairs.

Dolly came into the living room still drying her hands with a dish towel.

"He's so embarrassing sometimes," she said.

"I love your dad," I said.

"Was that a new song you were playing?" she asked.

"Yeah."

"Sing it for me."

She sat down next to me on the piano bench and I played "This World" for her after which she clapped quietly and said, "Nice," and then we started kissing.

"You don't think it's a little depressing?" I said.

"Of course it is," she said, her eyes still closed, "That's what I like about you," and we went back to kissing.

"Your parents," I said, finally stopping.

She rose and beckoned me upstairs to her bedroom.

We did start to make out a little bit on her bed and I briefly pondered getting my hands on her breasts but then pulled away which made her ask why.

"I just broke up with Claire," I said.

"So?" she said.

"I mean like 4 hours ago."

"Nyeah, it's weird I guess."

"Nyeah and–"

"What?"

"I don't want to be obligated to spend time with anyone," I looked as if to let her know that included her, "That's what what I'm trying to get away from."

"Ah," Dolly said, "yeah, so you said."

I shrugged.

"You suck."

"But you love me anyway."

"Something like that," she got up off the bed and held out her hands as if to help me up but I grasped her hands and pulled her on top of me instead.

We didn't touch lips but we were close enough to intermingle breath.

"You just broke up with Claire," she teased, "you're a free man in Paris."

"I feel unfettered and alive," I said.

She kissed me quickly and stood up.

"I should go home," I said.

She nodded.

"I'll walk to the bus stop with you."

We walked silently until Dolly asked, "Do you want to go to the movies next weekend?"

I thought about it.

"No obligation or anything," she promised.

"I dunno," I said.

"We won't make out. Friend date."

I shrugged.

"You don't even have to call me the next day. Unless you feel like it."

"Now you're lying," I laughed.

"OK, yeah."

"Chicks, man," I shook my head.

"Shut up," she said, "Don't be a chauvinist piglet."

I grabbed her by the wrists and we fake wrestled until she almost accidentally kneed me in the balls and anyway the bus came so we stopped because I didn't want the bus driver to accuse me of anything untoward with the young lady.

"Friends," she said as I got on the bus, "I'm cool with that."

I nodded.

"But can we still kiss sometimes?" she asked.

"Most definitely," I said as the bus door closed.

I'm sleeping with myself tonight

Saved in time, thank God my music's still alive

I got home to a postcard from Annie De Milo in Wales waiting for me on my bed. It must've arrived the day before and gotten jumbled up with the other mail. I presumed my mother found it and left it on my quilt.

It was a photograph of her town–Hay-on-Wye–with the Wye River in the background.

I didn't think she was actually going to write to me.

Hi, Lance!

I know it took me 6 months to send you a postcard but I have had so much schoolwork to do it's not even funny. (But it's not sad either). You know what? It snowed here and I got to go sledding on the heath! It was really neat. Right now I'm reading <u>Charlie & The Chocolate Factory</u>. *I totally understand Augustus Gloop because I really really really love chocolate. Please write back to me and tell me what you are reading and also tell me something interesting about it like I just did with* <u>Charlie & The Chocolate Factory</u> *only with the book you are reading instead. Now you have my address so you know where to mail it. Send me a postcard of Los Angeles with the Observatory in it! (or the Tar Pits but the Observatory would be better). OK?*

Your friend,

Annie De Milo

p.s. It's cool to live by a river

p.p.s. I still don't have an accent

p.p.p.s You're still a nimnork

I put the postcard on my desk and left it there until such time as a response fashioned itself in my head.

I went up onto the garage roof to get high and, as always, allowed myself to hope that Penelope Lagniappe would catch a whiff and climb up and join me.

I heard a familiar rustling of the bushes and smiled but instead of Penelope emerging, it was Buzzy climbing up and joining me.

His head was shaved.

"Dang, dude," he said, "Let me get a hit of that."

He sat down next to me and I handed him the mini-bong.

"Penelope said you'd probably be up here."

I looked at him in the dimming sunlight streaking through the bare branches of the sycamore trees.

"So where have you been, dude?" I asked.

"Brain surgery," he said.

"Whoa shit. Brain surgery?"

"No biggie," he said like the essence of old Buzzy.

He handed the bong and the lighter back to me.

"Still planning to marry Heaven Sender?" was the only thing I could think of asking him.

"We will have a miserable life together one day, yes," he said, "I wish I was Godfrey Dirth."

I couldn't gauge where he was mentally.

Did brain surgery cure him? Of what?

Was he still crazy?

Was the whole thing some kind of genius put-on and I was now being let in on the joke?

"Flippy Killbones still around?" I asked.

"You know Flippy?"

"You've told me about him, yeah. And I've heard him speak a few times. He kind of sounds like Bugs Bunny."

"Ah. Really? Dang. I only know some of what's going on. It's hard to describe. I know people look at me weird. I'm still me though."

"And the house next door?"

"You mean your house?"

"No the other house next door," I said all turned around backwards.

"Oh in the wilderness."

"Yeah that one."

"Yes, I live there now."

"Oh," I said.

"The people in the house next door finally let me in," he said.

Buzzy was under there somewhere. I could feel him trying to scratch his way out.

Finally, my curiosity couldn't resist inquiry:

"Dude, I just want to clear something up, be honest, are you faking this whole thing?"

"Does it matter?" he asked back, eyes closed, immersed in the infinitely rhetorical.

Small Change

1

Manifest Destiny And Beyond

Words & Music by Lance Atlas

I've been losing sleep over nightmares

I should have had and should be having

I've become the grudge you hold

And held so tightly smothered in your loving hand

Now after modest interruptions I continue to explore

The early hours, break of dawn, the sudden death of evening scores

Manifest destiny and beyond

A coast to coast voyage home

Permanent circle

The plane I search

The void I roam

Herein lies the key to unlock embrace

And watch it spoil with handling

Refusal solves these problems before they start

I will never love again

Active passion having passed I begin to find

The emphasis on the physical is just a state of mind

Manifest destiny and beyond

A coast to coast voyage home

Permanent circle

The plane I search

The void I roam

Lamp shade party lights

Cast a shadow in the darkness

Of my room

I sense implosion and erosion

I will make my way away across the fruited plain

And leave behind the monoxide trails aware of a new direction

Tonight I erase the blemishes from the future's past complexion

But my mother never told me where to start where to look where to find . . .

Manifest destiny and beyond

A coast to coast voyage home

Permanent circle

The plane I search

The void I roam

There was something different about that song.

A bonefire in the elephant graveyard.

An upshift.

An ascent into the epic pudenda of my muses.

I longed to be lost inside them.

Traipsing through language and mindplay and music, I would prostrate myself to Calliope and Euterpe and enslave myself to their demands. They would visit me amid the darkness whether in bed or on rooftops or on barefoot walks before dawn.

Aware of a new direction

I wrote the song as a kind of renunciation.

Other than making out with Dolly Ferris once in a while, I had vowed, post-Claire, to abandon my constant thoughts of the human female and refocus my attention on the heavenly muses instead and open myself to their transmission with steadfastness, resolve, and fidelity.

Of course within hours of completing said sung declaration of chastity I was performing cunnilingus on (and getting fellatio from) Taryn Rust with Pink Floyd narrating uncannily in the background.

Dang, dude.

I am a fucking slut.

And I like to be fucking slutty with other fucking sluts, real or imaginary.

So, the cunnilingus thing started because Aron's had sold out of *Animals* and I was dying to hear it.

"Maybe my dad will give me a ride up to Tower," I said to Taryn Rust– recently promoted to Assistant Manager–who had gone into the stock room to look for a copy back there but returned empty-handed.

"I'm sure Tower's got it though," she said.

"But my dad won't want to go tonight. It's Saturday and Tower will be crowded and he hates that parking lot even when it's empty."

"Yeah that lot gets cray-zee," she said, "I wouldn't want to drive up there tonight either. Go tomorrow morning, it'll be empty."

"But I want to hear it tonight."

"I've got it if you want to come over later."

My reluctance succumbed to the allure of new Floyd.

"Where do you live now?"

"On Willoughby, right near Poinsettia Park," she said, and she wrote the address down on a piece of scratch paper from the cashier's counter.

"What time?"

"Yeah? You're coming over?"

"I am."

"Coolness. 7:30?"

"OK," I said.

"Bigelow just gave me a lid of some sweet sinsemilla," she said, "so the journey will be well-fueled."

"I hope you have plenty of Count Chocula and half-and-half on hand."

"No duh," she said.

Because of our agreement last summer—the night she had given me my first and only blowjob—whereby I was expected to eat her out the next time we were in a position to be intimate and that would without doubt be tonight so I was tense about it.

Once again I would have to let Taryn guide me because I had no idea what I was supposed to do down there, or well maybe just the vaguest notion. I had thought it through a few times. But it remained a purely abstract geography abetted by occasional bits of porn in *Beaver Slam* magazine when I could get my eyes on it which hadn't been often lately.

I brought her a copy of *The Fan Man* because I had just read it and thought she'd love it and I was right, she did indeed love it, only she'd already read it.

She offered me wine and we talked about Horse Badorties.

"Horse is like if Holden Caulfield moved back to New York after he got out of Camarillo but didn't go to his parents' place and instead just started living in the Village," Taryn said.

"I didn't know you liked to read."

"I do. But I don't actually read all that much. Too busy with other things and of course listening to music comes first always. I dig it, though, when I settle in and tackle a book. I loved *Catcher in the Rye* in high school. I've read it like three times since then. I look at Holden completely differently now that I'm older than he is in the book. Mr. Beauregard said that would happen and it did."

"Didn't you love Beauregard?"

"Oh, hell yes, Beauregard knew how to groove on literature. And then Mr. Megiddo. Sigh. He brought it all alive," she said.

I nodded.

"My lord and savior, Mr. M.," I said.

I didn't want to be attracted to her mind also. Dang, dude. That could potentially ruin everything.

"I was totally high the first time I read *The Fan Man*," Taryn said.

"How else?"

"Horse Badorties is ready for the monsoon," Taryn opened an invisible umbrella.

She had a studio apartment whose walls were covered in music posters.

Neil Young–*After The Goldrush* era–was featured prominently on the back wall when you first walked into the place.

A Roxy Music poster that I had once seen at Postermat in Westwood and had since coveted–the one with Bryan Ferry in the black bejeweled jacket and Eno next to him in red and green and looking like an opiated angel–was mounted crookedly above the kitchenette.

A poster of the *Aladdin Sane* album cover hung over her sofa bed.

The first time I ever locked eyes with Taryn Rust was while listening to Mike Garson's piano solo on the title track when I was in 10th Grade, standing at her bedroom door, one of those immediate flirtations that happen like a fact.

Whoooooooo loves Aladdin Sane . . .

Her stereo sat against one wall, tall speakers on either side, surrounded by orange crates full of LPs.

There were also LPs stacked variously in every available corner.

"I'm really into Steely Dan right now," she said, "I don't know why, I just am. *Royal Scam*, dude," she paused for gravity, "Dude. *Royal Scam*. Have you heard it?"

"'Kid Charlemagne,'" I sang, "Yeah. Been through it several times."

"Dude," she wagged her finger at me, "listen harder. Go back to it. Harder."

"I will," and I would.

"Plus, their name turns me on," she added.

Dang, dude.

Her bong was situated in the middle of a footlocker that was functioning as a coffee table.

The only other thing on the table was the booklet from *Quadrophenia*.

Quadrophenia was another shared love of ours.

Copies of *Rolling Stone* and *Creem* were organized neatly in a mahogany bookcase.

She didn't have a television.

"I don't watch that shit anyway," she said. "When I'm at home I'm either eating, masturbating, or listening to music, sometimes all at once."

I looked at her.

"All at once," I said.

"Sometimes," she smirked and motioned to the bong. "Bowl's loaded, go ahead."

"You won't join me?"

"I took care of that before you got here," she said.

Animals was already on the turntable.

While I took a couple of hits from the bong, Taryn got down on her knees and lowered the needle.

"This is why you came, right?" she said, looking over her shoulder at me.

I coughed and nodded and then took another hit and coughed again.

The music diverted my attention from her ass.

If you didn't care what happened to me,

And I didn't care for you,

We would zig zag our way through the boredom and pain

Occasionally glancing up through the rain

Taryn came toward me and I got up and we embraced in motion, dancing I guess it was, approximately, maybe, spinning in the middle of the floor, kissing with our eyes open, zoomed in on each other.

You gotta be crazy, you gotta have a real need

I cupped my hands around her head and she reached down and grabbed my crotch, unzipping and unbuttoning and extracting the contents therein seemingly in a single motion.

You gotta strike when the moment is right without thinking

Taryn pulled my jeans down and I stepped out of them.

She knelt before me and took my cock into her mouth after licking at its underside a few times like a lollipop.

Dang, dude, I was in a fucking porno movie at that moment.

I held the top of her head as she bobbed on my cock.

It was really happening.

And after a while, you can work on points for style

Taryn made love to my cock with her mouth, lips, tongue, her hand on my balls, occasionally even tapping at my asshole with her pinky which at first freaked me out but then I thought it was pretty excellent.

And, dang dude, I almost came pretending it was Miranda—if I squinted just right it could've been her—but stopped myself because I wanted to be thinking about Taryn.

As with the first blowjob from Taryn I grew a little bored with her mouth after a while during this long stretch of instrumental wizardry that had me wanting to concentrate on the music instead of the head I was getting from this girl who knew what she was doing and who was into me and who loved music as much as I did and yet her mouth sucking my cock was far less interesting to me than what Floyd was doing on the record.

It stopped feeling good and instead became kind of annoying.

What rescued me was David Gilmour's soaring guitar solo, a comet ride through the cosmos and I was like Slim Pickens shouting "Yee–Haw!" bomb-back riding into Soviet annihilation.

My mind wandered until the dactylic rhythm of Taryn's lips and tongue brought me back to the grand satori.

When I came in her mouth I briefly pretended she was Miranda again but returned to Taryn mid-jolt.

The whole thing was borderline fictional.

And when you lose control, you'll reap the harvest you have sown

"Your turn," Taryn Rust said, a favorite phrase of hers, removed her shirt and pants, and pulled me onto the carpet with her, nudging my head cuntward.

So have a good drown, as you go down, all alone,

Dragged down by the stone

Her inner thighs were soft on my cheek and manna for my lips.

I inhaled and let my tongue touch enough to taste the tang, en route to the other thigh which I nibbled at while she hummed in approval.

Dang, dude, the inner thigh. Like the stuff up in Heaven, the Heaven you see in movies and cartoons.

"Play," she rasped and centered me on her clit.

And then I was in it.

While I let my tongue swirl around her circumference she took hold of my hands and moved them onto her breasts whose nipples I pinched gently in counter-rhythm to my tongue now up inside her.

It was no different from keeping track of the bass clef and the treble clef at the same time, dude.

My piano skills were coming in handy.

My hottest cantata.

She tasted like syrup from the sea, a kosher dill, finely aged parmesan.

Her right hand held my left forearm and occasionally she dug her nails into my skin and that was righteously erotic.

I let her steer.

She slowed me down and sped me up and called for me to introduce fingers into the vortex.

Her pelvis was thrusting up against my tongue and teeth and nose.

She winced, "I'm'na . . . na . . . na . . . nyeah . . . "

I stuck two fingers into her while my tongue stayed at her clit.

"Enh," she rasped, stiffened, held her breath, clutched my scalp and pulled my mouth off her, sort of went something like "ennnnhyeah," and relaxed with a guttural exhale and some satiated breathing as she squeezed my head with her thighs.

I worked my way up her body, circling her stomach, nestling in her breasts.

"I love that Roxy Music poster," I said, trying to kiss her.

"Wait," she stopped me and wiped my face with an edge of a pillow case from the sofa.

"OK," she said.

We kissed slow and deep.

I thought about how much I didn't want to fall in love with Taryn Rust.

How she was 19 or maybe even 20 by then.

How she did this with other guys I was sure.

How her brother was one of my oldest friends.

How her other brother was my pot dealer.

How our parents were friends.

How we could go months without talking to each other which was actually kind of perfect.

How we were both like cats, aloof but ready.

How holy shit I'd just gotten another blowjob.

How holy mackerel I'd just eaten a girl out and the swampy musk of her cunt lingered upon me and would permeate my dreams for weeks.

How instead of bragging I didn't want to tell anybody anything and wouldn't.

How every divine secret is thus sequestered.

I gotta admit that I'm a little bit confused.

Sometimes it seems to me as if I'm just being used

"I've got rubbers here," she said after a prolonged stoned silence listening to the music.

"I think that session took it all out of me," I said, looking down at my shriveled dick that didn't appear to be coming back for more.

"That was intense for sure," she said, "Yeah," and kissed me again. "Well, cool then," and then kissed me again, "Let's just hang."

We lay entwined on the carpet and felt ourselves breathing and thought about separate things.

Dragged down by the stone

When Side A ended, Taryn got up to turn the album over and then we reassembled ourselves.

As I pulled my pants back on, the change in my pocket spilled out and scattered across the room, which made Taryn laugh.

"Guys always do that," she said while I gathered loose coins from the carpet.

We listened to the rest of *Animals*, taking the occasional bong hit, sipping at wine, sometimes getting up and dancing but never for long before buckling under to cannabinoid gravity and ending up reclined on her sofa bed.

"I have to remember not to tell Dolly about any of this," I reminded myself because I was supposed to hang out with her the next day and didn't want to slip because even though Dolly wasn't my girlfriend she'd still flip a shit if she found out.

You know that I care what happens to you

And I know that you care for me too

So I don't feel alone on our way to the stone

Now that I've found somewhere safe to bury my bone

"I want your virginity, young pup," she said and raised her eyebrows at me.

"What makes you think I'm a virgin?" I said and then baa'd like one of the synthesized sheep on Animals.

"You're a virgin," she smirked, "But one of these days," she wagged her finger at me.

Taryn liked wagging her finger at me.

I could have called my dad to come pick me up from Taryn's place but it would've been weird telling him whose apartment it was which meant I'd have to lie, so instead I walked home down Willoughby, past KCOP Channel 13 and Bargain Circus, sifting the swirl of my thoughts, sifting and sorting.

Before I'd left, Taryn gave me a book in exchange for *The Fan Man* which she ended up keeping even though she'd already read it 'cause she didn't have her own copy.

"*Martin Eden*," she said. "You want to be an artist? Read this."

"Thank you," I said, blushing with reluctant love for her.

"When you're done let's get together and talk about it," she said, "You can read your favorite passages out loud while you're fucking me. How does that sound?"

I kept thinking about that phrase all the way home.

You can read your favorite passages out loud while you're fucking me

Taryn was my groovemeister and guide.

I was Grasshopper to her Master Po.

Gilligan to her Ginger.

Harold to her Maude.

Boy Wonder to her Caped Crusader.

Plato to her Socrates.

Sal Mineo to her James Dean.

I got home from Taryn's around 11 and my parents were already in bed which made me doubly glad I didn't call my dad to pick me up 'cause now I could sit on the front porch and smoke a bowl and I loved doing that but rarely got the chance.

I had this poem-like thing about the Sibyl of Cumae sloshing around in my head and I kept reminding myself to remember the images I was coming up with while I was recharging my synapses with this grass Bigelow Rust had sold me called Seminary. "'Cause it teaches you to be divine," he told me.

The Saturday night parade of ambulances heading west on Beverly en route to Cedars-Sinai blared and faded with predictable regularity.

Lives were ending, lives were being saved, lives were being disrupted, relatives and friends were freaking out, putting down what they were doing and dealing with the deaths and injuries and illnesses of loved ones, lives were being changed forever, but I heard only the sounds of sirens, calling from a distant shore, somewhere in the Aegean, somewhere near Delphi.

Buzzy Lagniappe came walking by and I wasn't going to say hey or anything.

I was enjoying being alone and thinking about my night at Taryn's and also the imagery that was coagulating in my head but I guess Buzzy smelled my doings or whatever 'cause he joined me on the front porch.

"Hey, dude, how's it going?" he took a seat next to me and reached for the mini-bong, "Don't mind if I do."

"Pretty good," I said, "Where you headed?"

"Back home. I was over at Whit's but he fell asleep and I want to watch *Saturday Night Live* so I left. What've you been up to?"

"Nyeah I just ate Taryn's pussy out and I think made her come and also got a blowjob from her and shot my whole hot wad in her mouth and some of it dripped down her chin," I said to myself and grinned.

"Eh, I dunno," I shrugged, "Learning."

"Sounds satisfying," he said.

"Immensely."

"Oh, yeah, I owe you 50 cents for that chocolate milk you bought me," he took out two quarters and laid them on the porch table.

"What chocolate milk?"

"Like back in 5th Grade, you know, when you were hanging around with Rose Benedict all the time. You bought me 2 cartons of chocolate milk when I didn't have any money and I never paid you back."

"I honestly don't remember what you're talking about."

"Well, I've felt bad about it. So here. We're even."

"Okie–doke, shmoke," I nodded.

Buzzy could still be way out there sometimes.

"You gonna watch *Saturday Night Live* tonight?" Buzzy said.

"Nah I think I'm gonna work on this poem I'm thinking about."

"All right then. It's time. Upward," he said, rising, "Unto the nethersphere."

"Right on"

"Take her slow."

"Always," I said.

"It's all in the slowness," he said, "That's where the love stuff is at, dig," and then he vanished in the darkness.

Buzzy's dad never left the porch light on past 10 because he thought it was wasteful.

Buzzy was back at Fairfax Spring semester and was lucid a lot more of the time, though occasionally he'd talk about the house next door and his spider friend Flippy Killbones and slip into voices.

He was still off, just not as often, not as far out as he had been like back in November and December before his alleged brain surgery.

I dimmed my bedroom lamp to an adequate ambience and scribbled out my poem which revolved around the Greek phrase *gnothi seauton*, something Megiddo had taught us a few days before and which hadn't stopped littering my thoughts since I'd heard it. I wrote the phrase on the front of my notebook.

We read a bit about the Sibyl of Cumae in class and, I dunno, the imagery, like the phrase, took hold.

I had no preconceived form in mind but the words came out in couplets.

The Sibyl of Cumae

Reports important portents to me

She mutters like a baby

Cryptic and elliptic maybe

She says, "You be The Oracle

Gnothi seauton, gnothi seauton"

I visit her at Delphi

The one they picks, the one they tell me

When her word emerges

Message from the demiurges

She says, "You be The Oracle

Gnothi seauton, gnothi seauton"

I want to be her lover

Although we do not know each other

Naked to the danger

We make it in the sacred chamber

Where she says, "You be The Oracle

Gnothi seauton, gnothi seauton"

And I say, "The people, the people

They're all inside me

The people, the people

They help me hide me

The people the people

They're all my mommy

I'm leaving the people

Before they drop me

I can if I want to

And they can't stop me"

I smell a sweet aroma

Then I go into a coma

The rest I don't remember

Beyond a sleepy dreamy tremor

I wake up in a prairie

Where my dead libido's buried

I come back to my senses

All alone but not defenseless

I am the master captain

In and of myself a bastion

And I say, "You be the Oracle

Gnothi seauton, gnothi seauton"

"You be the Oracle

Gnothi seauton, gnothi seauton"

I wrote *for Taryn* right below the title–"Gnothi Seauton"–but I ended up crossing out that inscription because I didn't really want to have any outward connection to her.

That night I jacked off to a panoply of females, switching every few strokes to a new face, and I couldn't really decide which one to finish with though I'm pretty sure it was Dolly who brought me home but not 100% positive 'cause I was very stoned and very tired.

I had given up the heavily scheduled FUCK–O–RAMA masturbation sessions for a more kaleidoscopic approach, faces on a carousel, spinning across my conscience, infinite variety, a bounteous bacchanale of scattered attention.

Sometimes I'd organize the carousel into set groups like "4th Period" or "Older Sisters" or "Girls On The Bus Today" or "Local News Anchors" or "The Waitresses At Norms" or "Wimbledon Semi–Finalists" or "The Brady Sisters" or "Teachers" or "Hygienists In My Dentist's Office" or "The Docents At LACMA" or "Dog Walkers on Beverly."

A day that had started with a renunciation of all sexual interaction ended with orgiastic slutfests, one real on a carpeted floor, one imagined alone in the dark after midnight sometime.

2

The next day the weather was January-cool, cloudy, raining on and off.

Dolly and I had made plans to hang out at her house and just do whatever.

We'd been hanging out together a lot since New Year's Day, had gone to the movies a couple of times, and when she and her family went to Disneyland and she was allowed to bring somebody with she brought me, but mostly we spent lots of enjoyable hours doing nothing, sometimes at her house, sometimes at the Tar Pits, sometimes driving around–she'd just gotten her license–talking about school and books and gossip and life, with the tacit understanding that we were just friends and nothing was going to develop romantically though we also seemed to have this other unspoken agreement that the occasional passionate smooching session didn't violate the promise because that definitely sometimes went on but we didn't talk about it afterwards.

"You want some hot chocolate?" Dolly said as we walked into the kitchen.

"Definitely, I dig your hot chocolate the most, you know that."

"It's the cinnamon," she said with casual confidence.

"It's the love, baby," I teased.

"Nyeah," she shook her head and scrunched her eyes at me which she often did though I never knew what she meant by it.

We sat at her kitchen table and drank hot chocolate and Dolly also made cinnamon toast which I thought was quite supreme in the set of all possible cinnamon toasts.

"It's the butter," she said, mid–chew, "That's what makes it so nummy."

"It reminds me of being in kindergarten," I said, "My mom would always make us hot chocolate and cinnamon toast on rainy days. Whitman Rust was in afternoon kindergarten with me and he'd come over in the morning to watch *Sheriff John* and eat lunch before school. Most days we'd have Swanson's chicken pies but on rainy days we had hot chocolate and cinnamon toast. I liked Sheriff John. I was never into the *Crusader Rabbit* cartoons, though. I thought those were pretty boring."

"How do you remember shit like that?" Dolly asked.

I shrugged.

"I don't remember anything about kindergarten other than 6th Graders sold us cartons of chocolate milk during recess and that I'd always get sand in my underwear."

225

"You went to Carthay."

"Yuz," she said and sipped her cocoa.

"I went to Melrose," I said.

"I know. We've talked about this before."

There were three stacks of pennies at one end of the table.

"My brother does those," Dolly said, "They all have to be exactly the same height. So he never adds to the stacks until he has another three pennies."

"Trippy," I said. "Don't they ever get knocked over?"

"Ha, like every day," Dolly said, "At first he gets upset and then he just rebuilds them."

I looked out into the backyard through the sliding glass door. The pool was covered.

"What are you reading right now?" Dolly said.

"Well, *Gatsby* for class and I'm about to start *Martin Eden* for my outside novel."

"I don't know that book," she said.

"Me neither," I said, "but Taryn said it was good so."

"Taryn?"

"Nyeah-um, Taryn Rust, Whit's sister." Dang dude. "I was at Whit's house and we were talking about books and his sister Taryn suggested *Martin Eden* 'cause it's about a writer or something," I said, fairly confident she didn't know that Taryn had moved out.

"You are such a geek," Dolly said, shaking her head and crossing her eyes.

"I prefer nimnork," I said, which reminded me I owed Annie De Milo a postcard still. I had the one she'd written to me on my desk but kept procrastinating about answering. "What are *you* reading?"

"*Gatsby*, duh, and also *An American Tragedy* for the outside novel."

"How is *An American Tragedy*?"

"It's really great but it also gives me a stomach ache."

"Why?"

"Ugh, it's just very painful watching all the bad decisions. It's probably gonna get even more painful. You should read it so we can talk about it."

"I might do that. I'd like to squeeze in one more book before we have to start reading for the term paper."

"Or why don't we read something together?" she said, "Like we did with *Dracula*."

"May be," I said.

"How about *Main Street*? Sinclair Lewis?"

I actually had been thinking about getting into Sinclair Lewis of late.

"That sounds cool, yeah."

"Shake on it," she said and held out her hand.

"*Main Street*," I said, shaking back, having the usual immediate regrets.

"You said you had a new song," she shifted.

"I do, yeah. It's different. 'Manifest Destiny And Beyond' it's called. If that's not pretentious enough for you please do let me know."

"Play it for me," she said and started to move into the living room.

"*I've been losing sleep over nightmares I should have had and should be having*," I played the song for Dolly Ferris on her dad's Steinway which always made my playing sound better than it really was.

She sat next to me on the piano bench and listened with her eyes closed, playing with my hair off and on.

"Dang, dude, Claire Farnaway did a number on you," Dolly said when I was done.

"Nah Claire was great. I think I did a number on myself," I said, "but the song's not really about Claire, except maybe indirectly."

"I'm not sure I see the connection to the concept of Manifest Destiny though," she said.

"Uhm," I hate when people call me on my bullshit, especially on my artistic bullshit, and double-specially when it's a chick and extra-specially when it was Dolly, "You know it's like fulfilling my true potential, spreading from sea to shining sea, but in my heart, or at least in my art. Plus I got *fruited plain* in there. But ultimately it's just a song. You know. It's not meant to be a topic for discussion in Mr. Sekhur's class or anything."

"My dreamy dreamboat," Dolly said of our AP US History teacher.

"Dreamy like Mr. Megiddo? I thought that was your current swoon."

"Sekhur's not dreamy like Megiddo, but dreamy in like that Egyptian-Jewish way dreamy," she explained.

"There's an Egyptian-Jewish way?"

"Absolutely," she said, "Like sort of French almost."

"What?"

"I know what I mean," Dolly said, "Forget it."

"So, are Egyptian Jews like descendants of the Hebrews who stayed behind in the Exodus?"

"Huh?" Dolly grunted.

"'Cause you know those dudes existed. You totally know there were some ornery-ass Hebrews who kvetched, 'Hell no, I ain't wandering in no desert wilderness for 40 years eating that funky fungus off the ground and doing whatever that stuttering lunatic dude in the robes tells us to do all the time. I'm staying right here in the bosom of Pharaoh 'cause that *goy* knows how to party,'" I said and was also kind of acting it out and saying it with my utterly bogus approximation of whatever the fuck an Egyptian-Jewish accent would sound like. I ended up sounding like Andy Kaufman.

"What the fuck are you talking about?" Dolly asked, dumbfounded.

Dang, dude.

Manny would have totally run with the Yid–shtick.

We would've ended up wanting to turn it into a sit-com.

I think that's an inherently Jewish tendency anyway, wanting to turn everything into a sit-com.

Our banter always ended up with one of us saying, "We should turn this into a sit-com."

Which would of course immediately render the thing unfunny.

And so we'd have to smoke another bowl and mine some new ideas from the ore chasm.

"I'm just playing," I said to Dolly and shrugged.

"It looks like it's not raining right now," she said, "we should go outside and walk around. Come on."

She started putting on her coat.

"Should we take umbrellas just in case?" I said.

"Umbrellas are for pussies," she said.

"You don't have a jewfro to deal with."

"Dang, you are such a girl, Lance."

"Nyeah nyeah," I muttered back because yes I am indeed very much a pussy when it comes to rain.

Beyond the vanity of not wanting wet poodle curls hanging against my head, I just simply hate the sensation of being outside with wet hair. It gives me a creepy skin-crawl like antihistamines do.

We left the umbrellas in Dolly's entry hall and ventured out into the gray L.A. day, strolling slowly along Commodore Sloat toward Carrillo.

"I love Los Angeles right after it rains," Dolly said.

"Yeah the smell of the pavement," I said.

"Almost as good as the smell of the sidewalk right when it starts to rain," Dolly said, "You know?"

"Yes! Barely wet sidewalk. I can smell it just by thinking about it. It's one of those smells."

"Like vomit," she said.

"I was thinking talcum powder, but yeah vomit's one too I guess."

"The smell of vomit makes me want to vomit."

"The smell of talcum powder makes me want to pamper myself," I camped.

"I love it when your little gay doppelgänger comes out. What's his name?"

"D'Artagnan, dahling," I said without hesitating.

"I love him," she said, "I totally want to go out with him."

"He carries an umbrella, you wouldn't like him," I said in my normal voice.

"Boo," she said, "You suck. I love you. Even if you are a rain pussy."

We came to Carthay Elementary School and gazed into the kindergarten yard.

"You wanna trespass?" Dolly asked.

I was reminded of my perfect playground date with Miranda Savitch in 8th Grade, the sandbox, the handball courts. That day had to remain sacred and singular.

"Nah not really," I said, "I'm cool just looking."

A crow sat atop the fence, stared us down, squawked, and took its scourge elsewhere.

"You went to elementary school here."

"Yeah, no big deal," Dolly said and I could tell she was disappointed I didn't want to hop the fence, but I didn't feel moved to change my mind because she'd be able to tell I wasn't that into it which would then bum her out and we'd both be miserable even though we both kind of already were at that moment.

"I wish it rained more often," I said as we resumed our walk.

"As long as you have an umbrella."

"Correct. And advance warning."

She didn't have to say pussy out loud.

Rainy days in elementary school were the best.

Blackboards and cloak rooms and hung up umbrellas and galoshes lined up along the wall.

The only bad part about rainy days at school was lunch because you stayed in the classroom and played the dreaded game "Heads Up, Seven Up," a wretched situation in which all but seven students in the class would put their heads down with a thumb in the air, and the seven roaming students would each touch a thumb, thereby "picking" that person.

The chosen people would, after "Heads Up, Seven Up!" was called, have to guess which of the seven had picked them.

I always hated that moment, for a variety of neurotic reasons, especially if I thought a girl had picked me, because what if I was wrong and then everybody might laugh ("why would she pick *you*?") or everybody (and she) might think I wanted to think it was her because I liked her or something.

Couldn't risk that kind of embarrassment or public revelation.

That's the kind of shit I always lived in fear of.

One time in 3rd Grade I was pretty sure Gina Dichlich had picked me but I didn't want to say I thought it was Gina because I didn't want her to think that I liked her so instead I said it was this girl Ramona who always invited me to her birthday party but I never went.

Gina Dichlich came up to me later and said her feelings were hurt because she'd picked me and I should have figured it out.

Dang, dude.

Shame is associated with those nascent crushy feelings at a very young age, those first tender tingles so easily trampled into humiliation.

And the more passionate the infatuation the more strident one's denial of it, to oneself, yes, sometimes, but especially to the object of one's very infatuation, in the presence of whom one might even feign dislike or indifference as a means of misdirection.

The tragic satisfaction of worship from afar.

Like the bright star in the Keats sonnet that guides and gives meaning but remains at a distance.

Not having to face the reality of anything mutual.

A series of sideways glances in order to avoid staring.

I've been doing that shit since before the girl from Zody's.

Hyper awareness of the other almost to the point of spying (though no one would ever know it given your strictly cultivated outward apathy).

Stilted nonchalance in any unavoidable interaction.

Unwarranted jealousy of any perceived challenge to your invisible, unspoken claim.

"OK, so I have this crazy idea," Dolly said as we were heading back toward her house.

"Marriage, ya wanna?" I said, invoking a common invitation to smoke a bowl.

"Haha, no," Dolly said, "Maybe later. But here's my crazy idea: I think you should audition for the musical."

"Right."

"No really. We're doing *Guys & Dolls* and we have too many dolls and not enough guys."

"No way."

"Oh come on, give yourself over to stardom."

"I'm not an actor," I said.

"Yes you are," she said and looked at me as if she'd figured out my whole persona was a sham.

"*Guys & Dolls,*" I said, thinking about it.

"Frank Loesser. Damon Runyon."

"Yeah yeah, I've seen the movie. I remember thinking the songs were good but Marlon Brando sucked."

"I think you'd love the lyrics."

"No no, I remember, I was impressed. Not quite Sondheim level but."

"Come on, that's like saying something's not quite Beatles level. Not quite Shakespeare level. What is? And what's the point? You miss too much good stuff thinking like that."

"Hey, Doll, I listen to everything."

"Except country," we said together on cue and laughed at the ancient cool nerd crew joke.

We just sort of started kissing on her front porch and for one very deep thundering instant it felt like she was my girlfriend.

We moved inside and made out on her living room couch for a while vigorously frenching with our jackets still on until her mom and brother came home.

We heard them enough in advance to separate and make it look like we were just talking.

My cock stayed stubbornly hard in my jeans though.

It was only early afternoon but I felt like going home and working on music.

"I think I'm gonna split," I said after her mom and brother left the living room.

Dolly offered to drive me home but I declined, preferring to take the bus and think about stuff.

"You sure?" Dolly asked, "It looks like it's gonna rain some more."

"I have my pussbrella," I said.

We kissed at the front door as I left.

"Call me later?" Dolly said.

I shrugged.

I didn't really want to.

Today was enough.

But, dang, dude, with girls it's never enough.

Girls always want to talk on the phone later.

Always.

"Fine, you don't want to call me later. I hate you," she said, "Go away."

She tried to close the door in my face but I stuck my foot in the threshold and blocked her attempt.

"Go away," she laughed and backed off as I pushed my way in and grabbed her by the arms.

"We had a nice day today," I said as she fought me feebly.

I touched her face while we kissed again.

"OK, now go away," she said when we finished and pushed me out the door.

I walked to the bus stop on Fairfax, letting my cock soften as pre-cum dribbled onto my thigh. I had to quickly adjust my dick so that it didn't get stuck to my boxers by crusting over 'cause, dang, dude, that shit hurts when you yank it loose or sometimes when it shakes itself loose while you're walking or even just crossing your leg or something. I hate that. It's like ten times worse than taking a Band-aid off your arm hairs.

I don't know if anybody saw me stick my hand down my pants to fiddle with the logistics. I tried to do it discreetly while I was walking down Fairfax but I knew it was possible somebody driving by'd catch me with my hand down my pants. I couldn't really control that. I made the necessary adjustments to my apparatus regardless 'cause, dang, dude, like I said, that shit hurts.

When I got home I hung out in my room and ended up writing a song called "Rain On Me," a song about the ongoing longing for rainfall that'd been hanging out in my head all day even while I was smooching with Dolly.

Rain on me rain on me rain

Keep pouring all day long

Rain on me rain on me rain

I love the sound of your sweet song

The wind is blowing harmony

The thunder plays a beat

Music fills the window sills

The sidewalk and the street

I feel like dancing in the mud

Or jumping prancing through the puddles

Rain on me

Rain on me rain on me rain

I wish the sun would go away

Rain on me rain on me rain

I want a cloudy drizzly day

Mom makes us all hot chocolate

And even cinammon toast

Chicken pie and buttered rye

That's the lunch I like the most

Although the sun is fun for play

The world looks better wet and gray

Rain on me

Rain on me rain on me rain

Let the water shower down

Rain on me rain on me rain

Splash my face and soak the ground

Come on rush in gush in cats and dogs

In buckets and in pails

Blue sky returns—I see the worms

The mushrooms and the snails

In the meantime I'll stay warm

And wait around for the next storm

To rain on me

I was getting into this pattern of writing songs in a single session that lasted as long as it took for the song to get finished.

Kind of the opposite of the way I was masturbating at that time.

I thanked the muses for their pennies from heaven, played "Rain On Me" through a few dozen times wondering what Manny would think of it, and then started reading *Martin Eden.*

I read the whole night, skipping dinner, finally falling asleep about 3am then waking up at 9 and going right back to it, not getting out of bed except to pee.

I spent the rest of Sunday, on into the night, captivated by Eden's dedication to his craft, pained by his disillusion, completely throttled by his poetic end, *And at the instant he knew, he ceased to know,* which I reached just before midnight and lay staring at that last pantheonic sentence, that perfect simultaneity of revelation and death . . . *And at the instant he knew, he ceased to know.*

I wanted to be that true.

I wanted to write a nipple-hardening closing line like that.

I ended up too tired to do my math homework but maybe Mr. Fudd wouldn't collect it.

I could fake my way through French by flirting with Madame Couchée and talking to her about Truffaut or Renoir, and luckily I had no homework in Chemistry over the weekend.

Because my 5th Period Cinema class was only a semester course, in the Spring I moved from 6th Period Chemistry into the 5th Period Chemistry class and thus had a free 6th, enabling me to go home at 2:00 which was a flagrant freedom.

Most of my friends were in the 6th Period Chem class, but Eddie Gurges was in 5th Period and we always had a great creative connection and a shared tendency to absent ourselves from the stream of life.

Those are the folks I have to be around. The ones who are often called elsewhere.

Lorelei Lux was also in Period 5. She too was often called elsewhere. It was the first time I'd had a class with her that year.

The chemistry teacher was named Dr. Meany, and he lived up to his name, especially if you sucked at science as badly as I did.

"Atlas, this is the first time I've received a lab report so bad I shouldn't even give it a grade. So, you're getting away with a courtesy F because I have no choice," he announced in front of everybody after making a cruel mockery of my lab report as an example of what *not* to do.

That was the only time a teacher ever made me cry in class.

I had the double embarrassment of my laughable lab report on public display as an example of ineptitude and of crying in front of my classmates.

I remember I faked sick the next day and my mother let me stay home even though she knew I was faking.

I didn't tell her about Dr. Meany making me cry.

I don't know if he felt bad about the incident or not, but when I moved into the 5th Period class Dr. Meany let me be lab partners with Eddie and Eddie was good at science so I was covered for the rest of the semester. I'd squeeze by with a C.

C as in CSUN.

Eddie was very into Lorelei Lux at the time.

"Dude you can see her whole vaginal apparatus through her jeans," he told me once during lab, "I'm in love."

I tried to dissuade him.

"You know that scene at the end of the *Jungle Book* movie when Mowgli goes to the edge of the jungle to look at the man village and sees a girl for the first time?"

"Not really," said Eddie.

"Well, Mowgli's eyes open real wide when he sees this human female and goes, 'What's that?' to his bear pal Baloo 'cause he's never seen a girl before, and Baloo goes, 'Stay away from those, kid, they're nothin' but trouble.'"

"Dang, dude, that's flagrant," said Eddie, "but pretty funny. Yeah. Chicks."

"Totally harsh, but, dude, it's true, and Lorelei Lux is trouble times ten. You really want to be with a girl who always speaks in riddles?" I asked him, "She'll write down everything you say in her little notebook and use it to make fun of you later."

"You think so?" he said.

"I know so," I said, "steer clear of the ones like that."

I had been trying to solidify my stance against romantic entanglement.

Whenever I'd see a couple walking down the street holding hands or smooching at the bus stop I'd think to myself, "I'm glad that's not me."

I love that feeling of not having to call someone later.

Girls are a fucking pain in the ass but they are also the best part of being alive so it gets kind of strenuous trying to maintain that sovereignty from them for long.

Dolly and I spent the next 2 weeks doing nightly readings of *Main Street* and then discussing the book on the phone.

Sometimes we'd gab for hours, always starting off with the book but then veering in myriad directions, from my latest musical endeavors to Dolly's enduring passion for tennis star Bjorn Borg.

"I will bear Bjorn's children one day," Dolly said any time the subject arose, "I swear it."

But inevitably talk would sway back to what was going on in Play Production, gossip I sometimes already knew because Mimi was also in Play Production and would report back first.

I was boggled by the political jockeying and backstabbing that went on, especially among the seniors vying for the leading roles, from friendly attempts at negotiated agreements not to try out for the same parts to ruthless subterfuge via both slanderous rumor and outright sabotage of auditions.

"It takes over your whole being," Dolly said, "If you do audition and get into the musical, you'll see, you'll see what it does. At the first rehearsal go ahead and say hello to your new social life."

"It's an all-consuming world," I said.

"Zackly," Dolly said.

I understood because just the prospect of being in *Guys & Dolls* was claiming a lot of my attention, and actually it was my sister Mimi–and not Dolly–who finally persuaded me to audition.

"I guarantee you'll get cast. You have a penis and you can sing on key," is how she put it, "You should do it. You might have fun."

"Me? Have fun? Never," I said.

It turned out my parents had the Original Broadway Cast album with Robert Alda and Vivian Blaine so I started giving it some serious listening and grew more and more enraptured by the songwriting. I hadn't had a composition lesson like that in a long time. Loesser's lyrics were brilliant and pyrotechnic, his melodies and song structures like a jungle gym to climb on. That score imprinted deep.

The afternoon of auditions I stood in the courtyard where nobody could hear me clearing my throat and singing "I'll Know," the tune I'd chosen to audition with.

Once proceedings were underway I joined the other prospects in the Rotunda, the distinct domed structure that was also the lobby of the auditorium.

Every few minutes, Deirdre Lux would appear at the door and call the next name.

When it was my turn I followed her down the long left-side aisle to the stage.

My path up the apron stairs felt like a kind of gallows walk.

Mr. Hill was sitting dead center about halfway back, to his left Pamela Turpin the choreographer and to his right Dr. Luft the orchestra teacher/conductor and musical director for the show.

Deirdre took a seat behind Mr. Hill and whispered in his ear a lot.

The day before, Deirdre had come into my Algebra 2 class with a summons and the whole class started whispering.

"D-Lux!" someone hooted as Deirdre handed the summons to Mr. Fudd.

"Shawn Wose," Fudd said, holding the summons forward, "to G–90."

"Mr. Hill wants to see you," Deirdre said to Sharon Rose, "it's about *Guys & Dolls* auditions tomorrow."

Murmurs fluttered throughout the class as Deirdre left with Sharon.

The Deirdre/Mr. Hill connection was the subject of much scuttlebutt among the Play Production crowd and had leaked over into other social circles that the theatre kids overlapped with.

Deirdre Lux was Mr. Hill's T.A. during his conference period which was totally weird.

"Who needs a T.A. during his conference period?" I overheard Miranda asking Dolly one day during English.

"He has a lot of paperwork to do for the production. You'd be surprised," Dolly answered.

Deirdre Lux was a year ahead of us, a 12th Grader.

In Junior High she'd been known as DeeDee, then just Dee.

Now she was called D-Lux by most people.

I still called her Deirdre.

I hate nicknames most of the time.

Buzzy was an exception because Buzzy was Buzzy and kind of always had been.

And Dolly was OK because it was almost like saying Dahlia anyway.

Most of the girls were convinced Deirdre was having an affair with Mr. Hill, but there was no verifiable evidence. Even her own sister claimed not to know.

Just before my audition, Sharon Rose asked Lorelei, who was waiting in the Rotunda with the rest of us, "Is your sister doing it with Mr. Hill?"

"I haven't the foggiest," Lorelei said with an English accent because Lorelei Lux always said shit like *I haven't the foggiest* with an English accent, "Not a bloody clue."

"Haven't you asked her?"

"Not really. It's not my bloody business, now is it? And it's not yours either, Sharon Rose."

"Why's she always in fucking G–90 with him at fucking nutrition and lunch also? And how the fuck is she his fucking T.A. during his fucking conference period? That shit's fucking crazy," Sharon pressed like a jealous

242

girlfriend.

"Maybe because they're fucking fucking," Jim Lord said as a joke rather than opinion.

"She helps him with stuff," Lorelei answered.

"Yeah, I bet," said Misty Winters.

"She's the assistant director of the musical," Lorelei said.

The girls around her all snorted.

The singing audition was *a cappella*.

Humming to find my note I launched into "I'll Know."

I'll know when my love comes along

I'll know then and there

I'll know at the sight of her face

How I care, how I care, how I care

After the song, I read for the part of Sky Masterson, though I knew I wouldn't be getting any lead roles because those were for the Seniors and other veterans of Play Production. I was neither. I was an outsider.

"Would you accept a non-speaking role?" Mr. Hill asked.

"Yes, of course," I said. By then I wanted to be in the show no matter what. I'd been hooked by the score. I had to be part of it.

"Thank you," Mr. Hill dismissed me.

I figured if I got cast at all I'd be in the chorus and I was cool with that.

I made my way back out to the Rotunda and then into the courtyard outside where I was supposed to meet Dolly after auditions because she'd offered to give me a ride home.

Dolly was stage manager for the show and was backstage with the techies who had already started building the sets.

While I was waiting, Lorelei Lux came up behind me and said, "Long time no speak, Lance Atlas."

"Hey," I turned, "Lorelei. Yeah we haven't crossed paths much this year."

"I know."

"But we're in Chemistry together now of course."

It was high-decibel weirdness that we were in Chemistry class together and hadn't spoken in there at all.

Lorelei was clutching her notebook like always.

"Interesting choice of song," she said.

"You heard it?"

"I didn't need to," she said and twirled her eyeballs hypnotically.

"How have you been?" I asked.

"I am tolerating the meaninglessness of existence right now," Lorelei said.

"But other than that, thespian life suiting you?" I asked, not wanting to get into a deep philosophical discussion with her.

"It provides a vehicle for hiding from myself, I guess," she said, "although I don't think that's ever all the way possible."

"Nyeah, we're all kind of stuck with ourselves," I said, "and each other."

Lorelei's eyes teared up even though she was smiling.

"Are you OK?" I asked.

"Yeah," she said, a tear dribbling down her left cheek, then she leaned into me and hugged me.

I patted her on the shoulders.

She started squeezing a little harder.

"Hug me back," she said.

I obliged.

"That's better," she snuffled.

I had never met this version of Lorelei before.

"You OK?" I asked again.

"It's good and proper to be talking to you again, Lance Atlas," Lorelei said, sounding more like herself.

While we were hugging I saw Miranda and Freddy walk past the auditorium holding hands.

"So did you enjoy *Pale Horse, Pale Rider* by, um," she backed away and opened her notebook and searched for the page, "Katherine Anne Porter?"

"Uh, yeah, it's great," I said once again taken aback by her knowledge of my doings.

"I know why you read that book," she said, "but I'm not going to tell you."

"Huh?" I grunted at one of Lorelei's typical crypticisms after which she started hugging me again.

"Hey," Dolly said, emerging from the Rotunda, "hands off, Lori."

"He's not your boyfriend, Dahlia Ferris," Lorelei said.

"I'm well aware of that, and he's not yours either, Lorelei Lux."

Dolly snorted and said, "Let's go, dude," gesturing to the student parking lot.

"Nice talking to you again," I said to Lorelei, "See you in Chem."

She held up her right hand and said, "How."

"Crazy-ass bitch," Dolly said as we walked together to her car, "What was she on about?"

"Nothing really," I said.

"Crazy. Ass. Bitch."

"That's the first time I've talked to her this year. Which is especially weird 'cause she's in my Chem class this semester."

"You're lucky. I have to talk to her everyday. She purposely calls me Dahlia to annoy me."

"I dunno, I just think that's how she likes to talk. And also I think Dahlia's a beautiful name. So nyeah."

"Nyeah nyeah."

"So what do you know about Deirdre Lux and Mr. Hill?" I just kind of threw in there.

"What? Like she's in love with him? Duh."

"No like are they?–"

"–I have no idea," she said, "but I doubt it."

"Why?"

"I just do."

I could tell Dolly wanted to stop talking about it so I shut up.

We drove to my house in mostly silence the rest of the way down Melrose and when we pulled up in front I wasn't sure if I was supposed to invite her in or what because I'm really bad at navigating those situations.

"I really loved reading *Main Street* with you and talking about it and stuff," she said.

"I really dug that book, yeah," I said, "Much more than I thought I was going to."

"Ugh," she rolled her eyes.

"What? You didn't like *Main Street*? I thought you said–"

"–No I . . . That's not . . . Nothing," she shook her head, "*Main Street* was great, yeah," she said. "I could totally see myself living in a town like Gopher Prairie."

"Haha, you?" I said.

"No for real."

"If you feel that way then I think you missed the point of the book. You would starve in that culture. You are too adventurous a soul, Dahlia. Dahlia Dahlia Dahlia. You are going to travel the world, dahling Dahlia."

That made her smile.

"I *am* going to travel the world," she said.

"Dahling Dahlia," I said again and stroked her hair.

"But I also long for simplicity," she said, "just getting up and going to work in a store and then coming home and eating dinner and thinking about things and getting laid every so often. Put me on a front porch and I'll gladly smoke cigarettes and watch the sky go by every night."

I let myself be in love with her for a solitary instant once again.

"Well, hell yeah, of course I get that part, the sitting and watching the sky thing for sure, believe me, dude, but I'm talking about access to art and literature and theatre and film and free expression."

"I'd miss that stuff, yeah, I guess," she said, "for sure."

"You're not a small town lady."

"I'm a big city broad."

"I love a dame who drinks from the bottle," I said with a Bogart-dentured overbite.

"But I loved doing the book thing together, Lance, really. And not because of *Main Street*, because it was with *you*."

"Me too. I'm glad we're friends," I said to her as I started to get out of the car because I couldn't think of anything else to say.

"We're not just friends," she said, pausing.

I looked away.

She let it go.

"You wanna gab later?" she asked.

"Uh, I have to do a bunch of reading for Megiddo's term paper. I really should concentrate."

I didn't actually *have to* do a bunch of reading. The thing is I *wanted* to do a bunch of reading that night. That was my preferred activity.

My mind was being reconfigured and gestated and whelped into a new realm.

3

When it had come time to get Mr. Megiddo's approval for the term paper, an author study, I proposed doing mine on the novels of Sinclair Lewis because I had really liked *Main Street* and also wanted to read *Babbitt* and *Arrowsmith*.

"Nobody reads Sinclair Lewis anymore," Megiddo sneered when I asked him, "There's better stuff to lend your attention to."

"Like what?"

"For you?" Megiddo said and walked over to the bookcase where he kept random books for use on outside novel essays.

"This is the subject of your author study," Megiddo said as he handed me *Tropic of Cancer*.

"Henry Miller," I said, looking at the cover.

"Know him?"

"No."

"This will loosen you up and spread you out," he said. "You are a Romantic, Lance. But you are too uptight."

Hey, dude, I thought, I have both finger fucked and eaten the pussy of Taryn Rust from whom I have also received two blowjobs. Who you callin' uptight?

"I'll start this tonight," I said, "Thank you."

"Let me know how you like it."

"As soon as I'm done."

"So tomorrow morning then."

I laughed. He smiled. He knew.

Tropic of Cancer was a lightning bolt to my forehead.

From the instant I read that phrase *We are all alone here and we are dead* I knew I had made contact with one of the mahatmas. I was rent.

The hero, then, is not Time, but Timelessness

The entire opening, written like a manifesto, was glorious and new and instantly liberating, speaking out loud the way I'd always thought to myself silently.

This is not a book. This is libel, slander, defamation of character. This is not a book, in the ordinary sense of the word. No, this is a prolonged insult, a gob of spit in the face of Art, a kick in the pants to God, Man, Destiny, Time, Love, Beauty ... what you will. I am going to sing for you, a little off key perhaps, but I will sing. I will sing while you croak, I will dance over your dirty corpse...To sing you must first open your mouth. You must have a pair of lungs, and a little knowledge of music. It is not necessary to have an accordion, or a guitar. The essential thing is to want to sing. This then is a song. I am singing.

And sing he did.

Henry Miller sang my private heart.

He sang a dirge for the future.

He sang my inherent sense of cosmic destiny, a bridge to anarchy, the sad fact of time moving irreversibly forward.

When into the womb of time everything is again withdrawn chaos will be restored and chaos is the score upon which reality is written.

I read until dawn when I had to take a shower and get ready for school.

I tried to get Manny to read Miller but at the moment he was obsessed with the guru Bubba Free John about whom he talked incessantly.

Manny's parents were letting him drive this crappy old Cadillac convertible they had, and one night we drove over to the Bodhi Tree, a spiritual bookstore on Melrose Avenue near San Vicente.

Being at the Bodhi Tree felt more like being in a house than being in a bookstore, a house where every room was filled with books. A dream house. I used to wish there were beds there too.

The Bodhi Tree carried the primary scriptures of the major religions and the many commentaries on them but also more obscure texts from lesser known belief systems.

In addition they had a ton of books on conspiracy theories, U.F.O. abductions, astrology, magic, and alchemy, as well as carrying an array of incense and incense holders, meditation pillows, a wide selection of tarot decks, Buddha statues, Sanskrit "Om" pendants and earrings and patches and decals and bookmarks, Shiva figurines, and even an actual crystal ball that cost like a thousand dollars or something.

Manny dragged me to the so-called Hall of Gurus, a corner of the store where sage wisdom was to be had amid harp music, herbal tea, and sandalwood incense.

He pulled a copy of Bubba Free John's book *Method of the Siddhas* off the shelf.

Originally captivated by the guru's spiritual autobiography *The Knee of Listening*, he was now reading everything the guy had written.

"Dude, he used to have his ashram right over on Melrose, up until a couple of years ago, like right next door to where Tuppence School of Music was. We were like right there, dude, standing in front of it the whole time. We could have hung out with the guru, us and our accordions."

I vaguely remembered that place and the big pictures of Bubba Free John in the front two windows, though I didn't know Bubba Free John's name back then, but the picture from the cover of *The Knee of Listening* was the same picture that was in one of the windows, so I semi-held onto that memory.

Manny and I had both been accordion students at Tuppence School of Music.

I started taking accordion lessons when I was five years old.

At age six I competed in the Western States Accordion Festival for the first time.

I did a duet with a red-haired girl named Shayna.

She was a good player.

We won a trophy.

But it might also have been one of those things where everyone wins a trophy. I don't remember.

Playing accordion was my entry into music participation rather than just loving through listening.

Tuppence School of Music was the brainchild of a guy named Skyler Tuppence who came door-to-door through the neighborhood, toting an accordion and convincing parents to sign their kids up for lessons at his school on Melrose.

It was affordable and close by and why not.

And, of course, he'd also sell each family an accordion.

Pretty soon just about every kid in the vicinity took lessons there, accordion, piano, guitar, woodwinds, everything.

It was a holy place to me.

I loved the smell of accordion wood and the inside of accordion cases and clarinet reeds that permeated the waiting area, where Skyler Tuppence's mother Margaret held sway at the front desk with demonstrative authority.

Mother Tuppence was a wise-ass chain-smoking raconteur, always entertaining, even to very little kids, though mainly she gossiped with the moms.

I felt kinship sitting in that room with all those other kids who loved music too, even though I never talked to them out of severe bashfulness.

Jinxy the guitar teacher often had seemingly nothing to do and would sit in the waiting area, sometimes reading a newspaper, sometimes consenting to schmooze.

"I need to put a little jasper in my rigmarole," he'd say and lean back and close his eyes.

I never saw him smoking but I knew he smoked because he smelled just like my dad.

Jinxy had long muttonchop sideburns and tiny round eyeglasses which sat almost absurdly on his long nose.

He was kind of a cross between Jughead from the *Archies* Comics (without the dumbass hat) and Shaggy from *Scooby Doo* (without the spindly beard).

He either wore thong sandals or went barefoot depending on the weather.

"Life is better when I feel like I'm standing on the earth," he'd say with his soles to the linoleum.

The guitar students especially hung on his words.

As a lowly accordion player, I was not part of that clique.

But that cat Jinxy was one of the first true freaks I knew.

We could never figure out what his story was.

Where did he descend from? When were his people coming back to retrieve him?

My first accordion teacher was a gentle giant of a man named Isaac Alero who brought great love to the music.

And he was shy like me.

So we didn't say much to each other.

But I understood his teaching.

For some reason he left the school fairly early on in my going there.

I never found out why.

He was just gone.

Someone said he went into the army and was sent to Vietnam but Mother Tuppence tutted no no that wasn't true.

I suppose they figured I was too young to understand so they just didn't tell me.

I missed Isaac for a while.

And then it became hard to remember what he looked like.

That's always a very sad moment in one's grieving.

When you lose the details of the face.

And also when you can't smell them anymore.

Skyler Tuppence, the man himself, became my teacher and exerted a tremendous influence over the way I listened to music early on.

He was infectiously impassioned and that shit's contagious, especially with a group of kids.

All the other teachers were called by their first names, but we always called him Mr. Tuppence.

I played in the accordion orchestra as well as doing solo competitions.

It was my first experience contributing to a group musical effort.

We did an all-accordion version of *The Nutcracker* once.

Mimi danced ballet in that production.

She was taking piano lessons from Mr. Tuppence, but the two of them didn't get along very well.

Mimi was known to put tacks on his chair and criticize his bad breath to his face.

Funny as hell. But not real conducive to musical evolution.

After my sister gave up piano and devoted herself to guitar, I started tinkering around on the spinet in our living room.

It was like discovering a native language after years of unknowingly speaking an alien tongue.

For a while I took both accordion and piano from Mr. Tuppence.

But by age 10 I had dropped accordion entirely and focused solely on piano.

I dug Mr. Tuppence's earth-jazz manner.

He taught me how to improvise and opened a new world to me thereupon.

I remember he gave me a progression of four chords.

"Play those chords over and over with your left hand and let your right hand do whatever it wants," he said.

I tried several times but just kept playing arpeggios of the individual notes in the chords.

"OK, keep playing the progression with your left hand and let me do the right hand."

As I held down the chords he played a variety of melodies over them.

"See? Have fun with it. Be free," he said, closing his eyes and continuing to play, "You know your scales, now use them."

Have fun with it. Be free.

Under his tutelage I made that crucial transition from my parents telling me to practice to my parents telling me to *stop* practicing.

And then, one day, when I was 12, without warning, we got word the school was closing.

A desolation.

My first brush with bankruptcy and failure.

They had run out of money and couldn't continue.

I walked up to the school a couple of days later and looked in the window and everything was gone.

Mr. Tuppence continued to teach me, first through another music school where he got a staff teaching gig, which was kind of sad, and then for a while at my house once a week.

But it wasn't long before he told us he was moving out to the Valley and wouldn't be able to teach in L.A. anymore.

More and deeper sadness.

Everything eventually goes away.

That night at the Bodhi Tree I got some nag champa incense and Manny got a Bubba Free John book.

Afterward we went to Cafe Figaro a little further west on Melrose.

All I wanted was some tea and their amazing creamed spinach and to steer the conversation away from Bubba Free John.

When we sat down we saw that Evelyn Childs was there with David Harkins, our British classmate. They were a couple of tables over, near the front window.

"Hey, guys," David said and waved.

Evelyn caught my eye and pointed at David and I gave a thumb's up and she blew me a kiss.

Evelyn and David had started going out so I wasn't hanging with her much anymore, but she had recently made me a tape with "Anarchy in the UK" on it and "God Save The Queen," which she was able to get because one of David's friends in England mailed him a bunch of 45s and the Sex Pistols were among them, and like with most of her tapes, unless she taped it off the radio, she held the microphone up to her stereo speakers while the record played.

"How's it going?" David asked, coming over to the table with Evelyn.

"Pretty good," Manny said, "We were just over at the Bodhi Tree."

"Looking at Bubba Free John books?" David said with laughing eyes.

"Good guess," I faked a cough to hide my chuckle.

"You digging the punk tape?" Evelyn asked me.

"It's great, yeah. I have to play it for Manny."

"You will dig it the most," Evelyn said to Manny.

"Right on," Manny said, "I'm sure. I've heard some of that stuff on KROQ, especially on Rodney."

"If you really want to get it take some speed first," she said.

"Only weed, no speed," I said, shaking my finger, "take heed."

"I dunno, dude, I might have to check that method out," Manny said.

"What have you guys been up to tonight?" I asked them both.

"We actually went to see *In Search of Noah's Ark* over at the Fairfax," Evelyn said, "The documentary."

"Quote unquote," I said.

"I thought it was brilliant," David said.

"But it's bogus," I said.

"Brilliantly bogus, though," David said, "You should see it. It's very sort of–"

"–Very sort of," Evelyn attempted an English accent, "Very sort of . . . everything is very sort of very sort of very sort of."

"Apparently this little phrase of mine annoys m'lady," David said.

"So that means you're, what, like a month into the relationship," I said.

"Bingo. You know the timeline," David said.

"Very sort of," I said.

"I hate it when guys stick together," Evelyn said.

"It's like clockwork."

"A clockwork orgy," David said.

"Only if you're a droog addict."

"It does take some people longer to get annoyed with each other," Evelyn said, "I don't think you're being fair."

"Nyeah, it only takes them longer to admit or confess annoyance. They're already annoyed though. They're just subtly freaked out about the consequences of noticing shit about their beloved that they don't like. As if even having those thoughts could contaminate the whole thing," I said, "That's what's up with that. It's all downhill thereafter."

Everybody was silent after I made my pronouncement and then David and Evelyn excused themselves to go back to their table

A little later Evelyn and I both got up to go to the bathroom and met in the narrow corridor where we had to wait because both toilets were occupied.

"Hey," she said, "How have you been? We haven't really talked in ages."

"I owe you a tape," I said.

"You do."

"I shall figure that out soon."

"Whenever, it's cool."

"You and David make a lot of sense," I said, nodding my head.

"So far," she paused, "He's hilarious and we dig the same music."

"That's important."

"The most," she said, "If your *music* don't jive then *you* don't jive."

"May be," I said, "I dunno. It helps, I guess, yeah."

"Dang, that reminds me, I need to get change for the cigarette machine," Evelyn said, pointing to the dispenser in the restroom corridor, conveniently placed so that minors could purchase a pack of Camel filters unseen. One of the reasons we'd all end up at Cafe Figaro. Norms on La Cienega also had one of those semi-hidden cigarette dispensers that we could use.

The ladies room became vacant.

"Great running into you," Evelyn said and went in to be about her business.

Listening to Evelyn's punk tape had, in fact, inspired me to write a punkish song called "The Garden of Hedon," very much the product of being in the early thrill of listening to the Sex Pistols.

No sign of water

No sign of land

No sign of morning

A sign of the times

Like a soft-sell billboard

In layman's language

It's so gainfully obvious

To people in our position

The workers are reclining

The management is lounging

The students are all scrounging

The teachers are resigning

They're all marionettes pulling their own strings

In their own space doing their own thing

In the Garden of Hedon

Self-portraits to which they masturbate

Pleasure first they advocate

In the Garden of Hedon

Dress for dinner

Dress to kill

Dress conformally

Favorite "wear-with-all"

Wallpaper fashion

Seduce the mirror

It's so gainfully obvious

To people in our position

The women are gaining

The men are losing

The parents are using

The kids are reigning

They're all marionettes pulling their own strings

In their own space doing their own thing

In the Garden of Hedon

Self-portraits to which they masturbate

Pleasure first they advocate

In the Garden of Hedon

Where the action is

Where the boys are

Where time is of the essence

Anywhere but home

History deletes itself

Theorize accordingly

It's so gainfully obvious

To people in our position

The old are reliving

The young are rehearsing

The crowd is dispersing

The loners are ungiving

They're all marionettes pulling their own strings

In their own space doing their own thing

In the Garden of Hedon

Self-portraits to which they masturbate

Pleasure first they advocate

In the Garden of Hedon

Manny said, "For sure we're doing that song in the band," after I played it for him and Yigal Frumkin.

We didn't have a band yet, but Yigal said he'd play drums for us if we ever got it together.

The day I played "Garden of Hedon" for Manny and Yigal I had gone over primarily to check out Television's *Marquee Moon*, what turned out to be a monumental album in the history of my listening and which Manny had just purchased at Aron's.

We had heard "See No Evil" on KROQ and were already enraptured by the double-helix guitar interplay that came spiraling out of the speakers, so we were eager to take in the whole thing.

After I played "Garden of Hedon" for them we made our sacramental preparations for listening to *Marquee Moon*, which involved a walk around the block with a stop to smoke part of a joint.

The alleyway behind the building where Liberace lived (in the penthouse) on Beverly Blvd. when he was in L.A. was a safe and private spot to have a toke and not be too paranoid.

"Dude, you know if Liberace came home right now and saw us he'd totally get high with us," Manny said.

"Yeah, and then blow us after," Yigal said.

Manny and I groaned at the thought of having our cocks sucked by Liberace. Though we both were able to picture it. Or at least I was. Dang, dude.

"Oh, man, dude, that is majorly wrong," Manny said.

"But funny," Yigal said.

"You get points for timing I guess," Manny said.

"I Am. The Man," Yigal chanted as we walked down the block back to Manny's house, "I Am. The Man."

Drummers.

We settled ourselves into Manny's room and he put on *Marquee Moon*.

Manny lay supine upon the bed.

Yigal and I were lying on the floor.

All the lights were off though the street lamp glowed outside Manny's bedroom window and lent a coal mine visibility. Fractured blackness turned high yellow.

"Is your sister home?" I asked Manny as the music uncoiled.

"Dang, dude. You have to ask that every time?"

I chuckled and shrugged.

"Just playing," I said.

"Lance has a hard-on for my sister," Manny said to Yigal, "even though she hardly even speaks to him."

"Leah? You better hope your dick is at least as hard as the pole she has up her ass," Yigal said, "or she won't even notice you're fucking her."

"Hey, that's cold-blooded, dude, that's my sister," Manny objected.

"Yeah, well," Yigal said, "Gotta tell it like it is sometimes, man. Your sister is freaky straight."

"In a major way," Manny laughed in acknowledgement, pointing at Yigal and inhaling with his signature croak, "She is pretty rigid."

"Dang, dude. I think she's sexy," I said.

"You think everybody's sexy," Manny said.

"Every woman is sexy eventually. It depends on your attention span. Even Ethel Mertz."

"When is Ethel Mertz sexy?"

"Like when she's singing? Come on, dude."

"I have never found Ethel Mertz to be sexy, dude. Ever. Even when she's singing."

"Oh, you just aren't paying attention to the right moments," I said, "the ones where she's caught up in the joy of the music, where you can tell how much she loves singing, when she can be herself instead of just setting up Lucy's next sight-gag, Ethel Mertz is damn sexy when she's in that particular groove."

I want a nice little boat made out of ocean

We fell silent and were all tripping out on the music which was, even upon first listening, embedding itself in the hippocampus jukebox, the stuff that's on constant rotation in the background of your brain no matter what else you're thinking about.

Gina Dichlich is afraid of the ocean I thought to myself.

I kept wanting to tell her that I was too but always forgot to when I was talking to her which was pretty much every day lately sitting next to her in English.

I'd been in school with Gina Dichlich since kindergarten but we never had the same friends so I never really got to know her very well even though I sat across the table from her for like three straight years. She was sassy and unafraid and we'd had some interactions here and there over the years. I

264

used to hang out a lot with this girl named Rose Benedict, especially in 4th and 5th Grade, and I think Gina and Rose didn't like each other or something, I don't really know, but there was a wall between me and Gina back then which was maybe finally starting to come down in 11th Grade.

Sitting next to her in Mr. Megiddo's class I got to know her mind a bit and was attracted to how serious she was behind the flirtatious affect. I got hip to her mask.

Gina was very deeply into Mr. Megiddo.

She was always at his podium talking to him at the beginning of class.

She organized an in-class surprise party for his birthday.

She knitted him a scarf for Christmas.

She wrote him notes during class and then left them on his desk on her way out.

She always sat next to him at assemblies.

She shushed other kids if they were talking during his lectures.

I'd have to bring up the fear of the ocean thing with her someday if I ever remembered while I was actually talking to her.

Tom Verlaine and Richard Lloyd were warping the woofers while I then suddenly got bent on thoughts of Miranda Savitch out of nowhere.

A couple of sentences from *Pale Horse, Pale Rider* had been hooking my brainwaves of late, to the point where I'd wake up with the lines in my head and they'd come to me in the shower or while I'd be walking to school.

Look, don't be afraid, it is nothing, it is only eternity

and

Now there would be time for everything

I deliberated with myself and then decided to give Miranda a copy of *Pale Horse, Pale Rider* for her birthday because I knew she would love it and I didn't care how awkward it would be I just had to get it for her.

I went up to Pickwick on Hollywood Boulevard because I knew they'd have it there.

"Make sure to call ahead so you don't waste a trip," my mother said before I left.

"Nyeah, I don't need to, I just saw it there the other day," I said.

"OK," she said, "I'd call though."

"N'I'm fine," I said, always eager to avoid using the telephone.

I took the bus to Pickwick Books, a really easy ride up Highland to Hollywood Blvd. and then it was just a block or so away.

I loved the warmth and the light and the vibe of Pickwick. It was a mainstream chain store, not an offbeat treasure like Dutton's or Papa Bach or Chatterton's, but I always always found great shit at Pickwick.

Often I dream that I am sitting on a hillside with an unobstructed view of the sky.

I'm in front of a big house that I know belongs to me but I've never been inside.

Down below is always a river.

And I swear the air in those dreams smells like Pickwick Books every time.

It was raining the day I went up to get Miranda the Porter book.

Los Angeles at its most beautiful.

Natively painted in grayness.

I had my pussbrella with me so I was safe just in case it rained.

They had a couple of paperbacks of *Pale Horse, Pale Rider* but they also had this eminently sexy black hardback edition which I knew I had to spring for.

At first I wrapped it in the comics section from the LA Times because I knew Miranda read them every morning or at least she used to. I was sure she still at least read *Doonesbury* so I made sure that one was on the front. But then I changed my mind and decided to give it to her unwrapped because I thought it would be slightly less awkward that way.

I was going to inscribe something on the title page but then chickened out about that too.

I didn't want to freak her out or anything.

I gave the book to her in Megiddo's class right before class started.

"Happy birthday," I said.

"Oh wow . . . thank you . . ." she said looking at the book and then at me and then down at the book again, "I wasn't . . . wow . . . um . . ."

The world looked so thin, between my bones and skin

There stood another person who was a little surprised

To be face to face with a world so alive

"I was really knocked over by it and I thought it'd be something you'd like," I said.

"Thanks, Lance," she said and held out her right hand which I held clumsily by the fingers.

When I went to sit back down in my seat, Claire Farnaway cleared her throat and looked at me and shook her head.

I'm pretty sure I was blushing.

The Television song "Venus de Milo" reminded me again that I still owed Annie de Milo a postcard. I had to take care of that.

"So Gatsby's belief that he can recapture the past, that Daisy has remained unchanged in the years since their romance is what?" Mr. Megiddo asked a little later in that same class.

"Delusional," said Miranda.

"Why?"

"She's a different person now."

"How so?"

"She's been living this extravagant life with another man for long enough that there's no way it hasn't changed her."

"Bitch been fucking someone else, dude," Buddy Feigenbaum muttered to his neighbors.

I put my head down.

For the first time I actually pictured Miranda fucking Freddy Snow.

And that was dog, dude. Flagrant in the extreme.

You know it's all like some new kind of drug

I still harbored that old image from 8th Grade of Miranda dancing with Freddy when we were practicing for the sock hop at Misty Winters' place in Park La Brea and it looked like they were fucking but this time I pictured them actually doing it and I was shuddering at my brain for allowing it.

My eyes are like telescopes

I see it all backwards: but who wants hope?

"Why is it," Manny asked from his perch on the bed, "that guys can say 'suck my cock' and mean it to be hostile but you'll never hear a girl use 'eat my pussy' in the same way?"

"Is that really what you're getting out of the music, man?" Yigal said.

"Nah've been meaning to ask that for a while," Manny said, "I think it's a major question."

"I dunno, 'cause it's just different, dude. Sucking cock and eating pussy are not the same thing," Yigal said.

"Duh."

"I'm talking psychologically," Yigal said.

"They're both about the female being penetrated, by cock or by tongue," I said, "the guy is in the position of power either way."

"You sound like Miranda Savitch," Yigal said.

"Ooh, face," said Manny, "And what about if it's not the female being penetrated but the female granting admission to her mystery? Like a gatekeeper. Deciding which pathetic little wormboy gets to experience the ultimate ecstasy."

"Tunnel of Love," said Yigal.

"*Then* who's got the power?" Manny asked.

"Or maybe she's not being penetrated or granting admission but instead she's devouring," I said, but Manny and Yigal had already gone back to the music.

I wanted to have a really deep intense orgasm when I got home later but I couldn't decide with whom.

My sex had gone totally prismatic and fractured and massively scattered.

I don't wanna grow up

there's too much contradiction

A week after I'd given Miranda *Pale Horse, Pale Rider*, she left an envelope on my desk in English class. I put it in my backpack for later reading.

I waited until I got home, ever the more to savor.

Divine transmissions.

I lay the envelope on my bed, took off my shoes, sat and looked at it for a while, and then, eventually, opened it.

Dearest Lance,

Thank you so much again for the book. I devoured it all in one gulp and think it's one of the best things I've ever read. Truly. All three novellas in the volume, but especially the title story. Gorgeous language. Powerful women everywhere. What the world needs more of. Plus, the extra obvious bonus. Haha. Good form, Sir Lancelot Link, Secret Chimp. Good form, indeed. Mostly though it made me feel really good to know I still show up in your thoughts as you are often in mine.

Love and stuff,

Miranda

Our relations grew sightly less glacial after that. Slightly.

I was listening

listening to the rain

I was hearing

hearing something else

270

I had to pee really bad but waited until Side A was over.

The title track was one of those transformative journeys that realign one's antennae.

During the long jam, when Verlaine and Lloyd bifurcate yet remain corollary, we were afloat in the realm of all things possible.

"Dang, dude, this is like the fuckin' Grateful Dead or something," Yigal said from deep space.

We lay in the dark silent for a minute or two when Side A ended.

"Wow," Manny said.

"Yeah," was all I could muster.

"Refuel for Side B?" Yigal asked.

"Wait I've gotta pee first," I said and hobbled to the john.

We walked around the block and smoked the rest of the joint we'd started earlier and then parked ourselves back in Manny's room for the next leg of the pilgrimage.

As Side B began to emanate, I slipped into this flagrant eyelid movie in which the image of two people fucking somehow turned into a giant land slug from dinosaur times.

I tried really hard to get back to the image of the two people fucking but I couldn't find them anymore.

And for a while it was just lily patch splotches of light in colors from another spectrum.

Never the rose

Without the prick

The music was tripping me out more than the weed was.

Dang, dude.

Television.

I woke up and it was yesterday

Manny, Yigal and I all three looked at one another in that moment, the singular moment of recognition that would eventually make us a band.

The world is just a feeling you undertook. Remember?

"Whoa, shit, dude," Manny said, "It's like a unified field, the way it all works together, every element."

You lose your sense of human

"This guitar playing," I said.

"Dang, dude, this is the kind of shit I want our thing to sound like," Manny said.

"I know a cat who can do stuff like that," Yigal said. "Emmet Beall. He's in 10th Grade. You know him?"

Neither of us did.

"Think he might be into it?" Manny asked.

"Em's the kind of cat who if he likes it he'll do it but if not no. He doesn't do shit he doesn't want to do and he doesn't play music he doesn't like to play. He's a cool cat, man. I've played in two different bands with him. We should jam sometime and invite him. He'll show up at least once. If he comes back a second time you know he's into it."

"Totally. Ask him," Manny said.

"Do you know a bassist?" I asked.

"There's this one dude who I think would really get it and dig it. Alain Yehudian. Very righteous cat from Montreal. 12th Grader."

"Handlebar mustache," Manny said.

"Yeah."

"I know that guy," Manny said, "Yeah. I once talked to him about *Lamb Lies Down* and he was on top of his shit, man. He knew what he was talking about."

"*Marquee Moon* occupied all of my listening for a long stretch of time thereafter and is still always sort of there.

The kind of music you don't need to be hearing to be hearing.

A couple of days later, under the sway of Tom Verlaine I wrote this tune called "Solid Air."

The cordial invitation spoke:

Dress polite and bring a joke

All gathered like nuts by squirrels

In separate lines for boys and girls

Binding manners, seats assigned

Topic boundaries well-defined

Strictly sneaking inside plaids and prints

Frankly reeking, posing subtle hints

Solid air

Suspended there

Makes no sense

All it makes is me cry

I'm caught in a lie

And I'm trapped in solid air

Compiling lifetimes cell by cell

Inmates outside wishing well

Held captive by the despot ones

With their ever mother loving guns

Daylight glimmers, open field,

Quick before the hole is sealed

Guards live orders in the halls

Like the algae that sings to the walls

Solid air

Suspended there

Makes no sense

All it makes is me cry

I'm caught in a lie

And I'm trapped in solid air

Hostage to the body cage

Written then assigned a page

Inaccurate conception marks another birth

A gravity-laden slave to earth

A thought for sore minds to expand

Disgorged before we understand

And in the moment that we know

We cease to be, we cease to grow

Solid air

Suspended there

Makes no sense

All it makes is me cry

I'm caught in a lie

And I'm trapped in solid air

And buried 'neath the fallout waste

The best laid plans of love and haste

I totally stole that 'inaccurate conception' image.

I got to school early one morning so I could talk to Mr. Megiddo about Henry Miller and my term paper before class, but when I went to his room Gina Dichlich was already there so I just stood in the doorway.

Gina looked over and saw me and said, "Thanks, Mr. M.," and left.

"Lance," Mr. Megiddo, "Yes, you were going to update me on your term paper."

"Yeah, it's going well so far. I'm loving Miller."

"I knew you would," he smiled, "Thought Miller might shift some things around for you. What have you read so far?"

"*Topic of Cancer* and *Tropic of Capricorn*," I said, "I don't know what to do for the third one. We have to have three right?"

"Yes, three novels for you to build a thesis around. I think *Sexus* would be good to do next. It kind of parallels some of the stuff in *Capricorn*."

"The pre-Paris years."

"Correct. It's part of a trilogy called *The Rosy Crucifixion*, but *Sexus* stands on its own nicely and goes well with the *Tropics*. Exponentially more sex in it."

"More?" I raised my eyebrows.

"Yes, believe it or not. But interestingly, Miller seems to get it all out of his system in *Sexus*."

"Cool, I'll do that one for sure."

"It's quite long, so you should start right away. Miller is still alive, by the way. He lives here in L.A. Pacific Palisades I think. Have you found his work inspiring?"

"Definitely inspiring," I said, "Yeah, for sure, but mostly in my thinking, not really in my actions."

"Well yes you're a bit young for those actions," Mr. Megiddo said.

"Some of them anyway," I said in fun, "But actually I'm thinking I want my thesis to be along those lines."

"What lines?"

"The idea of small changes being truer to human experience than huge drastic ones."

"In you? Or in the 'Henry Miller' character in the books?"

"Well, both, but I'm talking about the books as far as the paper goes. I love all the hyperbole and bravado and digressions and mind excursions and bold pronouncements and all that great riffing he does, but when you look closely at Miller's actions, he always pretty much does the same stuff. He's always hungry and horny and spends a lot of his time satisfying those urges and in between he walks around or sits around and thinks about stuff and writes."

"So what's your thesis?"

"Well, I don't have it exactly yet, but it's something like in Miller's works we see the mind can experience revelations and have visions of upheaval and personal revolution but the body is stuck taking one baby step at a time. And so change is ultimately always gradual due to the limitations of the body and the strength of habits."

"Work on that. It's a good start. Have you noticed that in *Grapes of Wrath* also?"

"No," I said.

"Well, synchronicity then."

I didn't know what he meant by that but then the early bell rang so I had a reason to end the conversation and first Gina then the rest of the Period 1 class started trickling in.

Gina talked to Mr. Megiddo at his podium again and I journeyed over to my desk where Claire Farnaway was sitting facing backwards talking to

Manny.

"Get out the way, woman," I commanded, "I need to take a seat and rest my feet."

"Whatever you say, stud," Claire said, stood up and moved to her own desk.

Miranda kissed Freddy goodbye at the door of the classroom and then said, "Hi, Lance!" as she walked past me.

That quick progression of events knotted up my stomach some.

Mr. Megiddo assumed his usual position in a student desk turned to face us.

"Don't forget there's a Librocubicularist Society meeting in here at lunch today," he said and opened his tattered copy of *Grapes of Wrath*.

He looked at us for a while without saying anything.

"Eventually Tom comes to realize that the individual, or even society, can only make small changes along the way," Megiddo said and looked at me and of course then I got what he was talking about earlier, "We make progress in little increments. The pace of evolution doesn't jive with our lifespans as a species. You won't be much different in your shroud than you were in your swaddling blanket. Maybe just different enough to notice that you're part of something bigger than yourself. That's what Tom Joad gets near the end. That he's part of a continuum."

"I remember Mr. Antolini saying something like that to Holden in *Catcher In The Rye*," I said, "the continuum thing."

"Yes, good," Megiddo said.

"What about the revelation of Christ? That changed the world drastically," Crystal Nabors countered.

"No doubt. Do you think Jesus changed the world overnight though?" Megiddo came back, "You think he was crucified on a Friday, resurrected on a Sunday and then on Monday everybody was a Christian? It took hundreds of years for that message to spread. Little increments. Evolution."

"It was only like 7 weeks before the Holy Spirit descended upon the Jews in the Holocaust," Crystal said, "That's not hundreds of years."

"The *Pentecost*," Mr. Megiddo said.

"That's what I meant to say, yeah," Crystal said and you couldn't tell if she was blushing because her face was always a little bit red, "and then they started spreading the gospel to the Gentiles."

"*Shiksa's* kinda right about the Holocaust thing though when you think about it," Buddy Feigenbaum said to Manny, "'cause that's when the Gentiles got involved and fucked it all up. They turned the coolest reform rabbi into a *goyishe* deity and we became the scapegoats they used to justify their Yidicide all over the damn place."

"Nah, man," Manny said, "It started way earlier. Gentiles were Gentiles long before they were Christians."

"*Goyim*," Buddy shook his head.

"And what about that final scene in *Grapes of Wrath*?" Mr. Megiddo had moved on.

"Ew," said Crystal Nabors, "that was nasty."

"I can speak directly to this," said Sharon Rose whose name we'd joked about throughout our reading of the book.

"It's worth it just to be able to say, 'Tell us about Rose of Sharon, Sharon Rose."

"Like you were saying before, she's part of something bigger," Sharon said.

"In what way?"

"She couldn't help her baby survive," Sharon was putting it together in her head, "but she can help the old man at the end by using the same resource."

"Her breast milk," Mr. Megiddo said.

"Yeah," Sharon answered.

"The milk of human kindness maybe," Miranda said.

"Yes, possibly," Megiddo pointed at her, "or just simply life."

"A land flowing with milk & honey," Crystal added, "the Promised Land."

"It's the continuum," I said, "The baby, at the beginning of its life is dead . . . the old man, near the end of his life, will go on . . . and Rose of Sharon is in the middle."

"The conduit," Megiddo added, "to life. Individuals die, but the life-force itself goes on."

"A little increment in the big saga," I smiled and Megiddo raised his thumb.

"Hope," Miranda said as the bell rang, "Hope for the future."

"Nice job today, guys," Megiddo said above the commotion as we all packed up to leave, "I'll give you the *Grapes* essay topics tomorrow."

As I was leaving, Mr. Megiddo hailed me quietly.

"Lance," he said and I turned my head, "A little increment in the big saga," he gave me another thumbs-up, "Title of your term paper maybe?"

"May be," I smiled and left.

After school that day I took advantage of a rare free afternoon and went to Farmers Market to find a postcard with the Observatory on it to send to Annie de Milo.

First I stopped off to see my dad in his podiatry cubicle at the back of the Beauty Shop, just to say hi but also because I needed change for the bus and he always had a ton of spare quarters in his pocket.

"Well, hey there, son," my dad said upon seeing me, using this facetious Sheriff Andy of Mayberry voice, "what brings you down to these parts?"

There was an elderly lady sitting in the patient's chair. My dad was working on her corns.

"Doing some postcard shopping. And I also need a little change for the bus maybe?" I held out my hand.

"Why the postcard shopping?"

"Oh, this girl I met who doesn't live here asked if I'd send her a postcard from L.A. with the Observatory in it and I know they've got them here somewhere."

"A girl, eh?" my dad leered.

"Haha, yes, but, no, you don't—"

"—Don't be embarrassed. They're all I thought about when I was your age. You remember how it is, right, Mrs. O'Malley?" my dad asked his patient.

"I don't much remember being young," Mrs. O'Malley smiled, "but then I also don't remember getting old. So."

"This is my son Lance. Lance, meet Mrs. O'Malley."

"Very nice to meet you, young man," she said and lifted her hand which I took.

"You know who her husband is?"

"No," I said.

"Ever heard of Walter O'Malley?" my dad asked.

"The owner of the Dodgers?"

"That is my husband, yes," said Mrs. O'Malley.

"Wow," I said, "I love the Dodgers."

"So do we, dear," she smiled.

I happened to have worn my dorky Dodgers batting helmet to school that day.

"Your father says you read a lot."

"Kind of, I guess," I said.

"What are you reading right now?"

"Henry Miller," I said.

"Oh, my," Mrs. O'Malley said to my father, "They let them read that in high school now?"

My father shrugged.

"It'll teach him more about the ladies than I ever could," he said, trying to joke.

"Dr. Atlas," Mrs. O'Malley scolded.

"Here," my dad said, standing up and reaching into his pocket, "here's change for the bus . . . and an extra buck so you can buy your girlfriend a nice postcard."

"Dad, she's not my girlfriend."

"All I'm saying is no harm in a postcard. 10 years from now, who knows, you'll meet again. Get her a nice postcard. And ask her about herself. Girls like when you ask them about themselves. Of course then you have to pretend to be listening when the start telling you."

"Dr. Atlas," scolded Mrs. O'Malley again.

"OK, dad," I said.

It was time to leave.

"Nice meeting you," I nodded and smiled in the direction of Mrs. O'Malley.

"I told your father whenever you want to come see a game just call me and I'll arrange some very good seats for you."

"Oh, wow," I said, "thank you. And thanks for the cash, Doc," I said like Bugs Bunny though it sounded more like Humphrey Bogart.

For some reason whenever I try to imitate Bugs Bunny I always end up sounding like Humphrey Bogart.

Just like when I try to speak with an Irish accent I always end up sounding like the leprechaun in the Lucky Charms commercials.

"I'll see you when I look at you," my dad bid his stock farewell.

I strolled through the Farmers Market keeping my eye out for Observatory postcards and found some over by the small newsstand next to the barber shop.

Not the big newsstand over by Kip's Toyland, but this pretty dinky set of rickety racks, one of which was a revolving stand that held postcards for tourists, and another with the *L.A. Times*, the *Herald–Examiner*, and a collection of the usual mainstream magazines like *Time* and *Newsweek* and *Life* as well as a very small selection of comic books and the latest issue of *MAD*.

The guy who ran the newsstand was this older Jewish dude named Milt Spilkes.

We didn't know much about him beyond his claims that he "used to be in vaudeville" (and he did have a Borscht Belt comedian's attitude and cadence when he spoke).

Sometimes he'd be really serious and philosophical, then other times he'd just set up dumb-ass puns like, "When I die, have a party and enjoy, don't be sad. No use crying over Milt Spilkes. B'doom–tshhh."

Spoonerisms were a cornerstone of his shtick. As was the verbal rimshot.

He was pals with my dad and always greeted me warmly and would often let me take the new issue of *MAD* for free when I was younger.

Milt Spilkes always had a lot to say.

"Doc's son," he nodded at me when I was checking out the postcards, "a pressure and a pilferage."

"Mr. Milt Spilkes," I doffed my Dodger helmet, "What's today's lesson?"

"Be open to hopelessness," Milt Spilkes said.

"Preach it," I said back.

"Life begins when it's all caving in on you," he said, "like the ordeal of your birth which is still kind of going on."

"Right on," I said, sort of digging what he was saying but also sort of being creeped out by it.

"What are you looking for?"

"I'm actually going to take this postcard with the Observatory on it," I said, reaching into my pocket for quarters and also a nickel and three pennies, "Here, I can give you exact change."

"This for your wall or are you sending it somewhere?"

"It's going to Wales," I said.

"To a special someone?"

"Haha no."

"Like I was saying: Be open to hopelessness."

"Will do," I said.

"And listen to Cole Porter."

"Oh definitely. I listen to *Ella Fitzgerald Sings The Cole Porter Songbook* all the time," I said, "That was my first favorite album when I was a little kid. I learn new things from it constantly."

"Good road," Milt Spilkes said, "I saw Ella with Oscar Peterson and Ray Brown at the Cocoanut Grove back in the day. Sublime as a dime in the prime of its time, b'doom–tshhh," he rimshat.

"Cool, man," I said and started to walk away.

"Hey, Doc's son," Milt Spilkes detained me, "This boy came by the other day who looked just like the fat kid from *Willy Wonka & The Chocolate Factory*, you know–"

"Augustus Gloop?"

"–Buzzy Lagniappe."

"Augustus Gloop is the fat kid from *Willy Wonka & The Chocolate Factory*."

"I thought it was Buzzy Lagniappe."

"Augustus Gloop," I assured him.

"Then who the hell is Buzzy Lagniappe?"

"Well, actually I live next door to a guy named Buzzy Lagniappe and he used to be fat and his real name is Augustus," I said from memory.

"That must be it then," Milt Spilkes said without knowing what he meant, "Anyway he told me to say hi to you. 'Say hi to Doc's son,' he said."

"Right on," I said, backing away.

My second escape attempt was intercepted by Dolly Ferris who came walking into the Market from the parking lot.

"Hey, buddy boy," she said and kissed me on the cheek, using her tongue to wet my skin slightly which made me shiver.

"Hey," I said. "Buddy boy?"

"It just came to me."

"Someone else used to call me that."

"Whatcha up to?"

"Just getting an Observatory postcard for a friend of mine in Engl–uh Wales."

"Who?"

"This girl named Annie."

"A girl?"

"She's a friend of a friend and anyway it's a long-ass story but she asked if I would send her a postcard with a picture of the Observatory on it."

"Cool, whatever," Dolly said, "You hungry for a doughnut? I was just about to go have one."

"Apple fritter at Bob's?"

"I'm buying," Dolly said.

"Let's do it."

"Can I interest you in a hot chocolate too?" she asked.

"Nyeah, maybe. It won't be as good as yours though."

"This is true," she said as she hooked her arm around mine.

We sat at a table in the Farmers Market courtyard and talked for a while about our term papers. She was doing hers on Sinclair Lewis as it turned out.

"I have loved *Babbitt* and *Arrowsmith*," she said, "and *Main Street* of course," and she touched my hand.

"I'm totally consumed by Henry Miller right now but I'm planning to have a Sinclair Lewis summer."

"Cool, you should," she said, "In *Babbitt*, even though it takes place in 1920, the politics are totally familiar, the same old tussle that's still always going on."

"The Deists versus the Puritans?" I said, "Didn't Mr. Megiddo call that the essential American tension?"

"Nyeah that and racism," she said, "Oh, and I want to read that other author he was talking about."

"Thomas Pynchon," I said, "Yeah. His name comes up a lot when Megiddo talks."

She seemed a bit restless and distracted.

"What's going on?" I asked her when I caught her smiling off into the distance.

"Nothing really. I got some very good news today but I can't talk about it yet."

"No fair," I said.

"I promise I'll tell you when it's for sure."

"You better," I said as she tilted her head onto my shoulder.

"Of course," she said.

"You want a ride home?" she asked.

"Nah'm just gonna walk I think."

"OK," she said without pressing it.

Normally she would've pressed it.

She was definitely off somewhere else.

We didn't kiss goodbye or anything.

On the way home I saw my dad hitchhiking near Genesee and Beverly.

"Oh, good, someone to walk with," my dad said as if I hadn't seen him hitchhiking and walking was his plan all along.

I smiled as we headed down Beverly.

"Did you find the postcard you were looking for?"

"Yeah," I said and showed him.

"Very nice of you to do," he said.

"Well, I should've done it a couple of months ago."

"True love waits," he patted me on the helmet, "So, when do you want to go to a Dodger game?"

"I'd love to see the Reds when they come to town. That's always a good game."

"I will give Mrs. O'Malley a call."

"Cool," I said.

I ended up catching a foul ball hit by Joe Morgan at that game.

We sat behind the Dodger dugout.

During the 7th inning stretch I went and found Mr. Beauregard and said hello to him.

It was strange to see him in a straw hat and usher uniform.

"Enjoying the game?" he asked.

"Yeah. I caught a Joe Morgan foul ball."

I pulled the ball out of my jacket pocket.

"I can get that autographed for you after the game," he said, and he did.

He brought it to me in Megiddo's class the next morning.

That ball occupies a sanctified corner in my underwear drawer to this day.

When my dad and I got to the front door we both realized neither of us had the house key on us.

My dad knocked in the familiar rhythm.

"Shave and a haircut," he sang as he rapped on the door.

"Two bits," I sang back and finished the knock as I'd been trained to do.

My mother opened the door for us.

"*Both* of you forgot your keys?" she said with mock exasperation.

"Nyeah I forgot to put it in my pocket when I put my pants on this morning," I said.

"Same here?" my dad said because he didn't really know why he'd forgotten his key.

She dismissed us with a wave.

"Do you want your change back?" I asked my dad.

"What change?"

"The money you gave me for the bus."

"Save it for another time," he said, grabbed the *Herald–Examiner* and a pen and headed to the bathroom where he would camp out for an hour or so. "Time to do the crossword puzzle," he winked.

I finished up my homework early and finally had a chance to write back to Annie.

Dear Annie of Milo and Venus,

Thank you for your great postcard. That picture of the Wye River is very beautiful. I hope to see the Wye in person one day. One of my favorite poems takes place near the banks of the Wye. Glad to hear you're liking <u>Charlie & The Chocolate Factory</u>. I have a great attachment to Augustus Gloop (and chocolate) myself. I have this friend Buzzy who's always getting mistaken for Augustus Gloop even though he's not fat—his real name is Augustus though. We have been reading <u>The Grapes of Wrath</u> by John Steinbeck in my English class. It has these strange little chapters that my English teacher calls "intercalary chapters." I will tell you more about them another time. They are very cool. Send me a postcard that has a picture of either a bookstore or a cheese shop (or both would be super). And of course let me know what you're reading now (and tell me something interesting about it).

Your nimnork friend,

Lance of Atlantis

4

Back in February, when the *Guys & Dolls* cast list was first posted on the door of G-90 a day or two after auditions, I was surprised to have been given a speaking role, Big Jule, the intimidating gangster visiting from Chicago.

I'm pretty sure I got the part because I was the shortest guy who auditioned.

That was Mr. Hill's sense of humor.

Sasha "No Shit" Sherlock and Bart Scribner were also outsiders in the cast.

Sasha got the part of Harry the Horse, my character's companion, the dude who brings me to New York from Chicago, and Bart was cast as Brother Arvide of the Save-A-Soul Mission.

Jim Lord, who'd been in Play Production since 10th Grade, was in the show playing the cop Lieutenant Brannigan.

This really good-looking senior named Conrad Lagoy played Nathan Detroit. He had that thing about him where you knew he was going to be a famous actor one day.

Sky Masterson was played by Elmore E.D. Sedgwick, Jr., who was a font of foul imagery shared willingly backstage while waiting in the wings for our various entrances with every lewd quip followed by a series of pelvic thrusts and the whispered word "Perversion."

"Bitch's coochie tasted like cheddar cheese and guacamole, the perfect taco," Elmore'd say, " . . . Perversion."

"I had a dream last night about nibbling on pig clits," Elmore'd say, " . . . Perversion."

"When two chicks bang their coochies together, you know what they call that?"

"Scissoring?" Jim Lord'd say.

"Nah," Elmore'd say, " . . . Perversion."

The two female leads were, as expected, seniors, Demi Mondesi, this mixed girl I'd seen in other shows, who was going to play Sarah Brown, and Jessica Bloom, who had starred in every play she'd ever been in since like nursery school and who'd, to no one's surprise, take the role of Adelaide, Nathan Detroit's long-suffering fiancée.

When I got the part, I had to ask my counselor Mr. Wood to program me into 6th period Play Production, which he did but was obviously bothered by the hassle.

"You sure you want 6 classes?" he droned, "I thought you said you only wanted 5. Isn't that why we changed your Chem class?"

"I didn't know I was going to get a part in the play," I said.

"Well, just be sure because I'm not changing this back," he huffed and handed me my transfer slip.

Walking into the auditorium as a new student in Play Production was even more stressful and awkward than it was when I auditioned in there the week before.

All the veteran thespians stared at me and Sasha and Bart as we joined everybody in the front rows to hear Mr. Hill talk about the production.

I noticed Diana Hitchcock wasn't in the cast, in the class, or even around school at all, but nobody ever said anything about it.

I just shrugged to myself and wondered where she was.

Rehearsal schedules were handed out, and, as Mimi and Dolly had warned, there were a lot of nights and weekends involved.

"This is the last time that's going to happen," Dolly said after the first day of rehearsal, "Getting out at 3. You'll learn to keep a sleeping bag backstage eventually, the closer we get to opening."

The following day we had a read-through of the script and when I got to my first line–"I come here to shoot crap! Let's shoot crap!"–Mr. Hill told me he wanted me to shout.

"You're a little man with a big voice and a big personality," Mr. Hill said, "That's how you intimidate. Go over the top with it."

It felt unnatural to be shouting every line and I was afraid it would make me look and sound ridiculous on stage, but I knew I had to listen to Mr. Hill and follow his direction, especially as a totally inexperienced newcomer to the stage.

Mr. Hill talked to us about the attitude he wanted the gamblers to display.

"Communicate it with your faces and body language," he said, "the pathetic arrogance of guys who think they're hot shots but are really just a bunch of small timers playing for very low stakes."

After we ran the scene with full blocking, the only note Mr. Hill gave me was, "I would just make one small change. When Brannigan is questioning you don't look directly at him; cheat to the audience, especially when you shout your lines," he gestured the angle, "about halfway between the Lieutenant and the first row of the balcony."

Jim Lord had his back to Mr. Hill and was darting a cunnilingus tongue back and forth at me to crack me up, though I was able to suppress my laughter until later.

Elmore E.D. Sedgwick, Jr. was in the wings just offstage, though in my line of sight, doing pelvic thrusts and whispering, "Perversion" just loud enough for us to hear.

A couple of months later, rehearsals were taking up more and more of my time and attention. I didn't have the energy to work on music which was in turn having a detrimental effect on my mood.

Lorelei was one of the Save-A-Soul Mission Band members, so she didn't have much to do at rehearsals, and my character was only in a few scenes and just 2 dance numbers, so we started sitting next to each other in the back row of the auditorium during the long lapses where we weren't needed.

"You're one of those people who knows how to be happy but doesn't know how to have fun," she said one afternoon, somehow always knowing precisely everything about me.

"Fun makes me sad," I said.

"Me too," she said, "Whenever I find myself having fun I feel like something is being forced on me."

"Same with me," I said.

We watched Turpin trying to choreograph the drunk Sister Sarah Havana dance sequence for a while.

"What are you working on right now?" Lorelei asked me.

"You mean music?"

"I mean anything. What are you working on?"

"Right now nothing," I said, "This is eating all my creative energy."

"Do you enjoy doing this?"

"Being in the play?"

"Do you enjoy doing *this*?" she gestured like a sorcerer.

"I like playing Big Jule," I said, "and I enjoy watching everybody work. But parts of my brain are complaining. I'm not writing any music these days."

"Jealous muses," she said, "Alack and alas, I know their song well."

I hadn't sacrificed my seed to Calliope and Euterpe in a long time.

That night I jacked off to a bunch of different girls heading toward Dolly as climax approached but I ended up releasing in the imagined vagina of Lorelei Lux at the crucial moment.

When I fell asleep Lorelei ghosted through all my twitchy dreams.

The German song my Nazi neighbor Frank sang every night in his kitchen window across the driveway from my bedroom infiltrated my half-slumber.

Ich weiß nicht was soll es bedeuten daß ich so traurig bin

A fitting soundtrack to my hypnagogic peregrinations.

A couple of days later, right in the middle of telling me about her father's obsessive-compulsive disorder, Lorelei reached into her purse and pulled out a Twix bar.

"You should give this to Mr. Fudd," she said.

"Why?" I asked.

"Silly wabbit," she said.

I thought for a moment.

"Twix are for kids," I said, "Haha. Wabbit. Fudd. Heh. Lorelei with the double reference."

"Be vewy vewy quiet," Lorelei whispered and then laughed to herself and jotted something down in her notebook while I watched Jessica and Demi rehearse "Marry The Man Today."

Lorelei had a way of making you feel like you were part of an experiment she was conducting.

A few days later, after we'd done "Luck Be A Lady" it seemed like 30 times, I stumbled to the back of the aud where Lorelei was waiting for me.

"That one looks ready," she said of the number and pulled out a pen in order to write on my jeans.

She inscribed on my thigh the word AMOEBA.

Above that word she wrote PARAMECIUM.

And even closer to my crotch she spelled out TRILOBITE.

Within a millimeter of my hardening penis she wrote LUMBER.

She looked at me, said "Lumber," and leaned across me to scribble more on my left thigh.

"What are you doing?" I asked as I touched the back of her head and pretended for a second she was giving me a blowjob.

"This is the magic number," she said, sitting up, "your portal to everywhere."

"That looks like a phone number."

"Call it," she said, "tonight. When you're done with your homework."

"It's upside down though," I said.

"Look at it in the mirror," she said.

For a second it made sense until I realized it didn't.

I called Lorelei that night, but when she answered the phone she very quickly told me she was busy and couldn't talk and then hung up really fast.

Right after I hung up with Lorelei, Dolly called.

"What are you going to do for your birthday?" she asked.

"I wanted to go to the opening of the new Woody Allen movie but my parents vetoed that even though they refused to say why so I'm gonna go out to dinner with my dad."

"Ah," Dolly said, "No party? You don't want to be celebrated?"

"Haha, no, I don't deserve it," I said.

"Oh, I know people who think you do," she said.

The next Wednesday was my birthday and my dad took me out to

Mirabelle. He attributed my mom and Mimi and Joy not joining us to "bad timing."

After dinner we went across the street to Tower where I picked up my own copy of *Marquee Moon* and also the latest Tom Waits album to which my dad's response was, "Nice jugs."

When we got home my mother, who was waiting on the porch, let us in through the sliding glass dining room door instead of the front door.

"What'd you get?" my mom asked as I walked in.

"*Marquee Moon* and the new Tom Waits," I showed her.

"Oh my," she said, looking at the cover.

She seemed distracted.

"Well why don't we go listen to it on the big stereo," she said and walked into the living room.

When I followed her into the living room the lights flashed on and a crowd of people yelled "SURPRISE!" and I was immediately most unhappy with this sudden disruption to my planned evening.

This wasn't just any old surprise party either.

Dolly and my sister had conspired to throw me a sweet sixteen, complete with sweet sixteen party games and other girly shit.

And, in fact, the only guests at this party were girls, which Mimi and Dolly thought was a very funny thing to do, only invite girls.

Dolly, Mimi, Joy, Claire Farnaway, Lorelei Lux, Sharon Rose, Misty Winters, Justine Balthazar, Arabella Mayflower, Evelyn Childs, Gina Dichlich, all the girls from the *Guys & Dolls* cast, my mom, and also my Aunt Serena was there (to keep my mom company I'm pretty sure, though that night she did give me a gift subscription to *Playboy* as a present along with a card that said *I hope you get a good fuck this year* which was pretty much the coolest and wisest birthday present and card of all time).

Miranda was even there.

Once the initial chatter settled down and I had greeted everyone, I edged my way toward the dining room where Dolly was standing and watching.

"Don't be angry," Dolly said before I could say anything.

She knew very well how much I hated that kind of shit.

"Why did you do this?"

"Because I love you and because Mimi and I thought it would be funny to throw you a girly sweet sixteen thing."

"Why?"

"Because you are a girl," Dolly teased.

"Which would make you a lesbian then, sort of, almost."

"I'm open minded," she said.

"Well, I love you too," I said, "and thank you."

"Lance Heaven," she said, indicating the party guests.

"Yeah. Who needs boys?" I said.

"Zackly," Dolly said, sounding too much like Miranda, "I'm glad you're not angry."

"I didn't say I wasn't angry."

"Lance! We want a picture with the birthday boy!" Claire Farnaway called from the living room.

Lorelei, Claire, and Miranda were sitting together on the couch.

"*Ménage a twat*, dude," I could hear Buzzy Lagniappe saying in my head.

I nudged myself in between Claire and Lorelei and Sharon Rose took the shot with her Instamatic.

I have no idea how that picture turned out.

The *Guys & Dolls* piano vocal score was on the music stand and I sauntered over to play a few tunes. By the time I was halfway through "I'll Know" pretty much every girl in the cast had surrounded the piano and began singing along. Lorelei stood directly behind me and rested her hands on my shoulders.

Jessica Bloom did a great version of "Adelaide's Lament" and then Demi Mondesi sang "If I Were A Bell."

All the girls joined in a raunchy rendition of "Take Back Your Mink" with all their hips moving like a giant Gaia and I was soaked in the preponderance of pussy all about me.

Lance Heaven indeed.

I looked over at Dolly.

She blinked back like Barbara Eden in *I Dream Of Jeannie*, not dancing but singing along.

The girls who weren't in the show must have been bored.

I saw Miranda talking to Arabella Mayflower who left not long after without saying goodbye.

To my relief, the *Guys & Dolls* interlude made it too late to play Sweet 16 party games, though I did open presents in front of everybody.

There was no card with Lorelei's present. She just wrote *From Lorelei* directly on the gift–wrap.

It was a can of Campbell's Soup-For-One.

"Minestrone," I said, "Thank you."

"Oh," my mom came into the living room holding a cardboard tube, "This was leaning up against the front door when I got home."

Inside the tube was the Roxy Music poster with Bryan Ferry in the black bejeweled jacket and Eno next to him in red and green and looking like an opiated angel.

No card, but it could only have been from Taryn Rust.

"Oooh, cool, who's that from?" Evelyn Childs wanted to know.

"No card," I shrugged.

"Secret admirer," Dolly said.

I looked over at her for a second.

The girls broke off into umpteen different side conversations and I wandered into the kitchen where I found Lorelei standing alone near the Sparkletts dispenser.

"Hey, Culligan Man," Lorelei said when I walked in to pour myself another cup of diet root beer.

"Soup-For-One," I said.

"I found the saddest thing of all time and wanted to give it to you for your birthday."

"Thanks," I said.

"You just ooze sadness, Lance Atlas. And aren't birthdays the saddest days of all?"

"Pretty much, yeah," I said, "I can't explain why though. But yeah."

"For me it's, like, I'm not special and don't deserve to be treated that way," she said, "so it makes me really uncomfortable, one, because I feel like I'm inadvertently fooling them somehow, but also because if they think there's something special about me worth celebrating then they don't really know me. Their love is for some fictional version of me."

I looked at Lorelei's reluctantly innocent face and wanted to kiss her very hard on the mouth when she said that.

Smart chicks, man. Foxy hotness.

"This year I plan to be completely alone on my birthday and not talk to anyone, including my parents," she said, "especially my dad."

"Wouldn't it be better just to ignore it? Like it's just another day?"

"I don't believe that's possible," she said, "Reality tingles on your birthday whether you're into it or not."

"Nyeah I guess," I said passively though I knew what she meant, "I get what you're saying. Yeah."

I wasn't ready for us to be all the way in synch yet despite the ineluctable fact of our eventual coupling.

"Isn't Soup-For-One the saddest thing of all time?"

"Yes," I said.

"Can you imagine shopping for that? Buying a product whose only purpose is to remind you how sad and alone you are?"

Lorelei had a mind that could go way dark, and the twisty nature of her behavior was a strong allure for me.

It was weird because Lorelei wasn't my girlfriend but it was definitely brewing and soon to boil over.

I didn't know how to act around her.

Plus I felt bad because Dolly had planned this whole party and everything and here I was totally falling for Lorelei.

I ventured back into the living room where Claire was still sitting on the couch and sat down next to her.

"Hey," I said and reclined.

Our hands were kind of playing with each other.

"I think I'm the only one in our class who hasn't turned 16 yet," said Claire.

"You're the baby," I said.

"I am," she said, "I used to be *your* baby."

"You were," I said and pointed at her.

"Isn't it weird how that changes and things aren't the same anymore?"

"I feel like change is always happening, like every moment," I said, "It's part of my problem."

"Problem? . . . singular? Um . . ."

"Shut up," I danced back at her.

"No, you shut up, you asshole. You dumped me. Grant me that victimhood, dude. You're the one who sucks in this used-to-be relationship."

"You are correct, sir," I said, "I accept full responsibility for the suckage."

"Waah," she pouted.

"What?"

"Waaah," she pouted again.

"Dude. Clarify. Be true to your name."

"You know. Us and all that stuff."

"Claire," I sighed.

"I know. I'm stupid. Never mind. Go away."

I started to oblige.

"No don't go away," she said and got me in a scissor hold.

Dang, dude, chicks just do not know what they fucking want.

I stepped out onto the front porch hoping I might see Jupiter and therefore know everything was all right.

The sky was overcast. The marine layer was arriving early.

"Hey, I think I'm gonna take off," Miranda said, joining me on the porch.

"Oh, hey. I'm glad you came tonight."

"Me too."

"Thanks for the book," I said.

She nodded and looked down.

Miranda had given me a hardback French edition of *Le Petit Prince*.

There was an inscription on the title page.

"Et quand tu seras consolé (on se console toujours) tu seras content de m'avoir connu. Tu seras toujours mon ami." —Antoine de St. Exupery

Bonne Anniversaire!

Miranda

"Did you have a happy birthday?" she asked after a silence.

"I guess. I just went to school. Had a chemistry test today."

"Right. We had one in Period 6 also. We miss you in Period 6."

"Amazingly I didn't have any rehearsal today. So then I went out with my dad and came home to this. I'm not that into birthdays."

"Yeah, I remember."

We were in that realm where nothing is connecting and there's this mutual desire to get out of the faltering conversation gracefully.

"See you tomorrow in Meggido's," she said and started walking to her car, "Bye, Lance."

I waved as she turned away and thereafter I wallowed in deep existential sadness with a tiny whiny groan I hoped no one could hear.

I was still out on the porch when everyone started leaving.

After a bevy of goodbyes and thank-yous and hugs, it ended up being just Dolly and me alone in my bedroom.

I put the new Waits on my stereo and we sat on my bed listening for a while.

Wasted and wounded, it ain't what the moon did, I've got what I paid for now

She got up to look at the stuff on my desk.

"What's this?" Dolly asked of a framed coin I had in a plastic stand.

"That's a mint condition Benjamin Franklin 50 cent piece," I said.

"I only know the Kennedy half dollar," Dolly said, "Cool."

"This was the one before that," I said.

"My grandfather always gives me Kennedy half dollars. 'Don't spend them,' he says every time he gives them to me. So now I have like 200 of them, I'm not kidding."

"Why doesn't he want you to spend them?"

Dolly shrugged.

"Maybe he thinks they'll be hard to get someday or something," she said.

"Keep them in mint condition," I said, "You never know."

"And a skull," she held the present my dad had given me on my 8th birthday, "and pyrite," she picked up the rock I got from Rose Benedict before she moved to Pittsburgh back in 5th Grade.

Dolly came over and sat back on the bed with me.

"So, hey, listen up. I've got something I want to tell you," she said.

I returned her gaze and waited.

"Um, the cool news I got a while back? I'm going to be spending senior year in France."

"What? Why?"

I'm an innocent victim of a blinded alley

"I'm going to be an exchange student," she said.

I was trying to imagine Dolly not being close by.

We had gotten really good at not falling in love with each other on a daily basis.

In that way she was the perfect girlfriend.

My gut ached.

Dolly could see it in my grimace.

"I know Lorelei Lux is on your radar," she said.

"I guess," I said.

"I see you guys sitting in the back of the aud together. I know what's happening. You can be corny and sentimental now about me leaving, but you will hardly notice I'm gone, dude," she said using her playful nature to mask her resentment.

I begged you to stab me, you tore my shirt open,

And I'm down on my knees tonight

"Whenever I think about doing something you're the first person I think about doing it with," I said.

"Aww, Lance. Likewise. You're my favorite. You know that."

"But you're leaving."

"Yeah. I have lots of things I want to do."

"Nyeah but."

"But what."

"Well . . . you're leaving," I pouted.

"I'm sorry," she said and closed her eyes, "I'll be back though."

We hugged for a long while and then eventually our lips and tongues met.

I put my hands on her breasts and squeezed them gently through the shirt.

"Press hard," she said and licked the underside of my teeth.

I couldn't wait to be alone so I could fantasize about fucking her.

A soft rain started to fall outside. I could hear it on my neighbor's driveway.

"Mmmmm," Dolly said biting on my lips, "The smell of rain."

My dick was into it but at the same time I wanted her to go home so I could get high and listen to the Waits record for real.

I broke off the embrace and lay on my back.

"What's wrong?" she asked, snuggling next to me.

"You're leaving," I said.

"I still want to keep doing what we're doing," she kept kissing my face, "Whatever it is we're doing."

I didn't play back.

"I'm not leaving until August. Late August."

I covered my face with my hands and didn't answer.

"I think I should head home," she said when Side A ended, "You know?"

I agreed.

We kissed sweetly at her car.

"What is it with you?" she asked.

"What do you mean?"

She narrowed her eyes at me.

"I dunno," she said, "Nothing. See you tomorrow," and kissed me on the cheek, "Happy birthday."

"I am glad for you," I said as she got into her car.

I was.

"And thank you for this party."

After Dolly drove off I smoked a bowl on the garage roof and called upon the muses to sing in me.

They descended from the heavens, through the telephone and power lines, approaching me in all their whetstone glory, with flute and writing tablet.

"Why have you called upon us?" Calliope asked.

"I can't decide where to go next," I said.

"Pussy Roulette," said Calliope.

"Pardon?"

"Play Pussy Roulette."

"What's Pussy Roulette?"

"When you jack off later–and believe me we'll be watching as we always do–spin your kaleidoscope wheel of current favorite females. Fuck each one as she arcs across your thought-stream. You'll end up ejaculating in one of them at the crucial moment. Whoever that is, the one who makes you pop off, she's the way forward."

"Oh, the carousel thing," I said, "of course. I didn't know it had a name."

I repaired to my bedroom, put on Side B of the Waits album and went to work on a round of Pussy Roulette.

My muses told me to.

I started out making my way through all the girls at the party.

Sharon Rose, in my bed. Fucking her was like fucking a Renaissance painting.

Misty Winters, really little, on my lap, facing toward me, forehead to forehead.

Justine Balthazar on the floor of the multi–purpose room at temple.

Arabella Mayflower, shiksa lips on my kosher beef.

Evelyn Childs, she and her sister, on their mom's bed (which I had very briefly seen once and memorized quickly for just such a purpose as this), *ménage a twat*.

I kept trying to make it happen with Gina Dichlich in my head but she eluded me, no matter how many times I circled back to thoughts of her bending over.

I worked another threesome with Jessica Bloom and Demi Mondesi backstage for a while.

And the roulette wheel kept spinning.

Taryn Rust appeared pulling me down onto her and into her, grinding hard against my rhythm to quicken the friction.

She's so good, she'll make a dead man cum

Then Leah Shepherd emerged, home on Spring Break, like always in her bedroom, pushing me away but eventually letting me.

Penelope Lagniappe on the garage roof jacking me off while I finger fucked her.

And out of the blue Diana Hitchcock made an appearance on the roulette wheel and I wondered where she was these days. I was on top of her and all scrunched up and humping.

Miranda Savitch showed up in a sweet lovemaking situation I think on her bed, but it was dark so I'm not sure, classically slow, holding hands, deep, tongues entwined.

And I wish you'd a known her

we were quite a pair

she was sharp as a razor

and soft as a prayer

so welcome to the continuing saga

she was my better half

and I was just a dog

I lay there riffing through the faces I fancied, the bodies I'd often throttled in my thoughts of late, trying to find the perfect pocket to deposit my wad in.

Then I suddenly got what the muses were doing.

They were mocking me.

Pussy Roulette was a simple projection of my inability to make deep and lasting relationships with anybody.

"You talk a good game, Lance Atlas. You make deep and lasting language. But you've got no capacity for the actual. Philosophy for you is nothing but a flirting technique," their voices sang to me.

"And also an escape hatch," I said, possibly out loud.

Eventually the roulette wheel slowed, and I began toggling back and forth between Dolly and Lorelei, Dolly and Lorelei, Dolly and Lorelei.

Dolly was my best friend.

Lorelei was my latest fascination.

Dolly was sensible.

Lorelei was cryptic.

Dolly was the best kisser on earth.

Lorelei was afraid of the very gesture.

Dolly's body was hot with longing.

Lorelei's body was pigeon-toed and always protecting itself.

Dolly bellowed yes.

Lorelei whispered no.

Dolly was leaving.

Lorelei wasn't going anywhere.

Dolly was Lorelei was Dolly was Lorelei was Dolly was.

Dolly was Lorelei was Dolly was.

Dolly was Lorelei.

Dolly was.

Lorelei . . .

I fell asleep to the cloistered image of my beloved as I thought she might look after humping herself to orgasm on my cock.

As the muses swept me into netherness, my Nazi neighbor Frank across the driveway crooned once again in a mellow tenor his nightly song while doing the dishes and gazing out his kitchen window:

Ich weiß nicht, was soll es bedeuten,

Daß ich so traurig bin;

Ein Märchen aus alten Zeiten,

Das kommt mir nicht aus dem Sinn.

Alack and alas.

I knew the song well.

Losing It

1

I was lost at the circus and couldn't find my way back to our seats.

All the aisles looked the same and I hadn't memorized any landmarks along my outbound journey to the men's room that might have guided my return trip.

I'd just had one of those stressful urinations where you realize there's a line of guys waiting to piss behind you and you're taking too long–because cannabis slows the stream down to an insufferably laid-back flow that can't be expedited–which makes you tense up and take even longer.

Unable to remember whether I should turn right or turn left out of the men's room, I just instinctively turned right and poked my head in at the top of each section all the way around the Forum.

I knew which row we were in, just not which aisle.

Later I realized I could've just looked at the ticket in my back pocket for the aisle number.

I should have turned left.

Instinct is unreliable.

I was at the circus because Dolly had called me up a few nights before and invited me and even though I hate the circus I couldn't resist the opportunity to hang out with her. Plus being high at the circus promised hilarity and revelation.

"One of my dad's clients gave him tickets," she said, "You want to go with me? We can be all aloof and ironic together."

"My two favorite poses. Let's do it," I said, "When is it?"

"Saturday afternoon."

"Oh, cool, we don't have rehearsal."

"Correct. Exactly."

Having time off from *Guys & Dolls* rehearsals was rarer and rarer, even on weekends now. We opened in a few weeks.

Whenever I went out with Dolly it felt like a date even though it wasn't.

The circus had come to the Fabulous Forum in Inglewood where normally the Lakers and Kings play, though I had also seen Cat Stevens there and Queen oh and Jethro Tull.

Dolly's dad's clients also gave him VIP parking, so we got to park close to the arena and also the seats were in the 2nd row which ended up freaking me out because all the overwhelming sadness of the circus was magnified by its intense proximity and volume.

My feelings were all a jumble because I was right on the verge of a full-blown romance with Lorelei Lux, so being out with Dolly, whom I still craved constantly, stirred up shameful feelings of betrayal even though Dolly and I tried as much as possible not to touch each other and also I wasn't really with Lorelei yet (we hadn't even kissed).

Still, that whole conflicted situation niggled at my belly throughout the afternoon.

The performance began with a parade of downtrodden animals and clowns.

"This is sort of depressing," Dolly said.

"Sort of?"

"OK, terribly."

"The ultimate circus stunt would be if they all came out and killed themselves because you know that's what they all really want to do."

"Sometimes I forget how demented you are."

She was in flirting mode.

"Wouldn't you?" I said.

"What?"

"Want to kill yourself if you were a circus animal?"

"I don't know. I'd probably try to find some way to enjoy it. Just like I find ways to enjoy your torturous company."

Dolly's eyes had this insidious sparkle that took me back to caveman days.

"Ladies and gentlemen, boys and girls of all ages," the Ringmaster said, breaking our groove, "Prepare yourself for the most elaborate waste of time you will ever witness, an appalling relic of our penchant for spectacle, an experience that each new generation is duped into thinking is fun when in reality it is nothing but human cruelty and grist for a thousand nightmares," or something like that, I don't remember his exact words.

The first act was a lion tamer named Cleo Dipchunk.

I'd have to remember to tell Annie De Milo about the lion tamer named Dipchunk in the next postcard. Maybe they were related or something. How many Dipchunks could there be?

"That lion is Winston Smith and we are his Room 101," I said.

"Did we smoke from the same bowl, dude? 'Cause you are out there today."

"And Cleo Dipchunk is O'Brien."

"So, do you think that the ultimate stunt here would be if the lion bit the tamer's head off in front of everybody?"

"No, that would be your own twisted praying mantis fantasy," I chided.

"Nyeah nyeah."

"You know you fuckin' dream about that shit," I said and started kissing her softly and wetly on the mouth but then twinged and pulled away.

"What's wrong?" she said.

"You're leaving," I pouted.

I was of course also nonplussed about Lorelei but I left that part out.

It was pretty fucked up.

"Ugh, is this what you're going to do for the next 3 months? Moan?"

"Nyeah probably I guess."

We came out of our mutual reverie as a gaggle of acrobats made a variety of human pyramids and in general defied gravity repeatedly.

They did this one inverted pyramid with one dude on the bottom holding up a triangle of bodies, each tier broader than the one beneath it.

"It's pretty amazing how they do that."

"I guess," I shrugged, "I feel like I'm dreaming it."

"Come on, you have to admit it's pretty damn cool," Dolly said.

"I dunno, I was just thinking about how the acrobats and the trapeze artists and the tightrope walkers are performing this yes pretty damn cool thing that they've learned how to do but the fact that they spend all of their time practicing that one thing, over and over again, all day every day, makes it all sort of a bummer. Like, for us it's an impressive 7 minutes or so that they're doing their act and then we move on to the next spectacle, but for them it's their whole life. They practice all day to get ready for that 7 minutes and then the next morning they have to get up and practice that shit all over again. Every day. Dang, dude. I dunno, it makes me sad."

"Yeah, but don't we all do that everyday in some way or other? I dunno, for me it's the animals."

"Oh man, totally. The melancholy in their eyes."

"I hate the circus."

"Me too."

"Why are we even here?"

As the acrobats dashed away and the tightrope walking duo of Clovis & Findhorn began their ascent up their respective ladders, a brigade of day-glo clowns came tumbling and skipping and juggling right up to where we were sitting and started pointing and laughing.

"Uh, dude, I think they're pointing at you," Dolly said.

"Nah," I said because why would they be.

"Our brother!" they yelled, beckoning, touching their hair, "Our brother!"

"I have to go to the bathroom," I excused myself.

I did have to pee really bad but I also wanted to get away from the clowns who were freaking me out the way the jack-in-the-box I got for my 3rd birthday did.

I would make my mother put the jack-in-the-box way up high in the closet so it would be far enough away that it couldn't hurt me, but I also wanted it to be visible so I could always look up and see how far away it was.

Sometimes I'd have my mother take it down and start winding it.

She was always careful to stop winding before the clown popped out because that would make me cry.

As if I would become the jack-in-the-box or something. Like I'd be stuck inside of a box and only be allowed to come out when the box-master so deemed.

To this day I don't like surprises.

Jack-in-the-box toys are sadistic.

I remembered Miranda Savitch raving over a hamburger at Jack-In-The-Box that day we trespassed on the Hancock Park Elementary School playground and played solitaire together in 8th Grade.

"Come back!" the clowns shouted as I made my way up to the foyer, "Our brother!"

"Cram it, clowns!" I wanted to be able to say to them.

Instead, I ignored them and continued my climb up the loge steps, pausing discreetly to look up the short togas of the usherettes who stood at the top of our aisle.

I cheered inwardly on behalf of my entire gender.

Dolly and I had gotten high in the car before entering the Forum and I was having trouble keeping track of basic geography, but I found the men's room eventually and urinated slowly into the trough.

I arrived back at our seats by divine trial and error to catch the end of the tightrope act, a stunt in which Clovis, the girl, sat piggy-back on Findhorn's shoulders while he rode a bicycle on the highwire.

Suddenly, in a literary moment of absurd cosmic timing, a decent-sized earthquake struck, not big by SoCal standards but certainly powerful enough to send Clovis & Findhorn plummeting netward.

Findhorn allowed himself to fall supine toward the waiting net, but Clovis spread into a swan dive position, abandoned to gravity and its constant mothering calm, purposeful, dropping in surreal slow-motion like Caesar's downturning thumb, completely alive for those few seconds before they both hit the netting—whose integrity had been compromised by the temblor, its brackets breaking loose from the stanchions thus rendering it useless—and with flat black finality slammed into the Forum floor and shattered inside.

An unexpected spectacle.

Shrieks, gasps, screams both guttural and shrill, exclamations of "Oh My God!" bounced across the echoing Forum air as the entire circus staff, trainers, stagehands, and performers alike, rushed to the center ring where the two bodies lay.

The arena hushed into a susurrus of disbelief.

Paramedics arrived and carried Clovis & Findhorn away on stretchers, their bodies not entirely covered, perhaps an indication of survival, though I couldn't see how.

Dolly and I had our arms around each other, and she was crying.

The ringmaster announced that the performance was cancelled and a full refund would be granted.

"Let's get out of here," Dolly said, and we walked thus enwrapped all the way to her car.

"Well, shit," I said as we headed down Manchester to La Brea, "that was fucked up."

"Oh my God," Dolly just kept saying through her tears as we drove, "I can't believe that happened."

After a long silence, just as we were coming up on Wilshire, I suggested, "Tar Pits?"

"Yeah," she said, "that sounds right," and she turned left at Wilshire.

We sat at the Tar Pits, 6th Street side, a blissfully coolish late afternoon in May, smoked a joint I had in the pocket of my sweat jacket, and talked about Clovis & Findhorn.

"They're probably dead, right?" Dolly said.

"That'd be my guess," I said, "though they weren't covered up all the way on the stretcher. When I saw that stabbed girl die in front of my house that time, they covered her all the way up."

"It's still a little unreal," she said, "I saw it happening in slow motion."

"Me too," I said, "And Clovis was in that swan dive position all the way down."

"What?"

"Clovis. The chick. She totally did a swan dive all the way down."

"Dude, that was the weed I think."

"Nah nah, I watched her all the way, she did it."

"O-Kay," she said dismissively, "Let me get another hit of that joint and maybe I'll believe you."

"Just think of all the kids who are gonna remember that shit forever," I said, "It's like part of their mythology now, like they're gonna tell their own grandchildren about it, the time there was an earthquake during the circus and the two tightrope walkers fell to their deaths. I know I seem like I'm making light of it. I'm just as freaked out as you are."

"Equally freaked, we."

"I just handle it differently," I said and we started kissing with tongues in full thrust.

I had been meaning to ask Dolly something for a while and so I brought it up post-kiss.

"Did you lose your virginity with Aaron?"

"Uh, yes," she said squinting her eyes at me not sure why I'd suddenly asked her that.

"I figured."

"Why are you bringing this up now?"

"Just wondering."

"Do you wanna hear about it?"

"Not really," I said (though I did sort of want to hear about it).

"It was at his house when his parents were in Palm Springs. Winter break, 10th Grade."

"You can spare me the rest."

"It was nice," she said.

"I'm glad."

"I'm presuming you and Claire never did it."

"Correct."

"Why not?"

"I wasn't into it," I shrugged, "And I don't think she was either."

"Did you guys do anything other than kissing?"

"Nope."

"Is kissing all you ever do?"

"Yep, so far," I said with images of Taryn Rust's mouth on my cock and my tongue on her cunt and the sounds she made when it seemed like she came while I finger-fucked her and the secret majesty of it all.

There was something else I'd been meaning to ask as a follow-up because I was curious and I was high.

"Did you have sex with Aaron when he was down here for Spring Break last month?"

"Lance, come on. Please," she snorted.

"Did you?"

"What makes you think that?"

"'Cause you've been acting weird around me."

"I've been acting weird around you because I've been watching you fall in love with Lori, dorkus."

"Sorry if that has bothered you," I said.

"Bothered me? Nyeah I dunno, more like realizing oh you won't be hanging out with me much anymore, like when you were with Claire."

"That's what happens," I said.

"Yup," she said, "but it's cool. You'll be back."

"Haha," I said, "Just in time for you to leave."

I made a pouty face that caused Dolly to bite my lower lip.

"You are fully aware of course that Lori is a crazy-ass bitch."

"You have warned me thus already," I said, "several times."

"Uh huh," Dolly sniped, "so just keep it in mind when you're trying to penetrate her force field. 'Cause, dude, it is dense and she stays deeply behind it."

"I dunno, I feel like she opens up to me," I said, "We talk and stuff."

"Lori is really good making it seem like she's opening up to you."

"But."

"But it's a trick," Dolly said and looked for a cigarette in her purse.

"Dang," she said, "I'm out."

"Here," I said and gave her my pack of Camel Filters.

"You are the best," she said and lit up.

"I don't know what went on in that house," Dolly said, "but both girls are responding to something. I mean, jeez, D-Lux is totally–"

She stopped herself.

"Totally?"

"Nothing," she said, "Anyway–"

"–But so anyway, did you?"

"What?"

"You know what."

"Have sex with Aaron when he was down for Spring Break?"

"You know it doesn't matter to me either way," I said.

"Shut up," said Dolly.

"But did you?"

She lay back on the grass.

After closing her eyes and waiting a few breaths, she said, "Yes," and covered her face.

I had started nibbling on her earlobe but stopped abruptly when she said that.

"But the thing is I didn't even want to."

"Then why did you?" I said, admittedly bewildered and palpitating a little though it didn't feel blackout dangerous or anything.

"I dunno," she shrugged, "Aaron really wanted to and I was just horny enough to say yes."

She paused to inhale the Camel.

"I didn't enjoy it."

"It makes no difference to me," I said, "Enjoy, don't enjoy, whatever."

"Ugh, you are such a pain in the ass," she snorted.

"But you love me anyway."

"I dunno. I'm reconsidering lately," she said and then started kissing me and she put her arms all the way around me as we lay on the grass together.

2

The first time I made out with Lorelei Lux was when the entire cast along with Mr. Hill went to see the film version of *Guys & Dolls* at the Tiffany Theatre up on Sunset a couple of days after the circus.

I sat next to Lorelei because we were an all but consummated couple.

"Did you hear about the tightrope walkers who died?" Lorelei asked me as we sat in the theatre waiting for the movie to start.

"Yeah," I said, not wanting to tell her I was in attendance at the catastrophe because I was there with Dolly and I hadn't yet gauged Lorelei's jealousy threshold, "Sucks."

"I wonder what it was like being there."

"Freaky, I'm sure. An earthquake? Crazy."

"Or jealous muses," she said twirling her eyeballs at me.

"What, like they should've been working on their juggling instead?"

"Or whatever their true call was."

"Who's the muse of juggling I wonder."

"Terpsichore, maybe? Muse of dance?"

"Can she cause earthquakes?"

"I don't know. She could certainly petition Zeus though."

"Or just fuck him," I said, "That usually works in terms of getting what you want in that particular pantheon."

"Ew," she said and turned slightly away from me, "Don't talk like that."

"Why ew?"

"I'll be back," she got up.

"Where are you going?" I asked her but she didn't answer.

Dang, dude.

Lorelei had pretty much commandeered my nightly masturbation fantasies and I figured that I'd go ahead and pounce in the dark during the *Guys & Dolls* movie because she seemed to be into me, not flirting in the traditional sense because nothing about Lorelei Lux was traditional but still receptive to my attentions. She wrote LUMBER on my jeans just a millimeter away from my cock and she'd also written her phone number and told me to call it. Provocative enough to signal interest.

"Where'd you go?" I asked when she returned.

"Payphone," she said, "I had to talk to my mother. Do you think this movie will be any good?"

"I've seen it," I said, "It's OK. Brando can't sing, but everybody else is good. I found the movie soundtrack in the $1 bin at Aron's. Some of the songs are different from the Broadway version. . . 'I've Never Been In Love Before' and 'My Time Of Day' aren't in the movie."

"Oh no, I love those," Lorelei said.

"Yeah, 2 Sky songs that Brando doesn't have to sing. But there's some other song he sings that's not in the play, I can't remember what it's called. Also there's no 'Bushel And A Peck,' the Hot Box Girls do a different number."

Dang, dude, I love that they are called the Hot Box Girls. I couldn't ever say that to Lorelei though. She was averse to raunch obviously.

And 'More I Cannot Wish You,'" I said.

"That song is kind of eh anyway."

"You think so? I think it's got a pretty melody. I like it."

"So you say, Lance Atlas," Lorelei said intently, "You like pretty things."

"I do," I said and thought again about how great an image Hot Box Girls is.

"Definitely worth watching, though. B.S. Pulley does Big Jule the way I would prefer to do it."

"He doesn't shout?"

"Right."

"Interesting . . . understated."

"Yeah. I've told you how I feel about the shouting thing."

"You have. But I think Mr. Hill's idea will work in the bigger context of the production," she said.

"So what's going on between your sister and Mr. Hill anyway?" I pointed to several rows in front of us where Mr. Hill and Lorelei's sister Deirdre were seated next to each other.

"They're close I suppose," Lorelei said.

Dolly was sitting on the other side of Mr. Hill.

"I don't really know other than she helps him with productions," she shrugged, "We don't talk much."

When Marlon Brando and Jean Simmons did "I'll Know," Lorelei leaned into my ear and whispered, "Your audition piece," at which I turned and kissed her on the lips though she had them tightly sealed. I forced my tongue into her mouth and felt her whole body relax into me, not touching me or holding me but going limp.

She moved her tongue but not really in any kind of dance with mine.

With my arm around her I moved my hand down through the top of her shirt.

Lorelei didn't wear a bra.

That was the first thing I learned about her beyond the words she wove.

She didn't push me away and so I took her nipple between my fingers and began kissing her on the neck and earlobe at which she pulled me back onto her mouth a trifle more engaged.

After that night Lorelei and I were just kind of together as a couple.

Nothing was ever said officially.

Sort of how it happened with Candy Stoner back in 8th Grade when we just started frenching at the Tar Pits and she was my girlfriend for the next 3 weeks until we just stopped frenching and then she wasn't anymore.

I called Lorelei later that night because I thought I probably should.

"You called," she said.

"I did."

"Goody. I'm glad."

"So, um."

"I liked the movie," she said.

"Me too."

"I liked it more than I thought I would."

"It took a while to get going but once it did, yeah."

"But you've seen that movie before."

"Yeah."

"It was my first time seeing that movie so it was different for me."

"I guess."

"A completely different experience for me than it was for you."

"Kind of. Not really."

"You've seen that movie lots of times before I bet."

"No just the once."

I pretended to think she was really talking about the movie because I could tell that's what she wanted me to do.

"You wanna hang out before school tomorrow?" I asked.

"No, not particularly. I'll see you in 5th."

"What about Nutrition? Lunch?"

"OK."

"OK?"

"Yes. I have to go," she said and hung up.

That was our first phone conversation as boyfriend and girlfriend.

Lorelei didn't seem much into seeing me on campus other than we'd sit together in the auditorium during Play Production when we could, though we were mostly in run-throughs by then so we were all backstage most of the time.

Occasionally we'd kiss in the wings.

Every time I saw her I wanted to kiss her but she wouldn't allow it when people were around.

The first few weeks of our romantic relationship were limited by the demands of *Guys & Dolls* rehearsals, though we'd sometimes find time to get together and make out on the couch in her living room.

I was never invited to Lorelei's bedroom.

Her favorite album was Neil Young's *After The Gold Rush* and she would put it on the stereo every time we made out.

It became the running soundtrack of our couplehood.

Still the searcher

must ride the dark horse

Racing alone in his fright

I became intimate with those songs and their arrangements, more intimate than I would ever become with Lorelei Lux.

Tell me lies later,

come and see me

I'll be around for a while.

I am lonely but you can free me

All in the way that you smile

A few days into my thing with Lorelei, Eddie Gurges dogged me about it in Chemistry with Lorelei standing a few feet away.

"For real, dude?" Eddie Gurges said to me as we set up our lab work.

"What?"

"'Stay away from those, kid. They're nothing but trouble.'"

"I did say that," I remembered with an appropriate sense of guilt.

"You talked me out of going after Lorelei so you could have her."

"Nyeah, it's not like that," I said, "Back when you told me you liked her I wasn't even talking to her. We got into each other during *Guys & Dolls* rehearsals. I didn't know it was gonna happen."

"Well, it sucks," he said.

"I'm sorry," I offered.

He shrugged.

"I hope she makes you miserable," he said, I think jokingly.

"I'm sure she will," I said, "Nothing but trouble."

That night on the phone I told Lorelei about Eddie.

"Back in January he told me he liked you and I talked him out of asking you out so now he thinks I did that on purpose because I secretly liked you."

"Didn't you?"

"No I was just anti-romance right after I broke up with Claire so I would've tried to talk anybody out of going out with anyone."

"Eddie told me you said I was crazy."

Dang, dude.

Girls keep track of everything.

Especially Lorelei Lux.

Her little notebook was a magnetic sponge for information, especially, apparently, as regarded me.

"What?" I asked aghast at being busted. Eddie had violated the guy code.

"I understood that as a diversionary tactic on your part," she said, "so that you could have me all to yourself. Quite brilliant."

I would gladly allow her to entertain that delusion forever.

"When did you first notice me, Lance Atlas?"

"Notice you?"

"As your destiny."

"Destiny?"

A concept to which I do not generally subscribe.

"I already know what the answer is."

"Well then what's the point of my saying it?"

"Because I want to hear if you're going to be honest or make something up."

"The aud I guess, during rehearsals a while back. It was a gradual thing."

"Wrong."

"Wrong?"

"That's not when it was."

"Then I don't really know."

"Yes you do."

"Jeez."

"Just say it."

I did not know what she was talking about.

"Uhh—m, New Year's Eve in 10th Grade maybe?" I guessed at an almost-kissing moment we'd had, "Dolly's patio?"

"I remember that night, but we were already deeply entwined by then."

"We were?"

I treaded a mess of memories of Lorelei's face and finally settled on one instance.

"The sock hop," I said.

"Yes."

"When we were spinning."

"Yes."

I remembered. We spun in a circle like elementary school kids.

Staring at Lorelei's face while we were spinning prevented me from getting dizzy.

"That's when you first noticed me," she said.

"I dunno. I guess yeah?" I said. "Is that when you first noticed me?"

"Oh, no. No. I noticed you long before then."

"When?"

"You don't know when?"

"No."

"Yes you do."

"I don't. Just tell me."

"7th Grade English."

"Ms. LaBouche."

"Correct. I told Miranda Savitch that you reminded me of the Little Prince, from the book."

"You what?"

My head was stunned by thunder.

"I told Miranda Savitch you reminded me of the Little Prince but she didn't know what I was talking about."

"What?"

I wanted to shriek it like when Harold realizes Maude has taken a suicide pill and she's gonna die and his shriek segues into the ambulance siren.

"She hadn't read the book," Lorelei said.

A whole cosmos was imploding.

"I loaned her my copy of the book so she could read it. She agreed with me when she was done."

"I don't . . ." I needed to hang up and vomit.

"Are you OK?" Lorelei asked.

"Yeah yeah," I said, "I have to get off though."

"OK. 'Night," she said and hung up.

Earth and sky were going to crash together from this blindsiding blow.

I lay in airless space not breathing, knocked out of orbit.

I wasn't quite hyperventilating but I was starting to see and feel stars. It's possible I lost consciousness.

I know that I became aware of my surroundings again and was able to stand up.

I didn't want to tell my parents about the episode.

I drank some water and decided to take a walk and get some night air.

The city soothed me and stoked me like a wilderness.

I would get these spasms of losing it, like total disorientation, but the torsion would subside and I would try to think it through rationally.

Had Miranda Savitch really plagiarized what I had always considered her first expression of love for me?

That note, *you remind me of the little prince! luv, miranda*, was my touchstone to the entire mythos of Miranda, a sacred text, a holy scripture, which now, in light of Lorelei's claim, was reduced to a forgery.

How was I to reconcile Miranda's *you remind me of the little prince!* with Lorelei's *I told Miranda Savitch you reminded me of the Little Prince but she didn't know what I was talking about?*

I felt like I was losing everything.

In addition to this latest plundering of my intimate mythology, I had also lost pretty much all of my songwriting time to either *Guys & Dolls* or Dolly or Lorelei.

I felt abandoned by the Muses and deservedly so.

And I was also going through withdrawal from the mind of Henry Miller, as I had finally finished and turned in my term paper on *Tropic of Cancer*, *Tropic of Capricorn*, and *Sexus*.

I had further solidified my thesis regarding the psychic and artistic growth in the main character's journey that outpaced the slower shift in his physical life, the idea that epiphanies are nothing but harbingers of a gradual change.

This one quote from *Sexus* hung perpetually in my head the whole time I was working on the final draft. Not because it had anything whatsoever to do with my thesis but rather because it looked right into me.

Every day we slaughter our finest impulses. That is why we get a heartache when we read those lines written by the hand of a master and recognize them as our own, as the tender shoots which we stifled because we lacked the faith to believe in our own powers, our own criterion of truth and beauty. Every man, when he gets quiet, when he becomes desperately honest with himself, is capable of uttering profound truths. We all derive from the same source. There is no mystery about the origin of things. We are all part of creation, all kings, all poets, all musicians; we have only to open up, only to discover what is already there.

I knew it for truth. Every day. Holding back. Not writing.

That day we turned in our term papers to Megiddo we also got into a discussion about *Death of a Salesman* which we had been reading out loud in class.

"Willie Loman is a loser," said Claude Moss.

"A loser by whose standards?" Megiddo asked, "and what has he lost? I'm not disagreeing with you."

"He lost his job," said Dolly.

"And his relationship with his sons really," Gina Dichlich added.

"And his marriage for the most part," said Miranda Savitch.

"Faith in himself," I suggested.

"Pretty much everything," Manny said, "in a major way."

"Good answers, all," Mr. Megiddo said. "What does it feel like to lose something? Or someone?"

"Achey emptiness," I said.

"Sadness and panic 'cause you want to get it back," Dolly said.

"You miss that person a lot," Miranda said. "It's amazing how close you can be with someone and then not."

"And that's painful," said Mr. Megiddo, "that lost intimacy."

"Oh yes," said Miranda, "and just kind of always there."

"In your stomach especially," Claire said.

"All things are impermanent," Manny interjected. "When the Buddha speaks of 'suffering' he uses the word *dukkha* which really means more like discomfort, discontent, like what Miranda and Claire are talking about. When you lose things and try to hold onto them, you know, like avoiding the fact that you can't hold onto anything ever, that's *dukkha*. It's all about letting go. Then there is no loss."

"Wow," said Mr. Megiddo, "Unexpected angle on it, Manny. Nice. I want to keep looking at this expression of *poena damni*, the pain of loss, when we get back together tomorrow. What does losing feel like? Your answers to that question will lead us back into Willy Loman's tragedy at its deepest level. Life is an ongoing negotiation, a compromise with the reality of existence, with our fellow human beings, and with the cosmos at large. And when we are forced to make these compromises, something is always lost in the deal."

I looked at Miranda and was puzzled by her difference now that Lorelei had raised the implication that her note to me–*you remind me of the little prince! luv, miranda*–was perhaps not genuine.

But on the other hand I held onto the possibility that Lorelei was being deceptive for some reason. She was well practiced at gathering inside information and then using it against people later. "Lori–Lies" the girls sometimes called her.

A couple of days after my fulcrum-shifting phone conversation with Lorelei, I went over to her house to fool around and see if I could start getting her a little more heated up about our bodily interactions.

"I'm here to ravish and ravage you," I said when she greeted me at the door.

"So you say, Lance Atlas," she walked into the living room and put on *After The Gold Rush.*

"How are you?" she asked and leaned in toward me and our mouths engaged in a soft quick kiss.

I thought of Miranda and all that was false.

Now that you found yourself

losing your mind

Are you here again?

Finding that what you once

thought was real

Is gone, and changing?

Lorelei's silent passionless love play was but a symptom of a decided and desiccating lack of chemistry between us.

Lorelei had a beautiful face and a pair of firm braless breasts that she let me touch and suckle, but with nary a motion to explore my body.

In my sexual fantasies I'd turn her into a slightly more enthusiastic partner, jacking off happily to images of fucking her on that living room couch.

As I'd never seen her bedroom it was difficult to imagine fucking her in her there.

Always the couch.

Such is my feeble sexual imagination.

Now that you made yourself

love me

Do you think

I can change it in a day?

How can I place you above me?

Am I lying to you when I say

That I believe in you

I believe in you

"I'm having the weirdest *déja vu* right now," I said after an extended session with her right nipple.

"Let it happen," she said, "See how long you can keep it going."

"Eh, gone already," I said. "What is *déja vu* really?"

"It's a universally felt sensation, that's for sure."

"I used to have this theory that you are remembering a dream. Manny says it's because all time is one moment and always already happening, but I don't know if that's him or Bubba Free John speaking. I also heard this one guy on KPFK say it was proof of reincarnation."

"I think it's probably more a synapse thing, a short circuit."

"'Splain?"

"You know how the normal path of experience is, first, perception, in the present moment while it's happening, and then, next, it gets sent into your memory bank?"

"Right."

"Well, I think in *déja vu* what's happening is there's a short circuit in the neural pathway, the experience simultaneously enters your present perception and your memory bank, so that you're living it and remembering it at the same time."

"A brain fart."

"If you must put it that way. It's like a single path crossing itself."

"The intersection of Curson and Curson," I said and thought of Miranda.

Lorelei never let me meet her parents.

She only invited me over when they weren't home.

"My father's not allowed to be alone with me," she said once.

"What?"

"Court order. Part of the divorce."

"Ah, I thought you live with both your parents."

"I do."

"But they're divorced."

"Yeah but neither of them wants to move out so they both live here but my dad is not allowed to be alone with me."

"Why?"

"I don't remember," she said.

"Where are they right now?"

"I think they went to the movies and then they're going shopping for groceries."

"Together?"

"Yes."

"They go to the movies and do the grocery shopping together," I said.

"They do pretty much everything together."

"But they're divorced."

"Yes."

"If they like doing pretty much everything together then why are they divorced?"

"I didn't say they *like* doing pretty much everything together, I just said they *do* pretty much everything together."

"But why?"

"Because they don't know how to do anything else."

"Why don't they just stay married?"

"Because my mother said the thought of being married to him, the thought that she was ever married to him, disgusts her."

"I don't get it."

"She spends a lot of time crying in her bedroom."

"Where does your dad sleep?"

"They sleep in the same bed."

"What?"

"I have no way of explaining any of this. I try to make sense of it and keep track of it in my notebook. My notebook is the evolving map of my personal circumstance, my experience of being alive in the world, the fact of being Lorelei Lux in this body at this time in the city of Los Angeles with these two parents."

"What's your dad's trip?"

"My dad's pretty obsessive," she said, "as I've told you."

"And he's not allowed to be alone with you."

"Correct."

"For unknown reasons."

"Oh, the reasons are known. I just don't remember them. Or it. Dee might remember more but neither of us brings the subject up. Marriage is a strange concept," she said.

"Yeah, it's just one of those milestones we cling to. I don't know, I sometimes think life is nothing more than birth, marriage, children, grandchildren, shuffleboard, and death."

"I agree, somewhat," Lorelei responded, "though I suspect there's a bit more to it than just those milestones."

"Or millstones."

"There's a rich in-between. Come now, you're an artist, Lance Atlas, you already know the richness. But, yes, milestones tend to define us, and, like you said, they can be millstones."

I was always thinking

of games that I was playing.

Trying to make

the best of my time

"Only Love Can Break Your Heart" played as I kissed her and lifted the bottom of her shirt over her boobs again so I could feel them up and get my mouth and tongue all over them.

But only love

can break your heart

Try to be sure

right from the start

I teased at her nipples with my teeth and tongue, but she didn't respond audibly or physically other than stroking the top of my head and giggling occasionally either out of nervousness or ticklishness but it was impossible to tell which.

Yes only love

can break your heart

What if your world

should fall apart?

"Birth, marriage, children, grandchildren, shuffleboard, and death, huh?" she said as she she pulled her shirt back down.

"That about sums it up, yup yup."

"Maybe you're right, Lance Atlas. Maybe it's all that bleak."

"I love you," I said.

"So you say, Lance Atlas."

"*I've been really trying, baby, trying to hold back this feeling for so long,*" I sang and held her hands in mine, "*And if you feel like I feel, baby, come on, come on, ooh, let's get it on.*"

"Don't call me that."

"What?"

"Baby."

"It's just a song," I said, "That wasn't me calling you baby. I thought it might make you laugh."

"Well just don't," she said, nudging me away.

I felt like going home after that.

"I need to go get some homework done," I said, "We've got nonstop rehearsals ahead."

"Yes, I must needs get to math problems on this goodly eve myself."

"What are you doing for the next outside novel in Megiddo's?"

"*An American Tragedy.*"

"Dreiser."

"Yes."

"Dolly read that a while back. She liked it but she said it gave her a stomach ache."

"Dahlia Ferris would have such a reaction, yes. I love Dreiser."

"Isn't that book like a 1,000 pages long?"

"Close to, yes. I read fast. What about you? What are you reading now?"

"*On The Road,* Jack Kerouac," I said and waved as I left for the bus-walk home.

Lorelei nodded goodbye.

3

A few days before, Mr. Megiddo had introduced us to the Beat Movement with "Howl," a conflagration of language that cleared my head for something new.

"Allen Ginsberg," Megiddo said, "The great breath again. It spends a long time inhaling, but oh my when it exhales, it exhales epic fire, the emanation of a happy dragon. Remember Walt Whitman from last semester, and last century? Well this is the most recent incarnation of that presence."

His reading of "Howl" was dramatic and riveting. Much that was unnecessary fell away from my head in the course of those minutes.

"angelheaded hipsters burning for the ancient heavenly connection to the starry dynamo in the machinery of night," Mr. Megiddo read and the words teased me, taunted me, welcomed me, enveloped me.

obscene odes on the windows of the skull

I sat beneath a waterfall, my mouth was open to the pouring forth.

who sweetened the snatches of a million girls trembling in the sunset

I sat in a lake of fire, my sex open to every ventilating dragon breath.

who dreamt and made incarnate gaps in Time & Space through images juxtaposed,

and trapped the archangel of the soul between 2 visual images and joined the

elemental verbs and set the noun and dash of consciousness together jumping with

sensation of Pater Omnipotens Aeterna Deus

Words about words about words about words. I became a bivalve in the deepest reef, living a perpetual witness-existence, there but to watch and wait, amazed.

to recreate the syntax and measure of poor human prose and stand before you

speechless and intelligent and shaking with shame, rejected yet confessing out the

soul to conform to the rhythm of thought in his naked and endless head,

the madman bum and angel beat in Time, unknown, yet putting down here what might

be left to say in time come after death

I was seeing neon, a glow like masterful flashworks, calling me to peek into the ark of the covenant.

"Isn't that something?" Mr. Megiddo said at Howl's conclusion.

"Hippy-trippy," said Buzzy Lagniappe.

"Out there," said Claire Farnaway, "Way out there."

"Not out there," Manny corrected, "In here," and held his fist to his heart.

"Lance?" Mr. Megiddo wanted my take.

"*I am speechless and intelligent and shaking with shame*," I quoted from the mimeograph in front of me.

Megiddo smiled.

"Here, we have time for something else before the bell rings," he said and handed out another poem. "Remember back when we were talking about what it feels like to lose something or someone? Here's another Ginsberg poem, one which, I think, captures it as perfectly as anybody in words. It's called 'Kaddish.'"

"Like the Hebrew prayer," Manny said.

"Yes. What is the Kaddish?"

"A prayer you say when you're mourning someone's death," said Manny.

"And is the Kaddish a prayer for relief from grief?"

"No, actually it's mostly a praising of God and also a prayer for peace."

"Which sort of ties into the mourning of death, wanting to be at peace with the loss."

"Totally," said Manny, "no more dukkha."

"You're a Jewish Buddhist," Megiddo said.

"A Juddhist," Manny said.

"Juddhist Priest," Jim Lord said and gestured Satan-horns.

The classwide laughter subsided and Mr. Megiddo continued.

"Ginsberg's 'Kaddish' is the poet mourning the death of his mother."

There were moments in the poem where Megiddo was choking up while he read and I wondered—I guess we all did—if he was thinking of some personal loss that still haunts him.

"*And you're out*," Megiddo intoned, "*Death let you out, Death had the Mercy, you're done with your century, done with God, done with the path thru it—Done with yourself at last—Pure—Back to the Babe dark before your Father, before us all—before the world.*"

He finished as the bell was ringing and said we'd break down both 'Howl' and 'Kaddish' the next day.

I stayed after class and told Megiddo how overwhelmed and affected I was by the Ginsberg poetry and thanked him for exposing me to it.

"I knew you'd like it," he said. "Go read some more of it."

"I was thinking of doing *On The Road* for my last outside novel essay," I said to him.

"Kerouac," he said, "yes, perfect. Read Kerouac and Ginsberg concurrently. It will definitely supercharge your brainwaves."

"Definitely, yeah. But thank you. You crack everything open for me, Mr. Megiddo."

"I try to do that for everybody," he said.

"Of course. I'm not the only one caught up in the holy spirit, believe me."

I looked over and saw that Gina Dichlich was waiting to talk to him, so I excused myself.

"Hey, you," she said and ruffled the top of my jewfro as I walked by.

Gina Dichlich had never touched me before.

I went and got *On The Road* from the school library during lunch and started reading it that night after rehearsal.

I was so into it I forgot to call Lorelei.

"You didn't call last night," she said when I saw her at Nutrition the next day, "10 demerits for you, Lance Atlas."

"Yeah, I-um, I was reading *On The Road* and just, you know how it is."

"A gentlemanly excuse."

"You should read it," I said, ignoring her barb, "It's amazing."

"Maybe I will."

"You should."

"What do you want to do this weekend?"

"Other than make passionate love to you on a mountaintop at dawn?"

"Don't be rude."

"I think we're pretty much tied up with rehearsals, aren't we?"

"I think you're right. Crap."

"Yeah, it sucks," I said, "'cause my parents are going to be out of town and I won't get to enjoy the freedom of the house without them there, not until late at night after rehearsal anyway."

My parents were making a rare foray away from home, Las Vegas for the weekend, and on such occasions my sister and I would trade off sleeping in their king-size bed and being luxurious.

On my night in the parental bed, I lay naked atop the quilt and called Lorelei on the telephone.

It had been a hard day of rehearsal and I wanted to talk to her outside of that context.

"Hey," I said.

"Hello, boyfriend."

"That's me."

"I know."

"What are you doing?"

"Writing in my notebook."

"About what?"

"Not you."

"Which means you *are* writing about me."

"You are wronger than you think you are."

"What are you writing about then? Tell your man."

"You don't get to know that."

"Top secret."

"The secretest. I've already told you too much about it."

"I think we should make love on a mountaintop, really."

"You're weird."

"Look who's caulking, Mr. Black."

"What does that mean?"

"It's my sister Joy's way of saying, 'Look who's calling the kettle black,' but it comes out 'Look who's caulking, Mr. Black.'"

"Interesting," Lorelei hummed.

"You have to come over and meet her one day."

"I will have to do that."

I couldn't tell if Lorelei was just being silent or if she was writing something in her notebook.

"So, what are you doing right now, other than talking to me?" she asked.

"I'm, uh, lying here naked on my parents' bed. Does that turn you on?"

"No, not really."

I was thinking about fucking her. I kept picturing it with my eyes closed and sort of playing with my dick. Not really jacking off. Pondering the possibility. The scenario was that she'd come over to meet Joy and then we'd end up fucking on my parents' bed. But I couldn't concentrate on the conversation and the fantasy at the same time.

"Well, anyway that's what I'm doing, my darling," I said.

"Don't call me that."

"Sorry."

"My father calls me darling."

I could think of no reply to that statement so we shared some more silence. It was part of our natural rhythm together.

"Sing me a song," Lorelei said, "lying naked in the dark on your parents' bed."

"How did you know I was in the dark?"

"Why wouldn't you be?"

"Zackly," I said. I was stalling 'cause I thought it'd be perfect to sing the opening of the Styx song "Lorelei" but I was having trouble remembering the words. Finally I grabbed a few.

"*When I think of Lorelei my head turns all around*," I sang all high and strained, what I remembered of the song from hearing it on the radio, "*As gentle as a butterfly she moves without a sound.* That's all I know from it, or, wait, no, the chorus, *Lorelei let's live together brighter than the stars forever.*"

"Impressive choice, Lance Atlas," Lorelei said, "Sing me the whole song one day."

"I will."

I didn't know how I was going to accomplish that because I didn't know anybody who owned it and I wasn't about to spend money on a Styx album.

"Now tell me a story," Lorelei says.

"I don't know any stories."

"Oh, you are full of stories, Lance Atlas. Let one out for me. Tell me a story you're never going to tell to anyone else ever again. It'll be mine and mine alone."

"Get me started," I said, "Spark the fire, Cap'n Flint."

"Aye, matey, tell me a story about . . ." I could never hear her breathing over the phone so there was just this silence as dark as the room, " . . . Tell me a story about the boy who had stars in his heart."

"OK, uh, there was this boy named, uh–"

"–Lance Atlas."

"Really?"

"Yes. Continue. I'm already getting bored. That's good. Boredom can get you through everything. Have you ever noticed that? Once you get good at being bored you never have to worry about being stuck somewhere with nothing to read. You always know what to do. Continue."

"All right, so this boy named Lance Atlas once knew this freak named Emperor Constantine. Emperor Constantine was his barber."

"Excellent. You know what I like, Lance Atlas."

"Emperor Constantine held court in a Melrose Avenue storefront called *Byzantium* between Martel and Fuller, overseeing a decayed empire of faded hippie impotence."

"Hippie impotence. Nice assonance."

"He resembled Uncle Norman Tinker from *The Courtship of Eddie's Father.*"

"Yes."

"The Emperor had a heaping swoop of brown hair held in place by The Dry Look because the wet-head was dead. Did you just snicker?"

"No."

"OK, so, there was also a bevy of beautiful women in tight bellbottom jeans hanging around the shop. Multiple love partners of Constantine without a doubt."

"Oh God."

"A vintage phone booth stood in one corner, beanbag chairs against the back wall, a jukebox that played Chicago and Three Dog Night incessantly. The room just reeked of incense and sex and hair products."

"Ew."

"As Lance Atlas–by now a teenager–sat in the Emperor's chair and gazed at the painting of a shackled Samson bringing down the columns of a building, he thought about the first time he'd come in for a haircut. When he was 4 years old. It was the first haircut he'd ever gotten from someone other than his mother. Emperor Constantine sat him in the chair with a booster seat and wrapped a bib around him that covered his whole body and he felt good and warm under that bib like he was safe there."

"I like that. Keep going."

"The snipping sound of the scissors was like music and he closed his eyes to listen but was stung within seconds by the slicing off of his upper ear by Emperor Constantine."

"Holy crap!"

"The top of Lance's ear flew from Emperor Constantine's scissors as he waved them in a panic. 'Oh my god,' he kept saying. Little Lance's mother was understandably freaking out. She held a towel to the boy's ear to try to stop the bleeding as he wailed from the seething pain. He couldn't remember if his mom paid for the haircut or not that day. She took the boy and the severed piece of his ear to the emergency room where they were unable to reattach the cartilage and he was told he would have to live with only a partial ear."

I had to pause for a moment to catch my brain.

"Don't stop," she said.

"I've already reached the climax, but here's the sweet denouement: The doctor said to him, 'You had to lose a piece of your ear, but we poured a whole bunch of stars into the wound so that the ear might not look perfect but it will feel perfect and work perfect and once those stars have done their job on the ear they'll find their way to your heart and that's where they'll stay forever because you can't ever lose stars once they're in your heart.' And always remembering what the doctor said, the boy grew up to be a musician with ears that, while not perfect, were certainly very very good. And the stars in his heart bring him light and warmth to this day no matter where he is and he loves knowing that he can't ever lose them."

Not a sound to be heard from Lorelei's end of the line.

Had I put her to sleep?

"The End," I said.

"You win that round, Lance Atlas. Bravo. Bravissimo. Just swell."

"Just for you, shweetheart," I bogarted.

"No, it's not. You're going to tell it to a whole bunch of other people too. Was that a true story?"

"You don't get to know that," I said with a vengeance.

"But the protagonist's name is Lance Atlas, Lance Atlas."

"Because you told me to name him that."

"You could have refused. It's your story."

"I'd never refuse you anything, baby."

"Ew, don't call me baby. I told you. You sound like my father."

"What can I call you?"

"Lorelei."

"No pet names?"

"I'm not your pet, Lance Atlas."

"But you are my girlfriend."

"That I am."

"I'd never refuse you anything, girlfriend."

Lorelei surprised me with a giggle.

"I made you laugh," I said.

"I love you, Lance Atlas."

"And I love you, Lorelei Lux."

"Hang on, I'm writing that down in my notebook."

"I do kind of have stars in my heart though," I said.

"Interesting . . . do tell, boyfriend."

"I have a heart murmur, you know, arrhythmia, and sometimes it feels as if there are billions of stars shaking around in my chest and sometimes even crashing into each other. I get these hot bursts and flutters."

"Wow. See? You are the boy with stars in his heart. And did you really have the top of your ear cut off?"

"Well, the barber did actually cut my ear when I was 4, but no pieces were severed off. I just bled a lot. And my barber's name really was Emperor Constantine, or at least that's what he called himself, and his barber shop was called *Byzantium* for real."

"Your mother kept taking you back to him even though he cut your ear?"

"My mom said she didn't want to make him feel bad. 'Everybody makes mistakes,' she said."

"Interesting . . . Your story almost made me fall asleep. A high compliment."

"And all-the-way putting you to sleep would be the highest compliment."

"Exactly. Without boredom there is no creativity. And there is no creativity without boredom."

"Symbiosis."

"You are correct," Lorelei said. "Now here's an unrelated question for you: When we were spinning together at the sock hop did you know we'd end up together like this?"

"Nyeah, I knew something was up, but it didn't seem like you reciprocated."

"That was by design."

"I understand how that works."

"I know you do."

"OK, now it's your turn to tell *me* a story," I said in order to shift away from the sock hop destiny plotline because I knew eventually I'd mythologize it into something it really wasn't just to jive with her internal narrative.

"Launch me, Lance Atlas."

"OK . . . Tell me a story about Lorelei Lux, the little princess who is the guardian of secrets."

"You're just trying to get into my notebook, good sir. I see right through your little ploy."

"It's not your notebook I'm trying to get into."

"Harumph. Very well then, you libertine," she said and I heard her breathe into the phone for the first time, "Back in the darkest days of the kingdom, when the King's enemies were many and his resources were few, there dwelt an enchanting girl, the daughter of the King himself, Princess Lorelei."

"Lorelei Lux."

"Princess Lorelei Lux, or just simply Princess Lorelei as most people called her, was a precocious child who loved everything she came into contact with, toys, dirt, food, bugs, even her fellow human beings. 'The Laughing Princess' as the courtiers and the townspeople alike referred to her because of her constant state of good humor, was, in those darkest days, assigned to be the Guardian of Secrets in a room for precious treasure hidden in the bowels of the palace. She was equipped with a bell and a ram's horn as signals for help should any invaders approach the room and attempt to plunder her booty."

"Heh. Booty."

"Don't heckle my story. Booty as in treasure."

"Dang. I was thinking of your nice assonance."

"Don't be inappropriate. Shall I proceed?"

"Yeah yeah. This is great. Sorry. You are a genius. Go ahead."

"One night Princess Lorelei heard her parents having a tremendous fight with voices loud and much slamming of doors. There had only been a short silence after the fighting subsided when Princess Lorelei saw her father storming down the corridor right toward her. 'What happened, Daddy?' little Lorelei asked the King. 'Nothing, baby,' he said, 'Daddy needs you to open up and let him in, darling.' 'But you told me not to let anybody in,' the Princess said. 'Except me,' said the King pushing his way in and locking the door. Once inside he began tearing the chamber apart, touching the treasure, grabbing it, putting his mouth on it. He was like a character in a cartoon saying, 'Mine, mine, all mine,' while he rolled around and pressed himself against the treasure and Princess Lorelei couldn't do anything about it. She pretended she was watching it from far away on a passing asteroid. 'Don't tell your mother I did this,' he warned the Princess, 'or I'll take your

353

treasure away forever.' 'You already have,' she cried and sat in her own shame and anger at herself for letting him in. For a while he came back every night to mess with the treasure until one night he just stopped coming and told her that everything was ruined. Ever since then the Princess only talks to the King when other people are around. The End."

Neither of us spoke for a phone eternity. At least a minute.

"I–um," I hesitated.

Dang, dude.

"Sorry," she said.

"No no," I said, "You got into it. You were telling it. It's a sad story."

"Yes," she said.

"Do you have that story written down in your notebook?"

"This notebook contains everything, Lance Atlas."

"I love you," I said and felt the bottomless depth of her darkness.

"You too," she said.

"I can keep your secrets for you if you want," I said.

"No no. They're mine mine all mine. I need them to stay hidden. Like wishes."

"I get it."

"I know. You have secrets too."

"Doesn't everybody?"

"I suppose even God has a secret."

"Dude, we *are* God's secret."

"You make me smile, Lance Atlas."

"Like a Cheshire moon on the beach?"

"Should I know that reference?"

"Nah. It's a secret," I teased.

"Oh, bother," she poohed.

"Tell me another story."

"No, I've told you too much already."

"Maybe tomorrow then."

"See you tomorrow, boyfriend," she said and hung up.

Sometimes talking to Lorelei Lux could be the coolest thing in the world.

4

I had spent zero time, outside of class, with the cool nerd crew, not even Manny, of late, what with *Guys & Dolls* rehearsals and Lorelei, but Whitman Rust and Claude Moss came up to me at Nutrition one morning and said, "Dude, we have to go to see *Star Wars* together when it comes out."

"I'm probably going to go see it with Lorelei," I said, "You know how it is."

"Chicks, man," bemoaned Claude Moss, "always fucking our shit up."

"Damn straight," seconded Whit, "But let's at least try to all go to the same showing so we can talk about it after," Whit said, "We all have to be there together to identify the iconic lines immediately. It's our sacred mission."

"And then repeat them endlessly to each other and all of our classmates," said Claude.

"My geeky brothers," I toasted and held out my fingertips for the touching.

"And we can hang in the car and get high right before," Whit added, "if you wanna drive with us."

"I've got my mom's station wagon that night," Claude said, "Buzzy and Manny are coming with us too."

"I'll check with the lady," I said.

The previews for *Star Wars* looked amazing, and I was definitely keen on the idea of being able to trade great lines from the film and talk about it afterward, so I ran the idea past Lorelei and she was cool with the hanging out afterward part, less so with the getting high before part, but she kind of had to deal with it because we got a ride from Claude.

"Nah'll abstain," I declined when Whit handed me the joint, "out of respect."

"Respect for the dead," Claude muttered to Whit but we could all hear him and they both laughed.

Star Wars was playing at the Plitt Theatre in Century City which wasn't one of the normal theaters we'd go to. We passed by the Avco on Wilshire where we were originally going to see it but the line was already too long so we went to the Plitt as did a lot of people as it turned out.

It was the first time any of us had paid $4.00 to see a movie.

"I hope we don't have to sit in the front row," Lorelei pointed out the line's length, "That gives me a headache."

"I'll battle for good seats," I said with false bravado and flexing my biceps which made Lorelei smile slightly.

Lorelei was at her most beautiful when she smiled. Her veneer came down and she was this electric sunflower, open and free instead of all turned in on herself.

"Knowing you we'll end up sitting separately at opposite ends of the front row," she teased.

"Have faith, woman," I said and flexed my muscles again.

In addition to Whit and Buzzy and Manny and Claude, Dolly was also there with Sharon Rose and Justine Balthazar and Misty Winters.

Heaven Sender attended with one of the Dirth twins, and they appeared to be double-dating with Evelyn Childs and David Harkins.

It was also the first appearance in public of Sandy Clay and Madeline Baker as a couple.

Miranda and Freddy were there too.

"I approve," Freddy Snow gave a thumbs-up to Lorelei and me as we held hands in front of the Plitt.

"Why, thank you," I said.

"Dude," he nodded and pulled Miranda closer to him.

"How are you guys?" Miranda asked.

"Good," I said as Lorelei pulled me closer to her.

"Nice," Miranda answered as she and Freddy started heading to the back of the line.

Lorelei, her arm hooked to my arm, started skipping in place.

"Lou lou skip to my lou," she sang and indicated I should skip in place with her, "Lou lou skip to my lou."

"Lou lou skip to my lou," I sang, "Skip to my lou my darling."

"Don't call me that," Lorelei said.

"Sorry. Forgot how the song ended."

I looked at her sadness and tried to kiss her but she tucked her head into my neck.

I've never known a deeper enigma than Lorelei Lux, an enigma which drew me in ravenously yet locked me out militantly.

For all of her stilted formality and cerebral sophistication, she possessed many childlike qualities.

Lorelei still had dolls and played chanting games I vaguely remembered from elementary school.

One time when we were hanging out backstage at a *Guys & Dolls* rehearsal, I thought she said, "Flea."

"Where?" I looked at my arms and chest as if for a flea.

"*Flee!*"

I stared at her.

"Now you say 'flee' back. *Flee!*"

"*Flee!*"

"*Flee fly!*"

"Repeat?"

"Yes. *Flee fly!*"

"*Flee fly!*"

"*Flee fly flew!*"

"Why are we practicing verb tenses?"

"*Flee fly flew!*"

"*Flee fly flew!*" I acquiesced.

"*Cumalama cumalama cumalama veesta,*" she sang and pointed to me.

"*Cumalama cumalama cumalama veesta,*" I dutifully repeated.

"*Cumalama cumalama cumalama veesta,*" she sang again and I answered:

"Cumalama cumalama cumalama veesta."

"Oh no no no na ta veesta," she sang on.

"Oh no no no na ta veesta," I echoed but then could not follow the rest because she segued into an elaborate string of fast nonsense syllables I was unable to keep track of.

Lorelei also loved saying goodbye by playing pat-a-cake or, even more often, the "Oh Jolly Playmate" hand game thing which I didn't know how to do so I was mostly lost and would just hold my hands up and let her do her thing.

"Oh jolly playmate, I cannot play with you," she sang the alternate version, *"My dolly has the flu and diarrhea too."*

It made me think of that schoolyard version of the Addams Family theme song.

The Addams Family started

When Uncle Fester farted

They really are retarded

The Addams Family

I never knew if those things originated on elementary school playgrounds or were cribbed from old issues of *MAD* Magazine.

"Does your dolly have the flu?" Lorelei Lux asked after one said chant.

I knew she was digging at me with the 'dolly' reference.

As had happened when I was with Claire, I stopped spending time with Dolly once I was fully involved with Lorelei.

We weren't talking on the phone anymore either.

"We should hang out," Dolly said when we bumped into each other on our way to the bathroom at the Plitt right after Star Wars ended, she to go pee, I to go wash my hand.

Making out with Lorelei during the film I'd started massaging her vulva through her jeans thinking maybe that would stoke some passion and she did grab my arm a couple of times, which was encouraging. Afterward she smelled my hand.

"Ew," she said, "Go wash."

I had gotten up during the credits to hit the bathroom before the crowds got there, and it was en route to doing due diligence at the request of m'lady that I encountered Dolly in the lobby.

I'd see her everyday in classes, and, as she was stage managing *Guys & Dolls*, we'd sometimes gab at rehearsals briefly. But that was it.

"Yes. We have to hang," I said.

"You know Lori's a crazy-ass bitch, right?"

"So you've told me," I shrugged.

"Stalled at 2nd base I'm guessing."

I shrugged.

"She lets you have at her nice perky titties but nothing else."

Dang, dude. How do chicks just know that shit?

"Lori," Dolly shook her head. "Anyway I've got nothing currently on the front burner, loverboy," Dolly said, "so when you're done playing Barbie and Ken."

"Barbie and Ken?"

"You know, sex without genitalia."

She blew me a kiss and slipped into the ladies room just as the crowd began to emerge from the theatre.

"Darth Vader Lives!" Buzzy Lagniappe yelped and intercepted my bathroom run.

It was great to see Buzzy going to public events and functioning.

Lorelei joined me and hooked my harm.

We all ended up at Ships on La Cienega.

Ships was mostly booths but we got the big table in the back so that we could all fit, though we had to steal a couple of chairs from nearby.

"Use the force, Luke," Manny said as he made Svengali gesticulations at the toaster.

There was a toaster on every table at Ships.

"I loved when Han Solo said, *'Either I'm going to kill her or I'm beginning to like her,'*" Whit said.

"Totally relate," Claude said.

I could too but obviously couldn't say that.

"*I have a very bad feeling about this,*" I said instead, in the voice of Han Solo.

"Han was the best character I thought," Miranda said.

"And the hottest," Dolly added.

"I thought you'd be more into Princess Leia," Manny said to Miranda.

"Excuse me?" Miranda said.

"I mean like she's powerful and independent and all that stuff."

"I thought Han was the best character," Miranda repeated without responding to Manny.

"The reluctant hero," I said.

"Defenly," said Miranda.

"That's most of us," I said, "isn't it?"

"Yeahzackly," Miranda slurred a little and we looked at each other boldly for a moment like nothing had changed.

"I mean, most of us are capable of being heroes but we'd all have to be dragged into it. Like Han," I said, "At first he's just in it for the money."

"But he responded when called upon," Miranda said.

"The moment it stopped being about the money is when he became a hero," I said.

"May be," said Miranda, again sharing an extended glance with me as Freddy put his arm around her.

"Harrison Ford was in *American Graffiti*," Sharon Rose said.

"Who was he?" Dolly asked.

"The guy in the cowboy hat who races against Paul Le Mat."

"Oh yeah, huh," Claude said.

"Paul Le Mat is the coolest," Whit said.

"Way cooler than Fonzie," Claude said.

Lorelei was completely silent the whole time we were at Ships.

Every so often she'd open up her notebook and write something down.

But mostly she just sat there, uncommunicative other than intermittently digging her nails into my kneecap under the table.

Eventually I got the hint that she wanted to leave, but we were beholden to Claude for our ride home.

The worst part of the evening was that when I held Lorelei's face to kiss her goodnight, she pulled away and said, "I thought I told you to wash your hand."

5

The 72 hours leading up to our first performance of *Guys & Dolls* we pretty much lived at school.

That week we were excused from our classes on Tuesday and Wednesday, and opening night was Thursday.

All day tech rehearsals on Tuesday then a complete run-through with tech on Tuesday night.

Wednesday day, mini–performances of "Take Back Your Mink" and "Sit Down You're Rocking The Boat" at assemblies for the student body every period.

Final dress rehearsal on Wednesday night.

Demi Mondesi, Mimi, Sharon Rose, Bart Scribner, and Lorelei came into rehearsal on Tuesday laughing loudly.

"So we went out looking for costumes," Demi Mondesi said.

Mr. Hill had sent them out to find Salvation Army style clothing for their roles as the Save-A-Soul Mission band, and the administration had agreed to let them leave campus.

"And we thought we'd go to the Salvation Army thrift store 'cause where better to get Salvation Army uniforms, right?" she giggled, "And the lady there said, 'Um, we don't carry Salvation Army uniforms here,' and we just went 'Huh? But this is the fucking Salvation Army store! You don't carry your own uniforms?' and she told us you have to join the Salvation Army to get a Salvation Army uniform."

"And this is funny?" Mr. Hill scolded, "We open Thursday night, and you have no costumes."

"No, no, we got them," Demi answered, "We went to Goodwill. They had a grip of Salvation Army uniforms," and they all pulled their duds out of plastic bags.

I felt uncomfortable about my performance and the way Mr. Hill wanted me to shout all my lines until I uttered my first line on opening night, "I come here to shoot crap! Let's shoot crap!" and the audience exploded with laughter.

Mr. Hill had made a good call.

Having the shortest guy in the cast play an intimidating thug named Big Jule who speaks in this booming scary voice hit just the right funny bone.

I wore plaid pants, a straw fedora, and a green necktie with a huge letter J– embroidered by Mimi–covering its length.

The rousing finale, our re-worked funked up version of the title song, brought the audience to its feet with hoots and whistles attendant.

When you see a guy reach for stars in the sky

You can bet that he's doing it for some doll

After the performance we all quickly removed our make-up and costumes and went out into the Rotunda to greet the members of the audience.

Miranda approached, smiling.

"I had no idea, Lance," she said, holding out her hand for shaking, "Bravo."

"Thank you," I said, holding her hand until Freddy dragged her away, barely nodding his acknowledgement in my direction.

As the end of the school year approached, my parents started noodging me about getting a summer job.

Manny was planning to apply for a job at the Hollywood Bowl and said I should come along and do an interview too 'cause it would be a very cool gig, just 4 nights a week and you got to hear all the concerts for free.

On a Saturday afternoon in early June I tagged along with Manny to the

Bowl.

There were hundreds of kids our age there, all filling out applications and waiting to be interviewed by one of the various managers who were seated behind a long table in the middle of a large empty room that was just below and behind the stage.

When our names were called, Manny was sent to the far end to talk to Herb Smeltz, the manager in charge of guest services.

I was instructed to see Javier Contreras, the house manager. The boss of the ushers.

"Hello," I said, "Lance Atlas."

We shook hands and he told me to be seated.

"Mr. Atlas," he looked at my application, "Your only other job was—"

"—Paper route. Delivering the *Herald-Examiner.*"

"Yes. Fine. How much do you know about classical music?"

"I love classical music," I said. He bore down on me with an intense and steady gaze. "But I'm not really that educated in it. I am a musician myself and a composer. Creating music is the most important thing in the world to me."

"If I put you on the 1st Prom, you think you can handle it? It's where our box seats are. Longtime season subscribers and a good number of celebrities and dignitaries from around the world. Mr. Metzger's box is there."

"Who's Mr. Metzger?"

"Gerhart Metzger is the President of the L.A. Philharmonic Association. El Jefe."

"I believe I can handle it."

"An usher on the 1st Prom is the face of the Hollywood Bowl experience. We expect you to be attentive, well-groomed, and charming even when

365

some of our more demanding patrons are being unpleasant to you, and I promise you that will happen occasionally."

"I look forward to the challenge," I said.

"Good good. I'm very pleased to offer you a position here for the summer. I'm going to pair you with one of our veteran ushers. She'll show you the ropes," he looked at me some more. "See you in a couple of weeks."

We stood, shook hands again, and I walked over to the door where Manny was talking to Gina Dichlich.

"Hey!" Gina said as I walked over.

"Hi!" I said. It was nice to see her there.

"What did you get?" she asked.

"Usher," I said, "1st Prom."

"Whoa, shit," she said, "Wow. I'm up on 3rd Prom I think."

"Did you meet with Contreras?" I asked.

"No, I had some other dude. His last name was either White or Black. I can't remember which."

"Was he white?" I asked.

"Yes. Very much so."

"Then his name is Black."

"You know him?"

"No, but haven't you noticed that most people named Black are white and most people named White are black?"

"I never . . . yeah, huh?" she said and laughed, "That's cray-zee."

Manny frogged his inhaled laughter.

"That's is so true," he said, "High–larious."

"What about you, dude?" I asked him, "What'd you get?"

"Runner."

"What's that?"

"The dudes who bring people the meals they ordered and we also bring them the collapsible dinner table thingies."

"Bummer," I said.

"Nah, it's cool, man. It's harder work and longer hours but allegedly you get lots of tip money so it's overall more lucrative I guess."

"Coolness. You're supplying the herb this summer then."

All three of us laughed.

"I just have to figure out how I'm going to get to and from here on a regular basis. Probably the Highland bus makes the most sense, don't you think?"

"I'd drive you," Manny said, "but runners have to get here earlier and stay later than the ushers.

"Where do you live?" Gina asked.

"Citrus and Beverly," I said.

"I just live over on Fuller and Oakwood–"

"–Oh yeah, I remember I ran into you that night on the corner a while back."

"Yeah," Gina said.

"With your friend Wendy."

"Right. You didn't want to smoke out with us."

"Dude, I was already way stoned that night. And did I tell you I ended up going to a hockey game with Wendy? I didn't know she was also friends with Rudy. She has to be a lesbo, right?"

"Uh, yeah," Gina said, her eyes a chasm I couldn't fathom, "But anyway I can totally drive you, no problem."

"Dang, that'd be excellent," I said, "I'll help pay for gas."

"Nah that's not necessary," she stuck out her hand, "I'm going that direction anyway. Just the company will be worth it."

"Cool then," I said, "Yeah, wow, thank you."

Although the energy at school was winding down, Mr. Megiddo was doing his best to keep things heated up.

"Last night I asked you to read the Thomas Pynchon story 'Entropy,'" Mr. Megiddo said.

"Did you notice the epigraph? Lance, you in particular should have picked up on it."

The epigraph was a quote from *Tropic of Cancer*.

"*A lockstep toward the prison of death*," Megiddo read. "What's the point of an epigraph?"

"Pointing toward or reinforcing the theme of the work," Miranda said from the back.

"Good. So with that in mind, what's this story about then?"

"Death?" Gina Dichlich said.

"Of a sort, yes. What is death?"

"Loss of life," Gina said.

"Yes. Loss of life for the one who dies. What else?"

"Loss of your presence for those who are left behind," I said.

"Yes. What else?"

"Loss of everything," Miranda said, "the ultimate death of the universe. We talked about entropy a little bit in Dr. Meany's class."

"Good let's start there. With the title. What is entropy? Miranda?"

"It has to do with how eventually matter and energy degrade."

"Degrade?"

"Lose their oomph and their order and tend toward chaos."

"Everything eventually loses its oomph," Megiddo said.

"Sort of, yeah."

"And becomes disordered."

"Yes, and boring."

"As someone who everyday becomes older and more boring and has less and less oomph, I can attest to the reality of this phenomenon," Megiddo joked. "I'm sure Dr. Meany would not be pleased with our watering down of the thermodynamic concept of entropy, but for our purposes here in English class in general, and with this story in particular, Miranda's description is fine. So, what is this story about?"

"Loss," I said.

"Anybody else?" Mr. M. asked.

"I agree with Lance," Miranda said and I looked back at her but she was looking at Mr. Megiddo.

"The loss of everything," Gina Dichlich said. "I feel like that's been the theme of, um, everything we've read this semester."

"Indirectly, yes," said Mr. Megiddo. "It's not only a general human experience, but it's also peculiarly American. So, yes, my approach to the literature has been biased toward that theme."

He read to us from the story:

He found himself, in short, restating Gibbs' prediction in social terms, and envisioned a heat-death for his culture in which ideas, like heat-energy, would no longer be transferred, since each point in it would ultimately have the same quantity of energy; and intellectual motion would, accordingly, cease.

"Callisto's ordered ecosystem, his apartment," said Megiddo, "is losing its energy to the chaos downstairs in Meatball Mulligan's place," Megiddo pointed out, "just as the little bird's delicate ecosystem is losing its life-energy to the bigger disordered cosmos which will rob the bird of its individuality and blur it into the whole."

"*The final absence of all motion*," I said, pointing out the line in the story.

"Yes. And what's that other line?" he searched his copy, "here: *The cosmologists had predicted an eventual heat-death for the universe (something like Limbo: form and motion abolished, heat-energy identical at every point in it)."*

"The loss of everything," Gina Dichlich repeated and looked over at me.

6

The penultimate event of the school year in the dramasphere was the bi-annual Thespian Snatch Breakfast.

Yes, they called it a "Snatch Breakfast," and I will confess that at the age of 16 the image of a "Snatch Breakfast" was the provoker of much horniness.

The phrase conjured up images of lapping Lorelei's vagina at dawn on a mountaintop with a Fantasia sunrise coming up symphonically just beyond the the rise of her mons veneris.

The Snatch Breakfast in reality however was quite tame: newly inducted members of Thespians, the student theatre arts honor society (sort of the equivalent of lettering in sports), were awakened by veteran members of the club at dawn, unannounced, and taken out to breakfast in their pajamas. Their parents were informed of the invasion ahead of time. First, to make sure the abductors would be able to gain entry to the house and, second, to make sure the snatchee wouldn't be sleeping naked.

I wasn't a Thespian, but I was allowed to attend because Lorelei was being inducted and I was her boyfriend.

She was wearing jeans and a t-shirt when we pulled her out of bed.

"Wow," she said as she began to sit up, feigning surprise even though her full dress betrayed her foreknowledge of the event.

"She probably really does sleep in her clothes, knowing her," I heard Dolly whisper to someone else.

I started to crawl into bed next to her and kiss her but she pushed me away and looked annoyed.

It was the only time I ever saw Lorelei's bedroom. I memorized as much of it as I could for later use.

Although Norms and Denny's and Canter's were open at that hour, they all had the wrong vibe.

In Los Angeles the only place to go for breakfast at dawn was the International House of Pancakes on Santa Monica.

I didn't care much for their pancakes—all pancakes paled in comparison to the ones at DuPar's in the Farmers Market—but I was fascinated by the so-called "Never Empty Coffee Pot." I pictured a magician's hand holding the brown plastic vessel, pouring it eternally, like one of Christ's miracles, into the void.

That coffee pot piqued my imagination.

It spoke to my wonder.

I've always been attracted to the infinite.

My favorite place to see it is in other people's eyes.

I don't remember much about the breakfast other than I sat next to Lorelei.

371

But I remember the coffee pot.

Would that I had a mind like the Never Empty Coffee Pot.

Then everything could be so easily lost.

After the Snatch Breakfast I got dropped off with Lorelei at her house hoping we might make out a little bit but I could tell she didn't want me there.

"My parents are home. This is the day my dad cleans the house. I have to go hide in my room before the noise starts."

"Noise?"

"I'm afraid of vacuum cleaners."

"When did that start?"

"When I was little I thought if I got too close I'd get sucked in."

"I know that fear."

"My dad is very thorough. He gets that hose all the way up into everything. So it's legitimately scary."

"All right then. Abyssinia," I said and leaned in to kiss her.

She giggled.

"I love you," she said, "I'm sorry."

"You're sorry you love me?"

"I'm sorry for being me."

"Oh, hush," I said.

"Hush yourself, Lance Atlas," she said and we kissed a little bit more before I began the homeward trek.

I went back to Lorelei's house the next day, a Sunday, and when we were making out on the living room couch, while I had my mouth on her breasts, she let me unsnap and unzip her pants, which surprised me, but when I got my hand down inside and caught the briefest feel of her slit with my middle finger she yanked my hand away and slapped my arm and looked at me with cold venom.

"Don't," she said and then made me go home.

Two strainful days with the girl.

A week after the Snatch Breakfast, the Thespian banquet took place at a restaurant called Papa Choux.

The new Thespians were given their pins, and Mr. Hill also gave out awards of recognition to various students involved in the Fall and Spring productions.

I was surprised and pleased to win a trophy for Best Character, which felt weird, as if Mr. Hill was giving that award to himself 'cause my performance was really his idea.

Elmore E.D. Sedgwick, Jr. won the award for Best Lead Actor for his portrayal of Sky Masterson, though many people felt Conrad Lagoy had given the superior performance as Nathan Detroit.

"I have just one word to say to you all," Elmore proclaimed as he accepted his award, "PERVERSION!" and he did a series of pelvic thrusts with his trophy held extended in front of his crotch.

Mr. Hill, who was always fine with raunchy humor came back to the mike.

"Two years ago—those of you who were here will remember this—we did Sweet Charity and during the first rehearsal with the orchestra Dr. Luft objected to Charity's line, 'I think I just screwed myself up' as being inappropriate in a high school play. So I talked to Aubrey Valadez, the girl who was playing Charity, about how to change it, and then we ran the scene again with her saying 'I think I just fucked myself up,' and Dr. Luft started yelling from the orchestra pit, 'Put back screw! Put back screw!'"

We all laughed at that even though we'd heard the story before.

Diana Hitchcock was in attendance even though she'd not been around all semester.

"Hey, whiteboy," she said to me as she walked past the table where I was sitting with Lorelei and Mimi and Conrad Lagoy (upon whom my sister was crushing at the time).

"Hey," I said, "Where have you been? I thought you'd be in *Guys & Dolls*."

"Oh, it's a long story. I haven't been in school this semester. I'll be back in September though. I was surprised to see you in the musical. I thought you were a jock."

"Yeah, well, I didn't want to wallow in my athletic mediocrity anymore. You know. How'd I do?"

"You were great! *Let's shoot crap!* Hilarious. Well done," she said, and moved over to Elmore's table to gab with him.

A couple of days before, Lorelei told me she wanted to perform a song at the banquet and asked if I'd accompany her on piano.

"Definitely! What song you wanna do?"

"You don't get to know that," she said.

"What? How am I supposed to accompany you?"

"Can't you sight read?"

"Yeah," I said.

"Then I'll give you the sheet music at the banquet."

I sighed and accepted this as one of the conditions of being Lorelei's boyfriend. Always defined by the things I wasn't allowed to know.

Luckily, thanks to lifelong listenings to my dad's Ella Fitzgerald albums, I was at least familiar enough with the song she wanted to sing–George & Ira Gershwin's "Lorelei"–to fake my way through it using the sheet music.

Although Lorelei obviously loved the irony of doing a song about her namesake, I'm not so sure she recognized the deeper irony that the persona of the lyrics was her psychic and spiritual opposite.

Or maybe she did.

Or maybe Lorelei's deepest secret is that she does indeed long to be "Lorelei."

I don't know.

She did sing "Lorelei" beautifully though in her sweet birdlike soprano despite the fact that it really called for a saucy smoky alto.

I want to be like the gal on the river

Who sang her songs to the ships passing by;

She had the goods and how she could deliver,

The Lorelei!

And each affair has a kick and a wallop,

For what they crave I can always supply!

I wanna be like that other trollop

Called the Lorelei!

Throughout her performance hung the beautiful incongruity of a song about a young woman longing for sexual abandon being sung by someone standing stiff as an opera diva.

Afterward, I sang my song "Rain On Me" to polite applause.

Jessica Bloom did a great version of "Dance 10, Looks 3" from *A Chorus Line*.

"Tits and ass, get the bingo bongos done," she sang and bounced her boobies, the image of which arose later that night in my addled masturbations.

As with most years, the last week of school was spent returning materials, getting old work back, and signing yearbooks.

In Megiddo's class, I passed my yearbook around and let everybody sign it who wanted to.

I was too busy signing other people's yearbooks to notice who was signing mine.

And anyway I always put off reading the signatures in my yearbook until the school year was over and everybody had already signed. It had become a sacred tradition.

The first one I came upon was Dolly's.

Dearest Lance,

I'm not really sure what to write . . . there's so much I want to say . . . Okay, well, let's start with I Love You! You've been a terrific friend to me this year and I hope it continues. Our closeness comes and goes (depending on your girlfriend status) but I always feel connected to you even when you are distracted. You'd better write to me while I'm away. I hope the coming year will be filled with happiness and that when I get back we can read a few books together and hang out and, well, you know . . . do what we do.

Love always,

Dolly, Bjorn, and the kids

p.s. Vive La France!

Claire had wrapped her signature in a circle around one of the many Eddie Gurges drawings strewn throughout the yearbook.

Lance,

Gosh, this has been the best year for me, & of course you know that you were a big part of it. Everything seems so far away now, but I'll never forget how special you were to me, & how knowing you has changed my life so much. I'm very glad that we're still friends because your friendship means a lot to me. I hope we always will be because I can really talk with you with ease. OK! I wish you all the best & I hope your summer's fabulous. Maybe we'll see each other now & then.

Bye now.

I love you always,

Claire (Turkey-Lips)

Lorelei took up 2 full pages, starting on a right-hand page then continuing on the facing left-hand page upside down.

Lance Atlas,

That part was comparatively simple. As you have probably not found out yet, I have great difficulty writing in other people's books because I'm so much more used to writing in my own. What do you say to a person you've known for five years without knowing? Well, I'll make a mad attempt. What I'd like to say is—we must have been predestined. Fate smiled upon us (as you must be aware of). Lance—I'm so glad that I finally really know you after all these years. You're a greater person than I ever imagined. You know you mean a great deal to me. Well, you may not know it—but I do! I hope you don't get tired easily of people who sink into the depths now and then and slip into a philosophical oblivion very often, because I plan to be around for quite a while. (Wouldn't it be a mind blower if our grandchildren were reading this someday?). Help—I think I'm going crazy—I hope you'll be around to go crazy with me in our little white round padded cell . . . (turn book over and continue on previous page) . . . I'm sure there has to be more to life than birth, marriage, children, grandchildren, shuffle-board and death. Our philosophy of life is just a mere outline of what life is really about. Life is all about people like you and me finding each other. I believe that our psychic powers were working overtime on that one. I do hope, however, that you will avoid letting the writing on your Levi's fade away. Someday you're going to look back on this signature I've written and say "What was she talking about?" But then you'll remember—"Oh, yes, I remember Lorelei, she was the crazy one who wrote things like LUMBER *on my jeans and said 'Wow' when she became a Thespian and was taken on a Snatch Breakfast at 6:30 in the morning–or was that someone else?" No, it was me and it still is. I know I must be impossible to get along with. Every time I think back to the 8th grade I think of us wandering around in the 4th dimension–not knowing each other's feelings. If we ever build that time machine we'll go back and visit us. Won't we be surprised? Don't let this scrawling mess fool you for one minute, Lance Atlas. I have very sincere handwriting. You know I really love you a lot. You're great!*

Love,

Lorelei

When I got through the entire yearbook, I realized that I hadn't seen any signature from Miranda.

I knew I'd given it to her to sign. Had she decided not to write anything?

Upon a second flip through the pages, I found a brief message on an obscure page that was mostly ads.

Dear Lance,

Even though we weren't very good friends this year, I thought about you a lot and I'm really happy for you. I hope we can stay in touch.

Love Always,

Miranda

I was surprised by how sad the cold emptiness of her signature made me, a fitting bookend to *you remind me of the little prince! luv, miranda.*

The day after school ended, Lorelei called me.

"OK, this is really bizarre," she said, breathing heavier than normal for

Lorelei Lux.

"What?"

"Are you ready for this?"

"I guess I'd better be," I said, "What?"

"Oh my god."

"What?" I asked more emphatically the third time.

"Mr. Hill proposed to Deirdre at graduation," Lorelei said to me, greatly disconcerted, "and she said yes."

"Whoa, shit. What?"

"My sister is going to marry Mr. Hill."

Dang, dude. It was real.

"Did you know this was going on? You can tell me now."

"No," Lorelei said, "She didn't even tell *me*."

"Wow."

"I thought *I* was a freak," she said, "but my sister is the *true* freak."

"That's pretty out there, yeah," I said. "How are your parents reacting?"

"Oh, my dad was just silent when they first walked over and told us right after the ceremony. Deirdre was just waving her ring finger at them and saying, 'We're in love!'"

"What can your parents do? She's 18 isn't she?"

"Yes," Lorelei said.

"So they're gonna get married."

"She said in September."

"How are you dealing?"

"It does not compute yet," she said, "It's very strange."

Word rippled through the student community and the parental network too of course.

Josh Hill had divorced his wife and was going to marry his student Deirdre Lux.

You felt like it was going to be in the paper or something.

No social gathering during the first 2 weeks of that summer failed to bring up the subject.

But after the initial flurry of flabbergasts and condemnations and rushes to judgment, eventually nobody really gave much of a shit.

Independence Day took precedence.

July 4th was on a Monday, and so a holiday weekend was observed.

I figured Lorelei and I would spend a bunch of time together, maybe go to the movies or the beach or whatever.

"On Saturday I'm going horseback riding with Sharon, Justine, and Misty. Girls only. But maybe we can do something Sunday."

"That'd be great. Beach?"

"Sure," she said.

"And maybe Monday go to the movies?"

"Uhm, I think I'm going to a 4th of July party at my uncle's house, but I'm not sure."

"OK," I said, increasingly bummed by her lack of enthusiasm.

It seemed like she never wanted to see me.

Later that day, evening actually, Lorelei called and said she was in the hospital.

"What? What happened?"

"Oh, I fell off my horse and messed up my face and broke my right arm. They're checking for internal bleeding. That's why I'm still here."

"Oh my god. Can I come see you?"

"No! I don't want you to see me like this. I forbid you."

"You're my girlfriend. I want to come see you. I want to bring you flowers. And chocolate. I wanna kiss it better."

"Don't be corny and cliché, Lance Atlas. If you love me you'll leave me alone."

"All right," I moped into the phone.

"No pouting," she said.

"I love you," I said.

"And I love you, Lance Atlas."

"Well, when may I see you?"

"They're sending me home tomorrow. I'll call you."

"So maybe tomorrow I can see you?"

"I said I'll call you tomorrow."

"You sure I can't bring you anything?"

"Sure."

"I want to see you!"

"All in good time, Lance Atlas. I'm tired, I have to go."

"Feel better," I said.

"Thank you. Good night," she said and hung up.

"Bye, baby," I said to the dial tone.

7

The first night of work, the Hollywood Bowl season opener, Gina came by and picked me up and so began our little carpool.

"I'm looking forward to learning more about classical music this summer," I said.

"Me too."

"It's really weird to see you wearing pants," I said.

"Well we have to, right?"

"Yeah."

"Eventually I'll figure out a way around it. I hate pants."

"Why?"

"I like feeling the breeze on me. It sends me soaring."

"Oh."

"Aer Lingus," she said and it took me a second to get the joke.

"You're not Irish."

"I'm half Irish."

"Ah, didn't know that."

"The lower half," she smiled.

"Haha," I blushed.

"I remember when you guys used to watch me on the monkey bars at Melrose," she said, "in what, like, 4th Grade?"

"I have no idea what you're talking about."

"Uh huh," she said, "Well, I hope you enjoyed it."

"Again," I feigned, "I have to plead ignorance."

"Dude, the 'Teacher, teacher, I declare, I see Gina's underwear,' was a bit of a giveaway, usually followed by 'I see London, I see France, I see Gina's underpants.'"

"That wasn't me," I said.

"You were there, dude. Busted."

We picked up our usher's jackets together but then had to part ways when she headed up to her station on the 3rd Prom and I stayed down on the 1st.

It turned out that the veteran usher Javier Contreras had paired me up with was Desirée Stoner, Candy's older sister.

Dang, dude. Older sisters. My leitmotif. Or rather life-motif.

"Hey, I remember you. Candy's boyfriend," she said when we were introduced as aisle-mates.

"Yeah, a long time ago. How is Candy? Still at Beverly?"

"Yup. What's your name again?"

"Lance."

"Right."

"Lance Atlas."

"Yeah yeah I remember. Candy talked about you all the time for a while. I remember when you used to come over."

"It was an intense 3 weeks, yeah. And what are you doing these days?"

"I go to Cal State Northridge."

"You live in the Valley?"

"Nah, I've got a place over on Franklin. I can actually walk to and from work. I commute to school during the semester. It's not so bad. I just get on the freeway right here."

"Cool."

"Yeah."

"I'll probably end up at CSUN also," I said.

"It's all right. You'll like it."

"What's your major?"

"Music."

"Oh, yeah, I remember. Cello," I mimed like most people do when they say the word for any musical instrument.

"Yup."

"My main memory of you is rocking out to The Who though. *Quadrophenia*, 'Dr. Jimmy & Mr. Jim.'"

"I like rock and classical. I like everything."

"Me too."

"Except country," we then said together and gave each other five.

"Welcome to 1st Prom, Aisle 4," she said. "Stick close to me at first and I'll show you how it's done, son."

Desirée and I were an excellent team, almost telepathic when it came to who was going to attend to which patrons, and she taught me, concert by concert, about music too, medieval, Renaissance, Baroque, Classical, Romantic, Modern and all their various subdivisions, the gamut.

One quiet night, Desirée, standing shoulder to shoulder with me amid a parade of patrons, whispered, "You are sexy times six."

"Haha."

"I'm serious."

"Shh."

"We should have sex."

"Desirée."

"I mean it."

"Desirée, we aren't going to have sex."

"Whatever you say, Master. I'm sorry. I should be spanked for my insubordination."

"You are weirding me out."

"Psych," Desirée snickered quietly.

"Funny," I shook my finger at her.

"Had you going though."

"Yes you did."

"You are a very trusting person."

"Yes. I usually presume people are being sincere."

"And if they're not?"

"Well, then they lose my trust."

"As it should be."

"You don't need to earn my trust. You can only lose it."

"Isn't that setting yourself up for a lot of disappointment?"

"My experience has been that people are mostly trustworthy."

"I've had a different experience. I've been hoodwinked and hornswoggled and horribly taken advantage of. I come to every relationship with a certain suspiciousness. Like I'm standing here wondering now, is Lance Atlas trustworthy or untrustworthy? And how do I find out?"

"You don't wonder that at all."

"Psych," she grinned again.

"And here I trusted you."

When I was on my break I'd have a nightly schmooze with Arabella Mayflower who was working at a concession stand on the 1st Prom.

I usually made sure to grab my snack at Arabella's kiosk.

Sometimes I'd get popcorn. Sometimes a hot dog.

Sometimes I was in the mood for a bag of trail mix they sold which, unfortunately, was packaged under the brand name "Funky Stuff," and which I was way too embarrassed to ask for.

"Let me have some of that Funky Stuff," I said the first time and blushed and after that Arabella very kindly had it waiting for me when I walked up so that I wouldn't have to ask for it out loud anymore.

"Oh, hey, Miranda told me to say hi," Arabella said one night, "I told her we were working together here."

"Ah, say hi back. What's she doing this summer?"

"Same as always, working in her dad's office."

"Which means reading a lot."

"Zackly. How are *you* doing? How's Lori?"

"Oh, fine," I said and shrugged.

"All recovered from her horseback riding injury?"

"Convalescing slowly. I actually haven't seen her in person since it happened. She won't let me come over."

"Sounds like Lori Lux, yup," Arabella nodded her head. "Miranda said she and Freddy are coming to something or other here, I don't remember what."

"Ah. Well, if they sit in 1st Prom maybe I'll see them."

"Oh, they'll definitely be in 1st Prom. Freddy's folks have had the same box for donkey's years," Arabella used a phrase I've never understood. Buzzy Lagniappe said "donkey's years" sometimes.

Arabella was really into the Dodgers so it was fun that summer to talk about them because they were having a great season and, though we didn't know it at the time of course, on their way to a World Series appearance against the New York Yankees.

"You still into Steve Garvey?" Arabella teased.

"He's a great player," I said. "My dad can't stand him. 'That guy's hiding something,' he always says about Garvey. I don't know. I love watching Steve Garvey play. His swing is a thing of beauty."

"Oh I agree," Arabella said, "with both you and your dad."

She always ended our conversations with, "Say hi to Lori," which I never remembered to do.

Weekdays I was going to Summer School because they were offering Driver's Ed and Driver's Training together so I could at least get my permit by the end of the summer and then start practicing for my driving test. There was no car for me to drive, we only had the station wagon and my mom needed that. But still.

One evening, on the way home from work, "After The Gold Rush" came on KLOS.

"I love this song," Gina said and turned up the radio.

Of course I said nothing and just her blast the song and sing along, but I was saddened by the reminder of the deepening schism between me and

Lorelei. I hadn't seen her in weeks even though we talked on the phone every night.

There was a band playing in my head

And I felt like getting high.

I was thinking about what a

Friend had said

I was hoping it was a lie.

When Miranda Savitch wrote *you remind me of the little prince!* did she mean it or was she simply plagiarizing Lorelei's observation?

I could not stop wondering this.

They were flying Mother Nature's

Silver seed to a new home in the sun

"Do you think this song will come true?" Gina said when it was over.

"In what way?"

"That we'll ruin the earth and have to find another habitable planet. Like we're going to lose all of this beauty?"

"I like to think we will acknowledge the danger and act to reverse it," I said, "I get too depressed if I think otherwise."

That night at the Bowl during the annual Bach Festival, someone walked past my post and up the aisle which was not allowed while the music was in progress. We were supposed to hold patrons at the foot of the stairs until a suitable break.

I looked up and saw the gentleman, dapper and bearded, kneeling in the aisle talking to somebody in one of the boxes.

I did my duty and went up to where the man was kneeling and asked him to come back down.

"Excuse me, sir," I said, "you'll have to wait until a break in the music to do this."

The bearded gentleman turned to me, eyes blazing, and said with a subtle and erudite accent, "Do you *know* who I *am?*"

"No, sir, I don't."

"Then I suggest you do your homework, young man, and let me go about my business here," and he waved me off.

"Lance," Desirée tapped me from behind and grabbed me by the arm, escorting me back down to the walkway.

"What the hell?" I said.

"Dude, that's Gerhart Metzger."

"Oh shit."

"Deep shit, more like."

"Oh, man," I said, "I fucked up."

After we were released for the night, we went to return our usher's jackets to the uniform clerk, a nightly ritual, and Gina pointed out 3 large photographs beneath a large printed sign that said Know Your Bosses. The faces of Herbie Smeltz, guest services; Javier Contreras, house manager; and, yes, Gerhart Metzger, President of the L.A. Philharmonic Association. I had never bothered to look before.

"I told Gerhart Metzger he had to go back to his seat while the music was playing," I shared with Gina on the way home.

"No fucking way."

"Yup."

"Oh shit, that is flagrant, dude!" and she gave me five, "Kudos for sticking it to the *Man*."

"If I'd known he was the *Man* I most definitely would not have stuck it to him. I hope I don't get fired."

I wasn't fired, but the next night I was stationed up on the 3rd Prom, most definitely a demotion, though the upside was Gina Dichlich worked on the 3rd Prom.

"Welcome to 3rd Prom, genius," she sassed me but then consoled, "It's not as uptight on this level. You know, people on benches, Kentucky Fried Chicken, Coors. None of that coq au vin and quiche and wine shit here, nuh-uh. This is rock and roll up here, baby."

Several times during the night, Javier walked past me and shot me a look I wasn't sure was apologetic or scolding, maybe a bit of both.

After the final segment of the program began and he came by to release us from duty, he walked with me to uniform collection.

"Message received?" he asked.

"Yes, sir. Thank you for not firing me."

He smiled and put his hand on the back of my neck.

"I've talked to Mr. Metzger and told him what a great asset you are and asked him to forgive your mistake. I had to bump you up to the 3rd Prom for tonight, but on Tuesday you'll be back on the 1st Prom."

"Desirée's aisle?"

He smiled again.

"You like that, hmm?"

"Very much," I blushed.

"Well, yes, Ms. Stoner specifically asked for you to be returned to her aisle as her partner, and she is one of our best, so it shall be."

"Thank you, Mr. Contreras," I said.

"Javier."

"Javier," I said and we shook hands.

"You're a good-looking boy," he said, "not like that fat kid from *Willy Wonka & The Chocolate Factory*, what's his name? Buzzy–"

"Augustus –"

"–Lagniappe?"

"–Gloop. Augustus Gloop is the fat kid from *Willy Wonka & The Chocolate Factory*."

"I thought it was Buzzy Lagniappe."

"No, it's Augustus Gloop."

"Then foo the huck is Buzzy Lagniappe?"

"Well actually I live next door to a guy named Buzzy Lagniappe and his real name is Augustus and he used to be fat."

"Ah, I thought wrong," Javier said, "Oh well. Have a good night."

Arabella Mayflower walked by as I was heading into uniform collections.

"Hey, did you see Miranda? She was here tonight!"

"No," I said, feeling the flop in my gut, "I was up on the 3rd Prom tonight."

"Oh, dang, that sucks," she said, "I told her where you're usually stationed and she said she was going to go say hi. Oh, well."

"Thanks for telling me though," I said without knowing why.

Gina was waiting for me when I came out of uniform collection.

"Did Contreras fire you?"

"No," I said.

"Scold you?"

"Not really. I'm being moved back to 1st Prom Tuesday night."

"Ooh posh, but dang," she said, "Really? I was excited to hang with you for the rest of the summer."

"Well, we can still hang," I said, "Like when we're not working."

"That'd be far out," Gina said, "But won't Lorelei get mad?"

I shrugged.

"She's recovering from a horseback riding injury and doesn't want me to come over, so I'm free to play elsewhere as I see it."

As we neared Melrose on the drive home, Gina turned to me and said, "Hey, you wanna get high?"

I thought about what I'd have to say to Lorelei to explain getting back from work so late.

"Yeah, cool," I said.

"I've got, at my house."

"Right on. Let's do it."

When I walked into Gina's bedroom I was grabbed immediately by her walls covered with these deeply surreal pastel drawings all done, I learned, by her, lots of celestial imagery, comets and stars and ringed planets.

"Art. I didn't know you were an artist," I said, scanning the walls.

"Yeah. All the way all the time."

And after that everything was different between us.

I had known Gina since kindergarten. Her name and her underwear had long been a simmering cauldron of phantasmic sex-thoughts for pretty much every penis-bearing human in her vicinity, me included, since time immemorial.

But now we were connected at the aesthetic level.

We were taking orders from the same bosses.

"Who's your muse?" I asked.

"Urania," Gina said without hesitating, "she gets all up inside me."

"Space, yeah, I see it," I said, pointing to her drawings.

"You're in it," she said and lay back on her bed, "Like Mr. St. Jerome always said."

She had started wearing a short skirt to work even though they weren't allowed, but I guess up on the 3rd Prom you could get away with stuff like that, plus she was Gina Dichlich and didn't take orders from anybody (except apparently Urania).

I could see her underwear and she didn't seem to care at all like she was still back in 4th Grade or something.

"I'm afraid of the ocean also," I remained standing, positioning myself to continue looking up her skirt.

"Huh? Where'd that come from?"

"In Megiddo's class, when we were discussing 'Bartleby.' You said you were afraid of the ocean."

"I am. Dang, you remember that? That was way back when I said that."

"Yeah. I do."

"Man, Lance, you know, I didn't think this would ever happen, us hanging out."

"Here we are," I said.

"I've wanted to hang out with you since like forever."

I didn't know whether I was supposed to lie down with her and start making out or not so I just kept standing and trying to look like I was checking out her drawings when really I was just wondering what the fuck to do next.

"You know, everyone thinks you have a thing for Mr. Megiddo," I said, testing the waters.

"Haha," she said, "That's pretty funny. Really?"

"Yeah, for sure," I said.

"I love Mr. Megiddo. He's given me all this creative confidence I never had before. He's my favorite person, the all-time coolest human ever."

"So you do have a thing for him."

"Like how?"

I duh'd her.

"Oh my," she sighed, catching my drift.

"So? Do you?"

This would determine if I was going to pounce or not.

"I need to let you in on a little secret," she whispered ironically loud.

"It's true! You like Mr. Megiddo!" I clapped my hands like a little kid.

"Can you keep it to yourself?"

"Of course," I kind of crossed my heart even though I don't believe in shit like that.

"You swear? You can't tell anybody."

I nodded emphatically.

Gina tucked her skirt between her legs thus ending my view.

"Well, the thing is . . . I like girls," she said matter-of-factly.

"But."

"I know."

"But your name."

"Haha."

"Dang, dude," I muttered and thought about it. I couldn't tell if it deflated me or turned me on.

Then the storyline came together.

Of course.

"Dude, oh, man, in 9th Grade, Samantha Coventry–"

"–was my girlfriend. Yeah."

I paused to digest.

"We were together like until maybe halfway into 10th Grade. She got way into witchcraft and stuff and that wasn't my scene at all. I just wanted to do my art. I was only going along with the witchcraft thing 'cause she was my girlfriend and I thought she was the coolest but after a while all that occult shit just weirded me out and turned me off."

I wondered if Gina knew about the Samantha/Ms. Cummings incident in 9th Grade.

She had to have heard about it.

"But everybody says you're a floozy," I said.

"People make shit up all the time."

you remind me of the little prince! luv, miranda

"But you're so. I don't know."

"Well, yeah. It's for the girls, dude," she said, "Does that gross you out?"

"What? That you're gay? No. I think it's cool. And kind of hot too actually."

"Ugh," she grunted, "*Et tu?*"

"I . . ."

"We're friends now," she made room for me on the bed.

I scootched in close, confused.

We lay facing each other and then ended up snuggling like seals on the beach.

It was one of those totally relaxed moments in the Eternal Now.

And, as it turned out, there was no marijuana involved.

We semi fell asleep on Gina's bed and when I woke up it was just after midnight.

Gina drove me home and made me promise again not to tell anybody she was a lesbian.

"I mean some people obviously know, but I'm not ready to be all the way out in the open about it," she said.

"Of course. I'm good like that. You can trust me with your secrets."

"That's why I told you."

"See you Tuesday night."

"See you then," she pointed at me.

I didn't know whether or not to call Lorelei even though I always called her as soon as I got home from work.

I calculated the risk of calling vs. not calling and decided it was wiser to call.

The algebra of girls.

"Sorry it's so late," I said when she answered softly.

"I was sleeping."

"Oops. I got held up and preoccupied and stuff."

"Preoccupied with Gina Dichlich?"

"I-um."

Jesus fucking Christ.

"Arabella said she sees you leaving the Bowl with her every night."

Dang, dude.

The gaping irony of this moment was supremely painful.

I hadn't told Lorelei that Gina was driving me because I didn't want to deal with explaining it to her. Now I was going to have to. And then some.

Plus, I felt totally duped by Arabella Mayflower who all summer had been telling me to "Say hi to Lorelei" when obviously she was talking to Lorelei the whole time.

"Yeah she, uh, drives me to and from work."

"And you didn't feel the need to share this information with me, your girlfriend? You're driving home every night with Gina Dichlich of all people, flooziest of all floozies?"

"I didn't want it to be a thing with you."

"Well now it *is* a thing with me."

"She. Is. My. Ride. To. And. From. Work," I said slowly and curtly like I get when I'm being all defensive and shit, "And she's not a floozy."

Dang, dude. This was bad.

I couldn't tell the truth about Gina. I promised.

So I had to let Lorelei suspect I was fooling around with her.

I had that madman feeling Holden Caulfield talks about.

"I'm very disappointed in you, Lance Atlas," she said and hung up on me.

I rolled a joint and went for a stomp around the block.

Whitman Rust and Buzzy Lagniappe were sitting on Whit's front lawn around the corner on Mansfield.

"Hey, dude, how's it going?" Whit said.

"Pretty good," I answered brusquely enough that Buzzy asked me what was up.

I shrugged.

"Chicks, man," Buzzy said.

"We're right, right?" Whit added.

"Gotta be," Buzzy said, "I know that perturbed look even in the dark."

"The bitch-done-fucked-my-shit-up look," Whit said.

"Yep," I admitted, "Though I mostly fucked my own shit up."

"Try some of this herb Bigelow laid on us tonight," Buzzy said.

"The fiercest Thai stick you have ever inhaled, dude," Whit said, "It'll make you feel like your bones are breathing."

I took a couple of puffs and, yeah, it was a rocket all right.

"Remember, dude, she's just a girl, it doesn't matter," Buzzy laid his age-old advice on me as I walked away.

"Later, dudes," I said, "Thanks for the puffage."

That night marked the first time I was unable to get an erection jacking off to fantasies of fucking Lorelei.

I tried for a while, even invoking the old reliable cunnilingus on a mountaintop at dawn, but after a while, when nothing was happening, I gave up and went to sleep.

8

After the last day of summer school was over I had to do some heavy duty rehearsing because my audition for the Songwriter's Showcase was coming up in a couple of days and I had not even decided which songs to sing.

I finally decided on "Rain On Me," "Manifest Destiny & Beyond," "Frailty & The Naked Wrist," "When Shall We Be Free," "The Garden of Hedon," and "This World."

The Showcase office and audition space was actually at somebody's house, either Ben Paraffin's or Ian Mulcahy's, I wasn't sure, though Ben was the one who auditioned me so I guess it was his.

He set up a mike, turned on his tape recorder and instructed me to play all the songs straight through, stating the title of each one before I began.

I played most of the songs on the piano, though I did "Rain On Me" on the guitar.

"'Rain On Me,' man," Ben said, "That tune's got some juice."

He just kept staring at me as I waited for a more elaborate assessment.

"Just out of curiosity, Lance. Every songwriter has a handful of songs he wishes he'd written."

"Or she."

"Of course. What are yours?"

"Oh man, um."

"Think for a minute or two. You know what they are. They are your templates. I'm going to grab a Coke. You want one?"

"No thank you."

Ben was correct in that 3 songs emerged before his return.

"Well?" Ben sipped at his Coke.

"Uh, 'Windmills Of Your Mind' is one."

"Ah, the Bergmans, and Michel Legrand."

"I love the melody and the lyrics for that song both for themselves and how they work together. It's like going through the same maze over and over again."

"Ha, that's a good way to put it," he said.

"I feel like I was born hearing that melody," I said.

"What else?"

"'Alone Again, Naturally,' Gilbert O'Sullivan."

"Nice. Yes."

"And also 'Send In The Clowns,' the Stephen Sondheim song."

"That's a weird tune, man," Ben said.

"Yeah, but something about it."

"Yeah yeah, I get it, man, excuse me," Ben said as the girl who answered the door when I arrived came into the audition room. She reminded me of Taryn Rust but with bigger teeth.

"Yes, Pam?" Ben said.

"Um, Elvis Presley died," she said.

"What?" Ben gasped.

"Just came over the radio. Elvis Presley died. Sitting on the toilet or something."

"Holy shit. Enormous."

We all just sort of sat there.

How could Elvis Presley be dead?

"Lance, listen, I've got to make some phone calls about this news. Ian and I will listen to the tape and you'll get a letter from us in about a month letting you know if you're going to get a slot in the Showcase or not. Cool?"

"Yeah, sure," I said.

"How old are you?" he asked.

"Sixteen."

"Well, keep working at your craft every day. And think about those songs you wish you'd written. Aim for that. Write some more like 'Rain On Me.'"

"Thank you," I said as I put away my guitar and headed out to the Melrose bus.

I called Lorelei when I got home to tell her about the audition.

"Dang, dude," I said, "Elvis Presley died. Did you hear?"

"Yeah, wow. My mom's been crying all afternoon."

"Mine is crying too. She loves Elvis. She was obsessed with him in high school."

"For us it would be like if one of the Beatles died."

"Yes, exactly."

"How are you feeling?"

"Oh, getting better but really slowly."

"Can I bring you something? I won't stay long."

"No, I don't want you to see me like this."

"I haven't seen you in over a month," I said.

"So?"

"I'm your boyfriend."

"Is there some rule?" she said.

"I think the rule is once in a while rather than never."

Chilly summer silence exaggerated the anger.

"Hey," I said, grasping, "A few days ago I finished reading *Sons & Lovers* by D.H. Lawrence. Did I tell you I was reading that?"

I had read Lawrence because back in June when I told Mr. Megiddo about my plans for a Sinclair Lewis summer he scoffed.

"Find something more adventurous," Mr. Megiddo said.

"But I like Sinclair Lewis."

"That's irrelevant. What would Henry Miller want you to read?"

"D.H. Lawrence," I said, "for sure."

Megiddo walked over to his bookcase.

"*Sons & Lovers*," he said, "Here. Read it over the summer. You can make it your first outside novel essay in A.P. next year. You are taking AP next year I hope?"

"Duh," I said and took the book.

Sometimes when you read a book it speaks directly to something going on in your life at the time which causes you to relate everything you read to said circumstance, and once you do that you are never thereafter able to think of the book without those associations.

In this case it was an onslaught of thoughts about Lorelei.

She shrank in her convulsed, coiled torture from the thought of such a thing. It was as if she could scarcely stand the shock of physical love, even a passionate kiss, and then he was too shrinking and sensitive to give it.

My dynamic with Lorelei. Totally. Trying to get my hands on and inside her body often brought about this effect. And this passage contained words I would never be emboldened to say even though they were an utter summation of our romantic circumstance together:

You see, I can give you a spirit love, I have given it you this long, long time; but no embodied passion. See, you are a nun. I have given you what I would give a holy nun—as a mystic monk to a mystic nun. Surely you esteem it best. Yet you regret—no, have regretted—the other. In all our relations no boy enters. I do not talk to you through the senses—rather through the spirit. That is why we cannot love in the common sense. Ours is not an everyday affection. As yet we are mortal, and to live side by side with one another would be dreadful, for somehow with you I cannot long be trivial, and, you know, to be always beyond this mortal state would be to lose it. If people marry, they must live together as affectionate humans, who may be commonplace with each other without feeling awkward—not as two souls.

My mind wandered as I read from Lorelei to every girl I'd ever been with except for Taryn:

There was some obstacle; and what was the obstacle? It lay in the physical bondage. He shrank from the physical contact. But why? With her he felt bound up inside himself. He could not go out to her. Something struggled in him, but he could not get to her. Why?

403

And through some of the book I was not thinking of Lorelei nor any other girl except Miranda:

The fact that he might want her as a man wants a woman had in him been suppressed into a shame . . .

Why couldn't he go to her, make love to her, kiss her? . . . Oh, why did not he take her? Her very soul belonged to him. Why would he not take what was his? . . . She had borne so long the cruelty of belonging to him and not being claimed by him. Now he was straining her again. It was too much for her.

Miranda that day on my front lawn a summer ago putting herself out of her misery.

"I marked this one passage I've been meaning to read to you 'cause it's totally cool and beautiful and I think you'll dig it. Can I?" I asked Lorelei while still on the phone with her.

She paused, "Go ahead."

"They felt small, half-afraid, childish and wondering, like Adam and Eve when they lost their innocence and realized the magnificence of the power which drove them out of Paradise and across the great night and the great day of humanity. It was for each of them an initiation and a satisfaction. To know their own nothingness, to know the tremendous living flood which carried them always, gave them rest within themselves. If so great a magnificent power could overwhelm them, identify them altogether with itself, so that they knew they were only grains in the tremendous heave that lifted every grass blade its little height, and every tree, and living thing, then why fret about themselves?"

She didn't respond right away so I just hung on.

"You like that book because it reminds you of Miranda Savitch," Lorelei said.

"I read it because Mr. Megiddo gave it to me and said it was good."

"He knew it would remind you of Miranda," she said.

"Well, actually it makes me think a lot about you mostly."

She just held the silence because she knew she was partially right–she'd read the book–and wanted to squirm me out.

"Would it be possible for us to have a conversation where Miranda Savitch isn't referenced in some way? Because that just about never happens," Lorelei said.

"What? You're the one who brought her up just now."

"I beat you to it, that's all. You wanted to bring her up."

"Thank you for telling me what I'm thinking and feeling, Lorelei. Really. How considerate of you."

I was gearing up for a struggle I no longer had any interest in.

I heard a muffling as she talked to someone else.

"I have to hang up," she said and did.

Dang, dude.

I didn't even get to tell her about the audition.

A few days later I finally convinced Lorelei to let me come over.

"It's our 3 month anniversary," I said.

"OK," she said, "My parents are going out tonight."

I brought her a red rose to celebrate the anniversary and gave it to her when she answered the door.

"Happy anniversary!" I said and tried to kiss her but she backed away.

There was not a mark upon her face, her arm was wrapped in a bandage, not a cast, and she moved awkwardly.

Lorelei looked distressed when she saw the flower.

"Oh, dear," she said, and took it, "Wait here."

She closed the front door and left me standing on the porch.

"Let's talk," she said, returning to the door without the rose, taking me by the hand and leading me into the living room.

She put Neil Young on the stereo.

Lover,

there will be another one

Who'll hover

over you beneath the sun

Tomorrow

see the things

that never come

Today

"Well, this bodes well," I said of the song.

She looked at me and then away.

"I don't like what we're doing," she said.

"Nyeah, I don't even *know* what we're doing anymore," I said.

"Exactly," she said, "I thought it was more than it was and recently I realized I was making a lot of it up, the whole mythology of us. You know? I don't enjoy it. I can't give you what you want. I don't know."

"You don't like making out with me."

"Nyeah, um, I just . . . I'm . . . I don't carry those feelings really. Not for you or anyone. It's hard to explain. And I don't want to have to explain."

"You're not into the way I look at all? Not curious about my body?"

"No," she shrugged, "I just . . . I don't know . . . I don't care about it. When people talk about that stuff, I don't know what they mean."

I realized that her barricade was impenetrable, inviolable, invulnerable.

I'm not sure how long she, standing, and I, sitting, listened to Neil Young without talking to each other.

I wanted to cry and yet I also felt tremendously relieved.

"Can I ask you a question?" I said finally, "Just for clarity's sake?"

"Sure," she said, standing across the room from me and looking out the window.

"Did I really remind you of the Little Prince in 7th Grade?"

She didn't answer.

"You told me that you told Miranda that I reminded you of the Little Prince in Ms. LaBouche's class."

"Well," Lorelei pondered, "it was actually the other way around."

"What do you mean?"

"Miranda told me you reminded *her* of the Little Prince. She was greatly enamored of the book at the time. And of you at all times. Even still, I'm sure."

"Nyeah," I grumbled, "She and Freddy are very together."

"Mark my words, Lance Atlas."

"Why should I mark your words? You lied to me."

"Reversed the truth, that's all," she said. "What does it matter now? What does anything matter, Lance Atlas? I mean, really? Isn't it all ultimately temporary and absurd?"

"Feelings, you mean? I guess."

"Everything," she said.

After another considerable silence, I said, "So, this is us breaking up."

"I don't know that there's anything to break, really," she said, "other than long profound telephone conversations. We can still have those. If you want."

I stood up and moved toward her.

I touched her back and she turned and fell into my arms, a deep bear hug, crying.

"I do love you, Lance Atlas," she said into my neck.

"So . . . let's keep trying," I said, "Maybe you'll wake up one morning and realize how devilishly attractive I truly am."

She shook her head.

"I can't give you that part of it. I have a severe malfunction as regards matters of the body. There's a glitch in my works."

I kissed her on the forehead and started to leave.

"Will you still speak to me?" she asked.

"Of course," I said because of course I would and what else was I gonna say anyway.

I cried a little bit on the bus and in my bedroom and called Dolly to tell her all about it.

"Crazy-ass bitch," Dolly said in response to the news, "I told you."

"Nah, she just wasn't into it. Or me. I guess."

"Come over," she said.

"I'm too sad and fucked up, my dear."

"Come out and play with me."

"I can't, D."

"What are you gonna do?"

"Well, first I'm gonna get fucking stoned off my ass, and then I'm gonna stay up all night and write a fucking song about how fucked up all of existence is."

"Writhe on the bed in pain," she said.

"Exactly, you know me well."

"I do. Maybe hang out tomorrow? Tar Pits?"

"I dunno," I said.

"Hey, I'm leaving in 2 weeks so you have to make time for me, bub. I've hardly seen you in the last 3 months. It sucks."

"I know how that feels. Yes. You wanna go see a film?"

"Yeah! What should we see?"

"I'd be into *Kentucky Fried Movie*. Chevy Chase."

"Right on," she said.

"It's a date."

"Yay!" I could hear her clapping. "Call me when you wake up."

"It might be later in the day if I stay up all night."

"Whenever. I have chores in the morning anyway."

I brought a legal pad up onto the garage roof with me so I could transcribe my despair as it attached itself to language.

I lit up what I figured would be the first of many bowls of brain-drenching Thai stick and lay back in communication with the Muses.

Calliope and Euterpe came to me in all forgiveness of my apostasy and prodigal wayfaring and reprobate behavior.

They gifted me with my first song in a long-ass time, at least the lyrics. The music would have to wait until the next day when it'd be OK to play the piano in the living room. I could already hear it in my head though. Heavy chords, dread-slow melody.

Life Is Wrong

The brutal brooding, the karmic trauma,

The frugal feuding, a plodding drama

Of contrived bedlam force.

Life lined with thistles and quick contagions,

Bruises and bristles and swelled abrasions,

A confined gristly course

I yearn to comprehend

And learn just what it means to end.

I'm weakened due to daily failures

And slow despond.

Life is wrong

The pilgrim process turns holy mission

Into a contest for prized positions,

Leaves foundlings floundering bereft.

We wander wistful, a waning nation,

Desire dismissal, seek out cessation,

Lost in sullen depths

I yearn to comprehend

And learn just what it means to end.

I'm weakened due to daily failures

And slow despond.

Life is wrong

Old age regretting what youth will learn next,

The pain of getting close to the vertex

Aimed at the rapid disintegration

And at the vapid slag of creation.

The old are shriven and reimbursed thus;

The young are driven by purer purpose.

One day, together, shriveled and flaccid,

All will graze tethered, complete, slaked, placid,

Drawn in one big breath

I yearn to comprehend

And learn just what it means to end.

I'm weakened due to daily failures

And slow despond.

Life is wrong

Perverse excrescence, dense-froze confessions

The icy essence of my expressions,

A sickly rhyme-whore's frost,

I want a wax place where time goes liquid,

An indistinct space, kindling the wicked

With reason to exhaust

I yearn to comprehend

And learn just what it means to end.

I'm weakened due to daily failures

And slow despond.

Life is wrong

Sure, one can employ taxing distractions,

Induct a decoy, perform exactions,

Baste in servile chores;

Still, hopes of utter annihilation

Move me to mutter endless negations;

On and on the drivel bores

I yearn to comprehend

And learn just what it means to end.

I'm weakened due to daily failures

And slow despond.

Life is wrong

I had written until dawn and didn't wake up until about 2pm.

I went over to Dolly's house not long after and then we drove to Westwood where *Kentucky Fried Movie* was playing.

The movie concluded with an unexpectedly hot and erotic sex scene, this couple making out on the couch and eventually intensely fucking.

"OK, that last scene was steamy as hell . . . fuck," Dolly said afterward.

"It was very well done, yes," I rasped in my own raging horniness, "very effective."

"So?" Dolly looked at me, "Nu?"

We kissed passionately at a red light, but when the dude behind us started honking because the light had turned green, I said, "I should probably get home."

"Ugh," Dolly snorted, "You suck, as always."

"I do. I know. I love you," I said and kissed her quickly on the lips.

9

When I got home, I spotted a postcard from Annie De Milo among the mail on the dining room table.

Dear Sir Lancelot of Atlantis,

Thank you for the Observatory postcard! I was so happy when it came I showed it to everyone. I originally got you a better postcard that had a picture of a bookstore with a cheese stall in front of it like you asked for, but I lost it in the mess of my room so I'm sending you this one instead which is just a bookstore but no cheese stall. Avalon Booksellers. It's one of my favorite shops in Hay because it has lots of King Arthur stuff. This boy Chad who's always mean to me gave me The Once And Future King *by T.H. White as a birthday present. I think his parents made him do that after I complained to the headmaster at my school about him being mean to me and calling me a 'poop tart.' My mother says he's only mean to me because he likes me but no way! Ew! I think I'm going to try and read the book even though it's hard because I'm really into King Arthur stuff right now. My parents said we are going to visit Tintagel soon because that's maybe where Camelot was. I'm so excited! What are you reading now? For your next postcard, send me one from Venice Beach. That'd be just dandy. And try not to be too much of a nimnork noogie-noo, OK?*

Your Welsh rarebit,

Lady Anne of Milo and Venus

I'd have to remember to tell her about the lion tamer Cleo Dipchunk when I wrote back.

Back in my bedroom I decided to torture myself and listen to the *After The Gold Rush* album and wallow in thoughts of Lorelei's face and braless breasts and her depth and complexity and withering distance and her indelible place in my attention.

Everybody's going out and having fun

I'm a fool for staying home and having none.

I can't get over how she set me free

That night at work I had a depressed conversation with Arabella at her concession stand following the break-up.

I was kind of pissed at her after finding out she had been shining me on about Lorelei.

"Well, you look like shit," she said when I walked up on my break.

I shrugged.

"Lorelei?"

I nodded.

"She broke up with me."

"Why?"

"It doesn't matter. I'm looking forward to Mahler's Fifth tonight," I said.

Arabella had no idea what I was talking about.

"Is Miranda happy with Freddy?" I asked randomly.

"How would I know?" Arabella sneered. "Who's ever happy with anybody really?"

Her words would reverberate.

After intermission the orchestra launched into an impassioned performance of Mahler's Fifth Symphony, another one of those immediate permanent jukebox pieces of music for me.

All night long, Desirée had been been pestering me.

"Laaaance," she had whispered during the first part of the musical program, several songs from *Das Lied Von Der Erde*, "my panties are creeping. Help me."

"What?"

"My panties are creeping."

"Like a bug?"

"Up my butt, silly."

"Oh."

I tried ignoring her for a while.

"You look sad," she said, "Why are you sad?"

"My girlfriend dumped me."

"Bummer," she said.

"Total drag, yeah."

"That girl from 3rd Prom?"

"What, Gina? No. We're just friends. She drives me to and from work."

"Walk home with me tonight. We can party. It'll cheer you up. I'll drive you home later. I've got a car at my place."

Mahler's Fifth Symphony underscored the rest of that night.

From the opening funereal march of the 1st Movement and the tempestuous careening roil of the 2nd through the playful dance of the the 3rd and the delicate elegance of the 4th to the locomotive climax of the 5th, my ears were coaxed and melted and lured and ravished by the complex beauty of Mahler's epic composition, as well as its structural similarities to the sex act, or at least as I'd fantasized it.

During the 4th Movement, Desirée leaned over and whispered, "If you come over later I'll play this for you on the cello."

"That sounds nice," I said, "OK. I'll come."

"Good choice," she whispered back and licked my earlobe which hardened all of my erogenous erectables.

After we were released for the night I met Gina in our usual spot and told her I was going home with Desirée and she seemed cool with it.

"She's cute," Gina said, "Go for it."

"Remember Candy Stoner?"

"Of course. Total fox."

"Yeah, well, that's her older sister."

"Rock and roll," Gina said, "Go get lost."

I walked with Desirée to her place off Franklin and Highland, the Franklin-Keys Apartments, a distinctly old Hollywood building with a fountain in front and an art deco lobby.

"My parents are helping with the rent while I'm in school. I couldn't afford it with this job."

"Nyeah, I was gonna say."

Her apartment was a large one-bedroom with an amazing view of Hollywood, very sparsely decorated. A poster of Angela Davis speaking at a rally and one of Jimi Hendrix at Woodstock were all that hung on the walls, both in the living room. Her cello stood on a stand in the corner. She also had a work desk in the living room but it was bare of anything resembling work.

"Angela Davis," I said.

"Yeah. I could have a natural that big if I dared."

"Why don't you?"

"My mother says it will prevent me from getting gigs as a concert cellist."

"Really?"

"It's a white white white white white white world," she said.

"Classical music? Oh, yeah, for sure," I said nervously.

"Haha, I'm talking about the *whole* world, though, dude," and she totally fucking kissed me on the mouth.

"Ah, yes."

She put *Sgt. Pepper* on the stereo.

"You get high?" she asked.

"Sometimes," I said, not sure what the right answer was.

"Cool," Desirée said and pulled a baggie of weed and a corncob pipe out of the desk drawer.

"Righteous."

"I mean, how could I not be a stoner, right, with my name?"

"Sometimes names can be misleading."

"But in a way, names define who we are, don't you think?"

"I don't know," I thought of Gina.

We sat on the couch and smoked a bowl from her pipe.

"Corncob," I said, exhaling, "Old school."

She nodded.

"So, Atlas, huh? What about *that* name? Does that define who you are? You've got the posture for it."

"Yes, I am condemned to keep the sky from falling for all eternity."

"Sounds like a shitty job."

"But someone's gotta do it," I pantomimed Groucho.

"Nah, dude, I say let that shit fall. Let the sky come crashing down so we can start all over," she said and started kissing me with full tongue, and, dang, dude, it felt good.

Our hands got quickly up each other's shirts and things went real fierce real fast.

Her breasts were reasonably small, an easy handful once I'd removed her lace brassiere, and I pressed them against her ribs and then caressed them gently.

Her hands were moving up and down my back, fingertips only on the way up, fingernails scratching all the way down.

My cock was painfully hard in my pants.

Desiree pulled me into her bedroom and onto the bed with her.

I got my hand down in her pants and a finger and then two up inside her all frothy and propulsive.

"Somebody knows what he's doing," she said with amorous cantillation.

I kept at her cunt while she unfastened my pants and extricated my pent up member.

She held onto my dick like a handle, not stroking it but just holding it like a stick shift, as I fingered her to crescendo.

"Come on, fuck me," she said right after it seemed like she might've come and yanked at my pants to remove them.

"I don't have rubbers," I said.

"'S'alright, I'm on the pill."

I pulled her pants off her and spread her legs wide, plunging my cock into her cunt–she cried out as I entered her–and finding there the biggest bliss we're born to, going back to where we came from, doing what makes us possible, like since all the way back in caveman days.

Cock-in-pussy was no longer an abstraction.

I was fucking.

The ecstatic passion and perfect leverage and wetness had me pounding at her pudendum barely a dozen times before ejaculating ferociously all the way up inside her, coming in her pussy during "Being For The Benefit of Mr. Kite," like right when Henry the Horse dances the waltz.

"I can go down on you if you want," I said, realizing I hadn't lasted long enough to take her anywhere.

"Buon appetito," she smiled and I submerged into a most satiating midnight snack.

Cunnilinguini al dente.

Her neighbors heard all about it.

I had lost my virginity to the proverbial older sister.

It wasn't Taryn Rust.

I succumbed to the wonder of shameless wanting.

"You want to hear that Mahler movement?" Desirée asked, getting out of bed afterward.

"Yeah, sure," I said.

We walked into the living room and I lay naked on the couch.

She sat on the stool behind her cello, spread her legs, took the instrument between them and began tuning.

"From Gustave Mahler's Fifth Symphony, the 4th Movement: Adagietto," she said and closed her eyes.

I was her toy. That cello was her lover.

I fucked Desirée Stoner after work several more times that summer, but when the Bowl season ended we never saw each other or spoke again.

10

Dolly was set to depart for her year in France at the end of August.

I was trying to picture an entire school year without her.

No Dolly in Megiddo's AP class, no Dolly in Play Production, no Dolly to hang with on the weekends, no Dolly at prom, no Dolly at graduation.

I wondered if she'd meet some boy and fall in love in France and lose all interest in even being friends with me.

Then I jumped way ahead in time and imagined her return next summer and how maybe, now that I had the Desirée Stoner experience under my belt, I would finally have sex with Dolly Ferris.

That projection led to a song about Dolly's homecoming, though it ended up being not about Dolly really but more about this ironic dream I had the night before about a girl who asked me out to dinner and a movie but then as we were on our way to the theatre she remembered that she was blind.

You never know where the muses are going to lead you no matter your earliest conceptions.

I finished the song the day before Dolly was to leave and since we had plans for one last hang I decided I'd play it for her now rather than welcome her home with it 10 months from now.

"I wrote a weird song," I told her when I arrived at her house, "Can I play it for you?"

"Of course," she said and led me into the living room.

I sat at the piano and, as always, she sat next to me on the bench.

"What makes it weird?"

"Well, it's sort a welcome home song for when you get back from France next year."

"And you're playing it for me now before I leave."

"Yeah. Like I said. Weird. But really it's not about you."

"How could it be? I haven't left yet."

"Zackly," I smiled and she smiled back.

I started playing the E–>Esus chords that opened my new song.

Dolly said, "Tell me not to go."

I continued to tinkle at the keys.

"Come on," she said, "turn this into a trashy novel."

"I will thrust my engorged member into your sopping wet honeypot," I proclaimed in the trashy novel language we often laughed about together.

And I continued to pound the chord progression of the song.

"No trashy novel, huh?"

"Nyeah. You need to go have your adventure, D. And I need to writhe on the bed in pain and write songs and stuff. I do love you."

She nodded.

"Just, you know, I can't do the whole thing," I continued.

"A divine tragedy," she said, masking her sadness with an ironic tone, "Now let me hear the tune."

"It's called 'The Death of Irony.'"

"That sounds like a Lance Atlas title if ever I've heard one."

"Hey, I am an *artiste*."

"Just play the fucking song," she said.

And I did so.

It's within my power to see you die

But I'll let you live I wanna watch you breathe

I'll settle for a countenance your blessing

Sigh when you decide you need to be relieved

So you're finally home again Marie

Did France teach that you can't learn how to know?

You can sleep while I give you my confession

Is it true French clouds dress up as mistletoe?

My friends are protagonized by every book they read

Their canned enigma can be cold

They pray to smallest ambiguities

This modern age is getting old

I laughed at those who said they knew you well

They laughed at me for never giving in

I vanished with my arid errant fortune

From the age of irony and sin

I came upon a wild unsightly girl

On a mission to rid the night of all its wrong

She seemed to understand the darkness

It let her live it kept her strong

She spoke to me of vision in a cage

She argued that a stigma can be kind

She asked me out to dinner and a movie

But after dinner she remembered that she was blind

She blamed this lapse on something she ate

Still I judged it irony and sin

I took her life and her missionary possessions

Then I laughed at her for never giving in

Have I sinned by killing sin this autumn night?

If so how will I hide my naked rage?

I'll change my name to protect the ignorant

And never keep true vision in a cage

So you're finally home again Marie

I know I'll have arrived once you believe

It's within my power to see you die

But I'll let you live I want to watch you breathe

The next day Dolly left for Paris.

I went with the Ferris family to the airport and had a tearful farewell with the girl.

"Dang, this is really happening," I said.

"Yeah," she said.

"I'm going to miss you."

"Likewise."

"You're going to have an amazing time."

"Yes," she said, smiling, "And I'm going to write to you all about it. In excruciating detail."

"You don't have to tell me about boys you make out with."

"Of course not. I know the drill. And you'll write back to me."

"Of course."

"And keep me posted about the multiple girls you're obsessing over at any given moment."

"Indubitably," I said like Fred Flintstone.

"'Cause unlike you I do like to hear about that stuff."

Dolly's parents started calling to her that the plane was boarding.

"Gimme a kiss I have to go," she said, and our mouths melted together one last time for a tender minute before she dashed off to the gate and then she was gone.

Dolly's dad dropped me back off at home afterward, and I made my way up onto the garage roof where I saw a jet ascending and heading east across the sky.

I pretended it was her plane even though she was probably somewhere over Kansas already.

I even waved.

Neil Young crept into my head.

When you see me

Fly away without you

Shadow on the things you know

Feathers fall around you

And show you the way to go

It's over, it's over

Who was I thinking about?

Dolly? Lorelei? Miranda?

I'd been working out this hooky anthemic melody and finally started to hear the lyrics, still foggy and bubbling, but ready for emanation, fruit of the rejection and abandonment I had brought upon myself.

The divine tragedy of it all hovered there for the capturing.

I needed only offer myself as receptacle and let the message enter.

The Muses infused me.

I was determined not to lose it.

The Divine Tragedy

Man's green earth plays tricks so clever

Jokeless mirth, a most tragic endeavor

To play the fool until the wild card's drawn

A magician's tool, he waves his hand you're gone

With a madman's skill he's desiring power,

To win, to kill within the hour

He changes clothes, he paints his face

He performs in shows, he pursues the chase

Off again in circles

That's life beneath the big top

Tightrope walk without a net

Is it purposely he's jumping?

Or accidentally he's falling?

Which is which is easy to forget

He decided not to pitch to their best hitter

They laughed a lot but the punchline was bitter

He disobeys their laws

He denies their cause

One last dramatic pause

Then he exits to their applause

Who would lie behind the back of danger?

Did an unknown twin die in the fabled manger?

Perhaps he lost the will to give

Or the winter frost decided him to ill to live

I learn to accept what I've been given

Appreciative tokens kept to adorn the house I live in

The distance grows in a figure eight

The winner knows to never leave the gate

Off again in circles

That's life beneath the big top

Tightrope walk without a net

Is it purposely I'm jumping?

Or accidentally I'm falling?

Which is which is easy to forget

Feeling man has a tragedy vision

Thinking man has a comedy mission

These stakes are real

I bet my one square meal

As my bluff's revealed

It's one shit deal

Off again in circles

That's life beneath the big top

Tightrope walk without a net

Is it purposely we're jumping?

Or accidentally we're falling?

Which is which is easy to forget

I will be your friend

What can you show me?

When we meet again

Will you still know me?

Will you recall

The barbed wire wall?

I broke your swan dive fall . . .

No I know you won't remember me at all

ABOUT THE AUTHOR

Barry Smolin is a native of Los Angeles, California. He is the author of *Wake Up In The Dreamhouse* (2011), a novella composed one sentence at a time on Twitter, *Always Be Madly In Love* (2011), selected poetry culled from the years 1988- 2010, and *Narcissus In The Dark* (2012), another novella, in addition to *The Miranda Complex Volume 1* (2016). Since 1995 he has been the host and producer of the radio shows *The Music Never Stops* (1995-2012) and *Head Room* (2012-present) on KPFK 90.7 FM in Los Angeles. He has also released four albums of original music under the name Mr. Smolin: *At Apogee* (2004), *The Crumbling Empire Of White People* (2007), *Bring Back The Real Don Steele* (2009), and *Heaven's Not High* (2013), as well as setting chapter 1 of James Joyce's *Finnegans Wake* to music in collaboration with the band Double Naught Spy Car as part of the "Waywords and Meansigns Project" (2016) and on an instrumental album *That Tragoady Thundersday* (2016). His music has also been featured on the Showtime television series "Weeds." He can be found online at www.mrsmolin.com